BURIED SECRETS

A DEREK REED THRILLER

Victoria M. Patton

Dark Force Press

Dark Force Press
www.darkforcepress.com

Book Layout © 2016 BookDesignTemplates.com

Buried Secrets/ Victoria M. Patton. — 1st ed.
ISBN 978-1-946934-24-6

Don't give up on your dreams.
And never let go of hope.

CONTENTS

CHAPTER ONE

"Home run," he chuckled as the bat swooshed through the air, impacting the man's skull. Droplets of blood spattered onto the wall; the pristine cream-colored paint now streaked with crimson red. Another blow, this time to the man's legs. The crack of bone splintering echoed throughout the room.

"I'm sorry," the man sobbed. "I'm so sorry."

Derek stood frozen as the man's screams pierced his ears. The lights in the library glowed against the dense haze of fog surrounding them. Squinting, he focused on the man with the bat. Outlines of a bookshelf and desk loomed in the shadows of the room. Derek's skin prickled as the hair stood on end. Although he couldn't see the victim's face as he slumped forward in a chair, he seemed familiar, known to him.

"Too late to be sorry now." The assailant lifted the bat over his head and laughed, his face obscured by a hooded sweatshirt.

Derek tried to move towards the victim. He had to save him and stop the brutal attack, but his legs wouldn't budge. He looked down; his feet melded into the wood floors.

A high-pitched cackle filled the room. "You couldn't save Chrissy. You can't save him."

Derek's eyes bulged. He blinked, squeezing them shut. "No. No. You're dead. You're not real." He muttered the mantra over and over.

"You too scared to look up, boy? You didn't think you could get rid of me that easy, did you?"

Derek's heart pounded, thumping like a jackhammer against concrete. The air in the room hung thickly, his chest constricted, making each breath a struggle. Lifting his gaze upward, his hands trembled as he reached for his gun. His fingers grazed an empty holster.

Josiah Craig removed the hood of the sweatshirt. One side of his face was eaten away by maggots, the other side partially caved in and unrecognizable. A warped smile greeted Derek. Roaches and beetles weaved their way through his rotten, blackened teeth.

"You're dead. You can't do anything to me."

"Oh, Derek. Are you sure about that?"

Derek closed his eyes, grabbing the sides of his head. "I left it at the grave. I left you at the grave."

A sickening howl bellowed out of Josiah. "You're as stupid as a bag of hair, son."

Derek took a deep breath, clinching his fists before he faced his demon. "Not this time, Josiah. Or whoever you are. Not this time." He turned away as the man in the chair called out to him.

"Stop him, or he will keep killing."

Josiah lifted his hand to his mouth. "Oh my. Where are my manners? Derek, let me introduce you to someone."

As Josiah slowly turned the chair around, Derek trembled. He swallowed several times, trying to coat his dry, burning throat. As the man in the chair came into full view, Derek gasped. "No. No. It can't be."

"Of course, it is. I told you, you can't run from me."

The man sat in a pair of boxers. Blood oozed from his head wound. Both tibias had compound fractures. Derek's stomach rolled as the sour taste of vomit hovered at the back of his throat. His legs shook under his weight. The last thing Derek saw was himself tied to the chair, with half his head bashed in.

CHAPTER TWO

Derek screamed as he hit the floor.

Lola jumped off the bed, darting towards him. Her head bobbed and weaved as she sniffed him. The boxer darted around the room, searching for intruders before returning to his side. She barked and nudged him until he acknowledged her.

Derek's breathing came in short pants, as he sat up. Sweat beaded on his forehead, tiny droplets ran down his face. His hand shook as he reached for the brown boxer. "Hey, girl. I'm okay."

Lola licked his face, nuzzling his chest. Her ears perked up as movement outside the sliding glass door caught her eye. Her huffing turned into loud barks as she went through the electronic doggy door.

"What do you see, Lola? Hmm?" Derek steadied himself, leaning on the bed as he got his legs under him. Staggering, he maneuvered towards the glass, sliding it open. The warm, fresh air filled his lungs. Phoenix in September was still hot. Even in the early mornings. He glanced at his new watch, 5:30 a.m. Groaning, he yawned. "Fuck, I'm awake. I might as well stay awake."

He leaned against the door frame, watching Lola run around his backyard. She occasionally stopped at the front door of the bungalow, at the back of his property.

His new resident, Agent Kyle Marcum, moved in a week ago. He needed a place to live, and it seemed like the perfect fit. The bungalow sat empty since his grandmother's death when Derek moved into her home. He watched as Lola crept around the small residence, probably looking for her new best friend, Squeakers, the cat.

"Lola, what are you going to do when Lizzy comes home and takes you back to her house?" Derek clapped for the dog to return.

She bounded inside, excited for the day to begin.

"Lola, if we could bottle your energy, I would make a killing." He slid the glass door shut.

The dog cocked her head to the side as if she understood.

"You hungry?" he asked her, grabbing his phone from the nightstand. Along with two pills from a prescription bottle.

Those two words were her cue. She took off running towards the kitchen.

Derek followed, turning on every light, pausing at each room before he passed the doorways. As he neared the archway leading into his spacious kitchen, he stopped, peeking around the edge before entering. He blew out the breath he held through taut lips. "I must look like an idiot." He frowned at the dog as she sat ogling him, waiting for him to fill her dog bowl. "What?"

She barked at him, trying to rush him along.

"I guess if you're not seeing a boogeyman, it must be safe to enter." He placed the two pills on the counter and grabbed the dog food from one of the bottom cabinets.

Lola's butt wiggled as her stubby tail shook at Mach speed.

"My gosh, calm down, dog." He chuckled at the boxer. Once he filled her bowl, he made some breakfast, starting with a pot of coffee. Grabbing eggs and bacon from the refrigerator, he placed the pan on the stove just as his phone rang. "Shit, this can't be good," he said as he looked at the caller ID. "Derek."

"Derek, you sound awake," FBI Assistant Director Fretz said.

"Well, you're calling me at 6 a.m."

"You sound more awake than usual. Why are you up?"

"Why are you calling me?"

"Ah, hell. I'm sorry. I've just woken up myself. There's been a murder."

"Um, okay. What does a murder have to do with me?" Derek took a mug from the cabinet, filling it with coffee. He popped the two pills in his mouth, hoping they would settle his nerves.

"I need your team to handle this one."

"I thought the Legacy Unit handled cold case files? Why do you want us to handle a fresh body?"

"If you remember, I said you may handle a recent murder case once in a while. Well, this is one of those times. Plus, someone requested you."

Derek stiffened. "Requested? By who?"

"Congressman Jackson."

Derek cringed. Lizzy's—hell, he didn't know what he was to her. Boyfriend or business partner. "Why did he ask for me?"

"His friend is the murder victim. Billy Edmond. The good thing, Jackson has been in Washington these last few weeks. He isn't on your suspect list."

"Yeah, that's great." Derek sipped his coffee. "I'm guessing I need to get to the crime scene?"

"Yes. The local ME and the Crime Scene Unit are holding the scene. The guy has been dead for roughly five hours."

"Who found him? Do you know how Jackson found out about the death?"

"Jackson received a call from the victim's staff. The only reason we are aware of this case is that Jackson requested the FBI, and you specifically, to handle it. The victim lives alone. His wife died a long time ago." The AD paused.

"Hello? Director? Is there something else? What are you not telling me?"

"Nothing. That's all I got. How quick can you get there?"

Derek glanced at the clock on the wall, double-checking the time on his watch. "Where is the scene?"

"East Valley region, Ahwatukee."

"Crap." Derek rubbed his temples. "At least an hour. I can get Agent Marcum to head into the office, and he can get going on the research of our victim." He paced around his kitchen.

"Is your entire team here?"

"I believe a few of them are in town. I'm not expecting anyone to report until Tuesday. Wait, maybe Wednesday. Anyway, why is this happening on a Sunday? Can't I just enjoy the weekend?"

"Um, you know today is Monday, right?" Assistant Director Fretz asked.

"Shit. I lost a day somewhere." Derek placed his cup in the sink and headed towards his bedroom. Lola in tow. "I'll call them. I have enough agents to get going."

"Keep me posted. I want to stay in the loop at all times. I'm texting you the address." Assistant Director Fretz hung up.

His phone pinged as he walked into his bedroom. "Damn, damn, damn." Derek opened the glass door, heading for the bungalow. Knocking on the door, he waited. He lifted his hand, ready to rap on the door one more time when he heard muffled noises on the other side.

The door flew open; Kyle stood wrapped in a towel. "Yo, boss.

What's up?"

"We got a case."

Agent Marcum scratched his head. "You mean like a new dead body case?"

"Yup. Special request for the Legacy Unit to handle it. I need you to go to the office. Make sure the computers are up and running, then run Billy Edmond's financials. That's our victim. Do as much as you can without crossing any lines. Find out if his money played a part in his murder."

"Okay. I got it. I'll leave in thirty," Kyle said, nodding.

"One more thing. This stays between us."

Kyle nodded again.

"I need you to tell me what connection he has to Congressman Jackson."

"Do you suspect the congressman?"

"No, but he asked for us to investigate. I have my suspicions why, but I would like to know his connection. It seems the staff called him first."

"Oh. No worries. I got you covered."

"Great. I'll touch base with you later." Derek turned to leave, then spun around. "Our secretary may or may not show up. I don't know who the AD is giving us or how soon. But, if she doesn't arrive before I do, I need you to call Agents Pillard, Finch, and Peterson. They're slated to be here tomorrow. Ask if they can get in today. It's okay if they can't. Don't worry about Mackle. He isn't coming until next week."

"No problem." Kyle closed his door as Derek walked away.

Lola ran around the yard doing her business. Derek entered his bedroom, sliding the door closed, locking it. Then scrolling through his contacts, he found Agent Felicia Rogers and Agent Kelly Warden's numbers, and texted them the address.

Back in the kitchen, he fixed the eggs and bacon he had set out earlier. The minute he sat down to eat, he heard the electronic doggy door open, letting Lola inside. Her nails clicked on the tile floor as she ran down the hallway, sliding to a stop at his feet. "Really? You must have a sixth sense when it comes to food."

She pawed his leg, begging for a bite. He shared his breakfast. Eating quickly, he locked up and left. As he waited for his garage door to open, he wondered about the shit storm about to unfold.

CHAPTER THREE

Monday 8 a.m.

Derek drove past an elaborate electronic key pad outside an open iron security gate. A Tudor house in vibrant colors of red masonry and robust dark wood sat at the end a long driveway edged with dark green hedges. From his car he could see three large chimneys. He wondered how many chimneys one house needed.

Exiting his vehicle, he blocked out the noise from several cops and crime scene techs milling around. He glanced back, letting his eyes scan the three-acre property. There had to be more security than one gate and keypad. *If he let in the killer, did he know the killer? Did the killer know who would be home? What about the staff?* The questions rattled around Derek's head.

Police officers congregated at the entrance, trampling anything of use outside the front door. He tilted his head towards the men, but didn't remove his badge from the back pocket of his jeans.

"How you doing?" Derek asked as he walked up the steps leading to the front of the house. No one asked for his identification. He shrugged. Maybe he looked like an FBI agent.

Standing at the edge of a long wrap-around veranda, he counted the number of wooden loungers lining the length of the structure. "Eight, do we really need that many?" Small tables between the loungers created intimate conversation areas. Something told him the wife did the decorating. He reached out and twisted the brass knob in the center of a wooden door. Stepping into the foyer, he let out a low-tone whistle.

Several chandeliers hung at various heights from a twenty-foot ceiling. Rich warm glows of amber light filled the entryway. A wide staircase curved as it rose to the second floor. It drew the eye upward to a large round window. A huge vase of pastel-colored flowers filled the frame.

Walking through the foyer, he stepped into a vast, open living room. A solid wall of glass spanned the entire length of the room framing the perfectly manicured backyard. Standing in the center of the space, he glanced around. A massive kitchen sat off to the right. To the left stood a double-sided fireplace. It broke the large area into two spaces.

Looking over his left shoulder, he cocked his head to the side. Voices drifted towards him, coming from the other end of the corridor. He followed the faint conversation.

He stopped outside an elf-like door. Leaning back, he glanced to his left. Another doorway just down from him blended seamlessly into the wall. His brow furrowed at the much darker wood of this door. His fingers followed the recessed design, studying the intricate details. The oak wood was smooth under his skin. He took a small step back, letting his eye follow the curve of the doorway.

He walked a few feet towards the end of the hallway. Two other doors on this corridor blended into the surroundings. Derek moved back to the odd door. *This was your special place, wasn't it? You set it apart from the rest of the house. A house your wife designed. But this was all yours.* He reached out, pushing the L-shaped handled downward. Stooping, he held his breath as he stepped into the room.

His eyes widened. A sudden heaviness expanded in his core. He blinked rapidly as he tried to process the scene from his nightmare. The man in the desk chair loomed in front of him. Derek's breath hitched as he squeezed his hands into fists to stop them from shaking.

"Ah, it's about damn time you showed up, Agent." A deep voice filled the room. "Personally, I can't believe they let you stay on the force."

Derek didn't avert his stare. "Shut the hell up. You should talk. Where did you get your medical degree from? A discount medical school?"

The other men stood in stunned silence as robust laughter boomed out.

A pair of big burly arms wrapped around Derek's waist, lifting him upward. "Seriously, Doc?" His feet thudded on the rich mahogany flooring as the doctor relinquished his hold.

"Man, it's good to see you!" Dr. Rory Callahan said, patting the young agent's face.

Derek couldn't help but smile. "It's good to be back, Doc. Have you seen Ronald? I mean, Dr. Chelsea?"

Dr. Callahan nodded. "Played golf with him just the other day. He cheated."

Derek walked around the dead guy as he listened to the doc. Strapped to his office chair, the victim wore a pair of pink thong panties, another difference from his dream. His heart rate sped up just a bit as he glanced at the floor. Instead of a wooden bat like the one from his dream, a metal bat lay at his feet.

"I don't know why I play with him." Dr. Callahan watched the agent. He glanced at his head CST. "Quincy, have you met Agent Reed yet?"

"No, sir. I have not." Quincy extended his hand when the agent looked up.

Derek eyeballed the gloves.

"They're clean." He smiled as he wiggled his fingers.

Derek took his hand. "Nice to meet you." He turned towards the doc. "Have you got anything, or are you just going to slough your work off on Quincy?"

"We had to wait for you. Assistant Director Fretz instructed us to touch nothing. We touched nothing. I performed a quick visual inspection," he said, replacing the gloves on his hands with fresh ones. He watched as Quincy did the same.

"What do you have so far?" Derek stepped to the side, letting the doc closer to the body.

Pointing to the garrote around the man's neck. "I think he died by strangulation."

"For crying out loud. That's all you got?"

Dr. Callahan laughed. "No, silly. Ultimately, the garrote killed him. He used the bat for pain. Although," he pointed to a few gashes on the head. "These would have killed him had our killer not strangled him." The doctor pointed to the discoloration in the man's limbs. "I won't know the time of death until I get him into autopsy, but livor mortis indicates he's been in this position for some time."

Quincy took one step closer. "They found our dead guy early this morning. According to what the cops told me, the employee spoke with the deceased around 8 p.m. last night."

"I'd be willing to guess death occurred between 8 p.m. and sometime this morning." The doctor giggled, smiling.

"Wow. You're a genius for sure," Derek said, frowning.

"What are you thinking, Agent?" The doc asked.

"If our killer started off beating the man to death, why would he stop and use a garrote on him? Also," he pointed to the bloody bat on the floor. "The bat. How many people bring a bat to murder someone and then also bring a garrote?" Derek glanced around. Walking to a shelving unit to the right of the desk, he examined one shelf. A photo of an older couple sat off to the side.

"What you looking at?" the doc asked.

"This couple, and this. It looks like Billy played baseball." He pointed to a picture. "The bat on the floor looks like the bat in the photo."

"The couple are Billy's parents." Doc Callahan turned towards his CSU team. "Dust around the shelf. Let's hope our killer left something behind."

"You got it, Doc." Quincy motioned to one underling to start on the task.

Laughter drifted down the hallway, coming closer to the office door. All heads turned towards the fluttery sound.

The door opened, and Agents Felicia Rogers and Kelly Warden entered.

Derek noticed all eyes fell on Felicia right away. Although Agent Warden had an attractiveness to her, her features were not nearly as striking as Agent Rogers'. The two agents couldn't be more opposite from one another.

"Agents." Derek stepped closer. "Dr. Callahan, these are members of my team. Agent Felicia Rogers and Agent Kelly Warden. Agents, meet the indubitable Dr. Rory Callahan, ME."

Agent Rogers, oblivious to the stares, smiled. Her straight, perfect white teeth blinded the doctor. He removed his gloves and shook her hand. Not wanting to be accused of a lewd thought, he spun his attention to the other agent, shaking her hand as well. "Nice to meet you two. How did you get so lucky to be stuck with this guy?" He pointed to Derek.

"Really? We're doing that?" Derek moved to the back of the victim.

Dr. Callahan quickly introduced the rest of his team. He had to hide his amusement at Quincy's reaction, who stared at Felicia. "Quincy? Quincy?"

The young CST turned towards the voice. "Hmm? I mean, yes, doctor?"

"We need to get Mr. Edmond on the floor." The doctor put on another pair of gloves as he waited for his team to prepare to move the body. "Make sure the bag is completely open. Don't remove the garrote. I want everything in the bag. I will remove it when I get him back to the morgue." He glanced at the three agents. "It is pretty tightly wound. I don't want to lose any materials which may be inside the wound track."

"Good thinking, Doc. I guess that's why they pay you the big bucks." Derek winked at his agents. "Did you have any trouble getting here?"

Kelly shook her head. "Not at all."

Derek liked both women for different reasons. They each held skills he needed. But where Felicia could go undercover as a model, Kelly couldn't.

Kelly's mousy brown hair sat at the nape of her neck, pulled into a tight bun. She wore dark business pants and a dark jacket. A simple white button-up shirt underneath. Her shoes were—sensible.

Felicia wore black jeans, riding boots, and a loosely fitted pink top. Not sexy in any way, but the way she wore it, she looked like she just stepped off the runway. Her jet-black hair was cut in a stylish bob. She wore light makeup, where Kelly wore none.

"You two, go find the worker who found him." Derek turned towards the CST team, his brow wrinkled. "Do you guys know who or where he is?"

Quincy nodded. "Yeah, it's the house manager. He's in the kitchen, or at least he was."

"Perfect," Derek said. "Find him. Have him explain the security and how it works. Our killer either knew the victim or knew how to get in."

The agents headed towards the doorway.

"Also, if there are any security tapes, videos, or drives—whatever, make sure we get those over to Agent Marcum. Confirm when the house manager last spoke with the victim." Derek patted his jeans and his shirt pockets. "Damn. Anyone got any gum?"

Dr. Callahan sighed, removing one of his gloves. "It's your habit. Can't you remember to bring it?" He pulled a pack from his pants pocket and gave a piece to the agent.

Derek waved him off as he took two. The agents were almost out the door when he called out to Felicia. "I want to know everything regarding this house. I need to know all the access points—any entrances, backdoors, or any way in or out, including pet doors. Find out the relationship between the house manager and the victim. See how close they were."

"You got it," Felicia said, following Kelly out.

When they were out of earshot, the doctor leaned into Derek.

"Wow. They are two very different agents."

Derek smiled. "Yes, they are. But don't let Agent Rogers pretty looks fool you. Her hands are deadly weapons. She is a martial arts expert and an amateur boxer. And Kelly's attention to detail, coupled with her ability to speak five languages, makes her a valuable asset." Derek knelt near the body studying the wounds before the tech's zipped the bad shut. "Quincy, can you throw me a pair of gloves?"

CST Quincy Silas pulled an extra pair from his kit and tossed them to him. "Here you go. What do you see?"

The doctor stepped closer to Derek, snapping on a new glove. "What is it, Derek?"

Derek pulled on the gloves. "I'm not sure." He angled his head, bending over. "I think something is under him. Can you help me roll him?"

The doctor motioned for the CSTs to open the body bag a little more, giving more room to roll the body. "You ready?" he asked Derek.

"Yup."

Together, they rolled the victim over on his side. The pooling blood had caused the back of the thighs and buttocks to turn black.

Derek pointed to a piece of duct tape caught between the man's butt cheeks. "Ouch. That had to hurt." He and the doc rolled the man back to his original position. "Please make sure you get everything off that piece of tape."

"Yes, sir," the doctor said. "Boys, zip him up. And let's get everything from the scene." Dr. Callahan raised an eyebrow at his favorite agent. "Are you done here?" He waved his hand in a circle after removing both gloves.

"Yeah. At least for now. I'll tape off the scene in case we need to come back for any reason." He smiled at the man he loved like an uncle. Derek removed a roll of crime scene tape from the open CSU kit, setting it on the desk. Along with Dr. Chelsea, the two men were there for him at the oddest times. "I really appreciate you holding the body for me. It really helps to see everything before it's altered. It helps me see the killer and what he may have wanted."

"My pleasure, Derek. You need to swing by the house."

Derek watched as the doctor's mouth moved, but it wasn't his voice he heard in his head.

"You need to pay attention. Every detail counts."

"Derek?" The doctor snapped his fingers. "Hello, Derek! Agent

Reed?"

"Huh? Why are you yelling at me?" Derek's brow furrowed.

"Dude, where did you go?" Quincy asked as he stepped up next to the doc.

Derek looked at the CST; he flinched back, not understanding the question.

Dr. Callahan reached out, taking his shoulder in a tight grip. "It hasn't been long enough, Derek. Are you sure you're okay to come back?"

Derek shrugged, moving towards the door. "Yeah. I am. Lost in my thoughts, that's all. Call me when you have something from the autopsy."

The doctor saluted the agent. "I will." Dr. Callahan watched him leave the room. Worried. It might be too soon for Agent Reed to return to work.

.

CHAPTER FOUR

Derek walked around the house. On the other side of the second living room, he found what might be the master suite. He opened one of the four closed doors in the room. It led to a walk-in closet. He stepped inside to find it circled around and exited into the bathroom.

"Damn. This bathroom is almost as big as my living room," Derek said, spinning around in the large room. Glancing at his feet, he let out a whistle. "This tile must have cost more than my house."

He got down on his hands and knees as he studied the pattern in what he guessed must be Italian marble. Etched swirly lines ran through the stone, not painted on. He rubbed his fingers in the grooves to verify his assumption. "Very nice." Oblivious to the clicking shoes approaching him, Derek continued his inspection.

"Ahem."

Derek didn't look up or answer.

Agent Felicia Rogers smiled as she watched her boss crawl around the floor. He caressed the etching like a man might follow the curves of a woman. Her amusement grew as he stood, now enamored with the fabric-like wallpaper. Derek Reed wasn't a drop-dead handsome fellow, but his wavy dark brown hair, along with his boyish looks, softened a very rugged square jawline, making him undeniably attractive. "Um, hey," she finally said.

Derek didn't look at her. "Did you speak with the house manager?" He caressed the raised pattern on the wallpaper.

"Yes. Agent Warden is speaking with him in the kitchen. She's— rigid. Likable, very likable. But very rigid." She sighed. "I don't mean to say anything bad about my team member."

Derek turned towards her. "I don't think what you said is bad. It's your observation. Never hold back on your observations."

His emerald green eyes sparkled in the glare of the bright bathroom lights. She kept her expression void of emotion, but the deep green color mesmerized her. "Well, please know I meant nothing disrespectful by it."

"None taken. Tell me what you found out from the house manager."

He walked through another doorway, different from the one he originally came through. Stepping into the bedroom, he opened the other doors. All of them were closets, except one.

The homeowner had built a fully loaded and decked-out safe room. A small refrigerator, satellite phone, and other electronics were available. "I wonder why he had this," Derek said as he glanced around.

Agent Rogers remained quiet. Unsure if her boss wanted her thoughts or not. After a beat, she continued telling him her findings. "The house manager arrived early this morning, around 7 a.m. Found the man of the house deceased and promptly called the police."

"Doesn't the house manager live here?"

"Yes, but he stays with his mother once a month. A place on the south side of Phoenix. She lives in a nursing home."

Derek glanced at her over his shoulder as he inspected the control panel in the safe room. "Did you ask him if he touched the body?"

She cocked her head to the side. "No. I didn't realize someone had touched the body before the ME got here."

"I didn't say it had been touched. I just wondered if you asked." He walked past her, leaving the bedroom, entering the large living room. "Did you find all the entrances and exits?"

Agent Rogers pulled a notepad from the back pocket of her jeans and flipped through the pages. "Yes. There is a door leading through the kitchen into a mudroom. Through there, you can enter a hallway that takes you out to the backyard and the swimming pool. The garage is at the end of the same hallway as our victim." She frowned at him. "You don't see the garage from the front of the house. It is almost like a carriage house, off the back porch."

"Veranda," Derek said.

Agent Rogers frowned at him. "Off the veranda, there is a pool house along with a walkway which takes you to the garage. Basically, anyone can get in." Felicia held her finger up. "If the alarm system is engaged, motion sensors track an intruder and alert the residents via a talking sound system."

Derek tilted his head to the side. "I guess someone turned off the alarm."

She nodded. "According to the house manager, when he arrived this morning, the security gate needed his code to open, indicating it had not been disengaged. However, the house system had been turned off."

Derek sat on the arm of a sofa. "What does that tell us?"

"I think..." Agent Rogers began.

"A few things. Either the killer knew the victim, and he let him in, which included the gate. Or the killer entered through the gate maybe as a delivery driver, or the killer knew the system and shut it off." Derek unwrapped the second piece of gum and put it in his mouth, along with the first piece, which had lost its flavor. "Actually, it tells us something else, too. Our killer knew the house manager would be gone." His lips pooched out. "Maybe not. The killer could have gotten lucky."

"I don't think the killer knew the house manager wouldn't be here."

"Then luck it is," Derek said.

Agent Warden entered the room.

"Agent, what did you discover?" Derek asked. He watched as Agent Kelly Warden reached into her inside jacket pocket, removed a small spiral notebook, and flipped through a few pages. Derek clasped his hands in his lap and adjusted himself on the arm of the sofa.

Before she spoke, Agent Warden stood up straight and cleared her throat. "The house manager, Mr. Norman Aleshire, explained he had left early yesterday morning. He had an appointment with a decorator." She looked up. "Mr. Edmond wanted things renovated in the home. From what I gathered from Mr. Aleshire, our victim needed a change. He wanted to breathe new life into things his late wife, Francine, had done to the house. Mr. Aleshire said Mr. Edmond felt stuck in the past."

Derek stood, moving towards the glass wall overlooking the back-yard. As he got closer to the glass, steps were visible. They led to a massive pool. "Anything else?"

Agent Warden continued. "Mr. Aleshire then went to his mother's. Mr. Edmond mentioned he expected a visitor. But the house manager didn't know who or in what capacity."

Derek turned around. His new agents stood side by side. He hid his smirk. Their differences were why he chose them. Derek felt a slight chill as cold air encircled him. He twisted his head to the side, seeing if he could hear an AC unit kick on. Nothing.

"Is something wrong, Agent Reed?" asked Agent Rogers.

"What?" he responded. "No. And you don't need to call me Agent Reed when it's just us. We can limit the formalities to when there are non-unit members around. Is that okay with you two? May I call you by your first names?"

Felicia smiled. "I would prefer it." She nudged Kelly next to her. "Do you mind, Agent?"

Agent Kelly Warden adjusted her jacket. "I don't mind being called Agent Warden. But since this is a small unit and since we will work in close quarters, I have no problem being addressed as Kelly."

Felicia smacked the tightwad on the arm. "A simple yes would have sufficed."

Kelly rolled her eyes. "Yes."

Derek clapped his hands. "All right, got any ideas what we need to do next?"

The two women gaped at each other.

"Um, aren't you the boss?" Felicia asked.

Derek laughed. "Sure." He checked the time on his watch. He twisted it around his wrist tapping the glass, when he felt as if someone nudged him. He glanced around, then back at his agents. "You two check with Mr. Aleshire. See if we need Kyle, Agent Marcum, our resident geek. You will meet him at the office. See if he needs to come here and get the security files or if we need to take the equipment."

Kelly pulled out a jump drive from her front jacket pocket. "He downloaded everything from the system for the last few days. He said if we want to go back further, he will give our tech guy the login information. He clarified that only he and Mr. Edmond knew the login information." She placed the drive back in her pocket.

"Good. Very Good. Meet me at the office when you're done here," Derek said.

Both women again glanced at each other, not sure what their new boss wanted.

"If you think you have gathered everything, then head out," Derek said. He rubbed his temples. "Listen. I'll tell you guys if I need something specific for you to find out or ask. But, as FBI agents, and I might add, you two are the best in your fields. I expect you to think on your own. Make sure our house manager doesn't have the room cleaned until we release the scene. I left a roll of crime scene tape on the desk."

He headed towards the front door. "Get you some breakfast on the way to the office if you haven't eaten. We will meet up there." Derek left the two FBI Agents with more questions than answers. But he had to see if these two could think on their own. If not, he might have to add babysitting to his list of job duties.

CHAPTER FIVE

Derek parked next to Agent Marcum's car. He stared at the office of the Legacy Unit. An old Catholic church, it didn't fit the modern city around it. Two steeples with crosses attached framed the building. Arched wooden doors with ornate iron handles greeted visitors.

The doors offered little in the way of protection, which led the FBI to add an electronic bolting system. One stipulation the city made when the Bureau took possession of the church was to maintain its original integrity.

Exiting his vehicle, he stepped up next to a smaller doorway off to the left of the front entrance. It required everyone who entered to bend down and step over a raised threshold. It allowed for the main doors to stay closed unless large items were delivered.

He punched in the code on a keypad, swiping his thumb across the print scanner. He pushed the door open, stepping inside. Closing his eyes, he inhaled through his nose. The scent of oils once used by the priests permeated the pores of the wood. As the day grew warmer, the fragrance released, filling the main room.

He walked to his desk at the back. All the desks were in the open. There were no cubicle walls or private offices. "Kyle?" Derek walked towards the small hallway leading to the kitchen in the back. As he walked down the narrow corridor, his head throbbed.

He reached out and braced himself against the wall. Lifting his hand to his still healing broken nose, he wondered if this caused his dizziness. A wave of nausea swept over him. Sweat beaded along his hairline and down his back. "What the hell?" He tried to take a step to regain his balance. His feet were rooted to the floor. He tried to call out, but he couldn't speak.

Derek's breathing came in rapid pants. Then, without warning, starbursts exploded behind his eyes. He groaned in agony, grabbing the sides of his head. A scene flashed before him. He stood in a kitchen. A newspaper laid on a table. His eyes drifted down to the front page. The words were smeared with blood.

He couldn't read anything. He reached out to wipe the blood off the page, but with every pass of his hand, more blood bubbled out of the ink. It oozed down the page like tiny rivers on a map.

"Derek? Derek? Hello?" Kyle called out to him.

In an instant, the image disappeared. Derek stood in the church's kitchen. His eyes darted around. He looked over his shoulder, turning back to Kyle. "How long have I been standing here?"

Kyle shrugged. "I don't know. I came up from the cellar and found you standing there staring at the table." He stepped forward and peered at the front page of the Phoenix Sun Times. "Did something catch your eye?"

Derek frowned as he scanned the paper for clues. "I don't know. Something must have. Sorry, did you say something to me, and I didn't answer?"

Kyle grabbed a soda from the refrigerator. "No worries. Did you buy all this?" He asked, pointing to the fully loaded fridge.

"Yeah." Derek's mouth watered at the soda in Kyle's hand. "I also bought a few munchies." He waved towards the cabinets.

"Nice. Thanks. I think I have an idea."

"Okay," Derek said. "Let's go back to my desk." He reached out, grabbing his arm as he leaned into him. "Have you found anything regarding Congressman Jackson's connection to Billy Edmond?"

Kyle shook his head. "Not yet. Give me some time," he said as he followed Derek to the front.

Felicia and Kelly entered the office.

"Hey, boss." Felicia smirked at Derek's reaction.

"Why do I have a feeling you wouldn't stop calling me boss even if I said pretty please?" Derek asked.

"Because you're a profiler, and you know human nature." Felicia giggled.

"Kyle, this is Felicia Rogers and Kelly Warden. I have already established we will call each other by our first or last names when we're alone. Agent is too damn formal."

He stepped up to both. "Cool. Call me Kyle or Bones."

Felicia narrowed her eyes at him. "Bones?"

He shook Kelly's hand. "Yeah, one of my favorite characters from *Star Trek*."

Kelly frowned. "Don't tell me you're a Trekkie."

"Don't tell me you have a problem with Trekkies?" he asked her.

She shrugged. "Not really. I guess I just never got into it." Kelly sat on the edge of an open desk. "I didn't watch much TV growing up."

Felicia sat behind her in the chair at the same desk. "What did you do?"

Kelly glanced at her over her shoulder. "Bowling. Traveled a lot. My parents were linguists for the State Department."

Derek stood watching the three new agents interact as he thought about the incident in the kitchen. The injuries to his face from Josiah Craig may have some kind of lasting impact on his brain. He made a mental note to call Dr. Chelsea if the visions continued.

"Bowling?" Kyle grabbed a chair from another desk and rolled over to her. "This, I got to hear."

Derek smiled. "Kelly won several junior bowling championships throughout high school and became a collegiate champion as well." He raised an eyebrow at her. "Weren't you also on the pro circuit?" He saw his agent's face light up with a genuine smile. He thought if she smiled more often, she might not look so—uptight.

"Yes. I played in a few competitions before joining the FBI." Kelly glanced around the room. "Does it matter what desk we take?"

Derek shook his head. "Nope. As you can see, they have the same equipment. Except for Kyle." He turned towards his resident geek. "You'll have some more equipment delivered in the next few days."

"Which brings me to what I wanted to talk to you about. The equipment I'm going to have will put out some heat. Now, I won't need to be on it every day all day, but I wanted to ask you something." Kyle rolled his chair a little closer to Derek. "Downstairs is a small cellar. It looks like a canning cellar. But it would be perfect to set up my equipment. It's got electrical outlets, too."

"Will it be too damp?" Derek asked.

"No. It's perfectly dry down there. No moisture." Kyle's knee bounced.

Derek watched as the excited young man waited for a response. "I don't have a problem with it. Just as long as you don't become a cave dweller and never want to venture out of it."

"Not at all. I took some measurements earlier. There's a storage room down the hall," he pointed towards his right. "There are some wooden tables. They look very sturdy. They're narrow, so I don't think I will have trouble getting them down the steps." He smiled at the two other agents. "Especially if I had some help." He batted his eyelashes at the girls.

Felicia stood up. "I'll help."

Kelly sighed as she stood. "Sure. Let's get it done now. Then we can start on this case."

Derek sat at his desk. "I'm going to call and check on our secretary."

Kyle stopped just before the hallway to the storage room. "We're going to get a secretary?"

"I mentioned it to you this morning."

"Dude, the sun hadn't risen yet. Do we even need a secretary?" he asked.

"Hell yeah. I refuse to answer the phone, take messages, and babysit you guys. I told the AD I needed a secretary if he wanted me to take this team over."

"Sweet," Kyle said as he walked away.

Derek picked up the phone when the alarm on the front door buzzed. He glanced at the giant monitor hanging on the wall. Separated into eight smaller screens, it showed the grounds and building. Security cameras surrounded the place. One of those smaller screens showed the front entrance.

He could see an older woman standing there. "Who the hell is that?" He pushed the intercom button. "May I help you?"

The lady looked upward towards the camera, unsure where the voice came from. "I'm here to speak with Agent Reed."

"Who are you?" Derek asked.

"I'm Emma Allred. Your new secretary."

"Oh, come on in." Derek buzzed the lock.

Emma Allred stepped into the legacy unit wearing a loose beachy pantsuit. She recognized Agent Derek Reed immediately and smiled at the man before her. Emma had been following his career for a while. She extended her hand. "You must be Agent Reed."

Derek squinted at her. "Yes, I am," he said, taking her hand. "I wondered when you would show up."

"Well, here I am." Her eyes lit up as she glanced around. "I like this place."

He scrutinized her. Her warm tone reminded him of his mother.

"Assistant Director Fretz told me to show up today. The bureau had me scheduled to come in next Monday, but he figured you could use my help now."

Derek scratched his head. "Um, yeah. Emma. Can I call you Emma?"

"Absolutely. I'm not an agent, but I am qualified to carry a weapon." She patted her purse. "I have one in here. And I don't like to be called Mrs. Allred. Sounds way too old."

"Great. Um." He turned towards the kitchen, then back to her. "There are three other agents here. The others haven't arrived yet. Agents Kyle Marcum, Felicia Rogers, and Kelly Warden should be right back up. They're helping Kyle move some equipment down to the basement." Derek's shoulders slumped. "I think I forgot to get you a desk."

Emma started to say something when the other agents entered the room. Kyle and Felicia were laughing. Kelly was not.

"Hello," Kyle said when he saw a lady standing there. His eyes darted between the visitor and Derek.

"Guys, this is our new secretary. Emma Allred. Emma, this is Kyle, Felicia, and Kelly."

"Nice to meet you." Kelly stepped forward to shake the woman's hand.

Followed by Kyle and Felicia.

Derek snapped his fingers. "Kyle, is there another desk back in the storage room?"

"Yeah, a big wooden one."

"Perfect. Let's bring it out here. I forgot to get a desk for Emma. Also, have you spoken to the other agents yet?"

"No." Kyle winced. "Not yet."

Derek smirked at him. "It's fine. Go get the desk."

"Felicia can help me." Kyle grabbed her and headed back to the storage room.

Emma walked to the front and then turned around. She scoped out some electrical outlets and did some quick calculations in her head. "I think if we put my desk here," she pointed to the wall closest to the small door. "I can be out of the way but still close enough for deliveries and guests if we ever have any."

"Sounds perfect. We can set up one of these computers, and I can get another one ordered. I have a few days before all the agents arrive."

"That should work." Emma turned towards the two carrying the desk. "Set it right here for me, guys."

Walking back to his desk, Derek observed as Emma took control of the room. She didn't order but asked nicely for Kyle to hook up a computer for her and if he could roll the massive printer/copier towards her desk. The other agents helped get her area and equipment set up.

Once done, they set to work on the rest of the office space. They rearranged everything. Equipment shuffled from one place to another and back again until it sat in the right spot. He didn't have to tell them to do anything. He didn't have to ask. If the rest of his team fit in as well as these guys did, this team just might work. If not, he could always request a transfer.

CHAPTER SIX

Monday mid-day

Derek watched as Emma made a few trips to her vehicle, leaving the little side door open as she went in and out. She put a few personal touches on her desk. He noticed her treatment of a photo frame. The way she lovingly wiped its edges before placing it in the perfect position. He couldn't see the picture, but the way she smiled as she looked at it told him it must be someone special.

He watched as Felicia and Kelly settled at their desks. Much closer to him, he could see Felicia had placed a picture of her and a few academy cadets and one photo of her parents. Her desk looked as if an F-5 tornado blew through.

Kelly's tidiness sat in stark contrast to her coworker. A three-tiered file organizing basket took center stage in one corner. She had a cup holding pens on the opposite side and a pad of paper in front of her keyboard. The only personal item was a small bowling trophy.

Derek made a note to requisition another computer by the end of the day. Glancing down, he scowled at his own desk. He had one photo of Lizzy and Lola. His files were stacked on one corner. He had yet to prioritize the cases they would be investigating. He had fifteen on deck, not including this more recent case the AD gave his unit.

He searched for a folder. "Where are you?" he mumbled, rummaging through his desk drawer until he found it. Michael Finch and George Peterson were in town. He pulled a piece of paper with their contact information. He sent the two agents a text asking if they could be here by 8 a.m. the following day. Derek didn't text Cary Mackle. He wouldn't arrive in town until the following Monday. Agent Frank Pillard was due to show up any day.

Derek stood. "Everyone, Emma, you too."

They all looked up.

"Yeah?" Kelly asked.

"What do you need?" asked Felicia.

Kyle walked in.

"Kyle, this is for you too." Derek came around his desk and leaned against it.

Emma came towards them with a notepad in hand.

"I will let the others know this tomorrow, but I'm going to have Emma set up a file system on the network. Each case we work on will be there for all to access. As we get our rhythm in this unit, some will work on one case, some on another, and we will assist each other on all cases.

"We need to see the notes and all evidence gathered at any point during the case. Make sure your notes are coherent. And any photos you come across, make sure those go into the files with an identifying label. If you have to write something on paper, make sure you input it yourself. Emma isn't here to type out your reports."

Derek lifted his head, sniffing. He could smell a woman's perfume. His eyes darted around.

"Um, is there anything else?" Kyle asked.

"What?" he asked, looking at his partial crew.

Felicia cocked an eyebrow at him.

"Oh, I'm sorry. I just thought of something. I think it would be great to have a weekly roundup. Every Monday, we'll go over each case we're working on. If you find you need something, let me or Emma know. She will know what to do. I have stocked the fridge and cabinets with a variety of snacks and drinks. From this point on, we can all pitch in. If you drink all the soda pop, replace it. It's that simple.

"There are a few rooms here with beds. There is also a communal shower. If you ever find yourself here late, too tired to drive home, you can stay here. I requisitioned sheets and blankets. Emma, I need you to check on those for me."

"You got it," she said, as she scribbled on her pad.

"We have a laundry room. I'm going to see if we can get a used washer and dryer and get the government to pay for it. If not, I will hunt a set down for us. I know we have places to live, but sometimes we may need to bunk down here. We will want to wash the sheets. None of us need to take them home." Derek crossed his arms. "Do you guys have questions or concerns?"

They all glanced at each other, shaking their heads.

"For now, I want us to concentrate on this current case. Congressman Jackson asked for us to work it personally. I want to put all our efforts into it. Then we will hit some of our older cold cases. I will not assign cases. You look through them and if one speaks to you, then work on it. If you can't find one you like, just pick one, or ask me and I will give you one.

"Okay, Kyle, I want you to go through all the house security files from our victim's home. I believe Kelly has a USB drive for you. If you need more, get the house manager's information from Kelly and contact him."

Derek turned towards Felicia. "I want you to contact the ME and find out what they have so far. If he hasn't started the autopsy, ask him when. I want to be there if possible. Kelly, I want you to hunt down everything you can on our victim. Ask Kyle if you need him to find out anything for you. Kyle is getting his financial information. I want you to gather everything else. Find out who inherits the Edmond estate. Felicia can help you with this. Between the two of you, I want to know everything Mr. Edmond has been up to.

"Get a list of his closest friends. We need to talk to them. Whoever he spent time with the last few days, I want to talk to them. See if his secretary or business people know who he met with last night. Emma, I will have a list of all the cases to you in just a few," he said, sitting back at his desk.

Emma walked to her desk. "Just shoot it over to me."

Kyle took the USB drive from Kelly. "I'll be in my bat cave." He grabbed a computer off one of the empty desks.

Derek smirked at the excitement in the man's eyes. "Don't forget to eat and drink."

"Yes, Dad." Kyle laughed at Derek's scowl as he headed towards the basement.

"Boss," Felicia covered the desk phone mouthpiece with her hand. "The ME said he's going to start the autopsy in thirty. He asked if you want him to wait."

Derek looked at his watch. "Tell him I'm on my way. Thank you." He quickly culled all the files he had picked to investigate. A few were from ten years ago, but most were under five years. He had started to investigate one case when the Bureau first placed him on medical leave after the Josiah case.

Something about it piqued his interest. Several couples had been found murdered in their homes. It appeared as if the couples had no connection to each other. At least according to the notes of the local PD and the FBI agent first assigned to it. And from what Derek read, very little investigating had been done on the case. He put the entire list in a desktop folder, including their current case, and sent it to Emma. Derek grabbed his phone and his keys.

Emma looked up at him. "Did you send me the file?"

"I did. You should have it. Set up a separate case folder for each file. See if you can find any case notes in the system and put whatever you find in each file. Some will have more than others; some will be pretty empty. Kyle can help you if you run into trouble. On my desk are some folders with notes on each case. I will put those in later, but they may give you some extra information on where to look for things." He smiled at the photo on her desk. "He's handsome."

She beamed a full white smile at him. "He's my buddy. I usually take him with me everywhere. Got him just after my husband died."

Derek watched as she gently touched the photo of a massive Harlequin Great Dane. "What's his name?"

"Marc Anthony." She smiled at him. "When I'm here by myself, would you mind if I brought him? He's very well behaved. I will clean up after when I walk him."

"No problem at all. Sometimes I'll bring Lola with me. She's my best friend's boxer. I often watch Lola when my friend is out of town."

Derek hid his chuckle at her excitement. He leaned into her. "Nice thing about not being at the FBI headquarters. We get to do what we want." He winked at her. "I told Assistant Director Fretz I probably wasn't the best guy for this task force."

"You're the best agent to be in charge of this unit. And I am so lucky I got this assignment. Thank you."

"I'm glad you're here, too. Text me or call if you need anything. I'll be back after the autopsy." He started to leave, "Wait," he said, snapping his fingers, "I need to get you the code for the door and scan your thumbprint."

He turned around, walking over to the control panel on the wall near the door. Opening it, a small board popped down. A digital print scanner blinked as he put in the code. "Okay, the code is 2242. But it is useless without a thumbprint."

He motioned for Emma to place her thumb on the scanner. "I already put Felicia and Kelly into the system the other day when they came into town." The lights flashed red, then green, telling him the system accepted the print. When he finished, he locked the panel. "Now, the outer keypad, you push the star button, then enter the code. You have fifteen seconds to scan your thumb. If you don't, you have to start over again."

He pointed to a small button just underneath the panel. "Push this to release the locks when walking out." He turned towards the main area. "Felicia, Kelly, do you have questions about the security panel?"

They both shook their heads.

He turned back to Emma. "If someone buzzes, you will see them on the big screen. The lower left corner is the front door area." He stepped over to her desk. "Each phone has this button on it." He pointed to a red button. "Pushing this unlocks the door."

Derek zeroed in on Emma. "I know you carry a weapon, but if you ever feel uncomfortable, don't buzz anyone in. If they have a delivery, tell them to leave it. Get it when you see them leave the parking lot." Derek smiled. "Any questions?"

"No. Not from me," Emma said.

"Okay. Emma, I'll be back after the autopsy. Call me if you need me before then." Derek walked out into the bright sunlight of the Arizona sky. The heat of late September hit him like a brick oven. His shirt immediately stuck to his body.

Starting his prized possession, a restored 2006 Jaguar XJ, he cranked the cooling element in the seats. As the cabin cooled off, he pulled out into Phoenix's mid-morning traffic and started his twenty-minute drive to the ME's office. Patting his pockets for some gum, he kept his eye on the road as he searched his middle console for a pack.

"Damn. I need to buy some gum." He pulled into a convenience store parking lot. Running in, he grabbed two multi-packs of various flavors. Back in his car, he tossed them into the middle console as he continued his drive.

He hummed a classic rock song playing on the radio. Stopped at a light, the same perfume he smelled earlier at the office wafted around him. The hair on his arms stood on end. Although AC cooled the cabin, he felt a definite drop in temperature.

Out of the corner of his eye, he saw the outline of a person in the passenger seat. Sweat beaded across his forehead. His pulse echoed in his ears. As he pulled into a parking spot in front of the Medical Examiner's office, he closed his eyes. "Please go away. Please." He blew out a long breath. He thought this wouldn't happen anymore after Chrissy. Turning towards his right, a woman sat staring out the front window. Blood covered her clothing and dripped from her chin.

Her skin blackened and blistered. The smell of her perfume gave way to a burning smell. She twisted towards him. Her brain matter oozed from a crack in her skull. Her one blue eye bore through him. The other hung from an empty black socket. Broken bones littered her body.

Derek squeezed his eyes closed. "You're not real. I'm having side effects from my injuries. Nope. You aren't real." He reached for his door. He felt an ice-cool grip on his arm. He looked down at a bloody hand touching him. When he looked at the older woman, her bottom jaw seemed to open hinge-like, wider than physically possible. An ear-piercing scream filled the car. Derek covered his ears, shaking his head. The vehicle shook right before his windows shattered, sending glass debris everywhere.

CHAPTER SEVEN

Agent Kelly Warden sat at her desk. *Impressive*, she thought, reading about Billy Edmond. He'd gone to one of the most prestigious private schools in Phoenix. He came from wealth, but he'd made his own money. Scrolling through the information, it became clear Mr. Edmond used his family's connections to build his fortune. Which, as best as she could tell, came from acquiring businesses and then liquidating them. "Well, if that isn't a reason to kill someone," she mumbled.

He'd gained several friends in the Arizona political society. It seemed Mr. Edmond had no political aspirations, but he liked hanging out with people in power. *Now, why would you do that if you didn't want to be a politician?* she thought as she scrolled through endless photos. Photo op after photo op had him hobnobbing with some of the upper echelons in politics and business. There were several photos with Congressman Jackson. Many of which referred to their long-time friendship.

Kelly considered the age difference and wondered what the two men had in common. She checked the congressman's whereabouts during the hours of Edmond's death. A news report showed him at an event in Washington. As she scrolled through some other photos of the two, she saw a photograph of a woman.

Agent Warden glanced at Derek's desk. She peered around. Felicia was on the phone and Emma sat at her desk. Kelly strolled over to her boss' desk. As she walked past, she glanced at a photo. Walking into the kitchen, she grabbed a drink and a granola bar.

Sitting back at her desk, she zeroed in on the woman on her computer screen. She had the same auburn-haired beauty in the photo on Derek's desk. Elizabeth Chandler and Congressman Jackson were a thing. Not sure what kind of thing. However, there were a few other men of Congress, wealthy men, and actors in pictures with Elizabeth. One image of her with Billy Edmond and Congressman Jackson caught her eye. Elizabeth stood between them.

"Knew our victim, huh?" she whispered as she scrutinized the young woman. Curious, if not skeptical, of her boss's connection to a socialite. A smile crept across her face. It didn't matter to her. But curiosity had the best of her. She had to figure out Elizabeth Chandler's connection to the case.

Her attention was brought back to their victim when she came across an FBI file on the man. Nothing incriminating, but it looked like he had an in-depth search done on him three weeks ago. Kelly tried to open the record. She couldn't get it to open, so she tried to find the source of the search.

Kyle walked in whistling. "Anyone getting hungry?"

Felicia checked at her watch. "I could go for some lunch. My day started too early."

"Kyle, come here a second." Kelly waved him over.

"What do you need?" he asked, moving to stand behind her.

"I was searching our FBI database for anything on our victim. I discovered a red level done on him three weeks ago. But when I tried to access the file, I can't get in. And I can't read the electronic signature of who opened the search. I can't get past a wall. Can you help me?"

"Sure. Let me have a seat."

Kelly traded places with him. She took a sip of the soda she had brought from the kitchen as she watched Kyle's fingers fly across her keyboard. He didn't have to henpeck like most men using a computer.

Kyle's brow wrinkled. "This is odd."

"What's odd?" Kelly asked.

"Whoever accessed this closed the file and put an electronic lock on it." He continued to scroll through the searches done on Mr. Edmond. Every other search and its results were readily accessible except for this one. "I can unlock this, but I would leave a cookie crumb behind. Not sure if I should do that. I imagine there is an alert on it. If I access it, it will notify someone. Let me research this. I'll fill you and Derek in later." He jotted some information on the file extension.

"No worries. I can get other information about Billy Edmond. It would be nice to know what they were looking for. I'd like to know if it had any bearing on his death." Kelly took her seat.

"I will have something later today." Kyle headed to his bat cave. "I'll be downstairs. If you guys go for lunch, let me know. Otherwise, call if you need my help again."

"Thanks," Kelly said without looking up.

"Thank you." Felicia hung up her desktop phone. "Kelly, I just got off the phone with Edmond's house manager, Mr. Aleshire. He gave me the contact information for the family attorney. If I can get the attorney to see us today, you want to go with me? We can bring Kyle with us and grab some lunch while we're out."

"Yeah. Sounds good," Kelly said.

"Great. I'll call now."

CHAPTER EIGHT

Derek fell out of his car when he pushed the door open. He checked his skin for glass and cuts. Nothing. He sat on the hot concrete, gawking at the windows of his car. Not a single broken window. His heart thudded against his chest.

A man walking by ran over to him. "Are you okay?" he asked, reaching out to help Derek off the ground.

Derek squinted at a young police officer standing in front of him. He lifted his hand. The officer leaned in closer to him.

"When are you going to stop him? It was an accident."

Blood dripped down the officer's face. Derek flinched, withdrawing his hand.

"Buddy? You sure you're okay?" The officer stood with his hand outstretched.

Derek's brow wrinkled as he looked at the officer. The blood was gone. "Uh yeah." He tried to smile and laugh it off. "A bee must have hitched a ride with me." He lifted one eyebrow. "I don't like bees."

"Oh, I understand. My wife is allergic to them. She can swell within a few seconds." He pulled Derek off the ground.

Derek brushed himself off. "Thanks. I must look an idiot."

"Nah. Just glad I could help." The officer walked into the ME's building.

Derek stood at his car. He peeked inside, looking for the woman. No sign of her and no blood, either. He thought he had seen her before, but he didn't know who she could be. He rested his hands on the hood of his vehicle. The nightmares were bad enough, but now these visions were coming when he's awake. He couldn't live like this. He patted his pocket, looking for gum. Realizing he'd placed it in the console of his vehicle, he opted to go without.

As he walked into the building, the officer who helped him chatted to a few other men. When he saw Derek, he smiled. Nodding, Derek stepped up to the reception. "Hi, I'm Agent Reed. Dr. Callahan is expecting me."

"Oh, yes. He told me to send you on in." She pointed to a metal door with a key card lock. "Just enter there; I'll buzz you in. Follow the red stripe. When it dead ends, go right, and you'll run into autopsy."

"Thank you." Derek followed the young girl's instructions, although he didn't need them. He had been there before. Walking down the corridor, he heard whispers and echoes of conversations. Brushing off the eerie feeling, he quickened his pace as he convinced himself the voices came from people in outlying offices. Soft jazz filtered down the hall. Derek smiled as he neared his destination. He knew Dr. Callahan's music. He pushed open the large swinging double doors.

Dr. Callahan glanced up. "Derek," he said. "I'm glad to see you." He looked towards the table. "I just started."

The garrote was still twisted around the man's neck. Derek studied the open wounds on the man's head. He looked up, smiling at the doctor. "These open cuts, they aren't deep enough to kill him?"

Dr. Callahan shook his head. "They would have knocked him out. Until I do an x-ray and see the damage, I can guess they would have killed him, but not immediately. Even then, they may only render him unconscious for a long time. The wire around his neck killed him." He pointed to the neck wound. "I waited to remove this last."

"Can you tell from the angle of the head wounds whether he sat or stood during the attack with the bat?" Derek glanced around. "Where is the bat?"

"The CSU has it. As for the head wounds," Dr. Callahan moved towards the end of the table. He swung over the magnifying light and examined the gashes. Stepping around the body, he studied the wounds from another angle. "I can hazard a guess. When I remove the scalp and examine the skull, I can tell more. Looking at the direction of the gashes and the way the skin tore, I'd be willing to guess Mr. Edmond sat while being hit with the bat."

Derek's brow wrinkled. "Back at the house, the wall behind the desk had blood spatter on it."

"Yes. From the direction of these cuts, I would say the killer stood in front of our victim." Doc raised his hands as if he held a bat. "Our killer swung left to right, striking Edmond at a downward angle." As he lifted the imaginary bat, he continued. "The cast-off would make sense."

Derek pooched out his lips as his brow wrinkled.

"What is it?" Dr. Callahan asked.

"I need to see the photos of the scene, but do you think these hits to the head could've been used to incapacitate him?"

Dr. Callahan shrugged. "Sure. It may account for the closeness of the wounds to each other. Rapid strikes would render him unconscious. I can make sure CSU sends the photos." The doc stepped back to the other side of the body, facing Derek. "These bruises here," he pointed to the man's arms, "these occurred while alive. I'm betting x-rays will show some fractures." He pointed to his legs. "These compound fractures also occurred while alive."

Derek's dream slammed into him. The man in the dream had compound fractures of the legs. How could he dream about a murder of a guy he didn't know? He looked up to find the doc staring at him. "What about the tape?" Derek asked.

"You okay?"

Derek nodded.

"Well, the tape is odd." He reached into a metal bowl resting on a cart next to the table. The doctor held up the tape. "I will send this over to CSU. Hopefully, they will find something useful on it." He placed it back on the tray. "The killer taped your guy's ass cheeks together. But he didn't stop there."

Dr. Callahan lifted the man's penis. "He taped his balls and then ripped the tape off. This tape is an industrial-style tape. The adhesive is extra sticky. When he ripped it off, it removed layers of skin from the balls and scrotum area."

"Ouch." Derek winced.

"Yeah. It's like some kind of hazing gone wrong," Dr. Callahan said.

"Sounds like a locker room prank. There is no way he sat in the chair while this guy taped his butt cheeks together. And it would be really hard for the guy to move with two broken legs. If we come back to my earlier thought concerning the blows to the head, the killer may have used those to incapacitate him. Our guy here is pretty big. My next question is, how did the killer get him in the chair after he used the tape?"

"I'll be running a toxicology screen. We can see if he used something to subdue Mr. Edmond, besides the hits to the head. As for getting him back in the chair, I would suspect a spike in adrenaline could account for the needed strength."

"Something isn't making sense." Derek closed his eyes, visualizing the room at the victim's house.

"What's not making sense, Derek?"

"Why would he go to all this trouble, with the tape and the bat, if he planned to use a garrote on the man?" Derek stared at the wound around Billy Edmond's neck. "This guy wanted him awake for the tape. He would want him to feel every hair and piece of skin being ripped off. Then he dressed him in panties. Then beat him with the bat. All of this is for humiliation. To put the killer in a place of power." He placed his hands on the table, leaning forward. "Our killer knew Billy." He looked at the victim's wrists. "I don't see any ligature marks."

"No. I haven't found any."

"You won't. If Billy knew the killer, there would be some trust. No ligatures needed. But the bat, he needed to use it to incapacitate him. And since he used the one from Billy's office, I have to wonder if the killer came with the intent to kill him or did something go wrong. Right now, I really got nothing."

He pointed to the body. "If you can tell me the order everything happened, it would really help me."

"Well, you don't ask for much, do you?" He laughed. "I will make my assessments of the injuries and try to give you some answers. I will make sure CSU sends you all their reports and photos from the crime scene. I know they also took a video. I will make sure you get them today. Maybe those will help you get some answers as well."

"I appreciate it." Derek started to leave, then turned around. "I want to ask you a hypothetical question."

Dr. Callahan raised an eyebrow at him. "Hypothetical, huh?"

Derek grinned. "Can a facial injury, say a like a broken nose and cheek, have adverse side effects during the healing process?"

Dr. Callahan put down his scalpel. "What kind of adverse effects?"

"Oh, like maybe nightmares or day visions, or auditory sounds?"

The doctor ogled his friend, although Derek was more than just a friend. Both he and Dr. Chelsea had a fondness for the young agent. "What exactly are you experiencing, Derek?"

Derek's head hung. "I said this was hypothetical. How do you know it's me?"

"Because I'm not stupid."

"You can't say anything to Ronald. I don't want to be pulled off duty again. Promise me."

Dr. Callahan's expression softened. "I won't mention it. Tell me what's going on."

Derek peeked over his shoulder at the door. "I've had weird dreams. And now they're happening when I'm awake."

"What kind of weird dreams?"

Derek shrugged. "I don't know. It's like pieces of several dreams, but they make little sense."

"Sometimes, our brain fills in parts of our memory with tidbits that don't make sense. It may be what you are experiencing. I know you had some memory loss from the injuries you suffered at the hands of Josiah Craig. Your body is still healing. Your psyche is going to be healing for a long time."

"Would my brain use current events to fill in the blank spots?"

"The brain can do a lot of things. It could be possible for your conscious mind to take current events or even past events and mix them with dreams, trying to fill the gaps of memory. Have you talked to Ronald since your last appointment?"

Derek shook his head. "When I got back from my family trip, I had to get this unit up and running. I didn't get back to Dr. Chelsea's office."

"Let's not forget you chased a serial killer while you were on forced medical leave. You didn't even have time off before you put yourself back under a severe amount of stress. Now you have this case, plus the responsibility of a new unit. You're stressed. Even though you may not think you are. All of this is taxing on a body that isn't one hundred percent."

"I'm sure that's what it is." Derek smiled at the man.

"Derek, promise me you'll call Dr. Chelsea if these visions get to be too much. Ronald will talk to you outside of the office, off the record. You know he would never do anything to jeopardize your career."

"I know. I know I can trust you and him." He stuck his hands in the front pockets of his jeans. "I need to get back to work. Make sure CSU sends over everything." Derek stopped again at the door. "Just out of curiosity, how well did you know Billy Edmond?"

Doctor Callahan shrugged. "His family came from old money. His dad had a law firm. Lawyers ran in the family. I remember when Billy graduated from Pepperdine with a law degree, his father expected him to come work at the firm."

"Why didn't he, do you know?"

"Billy liked to make his own way." The doctor laughed. "He had no problem using his family's connections, though."

"What kind of law degree did Billy get?"

"I think corporate law."

"Hmm, is that what his family practiced?"

"No. His father practiced criminal law. Very successful, too. Had one of the best firms in the country." The doctor twisted his back, stretching.

"How well did you know the family?"

"Not very well. Met Sr. at several city functions. Played a round of golf with him a few times for charity. Billy's parents died in a car wreck six years ago. It looked like an accident."

Derek scowled. "What do you mean it looked like an accident?"

The doctor pulled a stool over and sat down, looking across the body at Derek. "They'd been on a trip to Salt River Canyon and drove back via Apache Trail, State Route 88. They went off the road. Nothing but cliffs along that stretch of highway."

"You said it looked like an accident. What do you mean?"

"Eyewitness reports stated the car took a hard right and just went flying off the cliff. The investigation ruled out suicide, but no one could account for why the car took a header. Not much left of the wreckage, as you could imagine. With nothing to contradict the findings, it went into the books as an accident."

"What happened to the law firm?" Derek asked.

"Billy inherited it. I believe he sold it to one partner. He never wanted to practice criminal law. With no other children, their fortune went to him. However, by then, Billy had amassed his own fortune. No one has ever suggested or thought Billy killed his parents." The doctor stood and stretched again. "If you need anything else, let me know."

"Thanks for the information. Talk to you later, Doc." Derek made his way back to his vehicle, uncertain he wanted to drive it again. He bent down and checked the front and back seats. No unwanted visitors. That he could see.

CHAPTER NINE

Agent Rogers hung up the phone. "They can see us at 2 p.m." She checked her watch. "We could go eat first, then head over to the office."

Kelly lifted her head. "Okay. Let's call Kyle. See if he wants to take his car or ride with us."

Felicia pulled her phone and texted him. Within a few seconds, he responded. "Kyle said give him five minutes. He'll be right up."

Kelly leaned back in her chair. "Do you think you'll like this unit?"

Felicia sat on the corner of her desk. "Yeah. Arizona is taking some getting used to. At least the heat. But I like to snowboard, and we are close to skiing. Can't go wrong there. As for this unit, I like it. I like Derek. He's way better than the last boss I had."

Kelly's brow wrinkled. "What was wrong with your last boss?"

"Special Agent Jack Robertson. He thought he should be running the FBI. He had his nose so far up Director Fretz's ass." Felicia turned, smiling at Kyle. "Well, damn. Took you long enough." She grabbed her slim ID wallet containing her badge and her gun from her desk drawer.

"You want to drive?" Kelly asked.

"Um, you picked me up this morning; you have to drive." Felicia smiled at her. "Forgot, huh?"

Nodding, Kelly laughed. "I did."

"Am I riding with you, or do I need to take my car?" Kyle asked as they walked towards the door.

"We have to go see the victim's lawyer after we eat. Unless you want to go with us?" Felicia stopped at Emma's desk. "Emma, you want to go eat with us?"

Emma shook her head. "Thank you for asking. I need to run home."

"Okay," Felicia said as she followed the others out the door. "See you later."

Kelly unlocked her door.

"Where are we going?" Kyle asked, standing at his car.

Kelly and Felicia exchanged glances, shrugging.

"I don't even know," Kelly said.

"I know of one restaurant. It's Mexican. Best homemade tortillas ever," Kyle said. "Follow me."

"Sounds good." Kelly followed his red Kia Soul out of the parking lot. She cranked the AC in her old Ford F-150. "I know I should get a newer vehicle, but this one has a great AC and heater. And I own it outright. I just can't bring myself to buy a new car."

"I've had my Jeep Renegade for five years. Just paid it off. I'm not buying another car until the wheels fall off." Felicia pulled her phone from her pocket.

Kelly glanced over, dividing her time between the road and her new team member. "Where does your family live?"

"My mother died a few years ago. Heart attack."

"Oh, I'm so sorry." Kelly turned, following Kyle.

"Thank you. My dad lives in Marquette, Michigan. That's where I grew up." When they pulled into the parking lot of the Mexican restaurant, Felicia sent a text to Derek. Just in case he wanted to join them.

"My mom and dad live in Oregon. My brother runs the family business—hardware store. My parents are semi-retired." Kelly cocked her head towards Kyle as she exited her vehicle. "Where is your family located?"

Kyle held the door. "My mom and dad divorced. Dad lives in San Francisco, and my mom lives in Nebraska." He saw the long, sad looks on their faces. "It's not bad. They're best friends, and we often spend holidays together. They're just better off not being married."

They took a table at the back. After placing their orders, a comfortable silence fell over them.

"Where did you find a place to live?" Kelly asked Kyle.

"I got a sweet deal. Derek has a small one-bedroom bungalow on his property, I'm renting from him." He stuffed a chip loaded with salsa into his mouth.

Felicia grinned. "Teacher's pet."

Kyle scoffed. "Whatever. You're just jealous."

She laughed. "I am, actually. Although, I like my apartment. My bedroom has a porch facing the mountains. And my kitchen has a porch that opens right out to the pool. The best of both worlds." She swallowed a bite of tortilla. "Oh my gosh, these are so good."

"I told you. Best tortillas I've ever had." Kyle rubbed his hands together when their food arrived. "Mmm, this looks so good." Savoring his first bite, he glanced at Kelly. "Where's your place?"

She didn't hear him at first as she inspected her food. Kelly used her fork to separate each item, creating space between the food.

"Kelly?" he asked.

"Huh? Did I miss something?" she asked, taking her first bite.

"Where do you live?" he asked again. Sneaking a peek at Felicia, who watched her fellow agent in amusement.

"I found a small bungalow to rent. It's in a neighborhood near Felicia. It's a one-bedroom, with an extra small room I'm using as an office. I'm not a big fan of apartments."

Felicia moaned as she ate. "This is so good. It's delicious."

Kyle took a sip of his drink.

As soon as they finished their meals, the server brought each of them a sopapilla.

Kyle and Felicia smothered theirs in honey, while Kelly kept the honey and the sopapilla separate on the plate. Making sure the delicious treat didn't touch the sticky goo.

Felicia raised an eyebrow at her. "Do you have OCD?"

Kelly's nose wrinkled. "No. Why do you ask?"

"You don't like your food to touch. Anyone I've ever known who doesn't like their food touching has OCD. Take my uncle. Same thing with him. He is a neat freak. My aunt loves it. She never has to clean. He does the same thing with his food."

Kyle laughed as he signed his credit card bill, placing his card back in his wallet. "I can see from your desk, being a clean freak didn't rub off on you."

"Haha." She threw a sugar packet at him as she left money on the table. "I'm a little messy, but I'm not dirty. I keep things clean, just not very well organized."

"That's an understatement," Kelly said as they all headed out to the parking lot.

.

CHAPTER TEN

Derek received a text from Felicia as he walked into the empty FBI office. Pocketing his phone, he walked to the kitchen. He paused as he entered the hallway. "This is stupid. Now I'm scared to walk to the kitchen. Get a grip on yourself, Derek," he said.

Searching the refrigerator, he found the lunch meat and sandwich stuff he bought the other day. As he put together his lunch, he remembered what Doc Callahan had said about Billy Edmond's parents.

Sitting at his desk, he mulled around what he knew. Logging into the network, Derek opened the Billy Edmond case file. Emma had separated each agent's notes with a date and time of entry. He hoped his guys would follow this process from here on out. "This is fantastic," he said, smiling.

He jotted down the information on his notepad, then wrote out his conversation with the doc. He scrolled through the notes Kelly had entered. "Wait, what's this?" he asked as he read the notes. Checking his watch, he wondered when his team would be back.

He glanced up when he heard the buzz of the alarm. The monitor showed Emma entering, bringing Marc Anthony with her. A smile filled his face. He stood to greet the behemoth at the door. "Well, hello, Marc Anthony." Derek saw the sheer delight on Emma's face. "I see you didn't waste any time bringing him here."

"I'm sorry. I went home, and he looked at me like I had abandoned him. I shouldn't have gone home in the middle of the day. It's not something I usually do." She tugged gently on his lead while making a clicking noise. The dog sat right next to her leg. "Marc Anthony, can you say hello?"

The dog lifted his enormous head and howled.

Derek didn't have to kneel to scratch him. Sitting, the dog reached his mid-section. "Nice to meet you, Marc Anthony."

The dog head-butted his hip, almost knocking Derek off balance.

"He minds well, but the minute you give him attention, all those manners go out the door. All he wants is attention." Emma released the lead off his collar. The dog ran around, sniffing his new surroundings.

Derek went back to his desk. "Emma. Great job on setting up the file system. I hope my team can keep it up."

"If they have any trouble, I can input their notes."

"No. That's not your job." Derek said, taking a drink of his soda.

"I'm not sure I will have much else to do. How about this? If I can't do it, they can input their own notes."

"Well, let's see how efficient these guys are."

At that moment, Kyle entered the building.

Marc Anthony ran to greet him.

Kyle's eyes widened at the humongous dog. "Whoa, holy shit," he said as the creature bounded towards him.

"He won't bite. I promise." Emma laughed. "Famous last words of every dog owner."

"Hey, buddy." Kyle scratched his head. "Wow. Who is this?"

"This is Marc Anthony. I shouldn't have gone home today. I couldn't leave him."

Kyle left the dog lying next to his master as he made his way towards his boss. "I got a problem."

"Let me guess. It's the search done on Billy Edmond?"

"Yeah. Someone electronically locked the file." Kyle pulled over one of the free chairs next to Derek's desk.

Derek cocked an eyebrow at his resident geek. "Why do I have the feeling you're getting ready to tell me something bad?"

Kyle chuckled. "Not really bad. How do you want me to handle it? I can get around the lock, and I can probably do it without leaving tracks."

"And that would be illegal. Essentially, you'd be hacking our system." Derek leaned back in his chair.

"Well, I work for the entity I'm hacking. I have clearance up to third level security. Fifth level is reserved for the head of the FBI. Technically, I wouldn't be breaking into it."

"I think you're splitting hairs. Can you tell where the lock originated? Inside the system or out?"

Kyle sighed. "Inside the system. High level. But I can't tell which region, office, or personnel put it on there. See, each electronic lock has a series of numbers attached. Based on those numbers, I can usually tell the level and department. But this lock only has the level. Top tier. But no department."

Derek placed his elbows on his desk. "What does that tell you?"

"Basically, someone with one hell of a security clearance looked at

Billy Edmond."

"Damn." Derek dragged a hand through his hair. "This is going to be a mess." He sighed. "Have you found anything on Billy and the congressman's relationship?"

"Not much in the way of incriminating evidence. At least on its face. They had some major business deals. A few properties they owned together in Washington, along with a few businesses they invested in together. I got the impression they were working on something. I also found they were both in Washington when some high-level meetings occurred on the hill. I can't tell you if both were at these meetings, but both were in the area on the same days."

"Shit. Do you think any of this has anything to do with the electronic lock on the file?"

Kyle shrugged. "I couldn't say for sure. Do you want me to keep digging?"

Derek shook his head. "First, let me ask the AD. If he can't find out anything, I will ask Congressman Jackson."

Kyle's eyes widened. "Going to the big man, huh?"

"He asked for this unit to work this case specifically. I figure, if he wants answers, he will break down roadblocks. But I won't use that lifeline until I have to." Derek finished his soda. "I have a feeling, where this case is concerned, I will only get one bite at the apple."

"Okay. I'll wait for your instructions. I may experiment with the lock and see if I can pull any more information off it."

"As long as you don't break it and trip the alarm. I have no problem with that."

Kyle stood just as the girls came in.

Derek shook his head when he saw the young man's eyes light up at the site of Felicia. He wondered how long it would be before this became awkward.

The agents fawned over the big dog, lavishing him with kisses and scratches.

Derek rolled his eyes. When he brought Lola here, the two dogs would be spoiled. "Kelly."

"Yes, sir?" she asked, walking towards him.

"Kyle told me about the search done on our dead guy. I will make some calls on the file. For now, leave it alone until I have some answers."

"No problem."

"What do you guys have so far. Anything?" Derek asked.

Felicia sat in her desk chair, spinning as she answered. "We had a meeting with Billy Edmond's lawyer. He left most of his estate to Mr. Aleshire. Considered him family. His only family. He left a sizeable portion to his high school athletic team. Well, the school anyway."

Kelly sat next to her. "Yeah, and get this, he left a sizable amount to his former high school baseball coach. Who is now the headmaster of said high school. Not only that, but he left a sizable chunk to Pepperdine University, his dead wife's family, and charity."

Derek cocked his head to the side. "Did the house manager know he would get an inheritance?"

Felicia shook her head. "Nope. Billy made sure all the parties had no idea until his demise."

"Maybe this exonerates the house manager on motive. If he really didn't know. We need to make sure Mr. Aleshire hasn't withdrawn any large sums of money." Derek scribbled on his notepad.

"Do you think he put out a hit on his boss?" Kelly asked, leaning forward placing her elbows on her knees.

"Do you?" Derek asked without looking up at his agent.

Kelly frowned.

When she didn't respond, Derek tilted his head, staring at her. "Give me your honest opinion."

Her eyes met Felicia's. Kelly turned back to Derek. "No. I don't. From my conversation with Norman Aleshire, I didn't walk away with anything but an enormous amount of sorrow and loss."

Felicia agreed. "I got the same impression. And to be honest, I would automatically put him at the top of the list. But I'm not seeing it."

Derek rubbed his chin. "Okay. Let's put this theory on the back burner. If we see any evidence leading back to it, we can revisit." He paused. "If no one knew the terms of the will, then none of the beneficiaries had an obvious motive to kill Billy.

"After my meeting with the ME, I came away with the distinct impression the killer knew Billy. The injuries were very personal. And if we lean towards the theory that Billy didn't tell anyone about his will, where does that leave us?"

He glanced around the room, waiting for a reply.

"Someone outside his circle. But close enough to hold a personal grudge." Felicia spun around in her chair.

Kyle walked towards the basement, stopping just before rounding the corner. "I'll run everyone from the will. I can also cross-check them with each other."

"That sounds good. Run all of them. Deep run. Pull everything." Derek turned to Kelly. "Make sure he gets all the names."

"I can do that." She tapped something on her phone screen. "I took notes on this. I can forward the names to you, Kyle."

"I'll go downstairs and start the searches. I should have the security analyzed by the end of the day, too." He smiled at Felicia. "Are we still on for a beer later?"

"Yeah. You will have to take me home." Felicia looked at Kelly. "Unless you are going to come with us."

Kelly shrugged. "If you guys don't mind. A beer sounds good."

"Great." Kyle headed towards his lair.

Derek's thoughts drifted back to the bat at the house. He closed his eyes and remembered the photos of the baseball team. "Kelly, did you get information regarding Billy's high school?"

"Like what? What were you looking for?" She used her phone's stylus to tap something on the screen.

"The bat used on our victim appears to have been owned by the victim. I want to know everything about his high school baseball team. See if you can dig up when he played, who he played with, and if he has had any interactions with members of the team since high school. We know he left money to the coach or rather, headmaster. Maybe our answer lies with him."

Derek addressed Felicia. "I want you to call the headmaster and get an appointment with him tomorrow. You and I will go there." He thought for a moment. "Tell him we need to see him and don't give him a chance to dodge. Tell him we will be there at 10 a.m."

"You got it." She wheeled her chair back to her desk and began looking for his phone number.

"Also, get in touch with the wife's family. I want to talk to them, as well. I want to see if they can shed any light on our Billy Edmond."

"Do you want to see them tomorrow?" she asked.

"Yes. I understand they have been out of Billy's life since their daughter's death, but press the issue if they give you the runaround. See if they can see us at 2 p.m. or later tomorrow."

"On it," Felicia said, saluting her boss.

CHAPTER ELEVEN

With everyone working on a task, Derek dialed the AD from his cell phone. He walked down the hallway towards the sleeping quarters.

"Derek, how's the unit going so far?"

"Pretty good."

The AD laughed. "Well, let's hope it gets better than that. A lot of reputations are riding on your success."

Derek snickered. "They hitched their horse to the wrong wagon then. Listen, I need your help."

"Oh, no. This doesn't sound good."

"Okay, one of my agents searched the FBI database to find what she could on our victim. It seems someone ran a red level search on him three weeks ago. Can you find out who, what, and why?"

"I don't understand. Why don't you just open the file and see what's in there?" asked Assistant Director Fretz.

"It has an electronic lock. Why would there be a red level search on Billy Edmond? And why would they lock the file?"

Silence echoed over the line.

"Hello? Assistant Director Fretz?"

"Yeah. I'm here. This isn't good, Derek."

"I figured." Derek heard some shuffling, then a door close.

"Give me a minute. I'm going to call you back. Is your phone secured?"

"Yes. It is."

"Okay."

The line went dead. Derek waited for the ring. When he answered, the line beeped twice. He put in a unique code, allowing the call to be connected. "Why did you use your secure line?"

"I didn't think this would come up."

"Didn't think what would come up?"

"It has nothing to do with Billy's murder. Billy needed a third-tier security clearance."

Derek closed his eyes, trying to process. "Why would Billy Edmond need any level of security clearance?"

"He needed to give testimony in a land deal involving a local politician. The security clearance helped vet and clear him."

"How the hell is that not a possibility for his murder?" Derek paced the small bedroom. "Is this why Congressman Jackson requested me to work this case?"

"No. No one knew. This only just came down. It involves a massive land deal out west of Phoenix."

"The Balderro deal? Holy crap, are you kidding me?"

"Listen. No one knew about Billy's testimony against the landowner and the company wanting to develop it."

"Why didn't you tell me this upfront?"

"You weren't supposed to find it. No one was supposed to find it. It was a committee thing."

Derek sighed. "Who else knows about his testimony?"

"Me, Assistant Deputy Director Jessup, the head of the FBI, and Congressman Flannery, he's the head of the committee who called for the investigation."

"Oh, hell. I bet I'm not allowed to breathe a word of this. And I have to instruct my team not to pursue this."

"Yes. However, if during your investigation, you find anything pointing in this direction, I will get you clearance to see the file and see if it has any bearing on Billy's murder."

"This is crap. I won't cover anything up. If it leads towards this, I expect full disclosure."

"You'll have it. I promise. For now. Call off your dogs. Sometimes I wish you hadn't picked the team you did. I have a feeling these guys can uncover anything."

"Good. That's what I want." Derek sighed. "I like this team so far. I have four more coming onboard. I'll be eager to see how they fit in."

"Oh, sorry. I forgot to mention Frank Pillard won't be joining your team. He had a family crisis and asked to stay with his current unit."

"No worries. Mackle comes in on Monday. It won't be a problem."

"Keep me posted, Derek."

"I will." Dead air filled his ear. He pocketed his phone and walked back into the main room. He punched the intercom on his desk phone.

"Yo, boss man, what you need?"

"Kyle, come here if you can stop what you're doing."

"Be right up."

"Kelly and Felicia, I need to speak with you guys, as soon as Kyle gets up here." Derek glanced over his shoulder as he heard his geek's steps coming down the hallway. He turned back to the group. His heart stopped when he saw the chair in the corner, not blinking for what felt like a thousand minutes. When he finally closed his eyes, they were dry and sticky.

"Derek?" Felicia called out to him. When he didn't respond, her eyes darted between Kyle and Kelly.

"Derek?" Kyle snapped his fingers in front of Derek's face.

Marc Anthony began barking. The deep sound echoed throughout the church. All heads turned towards the dog, expecting to see an intruder.

"Marc Anthony? What has gotten into you?" Emma reached over and distracted the dog from barking at nothing but an empty chair. She shrugged at everyone. "I really don't know what's gotten into him."

"What? Huh?" Derek asked, snapping out of his trance. "Sorry, guys. I've been having some horrible headaches as my nose and cheek continue healing." He avoided looking at the winged chair sitting in the corner near Emma's desk. He had no idea why his mind brought her back. He had to consider running this unit, and handling this case were too much for his mind to process, and it needed a release.

"No problem. We all know about the case you worked on after the Josiah Craig incident and what a toll it took on you. You probably need downtime. Which means no cases." Kyle grinned as he sat on the corner of Felicia's desk. She smiled up at him, and his heart nearly pounded out of his chest.

Derek leaned against his desk. "I've been instructed to back off the locked file you guys uncovered today." All the agents looked at each other before focusing their attention back on him. "From what I know of each of you, this doesn't sit well. If anything we uncover leads back to the locked file, the AD has assured me he will grant us access to it. That's all I can offer you. Until then, take it out of the official record."

"I don't understand?" Kelly asked. "Why?"

"I can't tell you. I can say none of us in this room has the clearance for what is in that file. It pertains to a completely separate matter. However, I repeat, if you find anything pertaining to what's in it, I will get the AD to give us the intel. Until then, drop it."

Kyle squinted at him. "I don't like this."

"I know this bothers you three as much as it does me. Felicia, did you get us a meeting tomorrow with the headmaster?"

"Yes. He sounded nervous and kept asking me why the FBI wanted to speak with him. I didn't tell him the why. If he hasn't heard about our victim, I want to see his reaction in person."

"Good thinking. I like it. What about the late wife's family? What's her name?"

"Francine. Her parents are Loretta and Isaac Wallace. They live in North Central Phoenix, along the bridle path running along Central Avenue." Felicia whistled. "Prime real estate right there.

"Some major players live around there." Derek sat at his desk. "Did they agree to the time?"

"They did," Felicia said.

"Okay." Derek opened a few of the old case files, checking the notes. He glanced at Kyle sitting at one of the desktop computers typing at lightning speed. Derek peeked at the chair in the corner. Empty.

CHAPTER TWELVE

Monday evening

Derek pulled into his driveway. He sighed as he waited for his garage door to open. Lola's head rested on the window sill. He wondered how long she had sat there waiting for him. Probably most of the day. He had a doggy door installed a few weeks earlier so she could access the backyard. But he knew she hated being here alone. He hated being here alone.

Once in the garage with his car door open, he could hear the whimpering coming from inside the house. "Sweetie," he said, entering his home. He reached down, scratching her head. "Did you miss me?"

Lola ran around his legs, sniffing his pants and shoes. Along with his hands. She stopped and cocked her head at him.

He laughed. "Do you smell Marc Anthony? You'll meet him tomorrow." He walked towards his spacious living room. The rounded archways and ceilings helped circulate the cool air. The cooling tiles and the tile roof helped keep the interior temp much cooler.

He dropped his bag with his laptop on the table at the end of the entryway. He'd let everyone leave early today, but he planned on working here at home. Something about the five-year-old case nagged at him. "Before anything, I bet you're hungry, huh, girl?"

Lola's butt wiggled as her stub tail shifted back and forth. She pranced around, excited by the word hungry.

"Here you go." He watched her for a split second as she wolfed down her food. "Now, what am I going to eat?" he asked the dog as he stood in front of the open refrigerator. Scanning what he had to make, he opted for the left-over spaghetti. He grabbed the container of food, along with three beers. Placing the food in the microwave, he guzzled one of the beers, throwing the empty bottle away. "Man, that tasted good." He grabbed a bowl from the cabinet just as the microwave pinged.

Emptying the entire container of pasta, he took the two remaining beers and sat on the sofa. He turned on the DVD and let the last episode of Star Trek replay. Lola sat patiently at his feet, waiting for him to share, which he did. Breaking off a piece of the French bread he had brought with him from the kitchen, he tossed it to her. "Your mama is going to be so mad at me. She's going to say I spoiled you."

Lola nudged his leg, wanting more.

He opened and chugged half of the second beer. He ate most of his food, leaving several bites for Lola. Finishing off the beer, he put the bowl on the floor for the dog. Once done, he took the empty beer bottle and his dish to the kitchen. He placed his bowl in the sink, filling it with water as he threw his empty bottle in the trash.

On his way back to the living room, he grabbed his bag. Not really tired, or possibly overly tired, he went over the notes from the current case. He set his computer on his lap, sighing as he searched through what little evidence they had gathered.

Kyle had input his findings from the security tape. Not much of anything there. It seems the system had been shut off around 6 p.m. Derek quickly glanced at the report the ME had sent him. It looked like Billy died between 8 and 10 p.m.

Lola jumped up and snuggled next to him, resting her nose on his thigh, forcing him to push the laptop a little further away.

"Seriously, this is the only place you can lay?" he asked her as he rubbed her belly. Derek considered the timeline. He knew the house manager reset the system that morning when he came in. "That would fit. Lola?"

The dog's ears perked up.

"Tell me what you think. Why did someone turn off the system before our killer arrived? What would make Billy Edmond turn off his security?" Derek pulled his phone from his back pocket. Searching the file, he found the house manager's number.

"Hello?"

"Mr. Aleshire? This is FBI Agent Derek Reed. Do you have a moment for a few questions?"

"Yes. Whatever you need."

"Can you tell me if Mr. Edmond regularly shut off the security system?"

"Yes. There have been other times I have come back from my night away, and Billy had turned off the system."

"Do you know why?"

"Agent Reed, as business smart as Billy is...was, he wasn't technically savvy, especially when it came to our security system. Once armed, the code must be input every time someone enters and exits the home. On my days off, Billy often shut off the system so he wouldn't have to mess with it while he worked out, swam laps, or entertained friends. I tried to tell him not to. But he always kept the gate's system engaged. He argued it was enough. It uses a different code."

"I'm confused. Someone also shut down the camera system."

Aleshire chuckled. "And that was one of my issues with Billy. When he shut the system down, he shut it all down. Except the gate."

Derek heard a sniffle on the other end of the line. "I'm sorry I bothered you, Mr. Aleshire. I know this is a hard time for you. I really appreciate you taking the time to answer my questions."

"Don't be sorry. I want Billy's murderer caught." He paused. "I'm not sure why Billy might have shut off the cameras, unless it had to do with his expected visitor. Perhaps he wanted privacy."

"Was he seeing anyone?" Derek asked.

"I don't think so. He very much loved his wife. But I know he had a fling or two here or there. Nothing but a one-night stand on occasion."

"Do you have any of these women's names by chance?"

"No. I'm sorry. It is the one area I didn't pry. I think these interludes were for release, not a relationship."

"Thank you again."

"Anytime, Agent."

"Have a good evening, sir." Derek hung up and stared at his laptop. "Okay, Lola. There goes that mystery." He typed in a few notes into the case file regarding this conversation. Emma's system made it easy to put in updates and keep notes current.

"Lola, Emma is going to work out perfectly."

The dog raised her eyebrows, listening.

"Back to the timeline. If Billy shut it off himself, then I'm willing to bet he expected a visitor and didn't want to mess with the system. So, the killer comes in. I think they knew each other. What do you think, Lola?" he asked as he scratched her ear.

She groaned.

"I think I'm right too."

Scanning a few more notes, Derek knew the key to this may not lie in finding out who. That would take way too long... but figuring out the why may shorten the list. He made a note on his computer to have his new guys run down anyone who may have had a problem with Billy. Including any business deals gone bad.

Derek reached out to close his laptop when he saw the file for the case from five years ago. A case he shouldn't have pulled into the Legacy Unit. But curiosity had the best of him. And it had been the one case the director gave him permission to work on while on light duty after the Josiah Craig case.

Clicking open the file, he read the reports. The police detectives determined the first murder was a home invasion and processed it accordingly. The FBI stepped in after two more similar murders occurred.

The previous agent's report stated he saw no connection between the three murdered couples. At that point, the FBI stepped back. Derek also knew the agent covering the investigation had three weeks before retirement, and he didn't want the hassle of working a major case.

Looking over the crime scene photos, Derek saw that something didn't fit. One photo showed an overall picture of the first deceased couple in their bedroom. The wife died where she lay sleeping. Her head bashed in. "I bet she died instantly," Derek said, staring at the photo. Another photo showed the husband on the floor several feet away from his side of the bed.

Derek read the ME's report on the wife. She had one blow to the head. The ME said she died from a slow intracranial bleed. "But the killer only hit her once. Why?" he asked as he read through the rest of her report. His brow wrinkled as opened his last beer, taking a long pull. "If the killer wanted to kill them both, why would he only hit her once? Wouldn't he want to make sure he killed her?"

The detective's report said it looked like the husband tried to help his wife. But as Derek studied the photos, the placement of the body didn't fit with him trying to rescue his wife.

He scanned the rest of the report. The first detective on scene stated the husband had been struck while in the bed. But the pictures of the blood spatter on the walls didn't match up with his statement.

"No way it happened while he laid in bed." He searched for the CSU report. There was no mention of blood spatter, the angle of the blood spatter, or anything relating to the orientation of the body. "What the hell? Who investigated this crime scene?"

He went back through each case. The first murder was five years ago.

Nine months later, the second murder occurred. "Wait, how did I miss that?" He pulled each file sheet. "I'll be damned." The third murder occurred a year and a half after the first. "No fucking wonder they couldn't find any connections. They were looking at these as individual cases. Son of a bitch."

All things pointed to these cases not being related. But looking at them now, Derek could see too many similarities between them. The three murders took place in the victims' homes. The killer had used a bat or other cylindrical object to strike the couples. However, it didn't appear the wives were the intended targets. Injuries to the husbands were far more extensive. They all suffered before their deaths.

A random home invasion would not have the same MO in three different cases. Not to mention, there was nothing reported stolen. "Why the hell is someone going to do a home invasion, kill the homeowners, and not steal anything?"

Derek closed his computer, placing it on the coffee table. "This case is a clusterfuck." He decided to let one of the new agents, George, analyze the photos. The blood spatter would be the best place to start. If anyone could see the connection, he had a funny feeling it would be this guy.

He sat back on the sofa. With the computer gone, Lola inched her head up more onto his lap. He closed his eyes, listening to the Star Trek episode in the background. Stroking Lola's soft belly, her rhythmic breathing lulled Derek into a relaxed state.

He heard a muffled sound. Cracking one eye open, he didn't see anything. Derek thought of Chrissy. He thought he saw her at the office. But why? He still had nightmares about Josiah, but they weren't as prevalent as before. Nor have they been as scary—until last night.

He smiled at the memory of Chrissy. Her family sent him a card a few weeks back, thanking him for all he did to try to save her. As he thought about the Josiah Craig fiasco, an exasperated sigh escaped. "Don't go back there. It wasn't your fault." He heard his words, but he still didn't believe them.

Lola bolted up, growling. Derek jumped, his heart pounding. "Lola! You scared the crap out of me," he said, trying to slow his breathing. The hair on his arms bristled. He squeezed his eyes shut. "No, no, no."

CHAPTER THIRTEEN

The sofa vibrated as Lola's growls grew more intense, rumbling from deep within her chest. Derek rubbed his arms. They had a clammy sheen of sweat on them. The cool air blowing over him made him shiver. He squeezed his eyes tighter. "Not now. Please." He tried using the breathing techniques Dr. Chelsea had told him would help him deal with the stress. But he knew it wasn't stress.

"I have to face it," he said with his eyes still shut. "Maybe if I deal with everything, my mind will heal." He took a deep breath, exhaling slowly. After a few more deep breaths, he opened his eyes. "Oh shit. Why?"

Chrissy sat in the chair directly across from the sofa. "I could ask you the same thing."

Lola stared at the empty chair. She continued to growl but lost her protective stance.

"Lola, this is Chrissy. Stop growling. I have a feeling she's going to be here for a while."

The dog relaxed a bit more, but her stare never left the chair.

"So, why are you here? I thought I left you at the gravesite. Along with my watch." Derek twisted the watch on his left wrist. "My favorite watch."

"Don't like the new one, huh?" Chrissy asked with a devilish grin.

"It's a watch. Serves its purpose." He ogled the young girl. A slight smile pushed his cheeks upward. "At least you look good. I see you no longer look like you're dead."

"I guess I clean up nicely." Chrissy smiled.

With the bugs in her teeth gone, she did clean up nicely. "Why are you here?"

"You need me."

"No. I don't."

"If you didn't need me, you would deal with the nightmares."

Derek rubbed Lola's ears. Her growling had subsided, but her skin rippled with each touch. "How do you know about my nightmares?"

"Duh, you keep me in your head. Let's talk about them."

"I don't need to talk about them. They're just bad dreams."

Chrissy giggled. "So, you regularly dream of people being murdered?"

Derek laid his head against the sofa. "No. They only just started. It's a holdover from my injuries."

Chrissy laughed. Her young voice carried throughout the house.

Lola sat up. Cocking her head to the side.

"What the heck is so funny?" Derek asked as he patted Lola's head. "Calm down, sweetie. It's okay."

Chrissy's laugh lessened to a snigger. "Oh, man. You kill me. You don't really believe the words coming out of your mouth, do you?"

"Yes."

"Okay. We'll go with that. At some point, you'll realize it's more. But let's go with your theory for now. Either way, don't you think it's odd the nightmares are starting again with this case?"

"This case is stressful. Congressman Jackson asked for me to be in charge. I have a new unit, new people. It's a stressful time. Not to mention, I may be going crazy talking to a dead girl."

"Seriously? Stop thinking like that. Let's look at the dreams. Tell me about them."

He huffed out a breath. "Fine." He reached into his bag, grabbing a prescription bottle. Taking one of the blue pills with a sip of beer, he thought about the dreams.

"Those aren't going to help."

"What isn't going to help?"

"Those pills you keep popping. You don't need them either. They're clouding your judgment."

Derek glared at the young girl. "How would you know what they do for me?"

"I don't have to be a rocket scientist to see what you're trying to do. Just fucking deal with your shit and lay off the pills." She glared back at him. "Plus, you're not the same when you take them. You're... different."

He raised an eyebrow at her. "Different?"

"It's like your brain is numb. Slow. Off."

"Well then, they're working. Now, do you want to hear about my dreams or not?"

She glowered at him as she nodded.

"Um, let's see. In one, I'm in a library. Watching a man get beaten with a bat. By Josiah Craig. The man ends up being me. Another one happened while awake. I saw a newspaper ooze blood. And the third one happened in my car. A dead woman screamed and blew out all my windows." He snapped his fingers. "Wait, then a policeman with a bloody face spoke to me, and then the blood disappeared. And I keep hearing things." He smiled at Chrissy, winking, guzzling the last of his beer. "That's about it."

"What was on the paper?"

Derek shrugged. "I don't know. It was smeared with blood, and I couldn't read anything on it."

"How many times have you seen a newspaper?"

He shrugged again. "Just once. I stood in someone else's kitchen looking at it on their table. Oh wait, it also happened in the kitchen at the church. There was a newspaper on the table. That's what triggered the dream. Vision. I don't know."

"Okay, Sherlock. Don't you think it has some significance?"

"Probably, but not to this case. The Billy Edmond case."

"Are you sure about that?" Chrissy stood and moved to the sliding door.

Lola jumped down from the sofa and sniffed the chair. She looked back at Derek then at the chair again.

"Let's go outside, Lola. Go chase something." He slid open the glass door.

"What's the big collar on her neck for?" Chrissy asked.

"It opens the doggy door." He pointed to the far wall on the other side of the glass door. "This way, she can go in or out, but no one can get in unless they have the collar." He shook his head. This conversation seemed way too real. Maybe he needed a hobby or a workout routine. Surely that would help alleviate the stress.

"No, it wouldn't."

"What?" he asked her.

"You're not the workout kind of guy. Nor do you do hobbies. You like getting into people's heads. Unfortunately, this kind of work comes with a price." She turned towards him. "Now, who do you think is in the dream?"

"I don't know. The dead couples' cases have also been on my mind."

"Then that's where your head should be. From what I saw at the unit, your new team is quite capable of investigating this current case. You can focus on this cold case. I think you will be surprised how cathartic it may be. Not to mention, they obviously want your help."

He turned towards her. His jaw hung open. "Who wants my help? What the fuck are you talking about?"

Lola ran by barking and chasing *no-see-ums.* Those invisible creatures only dogs see and chase. He wondered what it would be like, to just chase shit all day and roll in the grass. Lay in the sun and have no responsibilities.

"The dead couples."

He grabbed the sides of his head as he shook it. "This conversation is crazy. I'm going crazy."

"Stop. You big baby. Think about it. You've been thinking about this case, even when you were on medical leave and chasing Cory. You were still thinking about this case."

"No, I wasn't. How would you know anyway?"

"Dude, I take up space in your head. You can't forgive yourself for my death. That keeps me tied to you. I know what the hell you're thinking about."

Derek avoided her stare. He heard a car door close. Glancing at his watch, he frowned. 10 p.m. "How did it get this late?" He waved at Kyle as he entered the yard through the back gate.

Lola had been engrossed in a frog who hopped around the back porch. At the sound of the gate, she bounded towards him. Her butt wiggled ninety miles an hour.

"Hey, girl." Kyle said, loving on the dog. As he walked to his bungalow, he waved at Derek.

"I like him," Chrissy said, smiling.

"He's a good kid. I like having him here. The bungalow is getting used, I get some money in my pocket, and he gets a really cheap place to live." Derek looked over and saw Chrissy smiling wistfully. "Please don't go over and cause trouble at his home."

She squinted at him. Her eyes lit with a twinkle of mischief. "I can't believe you would think I would do something like that. Plus, if I'm not real, why would you say that?"

"Covering my bases. It's late. I need to go to bed." The skin on his forearm tingled as if an ice cube rested on it. He glanced down to see her hand rested on his arm.

"Think about the three murdered couples as one crime. Not three separate crimes."

He tilted his head to the side. "I'm not sure I understand what you mean."

"The cases are connected. You already know that. Think about why. Who benefits from each of the men's death, and how are the men tied together?"

"But the wives were killed as well, not just the men."

"Yes. But you think they weren't the intended victim. Go back to the beginning. All the way back." She turned towards the far wall, then turned around. "I'll be back. You're going to need my help."

Derek watched as she vanished into a wispy puff of nothing. "I'm going to fucking need medication and a straitjacket. That's what I'm going to need." He called Lola inside and headed for bed. Too drained and too tired to shower. He stripped down to his boxers and crawled under the cool sheets. Lola took up residence on her side of the bed.

He drifted off when he received a text. A smile filled his face as he responded. *I love and miss you too.* "That was your mama, Lola. She misses us. Well, me anyway."

Lola snuggled up next to him, exposing her belly for him to rub.

"I bet she misses you too." Lizzy filled his thoughts as sleep overtook him. He really did miss her—more than he should.

CHAPTER FOURTEEN

Derek flopped from side to side, unable to get comfortable. Lola slept soundly next to him. He listened to her soft breathing fill the quiet bedroom. Too quiet. He couldn't even hear the usual night sounds outside his sliding glass door. Just Lola. She had decided to take her half of the bed out of the middle, squishing him to the edge. Tossing and turning for another few moments, he found a comfortable spot and drifted off to sleep.

In what seemed like seconds, his eyes popped open. His heart raced, causing pains in his chest. If he lifted his head, he would be able to see the end of the bed. But he couldn't do it. A sense of impending doom loomed around him. He trembled under the sheets, his breath lingering like smoke in the chilly air surrounding him.

"This can't be happening," he whispered. Derek squeezed his eyelids tight and readied himself. Taking a series of deep breaths, he peeked out from half open eyelids. Lifting his head just enough, Derek glanced towards his feet. Blinking, he gripped the sheets and squeezed his eyes closed again. "Please go away. Go away," he begged.

Derek opened one eye to find the dead man still there. His head was caved in on one side, his pajama shirt covered in blood. The ghostly visitor raised his hands and grabbed at his bulging throat. Three fingers bent backward, and his left wrist bent at an awkward angle. As the man's mouth distorted and elongated, he took a step closer to Derek. Gurgling emanated from the back of his throat.

Derek lurched back against the bed, drawing his legs towards his torso. He watched as the young man clawed at his throat.

Gagging, the man coughed up a newspaper roll. It landed on the bed, blood dripping from his open mouth. Saliva dripped on long strands from the man's chin. He started coughing again. The man began retching.

Another rolled-up newspaper landed near Derek's feet. A shriek-like howl filled the room as blood gushed out, soaking the bed. Derek covered his ears with his hands, burying his face in his pillow as a wave of crimson washed over him.

Derek bolted upright. His short raspy breaths echoed in the quietness as his eyes darted around the room. He clawed at his chest struggling for a breath. A sticky sheen of sweat coated his skin, his t-shirt and underwear clung to him.

Lola laid next to him, sound asleep, unfazed by his nightmare. Her fawn-colored fur was a bright contrast against the dark rich black of her muzzle. With no moonlight seeping through the window, she had a villainous look. Darker than usual shadows danced around the room.

"Calm down," he said, out loud, concentrating on regulating his breathing. Derek inhaled through his nose. He closed his eyes exhaling through his mouth. "It was just a dream." Derek rose from the bed, making his way into the kitchen. The cool floor under his feet gave him a slight chill even though the late September temps in Arizona were still in the nineties.

In the kitchen, Derek opened the refrigerator and pulled out a jug of iced tea. As he grabbed a plastic tumbler from the cabinet, his hand trembled, and goosebumps erupted on his arms. Hanging his head towards his chest, Derek spun around slowly. He was in a kitchen. It wasn't his kitchen. "What the fuck is going on?" he whispered. With his back to the counter, he glanced around. His stainless-steel appliances were now black.

A glass partition separated the living room and the kitchen. The home looked modern. Where Derek's home had rounded ceilings and arched doorways, this house had sharp edges and linear architecture.

A bright flash of light exploded in front of him. He lifted his hand, shielding his face. Derek shook his head, blinking several times. When his eyes adjusted, he now stood in someone's bedroom. A butterfly nightlight illuminated the room with a soft, warm yellow glow. The man who moments ago stood at the foot of his bed vomiting newspapers lay asleep in front of him. A noise to his right made Derek look over his shoulder, just as the bedroom door opened.

A dark figure crept into the room. A baggy hooded sweatshirt obscured his face. What looked like a metal pipe hung from the person's right hand. The intruder turned towards Derek. His face was warped and unrecognizable, filled with a crooked clown-like smile.

"Hey?" Derek yelled. "Wake up!" he screamed at the couple in bed. "Wake up!" It was as if a silent movie played out in front of him. He watched in horror as the intruder lingered at the wife's side. The figure lifted the pipe over his head. Derek tried to lunge forward, but his feet wouldn't budge. He yanked on his legs, looking down. Vine-like structures held him in place. The intruder threw his head back, laughing, but no sound came out.

The assailant lifted the pipe and brought it down on the woman's skull. The sickening thud echoed throughout the room as blood sprayed onto the wall. The husband stirred, turning towards his wife. The dark figure, much faster, stopped the man before he could get out of the bed.

The assailant leapt towards the husband, swinging the pipe, striking the man on the side of the head. Blood sprayed out on impact. The intruder lifted the pipe striking the husband again.

Derek lunged forward, this time his legs and feet followed his body. As his fingers grasped the weapon, he felt himself falling.

Derek jerked awake, soaked with sweat, pain radiated across his torso. His thudding heart felt as if someone was pounding on his chest. Lola laid on the bed sound asleep next to him. He swung his legs over the side, resting his head in his hands. "What the hell just happened?" breathing in and out through his nose, he tried to calm himself. Two distinctly fucked up horrible nightmares back-to-back.

"This is too much," he said. He opened his nightstand drawer, removed the bottle of pills, and took two. He started to walk to the kitchen but thought twice of it. Instead, he went into his bathroom and held his hand under the faucet. Popping the pills in his mouth Derek took several gulps of water. He splashed cold water on his face, running his wet hands through his hair.

He walked back to the bed and nudged Lola, making her move to the other side. He hunkered down under the covers, wrapped his arm around the dog, and pulled her closer to him. Derek buried his face in her fur, squeezing his eyes shut. He listened to Lola's breathing, blocking the memory of the dream from hell, slowly he drifted off to sleep.

CHAPTER FIFTEEN

Tuesday morning 7 a.m.

Derek entered the Legacy Unit with Lola in tow. He watched as she ran around the building sniffing every desk, chair, and object she could find. When she landed on Emma's desk, her ears perked up. He laughed at her raised eyebrows as she stared at him. "Yes. That is who I cheated on you with. You will meet him later."

Satisfied with the answer, she continued to learn all the smells of the building. Using his laptop, Derek logged on to the network. He thought about his conversation with his subconscious last night. Maybe Chrissy had a point. He did think those three cases were connected. What if he took the wives out of the equation?

Someone had to have a reason to want these men dead. If they didn't work together or have any visible connections to one another, something had to tie them together. "Of course, the local PD and that waste of an agent didn't really look for any connections. They deemed them all separate incidents," he said to Lola, who now laid at his feet.

He jotted each name down on his notepad. Three men, Albie Hawkes, Terry Curren, and Xavier Blackman. Derek started to set up a search to run each of the men, when he heard the alarm code. Lola jumped up and stood at the ready to defend. Or at least run to the intruder and beg for attention.

Derek glanced at the screen and saw Marc Anthony and Emma about to open the door. He looked down at the boxer. "Lola, I expect you to be on your best behavior."

She didn't take her eyes off the front of the room. Slight whimpers emanated from her as she trembled. Ready to bolt the moment her master gave her the okay.

Marc Anthony bounded in. He spotted Derek, stopped, and zeroed in on Lola.

For a split second, he saw Marc Anthony tilt his head to the side before it registered another dog sat in the room. Derek's lips formed a grin. "Good morning, Emma," he called out as he stepped around his desk. At the same moment, the big dog galloped towards Lola.

"Oh, my. Marc Anthony!" Emma rushed in, dropping her purse on her desk as the lead yanked on her hand. She almost fell forward before she regained control of the dog. "Stop that. You know you are supposed to wait to be introduced."

Marc Anthony's tail wagged. He whimpered and howled for his master to hurry up.

"Well, who is this pretty girl?" Emma asked, walking towards the brown boxer. She looked up at Derek. "I see you brought someone with you."

He chuckled. "I did. I figured they could keep you company and each other as well. This is Lola. Lola, say hi to Emma and Marc Anthony."

Lola barked, wiggling her butt. She and Marc Anthony exchanged sniffs and snorts. Once they got acquainted, they playfully chased each other around the room. They ran down the hallway and back to the kitchen.

Felicia entered with Kelly and Kyle in tow.

"Oh...hi sweeties!" Felicia said as the two dogs battled for her attention. "Who are you?" she asked, glancing between Derek, Emma, and the new brown boxer.

"This is Lola," Kyle said. "She's a pretty girl." He bent down, giving her a kiss on her nose. "You here to help protect us?"

Lola howled and wiggled. When Marc Anthony came over to get attention from Kyle, she readily moved to Kelly.

"This place is going to the dogs, that's for sure." Kelly laughed as Marc Anthony pushed Lola out of the way so he could be scratched.

"Do you guys mind if they are here?" Derek asked.

They all shook their heads.

"Not at all." Kelly sat at her desk. "This place is so much better than the regular FBI offices."

"That's for damn sure," Felicia said as she waited for her desktop to boot up.

Looking at his watch, Derek expected the new guys any minute. This will be the first time he has seen Michael Finch since he handled his sister's murder over ten years ago. He couldn't help but feel a little apprehensive. Michael's sister's case was one of his first as a profiler. He made several mistakes before he finally got the UNSUB'S profile right.

"Two new guys are on their way." Derek nodded at Kyle. "I would appreciate it if you would get their comps up and running. Get them logged into the network. Set up whatever computer is left over for Cary Mackle."

"You got it, boss." He smiled at Derek.

"I really hate you and Felicia right now," Derek said.

Both Felicia and Kyle laughed.

"I know." She winked. "You should have gone with us for a beer last night, Derek," Felicia said.

"I'll go next time. I promise," Derek replied as he walked into the kitchen. He could hear everyone talking in the main room. He grabbed a soda from the fridge, turned around, and dropped the unopened can onto the ground. His sharp intake of breath echoed in the empty kitchen.

A different man than the one from his dream stood before him. He wore blood-soaked pajamas. His right arm had a compound fracture. The man didn't say anything. He didn't move, just stood there.

Derek closed his eyes as he leaned against the counter. He pushed the panic down. This time when he opened his eyes, he studied the man. What he could see of his hair appeared to be dark brown or black. He noticed the man's square jaw line.

The dogs came running into the kitchen. Lola slid to a stop and growled. Marc Anthony thought she was playing and began barking.

When Derek looked at the dogs, the man disappeared. He bent to pick up his can of soda, tapping the top. He thought about putting it back in the fridge but decided to take his chances with it exploding.

Kelly turned towards Derek as he came into the room. "What did you do to the dogs?"

Derek sat at his desk, oblivious to her question.

"Yo, Derek?" Kelly called out.

"Hmm, what? Did I miss something?" he asked, peering around the room.

"The dogs. What are they all excited about?"

He shrugged. "Who knows? Lola barks at a lot of stuff that isn't there."

"Maybe she sees ghosts." Kyle attached a monitor to a desktop console.

Derek shook his head. "Don't start. There are no ghosts."

The front door buzzer sounded. The dogs who had just settled down jumped and raced each other to the front of the room, sliding on the concrete floor, trying to stop. Both whined at the door.

Emma shot a look towards Derek. "I think these are some more team members." She pointed to the TV screen. Two men stood at the door.

"Yeah, buzz them in," Derek said as he moved towards her. "Lola, Marc Anthony, give them some room," he said as the men walked into the building.

The others stayed in their seats, waiting to meet the new members of the team.

George Peterson, the oldest member of the team at forty-four, entered first, followed by Michael Finch.

"Holy shit," George Peterson said as the two dogs surrounded him. He held a box in his hands. "Wow. You are huge," he said, balancing the box in one arm as he reached out to pet the Great Dane on the head.

"He won't bite," Emma said from her desk. "His name is Marc Anthony."

"You must be Agent Peterson," Derek said, shaking his hand. "I'm Derek Reed."

"Nice to meet you," George said. "Nice to put a face to a voice."

"Same." Derek couldn't help but stare at the man. Well over six-foot with movie star good looks. His hazel eyes had a gold ring surrounding them. Derek took a step towards the youngest member of his team. "Damn, son. Look at you."

Agent Michael Finch smiled as he embraced Derek. "Oh, man. I can't believe it. I never thought I would run into you again, let alone get to work with the great Derek Reed."

Derek hugged the young man patting his back. "You grew up well." He stepped back, taking a good look at the man before him. "I'm proud of you, Michael." He hugged him again. He spun around to find the rest of his crew staring at him. He couldn't hide the chuckle.

"First," his eyes traveled between his two new members. "When it's just us, let's use our first names. Is that okay with you guys?"

"Yeah, no problem there," George said, nodding.

Michael agreed.

"Okay. Everyone this is George Peterson. He is our blood spatter expert. Oh, I forgot to tell you guys, Frank Pillard won't be with us. He had an emergency and decided to stay with his other unit." Derek placed his hand on Michael's shoulder. "This is Michael Finch. I met him on one of my first cases." He looked over. "Do you mind if I tell them?"

"No, sir. Not at all."

"Michael's sister was murdered when he was in high school. It was one of my first cases as a profiler." Derek paused for a few minutes. "That's what led Michael to join the Bureau."

Everyone introduced themselves, taking a few moments to shake hands.

"This is Emma. She's our secretary and Marc Anthony's mom. And this," he said, pointing to the boxer, "is Lola. She is my good friend's dog and I often take care of her. She and Marc Anthony will probably be regular fixtures down here."

Kyle pointed to the desks. "Have your pick."

"Wait, before you set up your space, I need to get your thumbprint." He motioned for them to follow him to the door. "The code is 2242." He opened the panel, dropping down the scanner. "If each of you would place your thumb here." He went on to explain how the security system worked.

Derek pointed towards an archway on the left. "Through there, you can find the kitchen and the basement, where Kyle has set up his bat cave." He pointed towards a doorway off to the right. "The bathroom and shower area, along with two bedrooms, are over there. Each has two twin beds in them. If you ever find yourself stuck here, there are sheets and blankets. Or there will be soon."

"Cool," George said. "I did a stint in this little west Texas town. Something similar to this. Can't tell you how many times we bunked in the office."

Michael smiled. "The place I'm living is about as rustic as this place. I landed this sweet cottage on a rancher's land just north of the city. My dad went to college with him. I pay him 500 dollars a month, including all the utilities. Plus, I get to help with the horses."

"That's so cool. I'm in an apartment. But, I'm right next to the pool." Felicia smiled at the men.

"Listen, I know I said we're going to work on this Billy Edmond case only, but I have a cold case I want to pull George in on with me." Derek turned towards him. "I need your blood spatter expertise."

"No problem. Whatever you need me for." George pulled a few things out of a box he carried in with him, placing a photo on his desk.

Felicia, who sat closest to him, gaped at the photo. "Holy shit." She scooted her chair to his desk. "When did you take this?"

Everyone else gathered around his desk, wanting a look.

"Wow. What a photo," Michael said.

Bright red blood coated a wall in what looked like a living room. You could see two covered bodies lying with only their feet showing. The group passed it around as George sat in his chair.

"I had just come out of the specialized class run by the FBI concerning blood spatter. I have a microbiology degree from Cornell, and my unit director thought I would do well learning blood patterns. Microbiology doesn't have much to do with blood. But it sounded fun, so I jumped at the opportunity.

"Anyway, this case came up. A father killed his three kids and his wife. They were hacked to death. At first, he looked like a victim. The investigation started moving in that direction. They called me in asking to help with the scene analysis.

"The guy stated there were two intruders. He also claimed to have a disability keeping him from raising his arm." George demonstrated the movement for the group. "After analyzing the spatter patterns and doing a lot of recreations in the lab, I was able to show the father had lied in his statements to the police. His alibi crumbled. With what we came up with in lab recreations, we showed exactly how he killed his family." He lifted the photo from his desk. "I made a copy of the original photo. To remind me of those three babies he slaughtered. All for money."

Everyone stood in silence.

"That's some crazy shit," Kyle said.

"People can be monsters." Felicia rolled her chair back over to her desk. Marc Anthony laid next to her feet, along with Lola. It seemed where one went, the other followed. She reached down and scratched Marc Anthony behind the ears. "Are you my handsome fella?" Not wanting to be left out, Lola sat up and begged for scratches too.

"In about an hour, we'll leave, Felicia." Derek motioned for George to follow him. "Bring your chair, George."

"Got it, boss." She winked at him as he scowled back.

"What do you need from us?" Michael asked.

Derek glanced at Kelly. "Have you run down all of our victim's acquaintances, business associates, and friends?"

She nodded. "I just checked the runs I set up last night before we left. I know Kyle is checking out the beneficiaries of Billy Edmond's will. But," she held up a finger. "It seems I have over sixty people who need to be looked at."

"Great. Divide up the list and let Michael help. I want you to see if anyone had a problem with Billy. Business or personal. Once we narrow in on a few people, we will begin the interviews. Break the list into two parts. Who was in town and who wasn't. That should cut it down."

"You got it." Kelly smiled at the two men. "There are snacks in the kitchen. We all chip in to keep the cupboards stocked. Get a snack or a drink, and give me a few minutes, and I will have some names for all of us."

"I could use a soda," Michael said, heading for the kitchen.

CHAPTER SIXTEEN

George rolled his chair over to Derek's desk. "What do you have?"

Derek opened the cold case file. "These are accessible via your computer. I wanted to go over a few things. While I'm gone, you can work your magic." He opened one picture of the three crime scenes. "Okay, so this is a case from five years ago. At least that's when the first murder occurred. Now, these weren't linked together. As far as each of the local PDs are concerned, these are three separate murders.

"They didn't all take place in Phoenix. One was in Tucson. I think that played a part in them not being connected. The FBI Agent who looked at these cases happened to be retiring three weeks after he got this file." Derek squinted at George. "I think he just didn't want to deal with this case. I can't prove it. Just a hunch."

George laughed. "I bet your hunches are pretty damn spot on."

"As I look at these scenes, I see similarities between the murder victims. The women were taken out first or at least immobilized first. When I started looking into this case, I thought couples were being targeted. But as I studied it more, I think the husbands were the targets."

George angled the laptop so he could get a better view of the screens. He zeroed on each photo showing the wives. He came back to the photos showing the entire scene, then the photos with the husbands only.

"What do you see?" Derek asked.

"I can see from these photos that the wounds inflicted on the wives were precise. As I look at each of the blood patterns near the wives, the killer hit them once. One strategic blow. Did the reports say whether the women died immediately or not?"

Derek shook his head. "In all three cases, the wives died slowly. The ME estimates thirty minutes to an hour."

George pointed to the blood spatter on the wall of the first case. "There is only one spatter pattern. There is no overlay from repeated blows. Your killer was precise."

"I think the blows to the wives were to incapacitate. Nothing more." Derek pointed to a photo in the folder. "He didn't care if they died. They just weren't the target. In this first case, the detective reported the husband was attempting to help his wife before the assailant struck him. I don't see that at all."

George lifted the glasses hanging around his neck. Looking at the photo on the computer first, he zoomed the image in and out, then pulled back to see the entire room. He then looked at the printed photo from the folder. "Can't see how anything in this photo would make the detectives reach this conclusion. Doesn't mean the detectives were shoddy they just made assumptions."

He pointed to the wall on the husband's side of the bed. "The angle at which the blood hits the wall and then drips down shows the first impact to the husband's head impacted his right side."

George stood and turned Derek's chair towards him. "I'm the killer, you are sitting on the edge of the bed or trying to get out of the bed, no doubt trying to get up and stop me, but you don't make it before I hit you." He raised his arm like he swung a bat.

"The weapon impacts your head at a slight upward angle. Blood sprays from the wounds at a slight upward arcing pattern from the point of impact. You can fall towards the foot of the bed, or you can crumple to the floor."

He studied the picture again. "The foot of the bed is cut out of the photos. Do the reports say anything about blood on or near the foot of the bed?"

Derek shook his head. "No."

"Then let's assume he crumples. As you fall, I'm going to hit you again. Or try to. This time though, my point of impact will be at a much sharper angle downward." He pointed to the overlapping spray of blood in another picture.

"There's cast-off from the bat and the blood from the first hit. That's these smaller droplets. The second impact is here. The blood spatter from the wound won't have such a rounded arc. As the first one."

George glanced at the photos one last time. "To me, it looks as if our guy may have hit him a few more times as he lay on the ground. He may have even dragged him a small distance to inflict more damage." George pointed to the ceiling in the picture. You can see the cast-off moved from the wall to there. Showing the killer changed how he stood and where he hit the victim."

Derek scanned the reports. "This seems to have been a cluster fuck of a mess. I think they thought home invasion and went with that conclusion. We could try talking to the detectives first on each scene, but I don't think it will get us much."

"I think you'd be right about that," George said. "Too much time."

"Let's come at this from the start. I know we only have the reports, but let's frame this as a more personal killing than a random home invasion and start from there."

George pointed to the photo. "I need to study the pictures more, but from what I see your guy may be left-handed."

Derek tilted his head to the side. "You think that because he was hit on the right side of the head?" he asked, looking at the pictures.

"More of an educated guess. Look at the wounds on the head, the way the skin is torn, and from the autopsy photos. It's the way it is bashed in. Also, these hits took some force. You wouldn't try to kill someone with a bat and not use your dominant hand."

"That makes sense." Derek searched the notes. "There is nothing in here about being left-handed. I can call Dr. Callahan and ask him." He glanced over the ME's report. "I don't know the doctor who performed the autopsy. But he will."

"I'll study the reports and really look over the photos from the scene. I'll have something for you," George said.

"You've already confirmed some of my suspicions. The other two cases are in this folder on the computer. Pull all the photos and see if you see any similarities. I need to see if the same person committed these murders. Based on what you come up with will determine our next course of action." Derek stood. "Felicia, you almost ready to go?"

"Yes, boss." She giggled, not looking at Derek as she typed something out on her computer.

Derek frowned at George as he, too, chuckled. He glanced down at Lola, who had sat up waiting to go for a ride. "You're going to stay here, sweetie. Hang out with Marc Anthony and the others." He bent down, scratching her ears. Turning to his agent as he grabbed his cell phone from his desk. "Let's go, Agent."

"Okay, Dad." She barked out a laugh. "You must be mad, calling me agent. That's like using your kid's middle name." She skipped behind him. "Will you buy me an ice cream, Dad?"

The rest of the unit laughed as Derek shook his head.

"You and Kyle are going to be my special kids, aren't you?"

She smiled, getting into his car. "Probably."

CHAPTER SEVENTEEN

Driving to the Londonvale Academy, he watched with dismay as Felicia checked out his car. She opened the glove box. Then the overhead bin holding his sunglasses and garage door opener. He cringed as she moved the seat back and forth. She adjusted the back of the seat to see how far it would lay down.

"You could sleep in this car." Her eyes were wide, and a smile showed off her rosy cheeks. Felicia looked over her shoulder at the rear seats. "This is one hell of a fancy vehicle," she said, raising the seat back to a sitting position. "Man, it has bucket seats in the back. This is too cool." She narrowed in on him. "Did you get it illegally?"

"What? No. Why would you ask me such a question?"

"You're a profiler in the FBI. Not a drug lord." Felicia ran her hand over the soft leather of the dash. "You stole it, didn't you?"

Derek rolled his eyes. "No. I bought it in an auction." He smiled at the memory. "Had my eye on it. I had a friend at the Arizona Highway Patrol who knew when it would come up for sale. Took off and spent the whole day there. Bid high out of the box and won it. Then I had it restored, and the interior redone." He sighed. "I love this car."

Felicia broke out in laughter.

"What is so funny?" he asked, pulling into the gated grounds of the private school.

"Men and their cars." She quieted her laughter as he rolled down the window. "They have guards at the gate," she said, leaning closer to him.

"Who are you here to see?" the guard asked, leaning into the window.

Derek held up his FBI credentials. "We're here to see Headmaster Russell McMillan. He's expecting us." He couldn't help but stare at the young woman. Strikingly beautiful. Her long black hair pulled in a loose bun, accentuated her high cheek bones.

The guard scrutinized the credentials, then checked a sheet on a clip board. A call came over her 2-way radio. She held up her finger to the agents. "Yeah, Mark, that's fine. Give him a citation. This is the third time he's parked in the faculty parking area. He needs to pay for this infraction."

"Okay."

The guard smiled back at Derek. "I'm sorry. These teens think they can park wherever they want. Go on in, Agent Reed," she said as she placed a visitor's card on the dash of the car. "Just hand this back on your way out."

Derek nodded as he drove through the gates. "I guess this is what growing up in the one percent can get you." Glancing in his review mirror, the guard stood outside the shack and watched them as they drove away.

"We don't have anything like this in Marquette, that's for sure." Felicia gazed at the number of Tipu and Arizona Ash trees. The large shade trees lined the curvy drive leading to the main building of the school.

As the car entered an expansive quad area, lush green grass filled spaces between buildings. The main building resembled a castle from the highlands of Scotland. Two large turrets flanked the ends of the main structure. Several battlements and crenels lined the roof area of the building. The deep gray stone façade made for a foreboding look against the backdrop of the dark green lawn.

"Wow. How much do you think this lawn costs to keep green?" Felicia's eyes widened as she gaped out the window.

Derek scoped out the other buildings. Not as large as the main building, but they all had the same stone façade. "This isn't a boarding school, is it?" he asked, glancing over at his agent as they walked towards the entrance.

"No. It isn't." She followed him through the wooden doors. Her jaw fell open at the sight of the foyer. "Wow!" She spun around, looking at the main stairwell leading to the second floor.

Carved out of deep rich wood, sculpted banisters lined the edges. Light fixtures resembling medieval torches lined the walls. Portraits of headmasters lined one wall. They were made to look like the old portraits of castle Lords.

On one of the walls, a plaque directed traffic to the main office.

As Derek led the way to the headmaster's office, several girls walked by, giggling as they saw the weapons on both he and Felicia.

"I'm so glad I'm not in high school now," Felicia said softly.

"You and me both." Derek pushed open a glass door leading to an outer office. An older woman sat behind an oddly modern desk.

Glancing up from her task, she smiled. Her eyes drifted to the weapons. "We don't allow weapons on the grounds."

Derek raised an eyebrow at her. "We're the FBI. We can bring our weapons on the grounds." He stepped closer to her desk. "I'm Agent Derek Reed." He pointed to Felicia. "This is Agent Rogers. We're here to see Russell McMillan."

The secretary's lip curled, making her left nostril flare. "Just a moment." She walked into the headmaster's office, shutting the door behind her.

"She is not friendly at all." Felicia glanced around the office. "I don't think we have the pedigree to get her polite side."

Derek snickered at his agent. "Maybe not. But I have the Federal Government on my side. We could make her life miserable."

Felicia smiled at him. "You are so mean, aren't you?"

He laughed. "Not in the least. But it would be fun."

The snooty secretary opened the office door and directed them inside. "Mr. McMillan is busy today. You have a few moments with him."

Derek leaned into the persnickety woman. "We have as much time as we need," he said as he shut the door in her face.

Russell McMillan stood, walking around his desk. "Harriet has been here a very long time. I often think she considers herself the headmaster. Please excuse her rudeness. I'm at your service, Agent Reed." He motioned for them to sit in one of four chairs facing each other.

They soaked in the large office. It was almost as big as his living room. An expansive set of book shelves covered most of one wall. Several pictures of the Academy's baseball team graced the shelves.

Derek stepped over to a wall. Something caught his eye in one of the photos, but as he reached for the photo, the headmaster spoke.

"Please have a seat. What can I do for you, Agents?"

Derek glanced back over his shoulder at Russell, making a mental note to ask about it. He took a seat. "We're here today regarding Billy Edmond."

A broad smile filled the headmaster's face as he chuckled. "Please tell me you aren't here because Billy has pulled one of his infamous pranks?"

Derek's brow wrinkled as he frowned. "No. I'm sorry, but Billy Edmond was murdered the other night." He watched as the emotion rolled across Russell's face. After shock, disbelief settled in his eyes. Then, maybe fear.

"I don't understand. Are you sure?" Mr. McMillan's hand trembled as he fidgeted with his shirt buttons.

"Yes. We're sure." Derek glanced at Felicia. She sat stone face studying Mr. McMillan's every move. He turned back to the headmaster. "Mr. McMillan, what can you tell me about Billy Edmond?"

He shook his head, shrugging. "I have no idea. Other than the occasional donor's banquet, I didn't see Billy very much. I guess occasionally, if I saw him out, we would talk about the good old days. The only other meeting happened a few years back. I helped him with a little league team he sponsored. He asked if I could give a few hours of training to the kids. That was the last time I spent any real time with him."

Derek scribbled in the notepad he had taken from the back pocket of his jeans. "Mr. McMillan, are you aware Billy left you a bequest in his will?"

Russell sat up. His back stiffened. His eyes darted between the two agents. "What? Why? Wait, do you mean me or the school?"

"Both, actually," Felicia said.

Russell shook his head, closing his eyes. "No. That can't be right. I can see him leaving something to this school. He loved this school. But there would be no reason for him to leave me any money. I just can't see why he would do that."

"You and he never had a close relationship?" Derek asked.

Russell McMillan blew out a harsh breath. "When Billy attended Londonvale, he and I were close. I was close to all my players, but Billy was special. He spent a lot of time here. His father and mother were often busy." He lifted his hands. "Don't get me wrong. Billy's parents were good people. They just had a lot of demands on their time. Billy would spend extra hours on the practice diamond."

"Was he a good baseball player?" Derek asked as he glanced at all the photos on the shelves.

"I wouldn't say that. It did keep him busy and out of trouble. For the most part." A whiff of melancholy fell over Russell. "Billy was our resident prankster. He always enjoyed pulling tricks on some of the players. Nothing harsh or meant to hurt. Just all in good team-building fun."

"Do you keep in touch with the other players?" Derek asked, pointing to the photos. He stood and walked to them. "It seems like you have several teams here."

Russell joined him.

Felicia took the opportunity to inspect the rest of the office. She walked to the other side of the room.

Russell pointed to three photos. This is the team from Billy's tenth grade year through his senior year."

Derek's heart rate sped up. He reached out for one of the photos. "What year is this from?" He held it out for Mr. McMillan to look at.

"Oh, Billy's senior year. They won state."

Derek had to set the photo back on the shelf to hide the shaking of his hands. "Do you have a copy of this photo?" he pointed to the picture he had just set down.

Russell thought for a moment. "Yes, I think I do." He walked to a file cabinet located in the corner to the left of his desk. He glanced towards Felicia on the far side of the room. "That was taken about seven years ago."

She stared at the large picture hanging on the wall. "Did you have some kind of reunion?"

Russell pulled a file from the cabinet. "Yes. We had a big donors party, and the entire baseball team attended." He turned to Agent Reed handing him a photo. "The team during Billy's senior year," he nodded in the direction of Felicia, "that's the entire team at the reunion."

Derek's ears perked up. He walked across the room. Standing next to Felicia, he had to stop himself from hyperventilating. His pulse raced as he stared at the photograph. His hands started to shake. "Holy shit."

Agent Rogers cocked her head at him. "Huh? Did you say something?"

He shook his head. "No. No. Just mumbling." Derek turned towards the headmaster. "Do you have an extra copy of this photo, as well? It would really help in the investigation."

Russell pulled the drawer back open. "I do. I can give you names from both photos, so you will know who you are looking at from the high school one to the other photo."

"I would really appreciate that." Derek stuck his hands in his pocket so he wouldn't fidget. "Did you have regular parties at Billy's, I mean you and the team?"

Agent Rogers watched her boss. His agitation, palpable. She laughed inwardly. *He probably forgot his gum.*

"The picture from seven years ago was the first donor's party. Billy had them most years. Usually in the summer. We would bring our families to Billy's house." Russell held the photos in his hand. "Oh, hang on." He placed them on his desk, opened the file drawer, and pulled another photo out.

"Does the whole team come?" Derek asked.

The headmaster paused. He tilted his head to the side before resuming his task. "I'm not sure I know. To the first party, yes. Two years later, a few weren't there. I didn't go for maybe two years. The last time I went was maybe a year or two ago. Not everyone showed up. I wasn't there last year. I had to go out of town. I remember Billy called me and asked me about a few of the men who had been on the team, but I can't remember who or why. I'm not even sure I remember when he called me."

"What about this year? Was there a party?"

The headmaster shook his head. "Not that I am aware of, anyway. I never received an invitation."

"You're getting a substantial amount from Billy Edmond's estate. I'm surprised to hear you say you and he weren't close over the last few years." Derek waited for Russell McMillan to respond.

Grabbing two papers he had printed from his computer, Russell stapled one set of names to one photo and the other to the next. "Trust me. I am just as surprised as you are. I didn't think we had the kind of friendship that would lead to being in the man's will. I mean, he invited me to the team party every year or two when he had one. But I assumed it was because I coached them, and I'm now the headmaster. Not due to a close friendship. I included an extra photo. It has the wives of some of the baseball team."

"Thank you." Derek took the papers from the man but didn't look at the names. "Well, I'm sure the lawyer for the estate will have some information for you. And I'm sure when they're ready to, they'll contact you." Derek turned to leave. "Out of curiosity, have you been out to Billy Edmond's house recently?"

"No, not recently. Except for the parties we just discussed, I haven't been to his home." Russell sat behind his desk. The weight of the news of Billy's death finally impacting him. "I just can't believe Billy is dead."

Derek remained standing. "Can you tell me where you were two nights ago?"

A quick flash of anger crossed Russell's face, that disappeared just as fast. "I was with my wife. We were at a fund raiser for a local art gallery. I can give you the names of the couples we were with."

"I'd appreciate the information." Derek handed him a business card. "You can email them to me." He saw the tears beginning to swell in the man's eyes. "Thank you for these." He held up the photos. "If we need anything else, we will be in touch with you." Derek followed Felicia towards the door. Before he walked out, he asked one more question. "Did Billy ever hurt anyone by pulling a prank? Or maybe there was one kid he picked on more than another?"

Russell McMillen shifted his stance. "I don't think I understand."

Derek's brow wrinkled. "It's a fairly straightforward question. Did Billy ever pull a prank, injuring, hurting, or embarrassing someone? Something which might cause someone to hold a grudge?"

Mr. McMillen stood up straight, adjusting his tie. "No. Never. I wouldn't let something like that occur. I didn't allow bullying then or now. His pranks were kid stuff." He glanced at his watch. "If you need anything else, please let me know. I have a meeting I must prepare for."

Derek exaggerated his nod, almost a half bow, as he opened the door to leave. "Thank you again for your assistance." As he walked out, the guard from the gate stood next to the secretary's desk. He nodded in her direction.

She barely moved her head in response.

Derek paid closer attention to the young lady's details. Her black hair now pulled back in a pony tail, pulling her face taut. The guard's deep green eyes were lackluster. Only now did Derek notice how much the guard slouched. He had the impression she wanted to hide her height. Blend in. The guard's stare followed them into the hallway.

Once in the car, Felicia turned towards Derek. "That was sort of odd."

"Which part?"

"All of it. What was up with that guard?"

"Not sure."

"What do you think about the way Mr. McMillen reacted to your question about a prank?" she asked.

"I think he overreacted. We need to find out why. Maybe someone on the team will be willing to fill in some gaps."

Felicia adjusted herself in the seat. "There is something else that seems odd."

"What's that?"

"C'mon. You know what I'm talking about. What's up, Derek?"

Derek turned, gawking at her as he drove to the gate. "I—what do you mean?"

"I could tell you were upset about something. And I'm pretty sure I know what it is?"

Derek's body stiffened. "What?"

"You forgot your gum, didn't you?"

Derek sighed a half chuckle. "Yeah, yeah. Am I that obvious?"

She nodded. "Yes. I could tell when you were looking at the photos. You were getting a little anxious or agitated. My uncle, who stopped smoking had the same symptoms as you. Have you thought of vaping? I mean, you could get the ones with no nicotine. Maybe it would help you. I know you chew gum because it helps with the cravings."

"I hadn't thought of that. I would think if I started using a vape, I would be one step closer to picking up a pack of cigarettes." He handed the dash card back to another guard at the gate and waited for it to open. "I think I should just stick to gum." Derek lifted his middle console, grabbing a pack. "I need to remember to carry a pack in my pocket." He glanced at his watch. "When is the family expecting us?"

"Around 2 p.m. Why?"

"Do you mind if we head back to the office and you can take one of the other agents with you?" he asked, pulling into traffic.

"Not at all. I have time to eat the lunch I brought." Felicia leaned back into the seat, snuggling against the cool leather. "These are awesome seats. They feel so cool against my skin."

Derek smiled at her. "Cooling elements. They come in handy here in Arizona." He turned on the radio thinking about the photos. He wanted nothing more than to get back to the office and find out if his hunch was correct.

CHAPTER EIGHTEEN

Tuesday early afternoon

Derek led the way into the Legacy office, Lola came running up to him. Her butt wiggled, bumping into his legs. "Hey, girl. Did you miss me?" He scratched her head.

Not to be left out, Marc Anthony made his way first to Derek then Felicia.

"Ooh, are you jealous, big fella?" Felicia crooned at him. As she walked to her desk, Marc Anthony followed right behind her.

Only George and Michael sat at their desks. "Where is Kyle and Kelly?" Derek asked Emma.

"Kyle is downstairs, and Kelly went to grab some lunch. I told them if they give me a list, I would go shopping then everyone could give me the money when I got back. So, make a list if there is something special you want. I figured I would go by Friday. If I can I will go tomorrow."

"That's great. I'll give you a small list," Derek said, heading to his desk and opening the laptop. Studying the pictures from the headmaster while it booted up, he caught himself tapping the face of his watch. "Shit," he said under his breath, realizing it was something he'd not done since burying the old one after the last case. He opened a desk drawer and rummaged for a pack of gum. "Oh, come on," he whispered. "Yes!" Derek almost squealed with the delight of a little girl when he found an unopened pack.

Felicia walked by, chatting with Michael on their way to the kitchen.

"Felicia, take Michael with you to the Wallace's house," Derek said without looking at the agent.

"Sure." She turned to Michael. "Did you bring lunch?"

"No. I was going to go get something," Michael said.

"We got stuff here." Her voice trailed off.

Derek stared at the photo of the baseball team in high school. Billy's senior year. Something seemed familiar about a few of the boys. He grabbed the photo from the first donor's meeting. He shifted his gaze between the two pictures. *This can't be. This is impossible.* He thought.

He'd previously seen two men in these photos. One in this kitchen earlier, and the newspaper guy. Both from his nightmares.

His knee bounced as he searched his computer for the five-year-old cold case. He scanned the three names, focusing on the list from the donor's party. "Get the fuck out," he said lifting his head and peering over the top of his laptop, making sure no one heard him.

He remembered the last photo, the one of the wives with their husbands. Pulling it from the bottom of the pile, he scanned the image. His head began to throb. He squeezed his eyes shut, then opened them and blinked rapidly. The woman who hitched a ride with him was not in the picture.

Derek dragged a hand through his hair as he sat gaping at his screen. He had been so sure she would be in this photo. "What am I doing?" He whispered under his breath. His mind played tricks on him. "I saw the crime scene photos, then my brain lumped it all together, creating the dream."

That's the only way he could explain this. He pulled on the ends of his hair, wishing he had his anxiety medicine to take the edge off. The one thing he knew for sure, Chrissy was right. The three cold cases were connected. He also knew it was simply pure coincidence that these cases were directly related to the murder of Billy Edmond.

He needed a moment to digest everything. Derek headed towards the kitchen for something cold to drink. Pushing his chair out to stand, cool air swirled around him.

Lola sat up from her resting place next to Derek's desk. Her ears perked up as she cocked her head to the side. The low guttural growl intensified.

Derek remained seated, reaching over and patting her head, leaning into her ear. "It's okay, Lola. Just relax, please."

Lola stared at him. She leaned a little towards the left and looked behind his chair. The hair on her back bristled. But she didn't bark.

Derek closed his eyes. "Go away," he said softly, hoping no one heard him. He didn't dare look up. He wasn't sure who or what would be standing there. A crushing blanket of fear engulfed him. He clasped his hands together to keep them from trembling.

He could hear Felicia and Michael laughing in the kitchen. George sat engrossed in a phone call with someone. Emma sat at her desk up at the front and paid him no attention. Out of the corner of his eye, Derek peeked to his left. A man in a bloody shirt and tie stood next to him. The man took a step closer to the desk. His head had a sunken indentation the size of a softball. The skin on his forehead had several gashes, all two to three inches long. Derek could see blood and brain matter oozing from the wounds.

Lola's growl became louder. Derek held his hand out, resting it on her head. The man pointed to the desk. His shirt sleeve was rolled up to his elbows, and his outstretched arm had a severe bend in it. Derek saw the fractured bone sticking through the skin. As the dead man stepped closer, Derek heard a buzzing sound. He swallowed, turning away and closing his eyes, not wanting to look at the man.

His chest tightened as he pushed out a breath through taut lips. Derek kept his gaze on his computer screen. Calming himself, he turned his head to the left. The bloody man's face was inches from his. The buzzing sound intensified as the man opened his mouth. A swarm of flies rushed out, flooding Derek's face. He waved his hands as he let out a cry. He lurched back in his chair, causing the wheel to get stuck on a cord, flipping him backward.

George turned at hearing the scream and saw Derek go down. "Woah," he said into his phone. "I'll call you back." He hung up, rushing to his boss.

Emma glanced up at the commotion. Marc Anthony barked, running in Derek's direction. "Oh my gosh," she exclaimed as she followed George to Derek's side.

"Derek? Derek? Are you okay?" George knelt next to Derek's chair.

Kyle had just walked into the kitchen when he heard the crash. He followed Felicia and Michael to the front of the building. As the three of them entered the main room, they stopped.

Derek still sat in his chair, as it laid on the floor. He stared straight up at the ceiling, not moving. His eyes were glassy and fully dilated.

George stared at Derek's face. "Derek?" he asked as he flashed a light in his eyes. He watched as the pupils constricted then dilated again when he removed the light. "Derek?" George patted his cheek. He took his penlight and flashed it in Derek's eyes again.

"Why isn't he answering? His eyes are open." Emma's voice was an octave higher than usual.

"I don't know. Someone, get me a damp rag." George continued to check Derek's pupils.

Felicia ran into the kitchen and soaked a rag. She reached into the freezer and grabbed a few ice cubes, wrapping the rag around them. She raced back into the room, sliding to a stop. "Here."

"Give me one of the ice cubes. You hold the rag on his forehead." George took a cube and ran it along Derek's cheek. "Derek?" He flashed the light in his eyes.

This time Derek blinked. He shook his head. Waving his hand in front of his face. "Get the light out of my eyes. Are you trying to blind me?" He reached up, wiping the dampness from his face. "What the hell? Why am I wet?" He attempted to stand.

"Whoa. You're not going to get up just yet. You were out cold," George said, placing a firm hand on Derek's shoulder.

"Huh? What do you mean I was out?" Derek squinted at everyone. "I'm okay. Really. If anything, I just bumped my head. Let me get up."

George stood. He motioned for Kyle and Michael to help him lift the chair with Derek in it. "Derek, stay there. Let us lift the chair."

The three of them set Derek back on the wheels of the chair.

The dogs sat staring at the group then ran off to play. Lola was oblivious to whatever had gotten her attention.

"Derek, what happened?" Emma asked, checking the back of his head.

"I just rolled back and caught my chair on my cord. The momentum sent me flying." He stared at everyone. "I promise, I'm okay. I'm just klutzy today." He stood and moved the cord for his computer. "I will, in the future, make sure this cord isn't where my chair rolls."

George studied the man. "You hit your head pretty hard. I think you should get it checked out. Even though your eyes responded to the light, it took you several minutes before you were coherent enough to answer my questions."

"I'm okay. Really." Derek smiled.

Felicia walked to her desk. "Well, that was exciting."

George raised an eyebrow at Derek. "You sure your head is okay?"

Derek sighed. "Yes. I feel like an idiot. But I swear my head is okay."

George sighed in resolve. "Before you decided to take a header, I was on the phone with a buddy of mine. If you consider me an expert in blood spatter, he is a legend. I sent him the photos of the crime scenes.

I saw something, and I wanted to get his opinion."

"Yeah? What did you find?" Derek asked. He started to rub the back of his head but stopped short. His head pounded, and he could feel the start of a headache—a severe headache. But he didn't want anyone to fuss over him.

George went to his desk, grabbed the file with all the photos, and then rolled his chair over. Mindful of the cord. "Here are all the pictures of this cold case." He spread them out. "Look," he pointed to each photo. "These patterns have similar consistencies. Whoever struck these victims held the weapon in his left hand. Which is what I thought earlier."

George leaned back in his chair. "I know you said you were going to have the medical examiner look at these, and my buddy is an ME. He determined the blows seemed to have elements which would lead him to believe the same person did all the attacks."

Kyle walked into the room.

Derek motioned for him to come over. "Kyle, I need your help."

"What do you need me to do?"

Derek highlighted the names of the three couples from the cold case. "I sent you a file with some names. I need you to find out everything about each person. Focusing heavily on the husbands for me."

"I can do that. What else, anything?" Kyle asked, munching on a granola bar.

"Yeah, run this list of names." He handed him one of the photos from the headmaster. "This is Billy's high school baseball team. I just got these, so I don't even know who is on it." Derek paused, breaking eye contact with Kyle. "Do a deep run on them. Find out where they are now. I want to know everything about them."

Kyle took the photo with the list of names. "No problem. I'll be downstairs," he said as he headed for the kitchen, the dogs in tow.

Derek turned back to George when his cell phone rang. "Hold on," he said, holding up his hand. "Derek."

"Derek, it's Assistant Director Fretz."

"Director. What's up?"

"I have some bad news. Cary Mackle won't be joining your team. So, you're going to have to make do with who you have."

"Oh. What happened?" Derek scooted towards his desk.

"It looks like his previous task force needs him on a drug smuggling case. That takes precedence over the Legacy Unit."

"I understand. No worries. The team I have is perfect. I think this is going to work fine."

"Great. Do you have any leads on the Edmond case?"

"Not yet. I think we have ruled out one or two people, which is a plus. We're still digging into his background, seeing if there is anything that stands out there. We're also looking at his business dealings. I'll give you something by next week. I'm sure Congressman Jackson wants answers," Derek said.

"Sounds good. Keep me posted."

"Will do." Derek disconnected the call. He looked over at George. "It looks like this is the team. Cary Mackle has to go back to his prior drug unit."

"I don't think we need anyone else." George looked up when the front door buzzed.

Kelly walked in.

"Guys," Derek said, waving everyone towards him.

Felicia and Michael were about to walk out the door when they turned around.

"Looks like this is it for our team. Mackle won't be showing up. I think this has worked out for the best. I'm not going to partner anyone up. We work together on cases. If you need help, just ask someone."

He looked over at Emma. "Our illustrious Emma knows most of everything going on. If I'm not here and you need something, I'm sure either she or Kyle will know what to do. I may be in charge of this unit on paper, but we operate as one."

Leaning back in his chair, he continued, "Let's get an update on where we are in the case." Derek turned towards Kelly. "Do you have all the names ready to go?"

"Yes. I am dividing the list between myself, Felicia, and Michael," she said.

"Good." Derek eyeballed Felicia and Michael. "When you two get back from the wife's family, get started on the names. Kelly, start with the business associates. I think you can whittle it down pretty quick."

She nodded. "You got it."

"I have Kyle running the names of the men on the high school baseball team. We can cross-reference those when he gets done. Some may be on your list, Kelly. I imagine Billy might have business dealings with them.

"I know from the visit with the headmaster today, seven or so years ago, Billy had a donors party at his home." Derek glanced at George. "Get the house manager, Mr. Aleshire's number from Kelly. Call him. Ask who besides the donors attended the event. Ask him if he has any records of the party or subsequent parties. Find out everything."

George scribbled on Derek's notepad. "No problem."

Kelly walked to her desk. "George, here is the number for Mr. Aleshire."

George tore off the piece of paper and rolled his chair back to his desk. "Thank you."

Felicia waved. "Be back soon." She and Michael walked out the door.

CHAPTER NINETEEN

Derek's fingers grazed the soft welt on the back of his head. He winced as the sharp pain radiated outward, intensifying the headache. *Maybe I did hit a little harder than I thought.* He checked his fingers for blood, then rummaged through his desk, searching for some pain reliever. Finding a bottle of Acetaminophen, he swallowed four without water.

His phone pinged with a text message. He smiled at the photo of Lizzy and her mom.

I miss you.

He texted back. *I miss you too. Are you having fun?*

Yes. I think my mom is getting tired, though. I may be home next week. I'll let you know the details later. I'll call tonight.

Okay. Talk to you then.

He set his phone down on his desk as Kelly walked up to him.

"Hey, um, I need to run something by you."

"Okay. What is it?" Derek asked, leaning back in his chair.

Kelly glanced at her feet.

"What is it, Kelly?"

"The woman in your photo has been photographed with Billy and Congressman Jackson," she said. "I found several business meetings with Billy and the congressman in which she seemed to be involved in."

"That's good work."

"Shouldn't we find out where she has been? She could be a potential suspect."

"I can tell you where she was the night Billy Edmond was murdered. She's on vacation with her family. Last week they were in France. This week they are in Italy." He cocked his head to the side. "Does that help?"

She cringed. "I didn't mean any disrespect. I've been trying to figure out how to ask you about her. I know you and she have a relationship."

Derek sighed. "There is no secret concerning Lizzy and I. We are very good friends. I've known her for a long time. It also isn't any secret what she does. She isn't a whore, though. She doesn't sleep with the men she's photographed with."

"I—I didn't imply...."

Derek held up his hand. "Don't apologize. I've wondered if anyone would ask about her. Feel free to check her out. The same investigative runs you would do on someone else. You don't have cause for a warrant, but you can do the same searches on her you would do on anyone else."

"I'm really sorry," Kelly said.

"No need, Kelly. It's okay. I know she didn't have anything to do with this case." Derek stood. "It shows me you aren't afraid to look under every rock. You knew I had a relationship with her, and you still approached me. I have no problem with you doing your job.

"I would only ask you wait for her to get back in town if you want to speak with her. She doesn't need to be bothered while she is on her trip. If you find anything questionable, I can kick this up to Assistant Director Fretz. He is aware of our friendship, and he can handle the questioning. This way, our unit stays transparent."

Kelly shook her head. "I don't see anything to make me think it will go that far. I just wasn't sure you were aware of her association with our dead guy."

Derek came around his desk. "When the AD asked me to handle this case on the request of Congressman Jackson, I knew there would be a good chance she would come up. I had to let the investigation proceed, though. So again, if you find anything, you can question her, and then if you feel it needs other eyes, we can get Fretz to do it."

"Okay. I have a lot of other people ahead of her who have more interest in Billy Edmond's death."

Derek crossed his arms. "Have you found something?"

Kelly sighed. "Nothing concrete. But he did have a lot of business with people who went to Londonvale Academy."

"I'm not surprised. They're part of the upper echelon of Phoenix society. I would probably be surprised if they didn't have connections over the years." Derek stretched.

Kelly walked back to her desk.

"Derek. I talked to Mr. Aleshire. He has some extra information. He is going to email me the party guest list," George said, spinning his chair to face him.

"Does he have anything else, like who declined, if anyone was angry about not being invited, maybe a fight, and we will have our killer in a few hours?"

George laughed. "I don't think he has that. But he does have a lot of information. He said he would send over everything. I told him I would go through it, and if I had any questions, I would call him."

"Perfect. Let me know what comes of it." Derek walked into the kitchen to get something to drink. He opened the refrigerator door, leaning against it. A rhythmic beat echoed against his skull. He rubbed the back of his neck, stretching, hoping the pounding would subside. He shut the door and spun around. "Holy shit." He clutched his chest. "Stop doing that."

Chrissy sat on the counter, swinging her legs. "Sorry. You hit your head pretty hard."

Derek touched the sore bump. "One of your friends showed up."

"He's not my friend. What? Just because he's dead and in your head makes him my friend?"

Derek leaned back, glancing over his left shoulder, checking to see if anyone was walking towards the kitchen. He then peeked at the door to the basement. It was open, and soft music came from downstairs. "He's not in my head. It's my subconscious trying to tell me something. I'm not sure what."

Chrissy smoothed out her dress. She had a ribbon around her neck, hiding the scar left by Josiah when he murdered her.

"I think if you let the visions guide you instead of fighting them, you might see the things from a different perspective." Chrissy fiddled with an empty can on the counter.

Derek watched as the can spun around. "Stop. Someone will walk in and see."

"No one is going to see it. Only you, stupid. How long will it take you to realize that?"

"Not true. Assistant Director Fretz saw you at the gravesite. When we were talking."

She laughed. "He saw what you wanted him to see."

"Just stop. This is too much. It's my head. The broken cheek and head injury from Josiah Craig haven't healed properly. Now, this bump, is just a—I need to have it looked at."

"Derek, relax. Think about what you have seen in the visions and dreams. They're trying to tell you something. C'mon. You see cases different than anyone else."

"These pieces aren't fitting together. Like this guy today, he wore a shirt and tie, not pajamas like the others. It's bits and pieces, and I can't figure out where they're coming from. I thought the woman I saw in my car was the wife of one of the husbands from the cold case. But she wasn't. I don't know who the heck she is. She isn't in any of the crime scene photos I've seen."

He crossed his arms. "I can explain everyone. I've seen photos from the past crimes. Mixed with the recent crimes, and with all my head injuries, my brain is pulling things together to fill gaps of memory loss." He sighed. "I'm stressed and distracted." Derek opened his can of soda and took a long sip. "I'm just distracted."

"Lizzy?"

"I don't know. Kelly talked to me about it. I don't know why I thought she wouldn't come up. The minute Assistant Director Fretz said Congressman Jackson asked me to handle this case, I should've known." Derek jumped at a noise behind him. Both Marc Anthony and Lola stood staring at him or the counter. He wasn't sure. Lola didn't bark, but her hackles were up.

He started to say something and realized Chrissy had left. "I can't believe I'm talking to myself again."

"Who were you talking to?" Kyle asked as he entered the kitchen carrying some papers.

"Huh?"

"I heard you speaking with someone. Who?" He grabbed a soda from the fridge.

"Um, myself. Running this case over in my head." Derek pointed to the papers in his hand. "What's that?"

"Let's go to your desk. There's something you need to see."

"Okay," Derek said, following him. He glanced back over his shoulder to see Chrissy waving at him as she spun around in the kitchen, fluffing her skirt.

CHAPTER TWENTY

Tuesday 2 p.m.

Felicia and Michael drove through the upscale neighborhood.

"I thought we may need to provide a DNA sample to get past the guard at the entrance," Felicia said, turning onto the Wallace's Street.

Michael whistled. "Looks like they pay for the protection. I mean, wow. These houses are something else. How much you think they go for?"

"Three to six million easy. Way out of our price range." Felicia turned into the drive at 55 Lexington Lane. "Oh, my." Her mouth hung open as she drove towards the smooth tinted stucco and brick gateway. Deep red roses covered the entire structure. No longer visible, trellises helped ease the flowers over the rounded archway. The patina on the metal gates gave a stark yet alluring contrast to the deep red of the roses.

"This is a heck of an entrance." Michael's gaze landed on the front doors located directly at the end of the driveway.

The dark wood had an overlay of sculptured metal. The square rigid frame softened as the eye moved upward to an arched window. A soft heather blue color trimmed every door and window, except for the front door. Sparsely placed bricks in the same color accented the walls. Tall pine trees framed the house. The same rose bushes from the entryway lined the walkway and front landscaping.

Felicia's eyes widened as she stepped out of the vehicle and spun around. "Look at this place. What, about seven thousand square feet?"

"Easy," Michael said as they walked up the cobblestone path. A smaller version of the design on the brick driveway.

She reached out to ring the bell just as the door opened. "Mrs. Wallace?" Felicia asked as she and Michael held out their badges.

"Yes. I'm Loretta Wallace. Please come in." She stepped back, holding out her hand as she ushered them in.

"Thank you for taking the time to see us, Mrs. Wallace." Michael looked in the direction of the husband, Isaac Wallace. "Mr. Wallace, I'm Agent Finch. This is Agent Rogers."

"We're devastated about what has happened to Billy." Mr. Wallace reached for his wife and pulled her into his side. "He and Francine were married for almost ten years. We thought of him like a son. Even more so after his parents died in a car wreck."

"Please have a seat." Mrs. Wallace motioned to a large overstuffed sofa. They took seats across from the agents. "Can I get you something to drink?"

Felicia shook her head. "No, Ma'am." She stared out the large sliding glass window at the resort-style pool and backyard. "Your home is beautiful."

"Thank you. We have a son and another daughter, along with their families who come here regularly." She smiled at her husband. "The grandchildren help breathe life into this home every time they're here."

"What can we help the FBI with?" Mr. Wallace asked.

"We're hoping you could give us some insight into who may have wanted Billy dead? Is there anyone Billy complained about?"

Mr. Wallace's brow wrinkled. "I don't remember any conflicts. Honey, I know you spoke with Francine more about her and Billy's life. Do you remember Billy mentioning anything?"

She sighed. "They had a good marriage. They were in love. No cheating. No fights. Financially, they both had their own money coming into the marriage. As for anyone being unhappy, I guess through Billy's business he may have made some people mad, but I don't remember him ever complaining about being threatened."

"How close were Mr. Edmond and his parents?" Michael asked, scribbling in his small spiral notebook he had removed from his pants pocket.

"Oh, yes." Mr. Wallace chuckled. "They had their regular father and son arguments. Billy's dad wanted him to work for his law firm. Billy had other plans, and over time, his dad accepted it. Neither of them let that come between them."

"Do you know if Billy was close to anyone outside of his wife? Did he have a best friend or someone from high school he may have confided in?" Felicia asked.

"I don't think...," Mr. Wallace started to say something when his wife cut him off.

"There was someone. I remember, about five years ago, someone from Billy's high school baseball team was killed. Billy took it hard." Mrs. Wallace smiled at the two agents. "I don't know many details. Billy kept it private, and Francine didn't push him on it."

"Do you remember his name?"

Both of them shook their head.

Mrs. Wallace's eyebrows raised. "I do remember Francine said Billy and the rest of the team had gotten together just a year or two before."

"The whole team?" asked Michael.

"I would imagine so." Mrs. Wallace leaned into her husband.

"When did Francine die?" Felicia asked.

"September 2017," Mrs. Wallace said.

"Did they continue to get together after the death?" Felicia asked.

"As far as I know. I remember before Francine died, she mentioned Billy having a party. I'm sure Norman, Mr. Aleshire, would know those details," Mrs. Wallace said.

"You were named as a recipient of Billy's will." Felicia studied their facial responses.

A hint of a smile tugged at the corners of Mrs. Wallace's mouth. "We don't need his money. We plan on donating it to animal rescue groups. Francine and Billy loved to support those groups."

Mr. Wallace sighed. "I'm sorry we aren't much help. Will you keep us posted? We would like to know how this turns out."

"When we can share any information, I will call you with an update." Felicia stood, nodding to Michael.

He stood and smiled. "We appreciate your time."

Mr. and Mrs. Wallace stood, walking the agents to the door. "Anything we can do, please call us."

Felicia and Michael got into the car. As she turned around in the large driveway and headed towards the street, she glanced over her shoulder. "I'm going to dream about this house tonight."

"Dream is about all you can do on our salary."

"Hell, I don't even think our salary is enough to pay for the dream."

CHAPTER TWENTY-ONE

Derek sat at his desk, leaning back in his chair. "Hold that thought," he said to Kyle as he answered his phone. "Reed."

"Derek, this is Dr. Callahan."

"What's going on, Doc?"

"There's been another murder. I think it's connected to Billy Edmond."

Derek grabbed a pen. "Where are you? I'll bring my team with me."

"1455 Central Avenue."

"You've got to be kidding me." He scribbled the address on a piece of paper.

"I wish. It's a mess too."

"I'm on my way." Derek hung up his phone. "Fuck." His head hung against his chest.

"Bad, huh?" Kyle asked.

"Worse." Derek sighed. "You were about to tell me something."

"The three guys you gave me, the cold cases...."

"Let me guess. They're on the baseball team?"

Kyle squinted at his boss. "Yes, how did you know?"

"I'm psychic. There's been another murder," he glanced up. "Wait, do you have the list of high school boys from the team?"

"Yeah," Kyle thumbed through the papers. "Right here."

"Look up Greg Burks. Is his name on there?"

Kyle shook his head. "Nope."

"Well, then I don't know why Dr. Callahan thinks these cases are related." Derek shook his head. "I guess we will find out when we get there." He stood. "George, I want you to come with me to a crime scene. Bring the pictures from the cold case file. Kelly, are you still going over the business contacts?"

"Yeah, not really getting anywhere, though."

"Good." Derek looked at Kyle. "I want you and Kelly to go over those names. Give her everything you have gathered on the entire team. Kelly, when Felicia and Michael get back, I want you to split those names between you and start talking to them."

George stood. "I just received several years of party lists from Billy's house manager. It seems the first party for the donors turned into a regular get-together for the baseball team."

"Save it for later. We'll go over it when we get back." Derek headed for the front door. "Kyle, if you leave before I get back, take Lola home with you, please. Her collar will let her in through the doggy door."

"No problem," Kyle said, nodding at him.

CHAPTER TWENTY-TWO

Tuesday 3 p.m.

In the car, Derek cranked the AC and the seat coolers. He glanced over at George, who stared at him with a raised eyebrow. "What?"

"How did you get this car?"

"I stole it from a drug dealer." Derek chuckled. "I got it at an auction. Had it restored. I'm guessing you think I got it by nefarious means."

He shook his head. "Not really. But you must get that question a lot."

"I do."

"Why did you agree to run this unit? I know most profilers are behind the scenes. They sit in locked rooms pouring over data, crime scene photos, and notes."

"Yes. That may be true of some. However, there are a few of us who go out on cases. Actually, work in the field. Especially when there are multiple murders and the local authorities are trying to get a handle on the case."

Derek paused. "I didn't like being in the backroom, studying photos and then relaying my findings. I wanted to be out in the field, in the scenes, getting my hands dirty. You get so much information from what you see. The smell of the blood. What the room looks like, where the murder took place. You can't always garner the same information from a photo or crime scene notes."

"How did you manage to get out of the dungeon?"

Derek laughed. "I bullied my way out. I had a case when I first started. I couldn't get a handle on the crimes from the photos. The notes regarding two identical murders, or what seemed like identical murders, didn't make sense." He drove through the streets of Phoenix. "I called the detective on the case, got some background, went to my boss and told him I was going. Then I went."

"Did you solve the case?"

Derek laughed. "Yeah. It's the only reason I didn't get my ass fired, caught the guy within a week. Not because of me. The detectives did a hell of a job."

"You glad you took over this unit?"

"Ask me when this case is over." Derek stopped at a traffic light. "What's with the twenty questions? You gunning for my job?"

"Hell no. I'm happy being a peon." George fiddled with his AC vent. "Do you know what we're walking into?"

Derek tilted his head to the side. "Unfortunately, I do." Light traffic made the drive to downtown easy.

George waited. "Well, what is it? Who got killed?"

"Greg Burks. Ever hear of him?"

George shook his head. "No. Should I?"

Derek followed along the outskirts of the city. Getting closer to downtown, the traffic slowly intensified. "His family owns one of the premier real estate groups on the west coast. They deal in properties worth millions. Even for a matchbox size apartment."

"Who would pay millions for a small apartment?" George looked at the buildings as they drove down the main streets of downtown Phoenix.

"The Burks build, sell, and rent a lifestyle. You buy the amenities one would expect to come with the property, not just the property. This particular place is a high-rise apartment building. But it's more like you're living in a luxury hotel. Everything is done for you. Maid service, laundry, and cleaning are all included in the purchase of the apartment."

Derek pulled under the covered drive of a fifteen-story apartment. "The first few don't have balconies. Once you hit the fifth through thirteenth, those have balconies overlooking either the city or the mountains, depending on which side you are on." He grabbed the file holding the cold cases.

As they exited the vehicle, a man came running out of the building. "You can't park here. You can't park here. Please move your vehicle."

Derek held up his credentials as he placed an FBI plaque on the dash of the car. "I'm FBI Agent Derek Reed. Where are Dr. Callahan and the police?"

"Oh, I'm sorry. I didn't know. They're on the penthouse floor. This is horrible. Just horrible."

Derek followed the nervous nelly into the building. "Can you tell me anything about what happened?"

Several large drop lights hung from the ceiling at different heights. Large pillars had vases filled with roses and exotic flowers. Derek counted eight of these elaborate flower stands located across the lobby floor. Three pairs of high-back chairs with tables between them commingled with cozy sofas spaced across the entire room. A bank of elevators sat to the right. One elevator entrance stood off to the side separated from the main bank.

The man used a special key card to gain access to the penthouse elevator. "Not much. I came on this morning after leaving yesterday at 4 p.m." He held the door open with his outstretched arm.

"Did you see Mr. Burks yesterday?" Derek removed a notebook from his back pocket.

"Yes. He phoned me earlier in the day and asked if Hutchinson, that's our Master Chef here on-premises could make Mr. Burks two steak dinners with appetizers and desserts and have it brought up to his penthouse around 7 p.m. I made the arrangements just before I left."

"I need the names of the person or persons who delivered the meal. Can you get me the information?"

He pursed his lips together, nodding.

"How about the names of any other employees who were here last night after you left and who may have seen Mr. Burks?"

"Yes. I can get you all the names. I will have it in my office for you when you leave." The man stepped aside as the door opened.

"Tell me your name?" Derek asked.

"Peter Montague. I have been the resident manager of this place since the Burks built it." He hung his head. "This is so terrible."

"Mr. Montague. I will be sending down a police officer, but in the meantime, do not let anyone into this elevator. Can you do that for me?"

"Yes. Yes, I can."

"Are any of the people from last night still on the premises?"

Mr. Montague squeezed his eyes shut, pinching the bridge of his nose. "I don't know. I think so. I will have to check."

"Okay, get me the list. If any of the employees are still here, make sure they wait for me. Okay?" Derek asked.

"Yes. I can keep them here. I will be in my office. Just ask the receptionist, and she will get me."

Derek watched Peter Montague hold back the tears as the lift doors closed. He and George stood in a luxurious foyer; another large vase of exotic flowers stood in the center of the entryway. Flanking either side of the marble table, two police officers greeted them.

"Who are you?" One asked.

"I'm Agent Derek Reed. This is my partner, Agent Peterson. Where is Dr. Callahan?"

"Let them in!" Dr. Callahan yelled from the other side of the frosted glass partition wall.

Derek smiled at the two police officers. "He sounds cranky."

One officer chuckled. "He is."

"I can hear you, Derek." Dr. Callahan leaned back and stretched.

Derek walked into the sunken living room. His chest tingled, restricting his breathing. He felt his pulse in his throat. He stood still, unable to lift his feet.

George looked at the wall closest to the body, studying the blood spatter and walked right into him. "Oh, sorry, Derek," he said stepping off to the side. He looked at the head of his unit. "Yo, Derek? Agent Reed?" he called out to him, nudging his shoulder.

Derek's posture slumped. He pinched his nose, trying to focus on what he saw. "Huh? Sorry. For a moment, I thought, never mind."

Dr. Callahan raised his eyebrows at the agent. His face had a slight ashen color. But as quickly as his color drained, it returned. "Derek, is something wrong?"

Derek shook his head. "No. You weren't kidding when you said it was a mess." He avoided eye contact with the ME. Instead, he focused on the man he had just seen in his office earlier in the day.

Greg Burks' left leg had a severe bend in it. Indicating a compound fracture. His left arm also had a compound fracture. Brain matter covered the wall and ceiling. Greg Burks' face was unrecognizable.

Derek blew out a breath. "His head is almost obliterated. This is a rage killing."

George smiled at the ME. "I'm George Peterson."

"Nice to meet you Agent Peterson. I'd shake your hand but," he wiggled his bloody fingers.

Derek glanced at the ME but didn't say anything. He moved gingerly around the dead man. He studied the wall and the bloody cast-off. "It looks like the first blow to the head occurred while he was either bent over or on the floor but not laying down." His finger pointed to the large spatter pattern low on the wall. "See here?"

Derek opened the case file he'd brought with him, glancing at the photos within. He handed it to George. "Do you think it's the same guy?"

George looked at the photos. Pulling them out one by one, he examined them. He kept looking at the body and the bloody wall. "Have you moved the body, Doc?"

"Yes. I rolled him so I could examine him. My guy over there has some photos. I made him take them before I moved him." Doc waved at his tech. "Get the camera."

"How was he laying?" George asked.

The doctor knelt next to the body. "When we came in, he was on his right side, facing the foyer. His right leg was at an awkward angle under him." He pointed to the camera. "Pull up the photos of the body, please."

The tech stood next to the two FBI agents and scrolled through the photos.

"Stop." George tucked the file under his arm. "May I?" he asked the tech.

"Sure." He handed the camera to the agent.

"What do you see?" Derek asked.

"I'm not sure." George put the strap of the camera around his neck, then opened the file again. He stepped to the front of the body and looked down at what was left of the man's head. Kneeling, he looked at the ME. "Could you turn his head towards you?"

"Of course." The doctor did as requested. "What do you see, Agent?" Dr. Callahan asked.

Derek squatted beside George.

George studied the photo on the LCD screen of the camera, then looked at the dead man. "See this?" He circled the small area of the man's head.

"You mean the only part of the man's skull not bashed in?" Derek asked.

"Yes. There doesn't seem to be any direct strikes against the right side of the head."

Dr. Callahan twisted the man's neck from side to side. "Once I remove the flesh and look at the skull, or at the least scan him, we should get a much better idea where he was struck. However, at first glance, that may be a plausible explanation for the lack of damage to this area."

"Okay, bear with me. This bolsters why I think your killer is left-handed. And yes, I think it's the same guy." George looked at the tech. "You want to be my victim?"

"Oh, yeah. It's what I live for." He chuckled. "What do you need?"

George handed the file and the camera to Derek. Stepping away from the body, into the middle of the room, he placed the tech where he wanted him. "All right. I'm the killer. I'm standing in front of Greg. I hit him on the left leg." He pretended to hit the tech.

The tech reached and grabbed his left leg, instinctively placing his weight on his right.

"See what he just did? He grabbed his injured leg and leaned to his right, shifting his weight, putting him slightly off balance. I bet your victim did this. I think this hit was to either incapacitate or distract Greg. Hitting Greg on the left leg, wouldn't be using his dominant hand and swing. Now at this point, I believe the killer stepped behind him." He moved behind the tech. "Continuing with the assumption our killer is a lefty, he wants to make sure this hit has all the power."

Derek squinted at George, then looked at the blood and brain matter on the wall. "His next hit would be to the left side of his head."

"Yes." He pretended to strike the officer on the left side of his head.

The officer fell onto his right side.

George reached down and helped the tech up. "Thanks." He stepped over to the victim. He pointed at the wall. "You can see the first hit to the head is at an upward arc. This first blow caused the blood you see here. You can see some of the cast-off here on the tile. As your guy swung again, the blood on the weapon landed on the tile." He pointed in the direction of the blood.

Dr. Callahan examined the victim's head. "The head has repeated blows on the left side and leading towards the top of the head."

"And that would make sense," George pretended to straddle the victim, "especially if our killer stood over Greg like this. As he swings, repeatedly hitting Greg, the cast-off from the weapon makes the arcs you see here," he pointed to the ceiling.

Dr. Callahan pointed at the victim's head. "There is a tremendous amount of brain matter in this area. The continued contact of the bat with the man's head would have been like hitting a ripe watermelon. The only way the brain matter could've gotten on the ceiling is from the repeated cast-off."

"Where is the weapon?" Derek asked.

"Haven't found one yet. I have techs searching the home." Dr. Callahan frowned. "You look like you have a question, Derek."

Derek looked up from the cold case file. "Do you know anything about a Dr. Reasor?"

Dr. Callahan's brow wrinkled. "I don't know him personally, but I know he filled in when other MEs were overloaded. He covered the entire state of Arizona. I know he complained about the time and travel. I think the state released him after about three years of working as a relief doctor."

"Was he good at what he did?" Derek asked.

"He was subpar at best. Why do you ask?" Dr. Callahan stretched his back.

"I'm revisiting three cases from five years ago. He never connected them even though he performed each autopsy on the murder victims. Granted, there was some time in between each murder and they did not all occur in the same jurisdiction."

"Why don't you give me the case numbers, and I'll look them up and see if I can give you any information. Do you think they're connected to these two cases?" Dr. Callahan asked.

"Kyle ran their names. They were on Billy's baseball team. George here looked at the photos and saw similarities between the cases. Same similarities he sees here. The problem, these damn cases were all mishandled. I think had this doctor connected these cases, they may have been investigated differently."

Dr. Callahan sighed. "I'll look up the cases and pull all the ME files related to the cases. Everything should be electronically stored. I'll go through the reports. I'll cull any information and send it to you."

"I would appreciate any help. I'm going to treat these cold cases as if they are new." He looked at George. "Let's get back to the office. We need to figure out how to approach all of these cases." Derek pulled his phone from his pocket and texted Kyle. It pinged back. "The team is still at the office. I'm having them wait for us."

Derek scratched his head. "Other than the injuries to our victim, what made you think this murder is connected to Billy Edmond?"

Dr. Callahan rubbed his chin with the back of his gloved hand. "Don't you know anything about Greg Burks?"

Derek shrugged. "No. Other than he and his family are realtors who overcharge. Why? What should I know?"

"Greg Burks was the batter on Billy Edmond's high school baseball team who hit the grand slam winning the state championship."

Derek's mouth fell open. "I didn't see his name on the roster of the team. How did I miss that?"

"Unless you knew the story, you wouldn't know about the name change. Back in high school, Greg went by the name of Greg Randolph. Randolph is his mother's maiden name. His mother remarried right after Greg graduated high school to Tennison Burks. Before Greg turned eighteen, Tennison adopted him. He wanted to make sure Greg was taken care of in the future, and adoption was the easiest way.

"I remember Billy's father drew up the paperwork as a favor to the Randolphs. They didn't want it going public and putting Greg in the spotlight for the wrong reasons. Greg's biological father lost his parental rights when Greg was a toddler. Billy's father helped with the court filings."

The bump on the back of Derek's head throbbed. He reached up and touched it, wincing at the tenderness.

Dr. Callahan's back straightened. "Derek, what's wrong with your head?"

"Nothing."

George wiggled his forefinger. "That's not true. He took a header earlier today. Knocked himself out when his head hit the floor."

Derek's shoulders sagged. The last person he wanted to know about the head injury was a doctor. Let alone Callahan. He looked up to see Dr. Callahan removing his bloody gloves and walking over to him. "I'm fine," he said, scowling at George. "Thanks."

George shrugged. "You need to have it looked at."

Dr. Callahan smiled as he spun Derek around. "Good thing I'm a doctor." He parted his hair, inspecting the large swollen mass on the back of Derek's head. The doctor peered over Derek's shoulder, looking at George. "What happened after he hit the floor?"

"His eyes were fully dilated and remained open. I shined a penlight in them, and they constricted. When I removed the light, they dilated again. It took several minutes before he responded to my questions." George stepped a little closer. "Does he need stitches? We didn't see any blood."

"No, but it is swollen. Very swollen." Dr. Callahan spun Derek around. He reached inside the white jumpsuit he wore to protect the crime scene, grabbing his penlight from his front shirt pocket. He flashed the light in Derek's eyes.

Derek squinted. "Seriously? Do you have to do that?"

"Quit acting like a five-year-old." He flashed the light a second time in each eye. "Your pupils seem to be responding. But the size of the bump on your head would normally warrant a CT scan."

"I'm not getting one." Derek stepped back. "No. I'm not going to the ER or any clinic."

Dr. Callahan rolled his eyes. "Fine. If you have headaches or trouble sleeping or staying awake, you will go."

"Okay. If I have any of those things, I will go." Derek gave George a dirty look. "You're on my shit list. Just so you know."

George laughed. "That's fine. I'll be on the list."

Derek glanced at the scene. "Please make sure I get copies of all the photos. And if you find anything in those reports, give me a call."

Dr. Callahan smiled. "I will."

Derek started to leave. "Doc?"

"Yes?"

"Don't say anything about the other three cases. I want to keep this under wraps as long as I can. Phoenix doesn't need to know a bat wielding serial killer is living among them."

CHAPTER TWENTY-THREE

Derek and George exited the elevator into the lobby of Burks' building. They walked to the reception desk.

"Good afternoon. How can I help you?" The young lady asked.

"Is Mr. Montague available?" Derek asked.

"Let me check for you." She picked up a phone and punched in a number. "Mr. Montague, you have..." she tilted her head towards Derek.

"FBI Agent Derek Reed."

"A Derek Reed up here for you. Yes, sir." She hung up. "He will be right up."

"Thanks." Derek turned, stepping away from the counter. He watched as residents milled about. Turning back to the lady, he caught her attention. "Were you here last night?"

"Yes. I worked until 8 p.m."

"Do you remember seeing someone come in looking for Mr. Burks? I understand he had requested dinner for two."

"If Mr. Burks wants a visitor to come up to his penthouse unnoticed, all he has to do is give them the code for the elevator. They wouldn't have to stop at the desk at all." A customer service smile plastered across her face.

"Okay. Do you remember seeing anyone who didn't look familiar to you?"

She sighed. "We have so many people coming in and out of here. The main elevators don't need a key or code, so anyone can just enter and go to the floor they need. We only require check-in if they are staying overnight and need to park their car."

Derek leaned into the counter. "Do you have anyone on that list? Anyone request an overnight parking pass?"

She pulled a sheet from a file folder. "It looks like we had three requests." Grabbing a pad and pen, she wrote the names of the guests, the parking space assignment, and the resident they were staying over with. "Here. The numbers are to the residents. You can call them and verify."

He smiled as he took the piece of paper. "Thank you. Do you know if the chef is around?"

She shook her head. "Not today. I know he had a wedding or something personal today through the weekend, if I am not mistaken."

Peter Montague rushed out from the back office.

Derek winked at the young lady behind the counter. "Thank you for your help."

"You're welcome."

"Agent Reed. Sorry, it took me so long." He stumbled on the carpet as he rushed over to him, catching himself before he hit the floor. "Oh, my. That was close." He straightened his jacket. "Here is the list of employees who were here last night. The chef is unavailable, but I did list his sous chef. He helped him prepare Mr. Burks' meal last night. I'm sure he can answer your questions."

"Thank you," Derek said.

"Do you guys have surveillance covering the elevators and the lobby area?" George asked.

Peter Montague feigned a smile. "We do." A slight snarl tugged at his upper lip. "I guess you're going to want those for last night?"

Both Derek and George nodded.

"Yes," Derek said. "I can have my tech guy come and get them, or if you can download it to a USB drive or cloud, we can get it from there."

Peter Montague moved behind the counter. He logged into a computer and typed a series of commands on a keyboard. "Give me just a minute. I need to go to the back and download it off the main security console."

Derek smirked at George. "Not sure he wanted to share that."

"I think he's worried about someone and privacy issues. He seems a tad bit uptight," George said.

Peter returned with a jump drive. "This has all the video from yesterday morning until this morning. If you find you need a wider time range, I can give you up to two weeks before I have to get it from our security company."

Derek took the drive. "Thank you, Mr. Montague. You have been very helpful. If I need anything else, I will contact you. I would like the crime scene left as is until I give you the go-ahead to have it cleaned. Also, no one is to enter the premises, not even any of Mr. Burks' family. The ME will place a lock on the door. Please make sure it is not breached."

"I will. No one will enter until you give the okay. There are no employees here from yesterday evening. But I have listed them on the sheet I gave you."

"Thank you," Derek said.

As Derek drove out, he saw George shaking his head. "What?" he asked.

George chuckled. "As nice as this place may be, I don't think I could live here. Seems way too snooty."

"I'm pretty sure you or I couldn't even afford this level of snooty."

.

CHAPTER TWENTY-FOUR

Tuesday 5 p.m.

As Derek pulled into the parking lot of the Legacy Unit, he glanced at George. "You were pretty quiet coming back. Something wrong?"

George waited for a moment before he asked his question. He finally looked at Derek. "Where did you go? Back at Greg's place. When you saw the body, it looked as if you had seen him before?"

Derek leaned closer to his door. He focused on the front of the building. Uncomfortable under the hard stare of his agent. "I had. I've seen him in the papers."

"No. It looked like you recognized him from somewhere else. Somewhere more personal."

Derek shook his head, frowning. "Nope. Just wasn't prepared to see him bludgeoned to death. Greg Burks' was a gregarious man. Whenever he did an interview on TV, you couldn't help but be drawn to him."

George squinted at him. "I think you're hiding something. I won't push it. But I hope you know you can talk to me. I'm sure the others on this team would say the same thing."

Derek stepped out of the vehicle and gave George a quick glance. "Thank you. I promise I'm not hiding anything. However, if I ever need to talk, I will let you know." Walking into the unit, Lola and Marc Anthony ran to them. "Hey, you guys." Derek scratched both their heads. "You miss us?" He didn't look at George as he walked to his desk.

Both dogs wagged their tails, nuzzling them.

Kyle exited George's seat. "I was using your computer."

"No worries," George said.

Derek sat in his chair, sitting the file he carried in on the desk. He handed the piece of paper with the names of the employees and the visitors to George. "Will you call all these? See if anyone saw Greg's dinner guest."

"I can do that," George said taking the papers.

Derek turned toward the rest of his agents. "What have you guys found out?"

Kyle sat on the edge of George's desk. "I ran all the members of the baseball team. I think we may have a problem."

Derek perked up. His gaze traveled across the faces of his agents. Kelly, Michael, and Felicia nodded in agreement. "What?"

Kyle sighed. "There are two other baseball team murders. Both happened in other states at different times. They never would've been connected. The local PD classified one as a robbery gone wrong the other a random hit and run." He nodded at Kelly. "You got the names?"

"Yeah. Arthur Brandis and Timmy Cowman. Arthur was found in his office after hours. And Timmy died after being run down by a car."

"How did the hit and run happen?" Derek asked.

"According to reports from the local PD files, a witness saw a speeding car traveling down the road towards the victim. The witness came out of his business, at the same time the car hit Timmy," Kyle said.

"Wait, a witness saw it?" Derek asked.

"The witness has a furniture business, which is located in the warehouse district of Portland. After hours, the area is deserted. According to the record, he left his business later than usual, saw a car speed up and run over Timmy Cowman as he exited his building. Killed him on impact," Kyle said.

"I'm guessing the witness didn't see the car or driver who hit Mr. Cowman?"

Kelly shook her head. "Nope. Nothing on CCTV, either. Cameras caught the accident, but the vehicle had no license plate."

Derek turned towards Kyle. "What about the other guy," he snapped his fingers, "Arthur Brandis?"

"The local PD believe someone broke into the office, thinking no one would be there. When they found Arthur Brandis working, they killed him during the robbery."

"Does it say what they were trying to steal?" Derek asked.

"Several of the man's files were stolen. He was a defense attorney in San Francisco. The detectives believe it had something to do with a case he handled. They never found any suspects." Kyle glanced over his shoulder at Felicia. "Did you speak with his family?"

She nodded. "Yes. They didn't think any of the cases he had warranted him being murdered. He handled mostly white-collar criminals."

"What years did they die?"

"Arthur Brandis died in 2016 and Timmy Cowman died in 2017,"

Kyle said, looking at the paper.

Derek pulled out the file from the headmaster. "Kyle, do you have the photo and list of names I gave you earlier?"

Kyle shuffled some papers around he'd been using at George's desk. "Yeah, here it is," he said, handing it to Derek.

He took the list of high school boys and the list from the first donor party. Taking a pen, he circled each of the players who had been murdered on both lists, and then circled the heads of the men on the donor photo.

"Okay. We found out today the latest victim, Greg Burks, was on this baseball team. He changed his name after high school. Billy's father helped his stepfather and mother with the necessary paperwork and helped keep it out of the papers.

"Counting up these deaths, we have seven dead from this baseball team. This photo is from the first donor party at Billy Edmond's house. It was taken roughly seven years ago, according to the headmaster at Londonvale Academy. It was the last time they were all together. Everyone on this team attended the first party." Derek pointed to the photo.

"I want to talk to everyone who is still alive. If they are local, go see them. If they are out of town, do a phone interview. I want their firsthand experience of the team. I want to know the dynamics of the team, who didn't like who, who stole whose girlfriend, and after our talk with the headmaster, I want to know if Billy pulled any pranks on someone and it didn't go over so well."

Derek walked around his desk and leaned against it. He pointed to the picture of high school boys. He glanced around the room at his agents. "Someone on this team knows something. We have nine men left to question."

Derek made eye contact with each of his team members. "Whoever is killing these men waited until five years ago to start their spree. Why? Did something happen at the first reunion? Did something happen during high school and then the first reunion set off our killer? I'm not sure. But, two years later, the killings started. And what does that tell us about the killer?"

"He's patient," Felicia said.

"Yes. He isn't in any hurry. He's waiting to kill when it is convenient for him. And by being patient, no one is connecting the deaths. It keeps him off the radar." Derek rubbed his hand through his hair.

"Remember, I got a bunch of stuff from Mr. Aleshire," George said.

Derek pointed a finger at him. "Go through it. Organize it by year. Make a complete list of who attended each of the parties. Our killer is associated with the team, someone on the team, or he is on the team."

Kyle stood, stepping over to Kelly's computer. "I will print all the information I have on each person still alive."

Derek looked at Felicia, Michael, and Kelly. "Each of you split up the remaining players. Call them and get some answers. Don't mention the other murders. Just tell them you need some questions answered. You can tell them it's in regards to Billy. It's all over the news. They already know about it, so let's use it."

Derek stood. "Before you call them, research each of them. Go in knowing as much as you can about each of them. We want to see if we can catch any of them in a lie or trying to hide something. Kyle, I need you to run each of these players against each other both dead and alive. Find out if they have anything in common. A club, a business associate, see if they use the same law firm. Find me a connection linking these players besides them being on the team."

He moved to his chair when the chime at the front door rang. Derek glanced at the screen. His eyes widened, then squinted at the visitor. His jaw tightened, and the veins in his neck throbbed, achingly so. "What the fuck is he doing here?"

The agents slowly turned their gaze from Derek to the front door as Emma buzzed in their guests.

CHAPTER TWENTY-FIVE

Lola and Marc Anthony ran to the door. As Congressman Jackson and his entourage entered the Legacy Unit, both dogs moved back, going into protective mode.

"Lola. Marc Anthony." Derek said in a stony tone. Both dogs immediately relaxed.

"Congressman Jackson, we really don't have time for this stop." A short blonde said as she looked at a PDA. "We need to get to your meeting." The assistant ogled the two dogs, stepping back as Marc Anthony moved to sniff her shoes.

"Claire, I know where I'm supposed to be. I need to take care of this." Congressman Jackson flashed a million-dollar smile at Emma. "Good afternoon. I'm here to see Agent Reed." He reached down to pet the dogs. "Are you this unit's watch dogs?"

"Not hardly. They are both harmless." Emma quickly turned in Derek's direction. "Agent Reed..."

"Congressman. What brings you here?" Derek asked as he extended his hand. He points to Lola. "Go lay down."

The boxer obeyed, followed by Marc Anthony, who doesn't quite understand why he can't meet the visitors. Both pout from their perches next to Emma's desk.

Congressman Jackson took his extended hand, squeezing nice and tight. "Derek. How's it been going?"

"Not bad. Why are you here?" Derek asked again.

"I had to come in town for a meeting at the capitol. Before I went there, I wanted to get an update on the Billy Edmond case."

Derek softened his stance. He may not like the congressman, but losing someone you care about isn't easy. "I'm truly sorry about your loss, Sir. Real quick, this is my team. Agents Rogers, Marcum, Peterson, Finch, and Warden. This is our secretary, Emma."

Each team member waved when Derek called their names.

The congressman smiled at each. "Nice to meet all of you." He faced Derek. "Do you have any suspects yet?"

"Not yet. We're still gathering the information. We're waiting to speak with a few of the players from the team who have had recent contact with Mr. Edmond. I believe I will have some information in the very near future."

"Congressman Jackson, we really must go." The blonde frowned at Derek. "We are on a very tight schedule."

"I understand. I'll walk you out, Congressman." Derek followed the blonde, who all but pushed the congressman out the door.

As the secret service and other personnel piled into the stretch limo, Congressman Jackson spoke. "Claire, I will be right there. I need a private moment with Agent Reed."

This time she didn't argue. The tone in her boss' voice, along with his icy stare, had her retreating to the vehicle. "Yes, Sir."

Congressman Jackson stepped to the side, indicating Derek should follow.

"What do you need, Congressman?"

"I know I'm not your favorite person. Especially where Elizabeth is concerned."

Derek held up his hand. "I like you fine. About as much as I like any other politician. Lizzy has nothing to do with my feelings for you or anyone."

"I can appreciate that. I asked you to take this case because I know you'll find out who killed my friend. I wanted to make sure you don't use my relationship with Elizabeth against me."

Derek snickered. "Wow. Not sure how I should feel about that statement. But let me clarify something for you. I couldn't really give a rat's ass about you. As for my job, I don't care where the cases come from or who asks for help. My goal is to stop murderers. Just because you used your position to move this case to the front of the line, I don't even care about that.

"At the end of the day, I would do the same thing for my dead friend. Mr. Congressman, the only time you ever have to worry about me is if you ever hurt Lizzy. Then, I don't care who you are or who you know. Am I clear?"

For a long moment, Congressman Jackson didn't say a word. Then he busted out in laughter. "Shit, son. As much as I want to hate you, solely because I know she loves you and not me, I can't. Anyone who can stand up to me deserves my respect. I helped get you this unit because I believe in your ability as an Agent." The congressman moved towards his vehicle. "I know you don't owe me a damn thing, and you don't report to me. But I would love any updates you can give me."

Derek took a step closer, holding out his hand. "I can do that."

Congressman Jackson shook it. "You really should go into politics, Derek. Washington could use more men with the size balls you have."

Derek stopped the congressman before he entered his vehicle. "I do need something."

Congressman Jackson closed the door and stepped closer to Derek. "Anything."

"One of my agents uncovered some information about Lizzy. She's been at several functions with Billy Edmond and both of you at the same time. I need an honest answer. Can anything regarding Billy blow back on her and hurt her?"

Congressman Jackson shook his head. "No. Any time Elizabeth attended a function, it was with me. She never had a relationship of any kind with Billy. He loved his wife even after her death. No one could ever compare to her. As for Elizabeth, she wouldn't do that out of respect for me. She knew how close we were as friends. It's coincidence she and Billy were at the same functions."

"Thank you. Don't tell her. If there is any reason my team thinks she should be interviewed, we will use Assistant Director Fretz to keep our hands clean. But I don't want Lizzy worrying. Not with her mother."

Congressman Jackson gripped Derek's shoulder. "I can agree one hundred percent with you on that. Thank you for telling me."

"You bet. I'll keep you posted."

Before Congressman Jackson got into his limo, he turned towards Derek. "We both love her. She has never made me any promises of happily ever after. She and I have a business relationship. I needed someone to go to parties and functions with me. And I pay her well for that privilege. She has always told me I hold a special place in her heart. She has never used me, and she never will. I know she will never be fully mine. Her heart lies with you. She just doesn't know it yet. But I love her. I can't help that. And I will never let her get hurt."

Derek was unable to form a sentence. His heart thudded against his chest. He knew Lizzy loved him; he just didn't know anyone else knew it. As he watched the congressman drive away, he wondered if this whole thing had been orchestrated as some kind of test. He doesn't think the congressman would come after him because of Lizzy. But he's been wrong before.

CHAPTER TWENTY-SIX

Entering the office, all work stopped.

"What did he want?" Kyle asked.

Felicia let out an exaggerated sigh. "I was going to ask the same thing. Tell me he didn't use his position to fuck with us or this unit?"

Derek shook his head. "No. He didn't. He actually wanted to see if I would send him updates. Which I told him I don't mind doing."

George cleared his throat, about to say something.

"And no, George, I'm not going to tell him everything. I understand him wanting to know where the case is. It's his friend. I think all of us would want the same courtesy. But hear me when I say this, I don't want any of our findings about the other murders and connections to our cold case out there yet. When it happens, we run the risk of driving our killer underground. I will update the AD when we have more information. As of now, only the ME is aware these cases may be related to the cold case. And that's how I want it to stay."

"Just making sure," George said.

Derek walked to his desk. Being mindful of the cord, he sat in his chair. He checked his watch. 4:30. He rose and went to the kitchen. Grabbing a diet soda from the fridge, he paced the small room. His brain didn't want to let the conversation with the congressman go.

"I don't know why you don't just ask her to stop. You know she would."

Derek frowned at Chrissy. "What makes you such an expert?"

She chuckled. "I'm a girl, idiot. At the end of the day, we want our knight in shining armor. That's what you've always been to her. You saved her once, and you love her. You have never judged her. She would leave it all for you."

"I won't ask."

"And that's why men are so stupid." She danced around him in the kitchen.

He looked back down the hallway at his crew. Turning back to her, he couldn't help but smile. "Chrissy, what would I do without you?"

"You'd be stark raving mad in a padded cell. Those pills you pop aren't helping. One day you will accept you're special."

"I'm not special. I'm an investigator."

Chrissy sighed. "If you say so."

He guzzled his soda. "Why are you here?"

"I told you to go back to the beginning. And you did. Sort of. But you're thinking too narrowly." She spins around. "I miss music."

"Come to my house, and I'll play music. You can dance around. How am I thinking too narrow? Narrow about what?"

"I can't do it all. You forget you keep me around to talk out your crazy shit. Think. Look at each dream or vision. Use them. They are connected."

"Um, are you okay?" Felicia asked as she opened the fridge.

Derek jumped, dropping his can. "Holy shit. I didn't know you were there."

"Obviously." She opened a bottle of water. "You talk to yourself a lot. Why?"

He threw away the paper towels he used to mop up the soda. He shrugged as he leaned against the counter. "Helps me see things from the victim's perspective. I hold conversations as if I am in their shoes. It's always helped me get clarification."

"It makes you look like a crazy person." She smiled at him.

"That's okay. When people think you're crazy, they tend to leave you alone. And as long as I get the job done, no one cares if I'm crazy. As long as I'm functioning." He walked to the main office. "We can pick this up tomorrow. Let's head home," he says to everyone. "Lola, you ready to go home?"

The dog wagged her stub tail, making her entire butt shake.

"What's everyone's plans for dinner?" asked Felicia.

Kelly yawned. "I have some unpacking to finish. And I'm going to bed early."

"What are you like eighty?" Felicia asked.

"No. I'm tired." Kelly stuck her tongue out at her.

"I'm having dinner with my landlord. Steaks out on the grill." Michael pulled his weapon from his desk drawer and clipped it on his belt. "You?" he asked Felicia.

"I guess I'm going swimming."

"You want some company? I'll bring dinner, we can sit at the pool." Kyle asked as he waited for her to gather her stuff.

"Sounds like a plan. I'll text you the address."

Everyone but George and Derek headed out.

"See you guys in the morning." Derek waved as they all left.

Marc Anthony looked back as Emma dragged him out the door.

"You will see her tomorrow. Now let's go home," Emma said as the door closed behind her.

Lola whined, looking up at Derek.

"Same for you. You'll see him tomorrow."

George laughed. "Looks like they're best buddies." He spun his chair so he could pet Lola's head. "What are you doing for dinner?"

Derek sat in Felicia's chair. "I don't know. I've eaten all my leftovers. I need to go to the store." He leaned his head back. "I'll order pizza. Share it with Lola. You?"

"There's a little sports bar down the block from my place. I might stop in there." He placed his hands on his bald head, interlocking his fingers. "You look like you got something on your mind?"

Derek frowned at his agent. "No. Well, maybe." He had to be careful what he said. He did have something on his mind. But he had to figure out how to make it seem like the information could be found by anyone.

"What?" George's eyes narrowed in on him. "And don't try to hide it."

"I'm not hiding anything. Dad."

"Oh, what a low blow." George laughed. "Just because I'm older than you. But if I were your dad, I'd smack you for not going to the hospital and having the egg on the back of your head looked at. How's it feel, by the way?"

"It hurts. Kind of achy. But not bad enough to warrant a trip to the ER or a doctor." Derek spun around in his chair. "Why don't you come over. If you feel up to going over some case notes."

"Sounds like a good plan. I'll stop and get beer." George stood stretching. "Any particular kind?"

"Nope. Just cold." Derek grabbed a few files from his desk. "Bring the file from Aleshire. I'll help you organize it. Maybe we can narrow in on something or someone."

George straightened the papers in a file folder. "Got it all right here. And there is a shit ton of information. I don't even know for sure what's important and what isn't."

"Then we can figure it out over pizza and beer." As they walked out the front door, Derek looked up to see Chrissy holding a newspaper. He cut a quick glance to George seeing if he noticed her. He pulled the door shut and punched in the code.

George stood at his truck, looking back at the old church. "This is a great building."

"I know. I think if the FBI ever walks away from this, I'm going to see if I can buy it." Derek pulled his phone from his pocket and texted George. He heard George's phone ping. "That's my address. See you there."

George saluted him as he drove out.

CHAPTER TWENTY-SEVEN

Derek loaded Lola into the car. She rested in the custom bucket seat like it was made for her. "You're so spoiled," he said, looking in the review mirror. As he drove out onto the main road, his phone rang through the Bluetooth.

"Hi, you." Lizzy's sultry voice filled his car.

Lola's ears perked up at the sound of her mama's voice.

"Hi to you. Lola is in the back seat. She's trying to find your voice and where it's coming from."

"Oh, Lola baby, I miss you." Lizzy laughed at the small howl-like squeak the dog let out.

Derek lifted his cell from the cradle, taking the call off speaker phone. "I took you off Bluetooth. She looks like she is about to cry. It's too tormenting for her."

Lizzy laughed in his ear. "Are you spoiling her?"

"What do you think?"

"I think she sleeps with you every night. And you like it."

"Well, she's as close to having you in my bed as I'm going to get. So, I'll take it. How's the trip and your mom?"

Lizzy sighed on the other end of the phone. "She's tired. But determined to fill her bucket list. The cancer is taking its toll on her."

"Will treatments help?" Derek's heart cracked at the sadness he heard in her voice.

"No. She's in stage four. Her doctor called today and told her he would make sure she was comfortable as the pain increased."

"When does he think that will happen?"

"No telling. She could have six weeks or six months. I have a plane on standby wherever we go. So, if she gets too sick, we can get home. She wants to die in her house."

"Enjoy this time with her and your sister. I know she appreciates this." Derek drove down his street. A few kids played ball. He slowed down, making sure to give them space. As he rolled past one of the groups, a young girl stared at him. Her pale face and sunken eyes were a stark contrast to the other kids. The hair on his arms stood on end.

"Derek, Derek, you still there?"

"Huh? Yeah, sorry, babe, some kids are in the street. Got a little caught up in watching them play. What did you say?"

She laughed in his ear. "God, I miss you. You and Lola. I have to go. We're on our way to breakfast."

He heard a muffled conversation. "Okay. Call me anytime. I don't care what time it is. Stay as long as you need. Lola is fine. I will go and check on your house. Don't worry about anything here. We miss you."

"I love you, Derek."

"I know. I love you, Lizzy." The phone fell silent. His heart ached. He pulled into his driveway and pushed the button to open his garage door. As it rose, he looked over his shoulder at the children playing. Derek tried to find the young girl. He closed his eyes and thought of the shirt she wore. It seemed dated. Like from twenty years ago.

"That doesn't make sense."

Lola sat up as he drove into the garage.

"Glad to be home, huh, girl?" He opened his door then let her out.

She ran to the edge of the garage. She didn't go out; she watched the kids play. Her hackles were slightly up.

Derek figured the excitement of the kids running around made Lola a little protective. He opened the door to his home. "C'mon girl, let's eat." He closed his garage door.

She bolted and ran to the kitchen, waiting at her bowl.

He filled it and grabbed a bottle of water from his as he placed an order for food on Henry's pizza app. Derek unlocked his front door for George and found his way to the sofa. Lola darted past him, almost knocking him over, as she ran to the doggy door.

He dropped his computer bag on the floor, fell onto the sofa, and propped his feet up on his coffee table. He closed his eyes. "It's nice to be home." He took several gulps of his water then held it in both hands, resting on his stomach. His phone pinged. Pulling it from his back pocket, he glanced at the screen. A text from Dr. Chelsea.

I heard about your bump on the head.

It's just a bump.

Meet me at my office at 7:30 a.m.

I don't want to.

I don't care. I don't have an appointment until after 9:30. I want to look at it.

Fine. I'll see you in the morning.

Derek sighed. "I'm going to kill George." Settling back, he relaxed. Closing his eyes again, he started to drift off.

His eyes popped open as his skin tingled. He placed his water on the coffee table and drew his weapon from his holster. He cocked his head to the side, listening for the noise that jarred him awake. Derek glanced out the back door. He saw Lola chasing her no-see-ums.

The shuffling noise happened again. This time louder. He crept down the hallway, hugging the wall. He peeked around the corner into the spare bedroom. He took a step over the threshold, then heard the noise emanating from his bedroom. The door was closed, but not latched. *I didn't shut this door.*

He eased it open. His gaze shifted around the room as he stepped inside. There was nothing in the main space. He crept to an alcove at the far end, opposite of the closet. He looked around the corner. Only his empty reading chair and lamp were there.

A scratching noise made him spin around. Derek saw a soft glowing light coming from the closed closet door. He reached out for the knob. Turning it slowly, he held his breath. As the door swung outward, a burst of cold air hit him in the face. The stench of urine made him gag.

The glowing light was gone. Only darkness and his clothes greeted him. Holstering his weapon, he stepped inside. He flicked on the light. "Lola, if you peed in here, I'm going to have to keep you out of my room." He shook his head. "She doesn't pee in the house." He sighed. *Something must have gotten in through the pet door.*

He rifled through his clothes hanging on the bottom rack. He moved further into the closet. The closet door slammed shut behind him as he lifted a box to look underneath, and the light switched off. Stepping over to reach for the door handle, he twisted the knob, locked. He stepped back, standing up straight. *This door doesn't have a lock.*

The breath he held rushed out. His pulse thumped in his ears. "Chrissy, if this is you playing a trick, it isn't funny." He cocked his head to the side. "I've literally lost my mind." He calmed himself. Switching on the light, the creepiness vanished. The light flickered then shut off. He flipped the switch up and down, nothing. "Great."

He started to turn the knob again when he heard the whimper. Turning slowly around, a rack of clothes swayed. He drew his weapon. He reached out with his left hand, pulling back the clothes.

"Derek? Where are you?"

Derek jumped, falling back at George's booming voice. A couple of empty plastic bins tumbled over as Derek lost his balance. Blinded momentarily by the bright light, Derek saw the weapon pointed at him. "Don't shoot, man, it's me."

"Derek?" George holstered his weapon then held out his hand. "What the hell? Do you hang out in your closet like this all the time?"

"Har de har har." Derek blew out a breath, thankful not to be alone. "I heard some noise in here, came in, the door shut, and I guess I tripped in the darkness trying to get to the light."

George raised an eyebrow at him. "What kind of noise?"

Derek shrugged as he exited. "An animal of sorts. I thought Lola came back here." He led George to the kitchen. His doorbell rang. "The pizza is here."

George removed two beers from the twelve-pack he brought and placed the rest in the fridge. "When I came in, I didn't see you anywhere. I figured you had to be here, so I went looking for you," he said as Derek set two pizzas on the counter.

Grabbing two plates from the cabinet, he handed one to George. He took one of the beers on the counter, along with one pizza, and motioned for George to follow. "Didn't mean to make you go on a hunt for me."

"I like this house." George admired the arched ceiling. "Very bright, airy, and cool."

"I inherited it from my grandmother. She had it remodeled. Put in a cooling system under the tile." Derek motioned to the coffee table. He

"I'm sorry about her passing." George sat on a chair adjacent to the sofa.

Lola ran through the doggie door, taking perch on the other side of the table, waiting for her pizza.

"No need to be sorry. She passed away several years ago." Derek eyeballed Lola. He glanced over at George. "She will stare at us until we give her scraps."

George broke off a piece of his crust, tossing it to her. "Good catch," he said, guzzling his beer.

Lola took a half a step closer to him.

"Lola."

She didn't look at Derek. He chuckled, shaking his head. "She's pathetic."

"I miss having a dog."

"Why don't you have one?" Derek walked into the kitchen.

"Grab the folder on the counter. I set it there when I went looking for you."

Derek grabbed two more beers and the folder, setting them on the table.

"Thanks. Too much trouble, having a dog. I traveled a lot. Kind of mean to put a dog in a kennel all the time."

"What about family? Any of them live near you?"

George smiled. "No. My father and mother still live in North Carolina." He reached into his wallet and pulled out a photo. "I went to see them just before I headed out here." He held out the photo.

Derek stared at the picture. "Your mother is beautiful." The woman in the photo had striking blue eyes which popped against silver-gray hair.

"She's technically my stepmother."

Derek raised an eyebrow cocking his head to the side. "That's an odd statement."

George laughed. "My mother died when I was ten. For a long time, it was just me and my father." He took a long pull of his beer. "Eventually, he started dating and met Catherine. They dated for two years and finally married." He sat back in his chair and chuckled.

"What's so funny?" Derek asked as he threw a piece of crust towards Lola.

"My mother's family remained close to my dad and me. I spent a lot of time with them after her death. She died of cancer. They weren't happy when my father started dating a white woman. It was the scandal of the family. My dad never saw color, though. He only saw a person. He treated everyone the same. He raised me to do the same.

"I was surprised by their reaction, too. I was about thirteen, maybe fourteen. Catherine helped me through those difficult teen years. Me and my mother had a routine. Every Sunday, we made a big family dinner. After she died, my dad tried, but it never seemed the same."

"If your dad is any kind of cook like my dad, I can completely understand."

George laughed. "He's an awful cook. Catherine found out about what me and my mom used to do. Before they were married, she came over every Sunday, and we cooked. I remember those days. They were some of the best times of my life. I don't think I would be here today if it hadn't been for her. I say, technically she's my stepmother, but it didn't take long for me to call her mom." He stared at the photo.

"What about your mother's family? Did they ever come around?"

George smiled. "Absolutely. It took a good year for them to do it. It was never about her being white. I realized that later. They were afraid they would lose me, my dad. We were the connection to their daughter. The color of Catherine's skin made it easy. It gave them something to latch onto. But when they saw what she did for my father and how she treated me, they finally accepted her. Now I don't think any of us can imagine life without her." George smiled.

"Family can surprise us, that's for sure. I'm not always proud of some of the things my family has done, but I bet they could say the same thing about some of the stuff I've done."

George gave Lola a big piece of a pizza. "She's a sweet dog."

"Since you're stationed here, you can get a dog."

George shrugged. "I might. Maybe I'll get a cat."

Lola's head cocked to the side at the use of the C-word.

"There's no cat Lola. Don't get excited." Derek opened a second can of beer.

George went into the kitchen, grabbed the second pizza and two more beers. He laughed at Derek's expression. "What? I don't want to get back up."

Derek loaded up his plate. "I didn't want to get up either." He reached into his computer bag. "Here is the information Kyle found."

"This folder has everything from Mr. Aleshire." George pointed to the folder in front of him.

Derek opened it. "Let's see what we have here." He fingered through the file, pulling out the party lists. "Here we have all the baseball reunion parties." He set them on the table. "I don't think we need to worry about this other stuff just yet." He set the folder aside. "I'm more concerned with getting to know the players on this team." He pointed to the lists.

George put the lists in chronological order. "Okay. Here is the list from the first meeting of the team at Billy Edmond's house."

Derek checked the date. "The first reunion took place seven years ago, 2014."

"Let's compare this list with all the other ones and who doesn't show up to the parties." George guzzled the last of his beer. Popping open another one. "These taste way too good."

Derek laughed. "I have an extra room. You don't need to drive home."

"I might take you up on your offer."

"This first meeting, everyone from the team showed up. Where's the list for the second meeting?" Derek asked.

"Here." George laid it next to the first list.

"This shouldn't be too hard. Aleshire put the names in alphabetical order." Derek read through the list. "It looks like everyone showed up to the second one as well."

George scanned the third year. "It looks like we have three who didn't come to the third reunion. Martin Lucey, Christian Dawson, and Albie Hawkes."

Derek snapped his fingers. He grabbed the list from the folder he had pulled from his computer bag. Searching, he smiled. "Our five-year-old case, the three murders, Albie Hawkes was murdered first."

"What were the names of the other two?"

"Terry Curren and Xavier Blackman," Derek said.

George looked through the list of names. "Okay. Terry and Xavier were at the third, but not the rest. When were those three murders?"

Derek searched his file. "Albie Hawkes died in late May 2017, right before the third reunion. The other two were murdered within the next year and a half."

"Okay. Didn't Kyle mention two more team members were murdered?" George asked, taking a bite of his pizza.

"He did. Timmy Cowman and Arthur Brandis." Derek looked over the party lists. "We only have five years of reunions."

"Yeah, Aleshire mentioned there were a couple of years Billy didn't have any. One, the year after his wife died. She passed away in late 2017. So, no party in 2018. He didn't have one in 2019. Mr. Aleshire has made a note here Billy had an event in Washington that year. And the party for 2020 was different. There were only a handful invited."

"Who was invited to this year's party?"

George flipped through the papers. "Greg Burks, Christian Dawson, Humphrey Archer, and Baily Hodgens. No other players. There were several notable politicians and upper crust at this party. But it doesn't seem to be dedicated to the baseball team."

"Maybe he quit having the team reunion and just selected a few of the players he had relationships or business deals with." Derek pulled a pad of paper from his bag and began to scribble.

George took the moment to grab some more beer. By the time he returned, Derek finished writing. "What do you have?"

"Here's what I've come up with." He handed him the pad.

George looked it over.

"The first column has the year of the reunions and who attended. The second column has who didn't attend that particular reunion. And the third has the names of those murdered and the year. I put them in line with the reunion years so we could see all of them at a glance.

George laid the pad on the table. He chewed on a bite of pizza, sipping on his beer. "We have nine remaining players, plus the coach."

Derek squinted at George. "What about the coach?"

"I think it's a safe bet he isn't the killer." George's eyes narrowed. "It's clear he has benefitted from Billy's death. But I actually think he benefitted more from him being alive." George pulled a piece of paper from the folder. "Aleshire has a list of donations Billy Edmond made every year. A couple went to the school and the athletic department."

Derek whistled. "That's a lot of money."

"Yeah, no kidding. I can't imagine they have benefactors giving those amounts each year to an athletic department. And if we go with the assumption, he isn't the killer, do we know for sure he isn't a potential victim?"

Derek leaned back against the sofa. He shot a quick glance to the chair. He snuck a peak at George, who studied the rest of the papers from Mr. Aleshire. Sweat beaded along his upper lip. He closed his eyes, willing her to go away. He looked over at Lola. Her ears were flattened, and she stared at the chair. He could hear himself pleading for her to go away.

"You okay?" George asked.

Derek's head spun around. "Yeah. Why do you ask?"

George cocked an eyebrow at him. "Umm. You're acting weird."

Derek brushed him off. "I'm just thinking." He glanced at Lola, who stared at him. She glanced at the chair, then back at him. He tilted his head towards her and was amazed when she just laid down at George's feet. The feeling of being watched disappeared. Derek breathed out a silent sigh. Thankful Chrissy didn't show up.

"Thinking about what?"

Derek took a long sip of his beer. "About what you said. About the coach being a potential victim. I think when we narrow in on why the players are being murdered, the coach's involvement will become clearer."

"Figure out the why? Don't you mean figure out the who?"

Derek shook his head as he finished off his last piece of pizza and guzzled the last of his beer. "That would be the easiest way. But we have no evidence pointing to anyone. The next best thing is the why. Every murder is motivated by something. It could be something similar about each victim, like hair color, eye color, or build. It could be a special date associated with each victim, which has special meaning to the killer. The motive doesn't even have to make sense to you or me, just the killer. And there is something between these players binding them to the killer."

"Sure," Derek pointed to the lists of names on the table, "this gives us nine people who may be our killer. That's if the killer is a player. Or we may have nine more victims. Either way, if we can figure out the why, we may be able to figure out the who."

CHAPTER TWENTY-EIGHT

Early Wednesday morning

George tossed in the bed. Not because it wasn't comfortable, but because something made him uncomfortable. Ever since he went to bed, he had a feeling someone lingered in the room with him. He laid on his back, listening to the deathly quiet house. No appliances kicked on. No outside noises. Just silence. Derek's house was too quiet.

He stared at the ceiling. Whatever or whoever didn't scare him. He just didn't like it. He remembered his grandmother telling him tales of their ancestors and their ability to see dead people. She called it the enlightenment. George wanted no part of it and quickly dismissed what his grandmother had told him.

He rolled to his side. He thought about Derek. He couldn't put his finger on it, but something didn't fit. Although he would never say the man could talk to dead people, he had a very odd streak.

George marveled at his ability to read people and evidence. That made him a genius. But his quirky personality and laid-back attitude made George uncomfortable at times. He had always been a by-the-book kind of agent, and Derek didn't seem to work like that. George didn't think the man did anything wrong, illicit, or illegal. It seemed more like Agent Derek Reed has his own way of figuring things out.

George cocked his head to the side. "What the hell?" He grabbed his watch off the nightstand. "5 a.m." He sat up. The yell happened again. He pulled his weapon from his holster draped over a chair in the room.

Opening his door, he heard Derek yelling at someone. "Who's he arguing with?" He stuck his head out, looking from side to side, scanning the hallway. A light glowed from underneath Derek's door. As he crept down the narrow passageway, his heart thudded against his chest. Holding his weapon next to his thigh, he moved closer to Derek's room.

Slowing his breathing, he stood outside the bedroom. He lifted his weapon. Reaching out he eased open the door. Ice cold air gushed at him. The door slammed shut. He wiggled the handle, but the damn thing wouldn't open. "Derek? Derek? Are you alright?"

He twisted the knob, and pushed against the door. A shriek came from inside. He stepped back about to kick in the door when it un-latched and creaked open. He eased it forward. His pulse echoed in his ears like a freight train rolling down the track. As he pushed the door fully open, lifting his weapon. Another gust of cold air brushed past him.

CHAPTER TWENTY-NINE

Derek felt the sticky sheen of moisture on his skin. His knees were drawn to his chest, a sharp pain radiated outward towards his arms. No longer in his room, he laid on the floor of a closet. Small and claustrophobic. There were flannel shirts and winter boots surrounding him. "Where the fuck am I?"

Derek tried to stand. His feet and hands were bound together. He yanked on the ties. Although they were loose, he couldn't free himself. The air in his chest thinned out. He struggled to breathe. Wheezing as he clutched his t-shirt, gasping for air. His lungs burned as if he had just run a sprint at the end of a race. His eyes darted around the small enclosure. He heard whimpering. *Was it him?*

He coughed, unable to catch his breath. The tightening in his chest felt as if a rubber band cinched around him. He was suffocating. He cried out, begging for help. "Please. Please help me." He screamed. His voice echoed, bouncing off the walls. The sound reverberated against his skull. It felt as if a thousand needles were pulsating against the bone.

Derek sunk into the wall as his pulse raced. He struggled for air. For a split-second, time stopped. The smell of urine overpowered him. He felt the wetness as it coated his skin. He moaned as the darkness engulfed him. His breathing slowed to a complete stop. His chest was frozen, unable to take in any more air. He struggled for a few moments before the pain lifted. The fear and suffocation vanished. And for a few seconds, a floating sensation surrounded him. Peace and calm washed over him as the last of the light dimmed.

As the door swung open, George stepped in. Derek laid curled up on the bed. If he didn't know better, he would've thought he had been bound somehow. His boss laid there moaning and crying out. "Derek?" he whispered.

He inched towards the bed. Lola sat staring at her master. She looked at George and back at Derek. He watched as she licked and nudged Derek's face trying to wake him. Quickly assessing his surroundings, George didn't see an intruder. Despite what every inch of his body told him.

He reached out and touched Derek's arm. "Derek. Wake up."

Derek's breathing sounded labored and heavy. George waited. When he got no response, he leaned over the edge of the bed. Derek's breathing had stopped.

He set his weapon on the nightstand. "Derek! He yelled as he rolled his boss onto his back. He listened placing his head next to Derek's mouth.

"Holy shit." He pounded on his chest. "Derek, wake up."

Derek gasped for air just as he felt the impact against his chest. He sucked in a deep breath. His eyes were wide as he watched George get ready to smack his chest again. He rolled to the side, falling off the bed. "What the fuck? Why the hell are you hitting me?"

George stepped back. He panted as he stumbled backward. "You weren't fucking breathing."

Derek jumped off the floor. His eyes scanned his bedroom. Relief washed over him. "Why are you in here?"

George walked to the door, and flipped on the overhead light. "You were screaming in your sleep. I thought somebody was in here attacking you." He dragged his hand down his face. "I think your house is haunted."

Derek sat on the side of the bed. "You're crazy." His head hung low. His chin rested against his chest. "I had a bad dream. That's it."

George shook his head. "Nope. Not buying it." He paced the master bedroom. "I've slept like shit. It felt as if someone sat watching me." He motioned towards Derek. "You were having a night terror. Not just a bad dream."

"What the hell is a night terror?" Derek stood. He glanced at the clock on his nightstand. George's gun rested next to it. "Is that your gun?"

"Yes. I thought you were being attacked."

"I think you are crazy. That's twice you have skulked around my house with your weapon." He rolled his lips, trying to keep from laughing. It didn't work. Derek busted out in laughter.

George ogled him. "This isn't funny. Something weird is going on in this house." He picked up his weapon. "Or something weird is going on with you."

Derek composed himself. "I'll fix us breakfast. I can explain a few things. That might make you think differently."

George followed him down the hallway. "I'm going to get dressed." He glanced down. "I feel foolish having breakfast in my boxers."

Derek laughed. "Meet me in the kitchen."

Lola bounded by, heading for the doggy door.

As Derek entered the kitchen, he glanced over his shoulder. He grabbed a bottle of pills from the cupboard. He took two. He pushed the bottle towards the back. Hiding it behind some spices.

He guzzled a bottle of water from the fridge. He didn't understand what he saw or felt in his dream. He had no idea what his subconscious tried to tell him. But he wondered if he wouldn't go crazy before he got the answers.

Cracking a few eggs in a cup, he chopped up some tomatoes and ham. He grabbed a jar of homemade salsa and set it on the counter. Taking the orange juice from the fridge, he grabbed an onion. Chopping it up, he then stirred the eggs, whipping them into a frothy mixture.

Setting a pan on the stove, he used half of the remaining butter, placing it in the pan. As the fat crackled against the heat, he poured in the eggs. As soon as they reached the correct firmness, he threw in the veggies. While those cooked, he threw in the last of his bread into the toaster. He turned back to the stove as George came into the room. "Perfect timing. It's almost ready."

George glanced over his shoulder. "Omelets? Nice."

"I can cook. But I'm too lazy to shop. So, my cooking is often limited. Although after this, I'm pretty much tapped out. I need to go to the grocery store."

George took a stool on the other side of the bar. He poured himself a glass of orange juice, sitting in silence.

Derek put the omelet on a plate. Splitting it down the middle, he slid half onto another plate. He grabbed the toast and buttered it. Setting a plate in front of his house guest, he smiled. "Dig in."

George took a bite. He reached for the salsa and added some to his eggs. "This is really good."

Derek bowed. "Thank you."

A silence crept in, the kind between a couple who was on the verge of breaking up.

Derek sighed. "Ever since the Josiah Craig case, I have some pretty gnarly nightmares."

George stopped eating. He swallowed his bite but didn't speak.

Derek forced himself to meet his house guest's stare. "No one knows."

"I can see how it could mess with your career," George said.

"My doctor knows. It doesn't interfere with my duties. It's just they are often very vivid. The injuries to my face were pretty severe. My cheek and nose were broken. And, he gave me a hairline fracture around my orbital rim. I relive those events over and over again. Sometimes they seem so real, I'm almost sure I'm right back in the carnival tent." Derek hid his eyes. He lied. And he was pretty sure George knew it.

"I heard you scream out. It sounded like you said, help me. At first, I thought you were arguing with someone."

"I'm sorry. I usually have a pretty good handle on it. Sometimes though, when I get into a case, I think my subconscious uses the dreams to distract me." He shook his head. "I can only imagine how crazy I must sound."

George finished his eggs. He slid the plate towards Derek. "Those were fantastic. And your secret is safe with me. I promise."

Derek placed both plates in the sink. He felt the heat from George's stare against his skin. "There's something else. What is it?"

George leaned forward, resting his weight on his elbows. "I think it's more than just dreams. One day when you're ready to share it with me, I'll be here. Until then, I promise, I won't mention this to anyone."

Derek smiled. His eyes met George's. "Does this mean we are dating now?" He wiggled his eyebrows at him.

George laughed. "You wish." He stood and stretched. "I'm going to head home and change."

"Take your time. Come in late. Don't worry about it. Crap."

"What?"

"Thanks to you, I have to go see Dr. Chelsea. He wants to check the bump on my head."

"Not my fault." George grabbed his keys and the folder he brought with him. "I should be there close to starting time." He walked to the front door. "I think we should do this regularly."

Derek winked at him. "I knew it. You want to be my boyfriend."

George laughed. "You are such an ass."

Derek watched as he walked out. He waved at George as he pulled out of the driveway. He'd told him most of the truth. He did suffer from nightmares, but they weren't always about Josiah. Remembering he'd forgotten to tell anyone at the unit he would be late, he quickly texted Emma.

As he slowly shut the door, he noticed the girl from the day before standing across the street. She waved at him. He lifted his hand to wave, then dropped it. It was 6 a.m. Why would a young kid be out playing at this time of day?

CHAPTER THIRTY

Wednesday 7:30 a.m.

Derek moped as he walked into Dr. Chelsea's office. When he texted he was on his way, the doc gave him the code for the office door. His assistant wouldn't be there, and the foyer would be locked. Usually, when he had to see the doc, the office bustled with patients. Today an eerie silence greeted him.

"Doc. I'm here," Derek yelled out walking towards the doctor's private office.

"I'm back here."

Derek followed Dr. Chelsea's voice. As he opened the door, Dr. Chelsea practiced his golf putt. "Really? This is what your psychology degree is doing for you?"

Dr. Chelsea shifted his weight, readjusting his grip on his club. "Most games are won in the short stroke. The elusive putt." He gently tapped the ball. He leaned slightly to the right hoping the motion would steer the ball as it rolled down the makeshift green.

Derek snickered when the ball stopped just short of the cup. "Well, looks like you have a lot of work ahead of you."

Dr. Chelsea took the seat across from his favorite patient. "Yes, I do. This is why I spent a ton of money on this little set up."

"You actually spent money on this?" Derek laughed as he pointed to the putting green. "You're a sucker, aren't you?"

"Pfft. A small price to pay to hone my skills." Dr. Chelsea rose from his seat. "How's the head?"

"Fine. Like I already told you." He tried to move his head around, dodging the doctor.

"Stop. What are you five?" Dr. Chelsea grabbed the sides of Derek's head. Gently and slowly, he dragged his fingers across the back of his scalp.

Derek tried to remain completely still.

"Doesn't hurt, huh?" Dr. Chelsea asked as he came around and stood in front of his patient. Lifting Derek's chin, the doctor used a pen light to test his eyes.

"Is this really necessary?" Derek asked as he blinked.

"Have you had any visions or nightmares since you hit your head?"

Derek started to say something.

"Don't lie to me, either."

"I don't lie, Doc."

"Sure, you don't. What's been going on?"

Derek squirmed under the stare of his friend. "I'm still having nightmares."

Dr. Chelsea sat back in his seat. "Before the bump on the head?"

"Yes."

"Has there been anything new since the bump? Any other odd symptoms?"

"No. Maybe. I'm working another case. One which involves Congressman Jackson and some high-powered people."

"I know you wouldn't think of taking a break."

Derek frowned. "No. That's why I came back early from my forced vacation. I can't stand sitting around doing nothing."

"I shouldn't have cleared you to work. I think you need more time. If you're still having nightmares from the Josiah Craig case, you need more time to heal."

Derek leaned forward, placing his elbows on his knees. Of all the people he can trust, Dr. Chelsea is one of them. "The nightmares aren't about Josiah."

Dr. Chelsea raised an eyebrow at him but remained silent.

"I have nightmares about the current case. Or at least I think it's about the case."

"Explain. This is where the maybe comes in, right?"

Sighing, Derek sat back. "I can't shut my brain off. I wouldn't even say they're nightmares. More like...."

"Visions?"

"Yeah. But not really. It's like I take pieces of all the different cases I've ever worked on, and they come together mixed with pieces of the current case. They never really make sense."

"Your brain is reacting to stress. You aren't going to be able to continue this pace for very long."

Derek shrugged. "The dreams sometimes help me see my case more clearly. So technically, they're helping, not hurting me."

"That's not true. Are you still talking to Chrissy, the dead girl?"

Derek wished he never mentioned her. "It's my subconscious. We already established that."

"Listen, the human brain can endure a lot. But at some point, it needs time to heal. The fact you're still using a dead girl to work out things inside your head is worrisome."

"What's worrisome? It's not like I'm going insane."

"Are you taking anything?" Dr. Chelsea pulled a pad from his pocket.

"You know I don't like medicine." Derek kept his eyes shielded from the human lie detector.

"Are you at least sleeping?"

"Not really. But again, it's the case."

Dr. Chelsea growled. "Exactly why you need to take a break. Let your brain and your body heal. You suffered a traumatic injury during the case with Josiah. Your body has not recovered. You really should've had the bump looked at."

"Nope. The minute I go in for a CT scan, I'm put on desk duty. I just got this team up and running."

"And you can sit at a desk and let them do the work for you."

Derek glared at his friend. "Are you going to report this and force me off the case?"

"Have I ever done that before? No. But, you have to check in with me. Weekly would be preferred. However, I will take every two weeks, if you come here."

"Fine." He watched as Dr. Chelsea scribbled on a piece of paper. "What's that?"

The doctor handed it to him. "Normally, I don't like to prescribe anything to sleep. But in this case, I think it's warranted for a short time. Are you taking anything? I know you had a prescription for Alprazolam right after the Josiah incident."

"I didn't like the way they made me feel."

"That doesn't answer my question."

"I still have some. I use them when I wake up and can't get back to sleep."

Dr. Chelsea stared at him. "Have you been taking it more than you should?"

"Only when I can't sleep. I may have taken one early in the morning."

"Derek."

"Listen, I'm not abusing my prescription. I would never risk my job. You of all people should know that."

"I do. But I also think you are using them to block feelings you should be dealing with. That prescription," he points at the paper, "should not be taken with Alprazolam. Ramelteon is used for insomnia. It helps you fall asleep. Your current prescription will also make you sleepy. Don't take them together."

"Maybe I just shouldn't take anything."

"I think you should stop taking the Alprazolam."

Derek nods. "I can." His eyes narrowed into slits. "I promise."

"I'm only giving you a thirty-day prescription. In two weeks, when you come back, I will reevaluate." Dr. Chelsea stood at the same time as Derek. "If I find out you're abusing any of these prescriptions, if the FBI doesn't find out, I will tell them."

"You would ruin my career?"

"If it means saving your life, you bet your fucking ass I will."

Derek tried to hide his smirk. "I promise, I'm not abusing them. I probably shouldn't be taking them, though. And you're right. I am using them to hide from things. Things I should just deal with. But I could use something to help me sleep."

"I'm trusting you. Don't make me regret it." Dr. Chelsea looked at his appointment book. "In two weeks, I have another morning like this. I want to see you at this same time."

"Okay. I'll be here. Can I go now?"

Dr. Chelsea stepped closer to him. "You are more than an agent in my care. You are like the son I never had. I care deeply for you."

Derek sighed. "I know."

Dr. Chelsea put his arm around him as they both walked towards the door. "This is why I have no problem kicking your ass into gear. Understand?"

"Yes, father." Derek laughed as the doctor shut his office door in his face.

.

CHAPTER THIRTY-ONE

9:30 a.m.

Derek parked at the Legacy Unit. He had stopped by the house and picked up Lola. His phone pinged with an incoming message from Lizzy.

Mom is tired. We're heading home. We should get into Cali by tonight.

That's great. When do you think you'll be back in Arizona?

I'm not sure. I'm flying with them to Philly. Get mom settled and speak with her doctor. Dad is anxious for her to be home. I'll keep you posted. Give Lola a kiss for me.

I will.

ILU

ILU more.

He couldn't wait to see her. And at the same time, he didn't know what she would be walking into with this ongoing investigation. His gut knotted. He also knew Congressman Jackson would want to spend time with her. Reminding himself of what he said, Derek took some relief in the fact the congressman knew Lizzy's heart belonged to him. He did hope one day her body would be his and his alone.

"Hey, boss," Felicia said without looking up.

"Good morning." Shutting the door behind him, he chuckled as Lola searched for Marc Anthony. "Where's Emma?"

"She had to take Marc Anthony to the vet." Kelly petted Lola's head. "Your pal should be back soon."

Derek settled at his desk. He looked over his notes on the baseball team. He never played many sports, but he had a few buddies who played football and remembered how close the team was. Derek also recalled a few pranks they pulled on each other. "What have you guys come up with on the remaining players?"

Felicia glanced up, speaking first. "I have Klint Kenyon, Christian Dawson, and Humphrey Archer. All of them live in this area. Well, these three live in Tucson."

"I have Baily Hodgens, Dwight Black, and Joseph Coombes. Joseph committed suicide during his sophomore year of college. Hodgens lives in Boston, and Dwight is overseas in London," Michael said.

"Do you know why Coombes committed suicide?"

Michael shook his head. "Not yet. I was about to look him up and see if I can get any answers."

"Figure out the best time to call London, and get ahold of Dwight ASAP." Derek leaned back in his chair. "Felicia, see if you can talk to them over the phone. Save yourself a trip to Tucson."

"I like that. I don't want to make that drive." Felicia spun around in her chair to finish researching her group.

Kelly looked at Derek. "I've got the last three. Gorden Padden, Julian Mousley, and Marin Lucey. Julian is a stuntman who happens to be on location in the Philippines. I did speak with his agent; she is going to try to get him on the phone for me. I told her to call me anytime, and I gave her my cell."

"Okay. This guy leads a fun life," Derek said. "You got anything else?"

"Martin Lucey is in jail. Seems he's been in trouble with the law since college. Mainly looks like white-collar crimes. However, he's been in jail this last time for over a year. His parents refused to bail him out with this last arrest. The other one, Gordon Padden, died of cancer five years ago. He lived in San Francisco at the time of his death."

Derek cocked his head to the side. "Wasn't Arthur Brandis in San Francisco when he was murdered?"

Kelly shrugged. "I think so. I can ask Kyle for sure."

"I'll go down and see Kyle. You guys get ahold of each of these men." Derek walked back to the kitchen and headed down the stairs. He imagined the nuns and the priests who lived here used this area as cold storage for veggies and canned goods. No moisture on the walls shows how well they built this church.

Derek followed the short hallway to the door at the end. An alcove sat off to the right. Standing shelves rested against the wall. A small half-moon-shaped window allowed light to fill the cave-like room. As he neared the open doorway, soft humming drifted out. Derek leaned against the door frame. Three large screens filled one wall—no doubt the source of the humming. A long wooden table held two desktop computers and one laptop. The position of the desk allowed whoever sat there, full view of all the screens. A printer and fax machine sat on a smaller table, lining the adjacent wall, creating an L shape.

Kyle sat in a chair facing the screens. He wore a headset and diverted his attention between the larger screens and his laptop. Derek watched, holding back his laugh. Even though his position allowed for him to see whoever may venture into his Star Trek-inspired office, Derek's young IT guy would first have to be able to hear the approaching guest.

Knocking on the door, he waited for Kyle to respond. He knocked on the door frame. When Kyle didn't respond, he ventured over the threshold. "Kyle?" Derek asked as he approached the desk.

Kyle glanced up when his boss walked in. He removed his head-phones. "What's up?"

"Can you tell me anything about Arthur Brandis?"

Kyle turned to the keyboard. "What do you need to know?"

"When he lived in San Fran, can you tell me who he may have worked with? Who his firm worked with?"

"Yeah. I told you the local police thought the murder happened because of something he worked on. The authorities found a few files were missing. I called the family this morning." He turned towards Derek. "I found something during my research that bothered me. I hope you don't mind."

"Mind you called the family?" He watched as Kyle nodded. "No. Not at all. Follow whatever lead you find. Always."

"I know Kelly called them but, okay then. Arthur Brandis had a law firm. He actually got his start working with—drum roll please—Billy's father."

Derek pulled over an extra chair from the corner. "No shit?"

"No shit. I couldn't believe the connection. It seems Arthur did summer internships at the senior Edmond's law firm every summer during law school."

"Nice gig. Don't law students struggle to get internships?"

Kyle shrugged. "I know it's hard to get one at a prestigious firm, let alone get one every summer."

"It's always about who you know in life," Derek said. "Okay, if we know Arthur and Billy had a close relationship after graduation, did any of the others who are dead have a similar relationship?"

"Yes." Kyle motions to the middle screen. "All of our dead guys kept in touch outside of the team reunions. Actually, Dwight Black and Baily Hodgens are in this group as well. It seems these guys got together regularly. They either went on trips together or had regular parties at each other's houses when they were still in the area."

Derek studied the list on the screen. "What about the remaining seven members of the team?"

"They don't have much to do with the inner circle of team members."

Derek's brow wrinkled. "Inner circle?"

"Yeah, every peewee or high school team I played on had an inner circle. These were the kids who always did stuff together. Outside of the team activities." Kyle tapped a button on his keyboard. The right screen lit up. "The coach is the one odd factor."

"How so?" Derek took a deep breath through his nose, holding it for a few beats before releasing it.

"He had communication with the inner circle regularly over the years. He also had regular contact with Billy's father." Kyle pointed to the screen. "I found communications from the coach to Billy's father via email. These communications go back to when the boys were in high school but ticked up significantly after the senior year."

Derek's eyes narrowed. "How did you get those communications? Do I even want to know?"

Kyle smiled. "Probably not. But I promise you it will stand up in court. Should it get that far."

"Oh, Kyle."

Kyle laughed. "I promise. Because Coach, or now Headmaster McMillan, was a beneficiary of Billy's will, I got a search warrant for the school's records. Now, I may have stretched that warrant to go back to the days when he coached, but it is all relevant to this case."

Tapping on the keyboard, the screen propagated with downloaded email files. "Something schools and universities, hell any company, don't realize emails are kept for years unless manually deleted. Making my job very easy."

Derek stared at the screen. Hundreds of emails littering the screen. "That's incredible."

"What's even more incredible is creating a filter pulling out emails with keywords. Words I thought might pertain to the murders." Kyle tapped the keyboard. "These emails, seem to discuss an incident which happened late fall, during Billy's senior year."

Derek sat up in his chair. "What incident?"

"I can't tell you."

Derek's mouth hung open. "Excuse me?"

Kyle laughed. "I can't tell you because the crafters of the emails made sure never to reference it except as the incident. The one slip up, Coach McMillan mentions a cabin. He makes the statement in an email just before Billy's parents died regarding a cabin. He wants to make sure no one will find out about the cabin. The response from Billy's father is a simple one line." Kyle highlights the email in question. "It's covered."

Derek read the entire email. "I want copies of all this. And all the other emails. Does McMillan reference the incident with any of the players?"

"Never." Kyle sat back in his chair.

"We need to figure out what happened without letting the headmaster know we know about it. Can you find out if our headmaster owns a cabin?"

"I've been searching his property records. I can't find a cabin listed among them. But I am still looking. I've incorporated his family members. I'm waiting on the results. I've pulled in his wife's family as well."

"As soon as you know anything, I need to know." Derek stood. "By chance, have you found any girls associated with the team?"

"Not sure what you mean. Like girlfriends?"

Derek shrugged. "Not sure what I mean either."

"I can run through the girls of the academy and see if anything pops."

Derek snapped his fingers. "That would be great. Let's do this, see if you can connect any girls to the boys, and see if they are still around."

"You think a girl or girls plays a part in why our killer is targeting these guys?" Kyle asked.

"I don't know. But with what you have found so far, I have to see at least if there is anyone outside this baseball team who may have a connection or be involved. It just seems logical the next leap would be girls. Maybe a brother is out to settle a score for his sister." Derek turned and headed towards the door.

"You got it, boss."

"Kyle, you do great work. This unit would be lost without your skills."

Kyle raised his hand, making the Spock hand gesture as a salute, beaming a bright smile from ear to ear.

CHAPTER THIRTY-TWO

Sitting at his desk, Derek read every email. He asked Kyle for the financials of the school and the headmaster. As he went through the numbers, he found something odd. "George?"

George looked up from his desk. "Yes?"

"Do you have the financial records from Aleshire?"

George grabbed the file folder on his desk. "Yes, right here. I haven't scanned the information into the computer yet. What do you need?"

"I'm not sure. Bring it over here."

Rolling his chair over, George perched himself on the other side of Derek's desk. "Here you go."

Derek glanced at the sheet then the records on his screen. He highlighted a few lines, then skimmed down the page, highlighting a few more.

Kelly opened her mouth to speak as her phone rang. "Agent Warden." Kelly's eyes lit up. "Thank you for calling me back." She stood walking to the kitchen.

Derek watched as she left the room. He turned back to his screen. Nodding at George, he turned his laptop, allowing his agent to see it without moving his chair. "These are the financials of the school and the headmaster. Billy's father made a sizeable donation to the school, Billy's senior year, just before graduation." He pointed to it. "Now look at the other donations."

George scans over the numbers. He looks up, squinting at Derek. "That's odd."

"It is. This first donation to the school, and specifically earmarked for the athletic department. Over the next few years, smaller amounts were made to the school, but the payments were made to the headmaster himself in the third year. As a consulting fee. What did he consult on?"

George slid his chair back. "I'll call Aleshire."

"Find out everything about the monies paid to the school, but most importantly to Russell McMillan. See if he knows anything about it. Also, ask him if Billy and the team ever went on camping trips to a cabin. During school and after school. I don't even know if Aleshire will know, but see if he ever heard of Billy referencing a cabin."

"I'm on it," George said.

Kyle walked around the corner.

"Kyle, have you found out anything on the cabin?" Derek asked, leaning back in his chair.

Kyle shook his head. "I can't find anything yet. I still have a few rocks to look under."

"Get me that information ASAP. Also, what about the girls? Anything pop yet?"

Kyle sat on the edge of Felicia's desk. "I'm running a program now. I should have something by this afternoon."

Derek turned his attention back to his screen. He picked up his phone to call Dr. Callahan when Kelly came bounding back into the room. "You got something?"

"Maybe. You remember I mentioned the stuntman, Julian Mosely? Well, that was him. He said he didn't have much to do with the team other than when they played. He only did it so it would look good on his college application and get girls. But he did say there was a pretty tight click between some of the players." She flipped through her notes. "Those would be all of our dead guys along with Baily Hodgens and Dwight Black. He also said that Coach McMillan was really tight with these boys."

"That falls in line with what Kyle just found," Derek said.

Kelly sat in her chair. "It looks like there were times the team went on little trips to help build team relationships, but after a few of them, he quit going unless they were related to games."

"Did he say why?" Derek asked.

"Yeah. It seems Billy liked playing tricks or pulling pranks on those who weren't in the clique. He pulled some on his buddies, but most of it seemed to be directed to the other boys at the academy. Sometimes the pranks were on the vicious side."

"Please tell me he elaborated." Derek placed his elbows on his desk, clasping his hands together.

"When I asked him about them, he recalled the last time he spent time with the team at one of these team excursions. The coach brought a few of the other dads. And one of the kids, Klint Kenyon, he couldn't swim. Billy and a few others blindfolded the kid and told him they had a surprise for him. They led him to the end of the dock and pushed him into the water.

"The kid struggled and nearly drowned. One of the dads ran down the dock and jumped in to save him. Klint called his mom to come get him. Billy and the others didn't really get in trouble. The coach told them not to do it again. Billy said he didn't know Klint couldn't swim. But Julian said he lied. Billy knew. He just liked watching the kid struggle."

"Did he mention where this took place?" Derek's foot bounced under his desk.

"No. He said it was a cabin. But he didn't know who owned it. He assumed one of the fathers did. He only went twice with the team. He said Dwight might know more. He was part of the clique, along with Baily." Kelly laid her phone on her desk. "He does have an alibi for these last two murders. He's been in the Philippines for over six months. He said he could prove he hasn't come back to the states during this entire time.

"Michael, don't you have Baily and Dwight?" Derek asked.

Michael nodded. "I do."

"Call them. Now. I don't care what time it is wherever they are. Ask them about the cabin. And the pranks."

George leaned forward. "Norman Aleshire said he wasn't sure about the money. He remembered asking Billy several times about it. Finally, Billy said Coach did some consulting for him and his dad. Mr. Aleshire said it was one of the few times Billy wouldn't give him the details. He left it alone and made the payments."

"I have Klint. I've been trying to reach him. He seems to always be out of the office." Felicia smiled at her boss.

"Call them and tell them if you don't speak to him in the next thirty minutes, where does he live?"

"Tucson."

"Tell whoever you get on the phone, if you don't speak to him in the next thirty minutes, Federal Agents in Tucson will show up at his home and work with an arrest warrant."

"Can we do that?"

"No. But he doesn't know that. I need answers." Derek motioned to her. "Do it."

"Done." She picked up her cell phone and headed to the kitchen for a drink.

Derek stood and rolled a white board from the corner over. "Kyle, print me pictures of all the team members."

"I'll be right back." Kyle jogged to his office.

Derek jotted the names of all the dead players, including Joseph Coombes, and added Gorden Padden's name at the end of the list with an asterisk. Next, he placed Billy's parent's names on the board, along with coach Russel McMillan. Lastly, he listed the living players, with Dwight and Baily in a separate column.

Felicia walked into the room. "Sometimes, I love this job."

Kelly laughed. "Why? What did you get to do?"

"This little snotty secretary I kept having to speak with took an attitude with me. Giving me some crap about how important Mr. Kenyon was, and he had other things to do. So, I told her exactly what Derek told me to say." A sly grin filled her face. "I may have thrown in she would face obstruction charges for her part in making my day harder than it had to be."

"Ah, that is a perk of this job. Threatening people." Kelly smirked at her friend.

"You're just jealous. You didn't get to do it."

"I am actually," Kelly said.

Kyle came back into the room. "Here you go, boss." He took his perch back on Felicia's desk.

Derek placed the pictures on the board. Under the names, he pinned the pictures of the boys. "These boys had close friendships. As Kyle said, an inner circle." He points to the other players. "Gordon Padden died of cancer. Martin Lucey is in jail and has been for over a year. I feel confident ruling him out as our killer. Julian Mosely also seems to have an alibi, and Coombes committed suicide. That leaves us with team members Klint Kenyon, Christian Dawson, and Humphrey Archer, one of which may or may not be our killer."

George pointed to the picture of Russell McMillan. "He may not have been part of the pranks, but he definitely facilitated them. He didn't seem to punish the kids, and he received a lot of money from Billy and his father. Throughout the years, especially after the incident at the cabin. I don't know what it means yet, but I think it has a major part to play in this."

"Yes. I agree," Derek said. "George also pointed out the coach could very well be a victim. And I have to agree with him. These other three team members could also be victims."

"I think from the amount of money the headmaster received, he benefitted from Billy being alive more than dead." George glanced around the room.

Derek dragged a hand through his hair. "We need to contact Hodgens, Black, Kenyon, Dawson, and Archer. We need to know about these pranks, and we need to know about this cabin or wherever they went for those team building trips. We need to know if someone else outside the team may have received the brunt of Billy's pranks. I think someone is holding the members of the team, at least some of them, accountable for something. But at this moment, I have no idea what or if I am even in the ball park of possibilities."

Felicia's phone rang. "Here we go. Hello, Klint Kenyon. Thank you for calling me back." She stepped to the side.

Derek watched her body language as she listened.

Felicia snapped her fingers, getting everyone's attention. "Klint, I need to put you on speaker phone. I'm in a room with several other agents." She pushed a button and spoke. "Klint, I have you on speaker."

"Uhm, okay. Agents."

"Klint, can you tell me again what you were just saying about the pranks."

"Yes. Billy played pranks on teachers, other students, workers at the academy. A few of those got him in trouble and cost his father lots of money."

"Klint, this is Agent Derek Reed. Can you tell me about the prank he played on you at the lake?"

There was a long pause.

The agents looked at each other.

Klint continued. "Billy knew I couldn't swim. He and the others threw me off the end of the dock."

"Did anything ever happen to the boys?" Felicia asked.

"No. But, I guess the school worried about a lawsuit, so Billy's dad paid my tuition for the remainder of the year. He explained it to my parents as his way of apologizing for his kid's behavior. But I knew it was a payoff. My dad did too."

"Did your dad want to press the issue?" Derek asked.

"Yeah. But I told him it would only make it worse. He took the tuition money. We didn't need it. My dad donated a lot of it to charity."

"What was it like for you after that?" Felicia asked.

"The guys left me alone. I'm sure the Coach and Billy's dad had something to do with their lack of interest. I got to finish out my time on the team and at school immune to Billy's pranks. Others weren't so lucky."

"What kinds of pranks?"

"One prank he pulled caused one of the teacher's convertible to be damaged by a bucket of paint. That prank cost his dad several thousands in repairs."

"Did anyone ever get hurt?" Derek asked.

"I wasn't at a lot of the team stuff. After the lake incident, I did enough to stay on the team. But I heard about a prank involving some girl. I don't know who. It happened when I wasn't around."

"Do you have any information about it? Something?" Felicia asked.

"I don't. All I can tell you is Baily or Dwight might know. They were definitely part of the chosen few. There is one odd thing. Billy was known for bragging about his pranks. Often to the point of tortuously making the victim relive them. But after the incident with the girl, no one spoke of it. Not one word. And if any of us brought it up, we were threatened with bodily harm if we mentioned it."

"Do you know when this happened?" Derek asked.

"After the season. I know this because I quit hanging out with the guys as soon as the season ended. I had decided I didn't want anything to do with most of them. Some of the others, like Christian Dawson, Humphry Archer, and Marin Lucey, I still hung out with once in a while."

George leaned in towards the phone. "Klint, this is Agent Peterson. Can you tell me who on your team got picked on the most by Billy?"

"Billy spread it around. He wasn't too selective."

"Who hated Billy the most?" George asked.

"Hmm. Humphrey Archer and Gorden Padden didn't like Billy or the other elite team members very much. Humphrey stayed away the most. He only played the games. He didn't want anything else to do with the team. For a while, Gorden tried to fit in. Get into the clique. But he just never really fit in." Klint paused. "There was another kid. Not on the team. Billy tortured him daily. I can't remember who, but after the girl, Billy changed his attitude. He started being nice to the kid. Kept some of the other seniors from harassing him."

"Did you ever find out why?" Derek asked.

"No. The kid seemed really glad to be able to hang out with the team."

"Before we let you go, can you tell me if there were any girls who were always around?" Derek scribbled on a piece of paper while he waited for a response.

"It's a shorter list if I tell you who wasn't around," Klint chuckled into the phone. "I don't remember too many of the girls, but Alesha Morrison and her best friend, Katy Preston, they were always around the team. Oh wait, I remember there being another girl."

"Who?" Derek asked.

"Oh, man. I can't remember. But she wasn't like a groupie. She hung around a lot with the kid I just mentioned, the boy. I wish I could remember their names. I remember, one day, she quit hanging around. Never saw her again. I think she may have left school. If I remember, I can let you know. But Dwight might know. He was Billy's right-hand man back then. I remember the girl hung around with Katy and Alesha when they let her."

"Did Alesha and Katy have a beef with any of the boys on the team?" Felicia asked.

"I don't think so. I found them annoying. I think Alesha had a crush on Dwight. Katy road her coat tails. Alesha was one of the richest girls in our school. One more thing I heard during college, Arthur Brandis helped at Billy's dad's law firm. Something went down, and Arthur almost didn't get his license to practice law. Again, Dwight might know about it. Hey, if that's it, I really got to go."

"Klint, are you aware Joseph Coombes committed suicide?" Derek asked.

A long silence filled the line.

"Klint?" Derek asked.

"Yeah. I didn't go to the funeral. I heard he was really depressed. I remember something about a girl. But I don't know who or what happened." Klint sighed. "Joseph was a nice kid. He started hanging with the popular kids. You know Billy and the others. But after the season, something changed in Joseph. He became a little more withdrawn. I thought when he went off to college he'd be fine. I thought it would help things. I guess it didn't."

"Thanks, Klint. If you think of anything, please call Agent Rogers. Any help you can give us will help us find who murdered Billy." Derek glanced at his team.

"You know something, Agent? I wasn't surprised to hear Billy was murdered. Everyone always thought he was a good kid and a great pillar of the community. But he wasn't. He pissed off a lot of people and had to have his dad bail him out a few times. To be honest, if Billy didn't have money, his ass would've been in jail."

"Thank you, Klint. One last thing. Where have you been this week?" Derek asked.

Klint chuckled. "I guess I'm a suspect, huh? Here in Tucson. I've been in major business meetings all week. I can get you the dates and times, and a few were actually recorded."

"I'd appreciate the information. Just email it to me at Reed@thelegacyunit.com."

"I'll have my secretary send it right over," Klint said.

"I appreciate you getting back to me," Felicia said.

"No problem."

The line went dead.

Derek glanced around the room, zeroing in Kyle. "I need you to find out if what Klint told us was true."

Kyle nodded as he wrote on a pad of paper. "I got it. I'm going to do a deep dive on Arthur, and I will look for a girl who left the school. I'm also going to hunt down any criminal records the father had shoved under the carpet. Hopefully, if I find the girl, I might be able to narrow in on the kid Klint referenced."

Derek nodded. "Hunt down Katy Preston and Alesha Morrison."

Kyle's eyebrows furrowed. "You think they're involved, don't you?"

"Not sure." He nodded at Kyle. "Get to work." Just before Kyle was out of earshot, he called out. "Thanks, Kyle. If you hit a road block, let me know. I'll call the AD." He turned back to Michael. "You need to get ahold of Dwight and Baily. Threaten both if you have to. And see if you can gather any information on Joseph's suicide."

Michael nodded as he made a few notes.

"I can help with the threatening part," Felicia said.

Michael laughed. "And let you have all the fun? I don't think so."

CHAPTER THIRTY-THREE

The air in the office crackled. Derek rearranged the photos of the baseball team, grouping the popular and non-popular players, hoping to ascertain what dark secret these boys harbored. His gut told him it revolved around a girl. He needed to discover which girl. As he stepped back, he had the sensation of being watched.

Closing his eyes, he took a deep breath. He gave sidelong glances around the room as he tapped the face of his watch trying to calm his anxiety. No one lurked in the corners. But his body reacted to something or someone. He turned back to the whiteboard, letting the evidence speak to him.

From the conversation with Klint, Billy's true personality started to shine through. He thought of calling the congressman, but he had no idea how Jackson would respond to him insinuating, his friend was an asshole. He would be willing to bet the congressman had no idea about Billy's high school endeavors to terrorize his former classmates.

Billy was a bully. He was mean and calculating. He used his standing in the community, even as a kid, to get away with things. Derek held strong to the belief a prior bad act from high school got the man murdered, along with the others. But to be sure, he had to call the AD.

Reaching for his phone, he silently slipped from the main office to the back of the church and entered one of the small bedrooms. He used a security code to access a secure line.

The AD picked up on the second ring. "It must be important for you to call me on this line."

"It is. I need to know something. I don't want to chase a lead if it has nothing to do with this case. It will cost me and my team valuable time."

Assistant Director Fretz sighed into the phone. "It's about Billy, isn't it?"

"I need to know if during the security clearance request if anything from Billy's past came up. Anything involving his father and the academy."

"I can't really tell you what we uncovered during the background check."

"I don't need to know anything about the land deal and the case. I'm specifically looking for something his father was involved in when Billy attended Londonvale Academy."

"Nothing inhibited him from getting the clearance. That's all I can tell you." The AD paused. "If the father had been involved in anything, he hid it well enough we didn't find it. I should rephrase that. It didn't warrant further action on our part. The security clearance went through. And I wasn't supposed to tell you that."

"Okay."

"Do you think an incident from the past is the reason he was murdered?"

Derek rubbed the back of his neck. "I'm not sure yet. And I would rather not say until I am more certain."

"You mean until you have evidence proving your theory."

Derek laughed. "I don't even have a theory yet."

"Do you have anything?"

"I might. Thanks for the information."

"What information?"

Derek shook his head when the AD hung up. He walked back into the main room. Emma had just entered, and Lola ran towards Marc Anthony. "Emma. Is everything okay?"

She waived him off. "Yes, my baby just needed his vaccinations. I bet Lola has been missing her best buddy."

Kelly laughed. "She sure has. I think seeing Marc Anthony is the best part of her day."

The two dogs danced around each other, wiggling their butts. Lola sniffed every inch of the big dog.

Marc Anthony stood perfectly still as she investigated the smell of others on his fur.

"They have become best friends, haven't they?" Derek asked as he leaned against his desk.

Emma smiled at him. "They have." She watched the dogs for a few moments. She looked at Derek, wanting to say something. Instead, she moved to her desk. "Have you solved the case?"

Derek laughed. "Not hardly."

She looked up. Watching the other agents as they worked on the task at hand. "I have no doubt you will."

Derek walked around his desk and sat staring at the whiteboard. "What am I missing?" he said under his breath. He had all the players and knew the murders were connected. But he had no idea why or who would be next. The only thing he knew for sure was there would be a next.

CHAPTER THIRTY-FOUR

Wednesday mid-day

Kyle sat at his desk. Years of emails scrolled across his screen. The program he set up searched for a specific combination of words. He had a handful of emails from Coach referring to the cabin, but he needed a specific reference to a young girl.

Glancing at his screen, he continued to search the school records for files of girls who left unexpectedly during the four years Billy Edmond attended Londonvale Academy. His brow furrowed when something caught the corner of his eye. He turned towards the door, expecting to see someone.

He removed his headphones. "Hello? Is anyone there?" Kyle waited; his head cocked to the side. Shrugging, he went back to his research. His eyes drifted toward the doorway. He rubbed his hands on his jeans, shivering due to a slight drop in room temperature. He shook off the uneasy feeling, chalking it up to long hours behind the computer.

As the endless emails drifted across the screen, he sat back and closed his eyes. The uneasy feeling crept down his legs, making them throb. He bounced his knees as he fidgeted in his seat. He breathed in through his nose and out of his mouth. Concentrating on the sound of his breath, he let his mind relax and drift. A soft, inaudible whisper filled his ear. He bolted upright just as his computer beeped.

He scanned the information. His heart raced as he read through the news report. An obscure article in a small-town newspaper outside Tucson mentioned the unexpected death of a young high school girl. His heart thumped in his chest. "This has to be her."

He printed the article and ran up the stairs.

Derek heard hurried footsteps approaching. Goosebumps littered his arms as anxiety crept over him. He clinched his hands into fists, hoping to dissipate the electricity pulsing through him.

"I got something," Kyle said as he rounded the corner. Practically sliding across the floor, he stopped directly in front of Derek's desk.

Derek squinted. "Show me."

"First, here is Katy Preston and Alecia Morrison's information," he said, handing him a piece of paper. "I haven't called on them yet. Wasn't sure if you wanted me to do it or not." He held out the article. "I think this is the girl."

Derek swallowed several times, resisting the urge to run. His mouth felt like dried cotton. He stared at the picture of a newspaper clipping, taking from the Sun Times. Front and center sat a photograph of a young girl.

He slowed his breathing down as his heart pounded against his chest. The girl from his neighborhood stared back at him, the one he had seen playing outside at 6 a.m. He gave a sideways glance to Kyle to see if he noticed his reaction. "What makes you think this is the girl?" He asked, trying to control his hands and keep them from shaking.

"Other references have come up to girls who have left the academy, but this is the only girl who died." Kyle tapped the desk. "It seems she had been with two of her girlfriends. They don't name them in the article. The girl's name is Casey Redding. The article says she attended a prominent scholastic academy when an unfortunate accident happened."

Derek tilted his head. "You think Katy Preston and Alesha Morrison are the two friends?"

"I'd be willing to bet money on it." The corners of Kyle's mouth turned downward. "She had an asthma attack."

Derek's stomach churned as acid crept up his throat, causing a searing sensation. He took a deep breath, barely reading the article. The dream he had the other night flooded his thoughts. "It doesn't say where, why, or what happened."

"Nope. Just states it was a tragic accident." Kyle sat on the corner of Derek's desk. "I went through the digital archives of the paper from the entire year. No other article ever mentioned the girl. And the author of the article left the paper three months later. I smell a cover-up."

"Hunt down the man who wrote the story. See if he will give you any information on it." Derek laid the copy of the article on his desk.

Kyle's eyes lit up. "I'm on it," he said as he trotted off to his cave.

"Listen up," Derek said. "Kyle found the name of a girl. It could be the one Klint mentioned. Casey Redding. It looks like she died in a tragic accident. She had an asthma attack."

George leaned forward on his elbows. "Tragic accident? Or maybe a prank gone wrong?"

Felicia nodded. "Given what we know of Billy, I'm voting for prank."

Kelly rolled her chair forward. "How did he cover it up, though?"

"That's what we need to figure out." Derek dragged his hand down his face. "Michael, tell me you have something from Dwight or Bailey?"

"Bailey Hodgens said we can talk to his lawyer and hung up on me. I still haven't reached Dwight Black. I was just about to call him one more time today," Michael said, nodding towards his cell.

"Get on it now. And give me Bailey's information. Do you know what kind of law his lawyer practices?" Derek crossed his arms.

"I believe he's a tax attorney." Michael handed Derek a piece of paper with the name and number of Bailey's lawyer as he stepped out of the room.

Derek frowned. "Kelly, get ahold of Casey Redding's family and see if they will tell you anything."

"I'm on it." She turned towards her computer, and accessed the main file holding the case information and notes and pulled everything Kyle had uploaded regarding Casey Redding.

Derek's breath hitched in his throat. Casey Redding stood in the far corner of the room. She pointed to the front of her t-shirt. The same one she wore the first day he saw her. Derek didn't understand what his brain tried to tell him, and he couldn't make out what the girl's shirt had on it.

Emma, who had stepped out with the dogs, walked back into the building.

Lola bounded around the desks, making her way to the corner. She sniffed the area but didn't bark. She sat and stared at the corner.

Derek watched as the vision of the young girl faded away.

"Hello, Derek?" Kelly stood in front of him, waving her hand.

"What? What's up?" he asked.

"Where were you?" she asked.

"Thinking about this case. What do you have?"

Kelly flipped through her notes. "I spoke with the mother. She's in a nursing home. She told me Casey had been invited to go to the lake with two of her classmates from Londonvale academy. She couldn't remember their names but remembered one girl came from a very wealthy family."

Derek glanced over Kelly's shoulder as she spoke, checking the corner for Casey.

"Her husband kept many of the details from her. She had a nervous breakdown after her daughter's death. But she remembers hearing her daughter got locked in a closet and didn't have her rescue inhaler on her."

"Does she know which lake?" Derek asked.

A broad smile filled Kelly's face. "She sure did. Lake Pleasant."

"George?" Derek called out.

"Yeah?" George said, turning towards his boss.

"Call Norman Aleshire and ask him if Billy or his father ever owned any property around Lake Pleasant."

"You got it," George said.

"And check the archives of the school. See if they own any property near there."

"Emma, would you order us something to eat?"

She glanced at everyone. "Chinese?"

"Sounds good." Kelly looked at her watch. "I didn't even realize lunch had passed."

Derek walked over to Emma's desk. "Call Yangs. They deliver," he said as he handed her his credit card.

"I love Yangs." She pulled up the menu online, jotting down several dishes to order.

Derek took a deep breath as he sat back down and called Bailey Hodgens' lawyer.

CHAPTER THIRTY-FIVE

"Fleischer Law offices, may I help you?"

"This is FBI Agent Derek Reed. I need to speak with Mr. James Fleischer."

"I'm so sorry. He is on another call...."

"I don't care if he is talking to the President of the United States. You need to tell him I am holding. If he doesn't take my call, I will have FBI agents pick him up within the hour and transport him to Phoenix. Have I made myself clear?"

"Um, just a moment."

Derek sat and listened to instrumental 80s music while he waited. He really didn't have the authority to pull off his threat, but he was pretty sure Mr. Fleischer didn't know that. Or at least he hoped he didn't.

"This is James Fleischer."

"This is Agent Derek Reed with the FBI. You have a client named Bailey Hodgens who refuses to speak with us regarding an ongoing murder."

"I don't believe my client can help you with your investigation."

"How would you know if you don't know what we are investigating? And if you know what we are investigating, I have to wonder if Mr. Hodgens has something to hide regarding said investigation. Did I mention this was a murder investigation?"

A brief silence filled the line.

"I really don't know how Mr. Hodgens can help you."

"You don't know what it's about. Unless you're psychic. And in that case, can you give me the numbers for the next lottery pick?"

"Mr. Reed..."

"That's FBI Special Agent in Charge Reed."

"Maybe I could help. Can you tell me what you want to speak with Mr. Hodgens about?"

Derek thought about his next move. "Listen, Mr. Hodgens may hold information which may help us with a murder case. He knew the deceased, and we believe he has knowledge of events which occurred when he and the deceased were in high school."

"I would need a guarantee Mr. Hodgens won't be held responsible for said events. If said events even occurred."

Derek smiled inwardly. "Are you his criminal attorney?"

"No. However, I represent Mr. Hodgens' best interest."

"We have no reason to believe Mr. Hodgens had any direct involvement with an incident during their senior year. But, if he continues to evade questions regarding this investigation, we may have to look at what he may or may not have been responsible for. I'm sure he doesn't want that. We are merely searching for answers."

Another long silence filled the phone. "I will allow Mr. Hodgens to conduct a phone interview. But if I feel you are trying to pin whatever you think happened on him, I will pull the plug immediately."

"I understand. But I need this to happen within the next thirty minutes. Or there will be no concessions made for Mr. Hodgens."

James Fleischer sighed into the phone. "I'll call you back on this number. It may take an hour or more for me to set it up. But I will call you back."

Derek scoffed at his phone as the line went dead.

Several of his agents looked at him. He simply waved them off. "Give me a chance to speak with the man." As he waited for the callback, he stared at the photo of the young girl. She wore a different shirt in the photo. *Why couldn't it be easy? Just one time.* He sat back and closed his eyes, concentrating on a dead girl.

CHAPTER THIRTY-SIX

Kyle finished his egg roll as he called the last known number for the reporter. His fingers tapped the desk as he waited. "C'mon, make my day, please." He cracked open his fortune cookie. *You will get great news, and you will rejoice.* "Let's hope so," he said as he placed the fortune on his desk.

"Hello?"

"Mr. Jessup? Arland Jessup?"

"Yes, who is this?"

"I'm FBI Agent Kyle Marcum. I need to ask you a few questions."

"FBI? What the heck does the FBI want with me?"

Kyle leaned back in his chair. "I need some information on Casey Redding. You wrote a story about her several years ago."

Dead silence filtered through the line.

"Hello? Mr. Jessup?"

"I haven't heard her name in a long time," Arland Jessup said.

"I need to know everything you found out about her death. Can you tell me about the story you wrote?" Kyle's fingers tapped the arm of his chair.

"Some kids found her dead at a cabin out by Lake Pleasant. Everyone involved said the same thing. She had a tragic accident. Somehow, she had gotten locked in a closet. The poor girl had a huge fear of the dark and freaked out. Causing her to have a severe asthma attack."

"Did you interview any of the kids involved?"

"Yeah, but my editor wouldn't let me print any of it. He allowed me to give a very undetailed account of what happened."

"What did the kids tell you?"

"All the kids made the same statements. They didn't know she had asthma, and they didn't know she was actually in distress. They stated they thought she was just acting for attention," Arland said.

"Didn't that seem odd to you?"

"Heck yeah, it did. But when I approached my editor about it, he told me not to pursue it. He even asked for all my notes on the story."

Kyle sat up. "Why would he want all your notes?"

"I have no idea. I asked him why, but he said he just wanted to read over them. He said he would give them back. But I never saw them again." Arland sat quietly. "It seemed to me someone had some kind of leverage over my editor. He never acted like this with any other story I investigated. This one took on a life of its own."

"What do you mean?" Kyle asked.

"After I reported the story, I continued to investigate it. On the side, off the books. I found out the kid involved, Billy something...."

"Billy Edmond?"

"Yeah, his dad had some heavy political strings, and he pulled them. Kept anything about his kid from ever coming out. I couldn't even find out who owned the cabin it happened in. All the records pointed to a shell company."

"Do you remember the name of the company?" Kyle's leg bounced under his desk.

"Yeah, and I can do better than just a name. I kept a copy of all my notes. I can send them to you."

Kyle jumped up from his seat. "You're kidding? That would help us a lot. Send everything, even photos."

"No problem. I have everything in a file on my computer. Where do you want me to email it?"

Kyle had to think for a moment. "KMarcum@thelegacyunit.com. I really appreciate this. Can you tell me why you left the paper three months later?"

"After seeing how easy my editor rolled over for this guy and buried the story, I couldn't stomach it anymore. I retired, and now I write crime novels."

"Thanks for your help with this. If I have other questions, I may call."

"Call anytime. There is one thing."

"What's that?" Kyle asked.

"The shell company never existed. I couldn't find any information on it anywhere. If it ever existed, they scrubbed it from every record."

Kyle stood prancing in place. "Thanks. I really appreciate all this."

"Keep me posted, if you can. I would really like to know what happened."

"If I can, I will." Kyle hung up and searched his email for the needed file. Nothing. He tapped his foot on the floor, leaning over the computer. "C'mon." He refreshed the screen, and the email from Arland popped up. "Yes," he said as he opened the file.

CHAPTER THIRTY-SEVEN

Derek threw away his paper plate. His stomach full of Yang's Chinese food. He would have to work hard not to take a nap. The dogs were full and happy too, both napping on the floor. He laid his head back against his chair. Relaxing when his phone vibrated against the desk. "Agent Reed."

"I have Mr. Hodgens on the line with us. Again, Agent Reed, if I think you are trying to pin anything on my client, I will cut this call short."

"Understood. Mr. Hodgens?"

"Yes, Agent Reed?" Bailey responded.

"Can you tell me about the incident which happened at the cabin?" Silence filled the line.

"Go ahead, Bailey," the lawyer said.

"We had a party up at the cabin," Bailey said.

"Who owned the cabin?" Derek asked.

"I don't know. I didn't really care. Billy got the keys and said we could go up there. We invited a few girls and the baseball team. I think a few other guys showed up," Bailey said.

"Tell me about Casey Redding," Derek said.

"Listen, I had nothing to do with her. I was making out with Aleesha Preston. Billy, Greg, and Arthur did that." Bailey sighed into the phone. "They thought it would be funny to put her in the closet. They blind-folded her and told her they had a surprise for her. She had a crush on Greg, so she would've done anything he asked."

"Who brought her to the party?" Derek asked.

"I think she came with Katy and Aleesha. They weren't great friends, but I think they were in a club together, or the girls worked with a club she was in. I'm not sure," Bailey said.

Derek's pulse raced. "What club?"

"Hell, I don't know," Bailey said.

"Bailey, can you tell me about Coach McMillan?"

"Shit, that guy is the worst of them all."

"What do you mean?" Derek asked.

"He portrays himself as this great guy, team player, all about the kids. He's only out for himself. He'll do anything for money," Bailey said.

"Did he help cover-up what happened to Casey?"

"I don't know for sure. I know Billy's dad had everything swept away, so no one, especially his kid, would get into trouble. Billy bragged about it after it all went down. How he could do what he wanted and not face any consequences."

"Can you tell me about a kid Billy protected after the cabin accident?" Derek asked.

"What kid?"

"Klint mentioned a kid Billy protected after Casey's death. Kept the other players and jocks from messing with him."

"I don't know who you're referring to. Billy didn't protect too many kids. One thing he loved more than anything was exposing someone's weaknesses. He definitely didn't protect anyone. Unless he had something to gain."

Derek's thoughts bounced all over the place. Something wasn't adding up. "Tell me what happened the days after Casey's death?"

"I don't know. Shit, it was so long ago." Bailey fell silent for a moment. "I remember Billy was adamant that no one speak of the cabin. It was also the last time we all went there." He paused again. "Wait. I remember something. After the girl died, there was this kid who hounded Billy about it. I don't remember the kid, some loser. But he said Billy would not get away with it like he did everything else.

"Billy was furious too. He kept saying he was going to have to shut the kid up if he didn't keep his mouth shut. Then one day, the kid stopped. He stopped harassing Billy. Maybe that's the kid you were talking about earlier."

"Can you tell me anything about the kid?" Derek asked.

"Not much. I remember a few months later, the kid was driving a new sports car. They never spoke, but Billy seemed really uncomfortable around the kid. Something I have never seen from Billy."

"Listen, Bailey. I may have other questions. Please don't make me chase you down again. I think you and your lawyer can see we are not after you for Casey's death. But we need to connect the dots to figure out who is killing most of your high school baseball team."

Bailey gasped. "Wait, you think these deaths are because of what happened to Casey?"

"I don't know. I do know someone is going to great lengths to make a point."

"Do you think I have something to worry about? I mean, do you think this fucking psycho is going to come after me or my family?"

"I don't know, Bailey," Derek said. "But I would definitely take precautions. Before I let you go, can you tell me anything about Casey?"

Bailey sighed. "She was a real cute girl. Super nice. Not like Aleesha or Katy. Her family had money, but they weren't super rich. I know she tried to hang around with Katy and Aleesha, but they made fun of her when she wasn't there."

"Why did they invite her to the party, then?" Derek asked.

"I don't know. I figured it was their one time to be nice. But it seemed kind of weird. I remember they didn't talk to her much at the cabin. I think that's why Greg and Billy played a prank on her," Bailey said.

"I don't understand," Derek said.

"From what I found out later, she was trying to talk to Greg. He was interested in another girl. I'm guessing they put her in the closet to get her out of the way—maybe."

Derek wanted to punch this guy. He knew exactly why they did it. He just didn't want to make himself look bad. "Did you help get her into the closet?"

"Agent, I think you are treading a little too close for comfort," Bailey's lawyer said.

"Mr. Fleischer, I'm just making inquiries. Bailey, have you told us all you know? We need to solve the murder of one of your best friends from high school. Several murders of several of your best friends from high school. I would think you would want to help." Derek tapped his pen on the desk.

"Bailey, you don't have to answer," the lawyer said.

"I don't mind. I had nothing to do with it. I wasn't inside when they did it. Aleesha and I came back an hour later. When we came up to the cabin, several kids were leaving, like in a big hurry. Billy said Casey had an asthma attack, and they think she's dead. It wasn't a few moments later the paramedics showed up along with the police. I told them I wasn't there, and me and Aleesha left."

"What about Katy?"

"Katy had left earlier with another guy. She wasn't even at the cabin when it happened," Bailey said.

"Is there anything else, Agent? I think Bailey has answered your questions."

"Not at the moment. But I may need to speak with you again. Thank you for your time. I appreciate it."

"No problem," Bailey said, then hung up.

"Thank you, Mr. Fleisher. I appreciate your help with this."

"You're welcome. I just ask if you need to speak with him, you will call me first."

"I can do that," Derek said. He laid his phone on the desk. Everyone in the room stared at him.

"Well?" asked Felicia.

"Well, what?" Derek asked, smirking at her. He turned towards George. "Did Mr. Aleshire have any information on the cabin?"

George shook his head. "He said the only cabin the family-owned was in Lake Tahoe. I wouldn't call it a cabin, either. I pulled up the pictures on Google Maps. It's a sprawling log house; looks like a ski lodge."

"Really, Derek? Are you going to fill us in?" Felicia asked again, glaring at him.

Derek laughed. "Okay. Okay." He ran through what he learned about Casey's death. "We need to call the local police up there and find out if they have any records. Hopefully, Kyle finds something out."

He watched his agents out of the corner of his eye. He pretended to work on his computer. His mind raced. He knew the club Bailey mentioned had significance. But he had no clue what club to even look for.

He sat still with his eyes closed, concentrating on Casey's t-shirt. The mental picture was fuzzy. He couldn't make it out. He scanned all the photos he had in the file. No one wore a shirt like hers. Why couldn't he see it?

CHAPTER THIRTY-EIGHT

Kyle ran up the stairs. "I got it," he said, running into the room. Derek looked up. "Got what?"

"I got the file from the reporter." Kyle laid a folder on Derek's desk.

"The reporter gave you his notes?" he asked, reaching for the file. He read as Kyle talked.

"Yes," Kyle explained what the reporter told him. "He said his editor had to have been paid off. When he took the notes, he never returned them. A good thing for us, the reporter made copies."

"Kyle, did you call the police up in Lake Pleasant?" Derek asked.

"I did. No one there had any answers. The officer in charge said he had no records on file. He remembered the case and remembered his sergeant at the time said it had been an accident and told everyone the case was closed." Kyle sat on the edge of Felicia's desk.

"Sounds like they involved the local PD in the coverup," Kelly said.

"But how?" Michael asked.

"Money and power," said George. "You'd be surprised what those two things can do for you."

Kyle's eyes were wide. "George is spot on."

"What do you mean?" Derek asked.

"The reporter said he traced the cabin back to a shell company. But he couldn't find any information about the company. He stated if the company ever existed, it had been scrubbed from everywhere." Kyle smiled.

Derek raised an eyebrow. "Do you have the name of the company?"

"Yeah, Pink Diamond Industries." Kyle watched as his boss flinched. "Something wrong, Derek?"

Derek had palpitations and his shirt stuck the light sheen of sweat on his back. He shook off the overwhelming feeling of dread that surrounded him. "No. Just thinking."

"I'm getting ready to hunt it down. I may need to cross some lines," Kyle said, taking a small step back.

Derek knew what he meant. "Don't go too far over and keep records. If we have to, we will beg for forgiveness later. What about Dwight? Anything?" Derek asked, turning his attention to Michael.

"Nothing. I can't reach him at all." Michael scrolled through his notes. "I called his parents. They now live part-time in Arlington, Virginia, and part-time here. They're in town this week. And they haven't heard from him in a while."

"Okay. Track his whereabouts. Use his personal information, social and anything else to find out his movements over the last month. Let's see if we can find him." Derek's gut told him the hammer was about to drop. A key piece of evidence stared him in the face, yet he couldn't see it. Or maybe he didn't want to.

"If you need help, let me know, Michael." Kyle took Felicia's fortune cookie off her desk. "I can run a simultaneous check while I'm hunting down this company."

"Don't you dare eat my cookie," Felicia snarled as her eyes narrowed in on him.

"Man, you're scary," he said as he set the cookie back down.

"You aren't the only one with some computer skills," Michael said, cracking his knuckles. He pulled up the Fed's database and signed into the US Embassy in the United Kingdom. If Dwight were working over-seas, he would have to have a visa. Combing through several files, he found what he needed.

As he read the file on Dwight Black, his heart rate sped up. He looked up, catching Kyle's eye. "Come here."

"What's up?" Kyle asked as he stood behind Michael. "Oh."

Derek knew that tone. "What? What's going on?"

Everyone else in the office stopped what they were doing.

"Um, well. We may have a problem." Kyle nudged Michael out of the way.

Michael sat on his desk. "Looks like Dwight left London four weeks ago."

Derek straightened. "How could we miss that?"

Michael blinked. "I don't know. I didn't think of searching to see if he traveled. I—I only just now thought of checking the embassy. I messed up. Damn." His head sunk into his shoulders.

"Listen," Derek said. "You would've caught it. Don't let it eat at you." He walked around his desk. Marking on his whiteboard. "Do you have his travel itinerary?"

Kyle nodded. "Yeah. It looks like he boarded a flight from London and landed in Washington, DC. He then hopped another plane to Dallas." Kyle frowned. "What the hell was he doing in Dallas?"

Derek pointed at Kelly. "That's what you're going to find out. Call his parents and ask them if they know of any business dealings he may have had in Dallas. Do not raise suspicions. If they ask, just tell them you're gathering information."

She nodded. "You got it."

Derek walked towards Michael, laying his hand on his shoulder. "If this is the only mistake you ever make, then you have nothing to worry about. And there are way worse mistakes that will have far greater reach and cause more harm than missing something like this. Now clear your head and get to work."

He moved to Kyle. "I need you to tap into every surveillance feed and follow Dwight from airport to airport. You can tap into the CCTV feeds of the city. I'll clear any roadblocks."

"You got it. I'm going downstairs. My equipment down there is better suited for this. I should have something on the company soon, too." Kyle quickly grabbed the fortune cookie off Felicia's desk while she spoke on the phone. He laughed as she flipped him off and snarled at him.

Michael sat in his vacated chair. He pulled up the file on Joseph Coombes. Knowing he missed something with Dwight Black, Michael wanted to go back over Joseph's suicide and read through all the notes from the college police department and the local ME's office.

As he scanned everything in the file, he reread the suicide note. This time, it took on a different connotation. The note referenced a girl. Joseph said he couldn't go on knowing he caused what happened. He said he was to blame. As Michael read, his heart sank to his stomach. He opened another file. The ME's report had an overdose of benzodiazepines as the cause of death.

Michael looked over the history of Joseph Coombes. From the notes gathered by the local police and the campus police, friends and his college roommate all said he was a health nut. He didn't even drink. It seemed like such a stretch to drug use. It nagged at Michael. He looked up to see his colleagues working in silence. He watched each one before turning his attention to his boss. He remembered his sister's murder and the impact Derek Reed had on him. He turned back to the computer. He had no proof, but he just couldn't let it go. *What if they were looking at this all wrong?*

CHAPTER THIRTY-NINE

Michael took a deep breath, then spoke. "What if Joseph Coombes didn't commit suicide?" He exhaled, letting his words hang in the air. He swallowed when everyone turned towards him.

Derek sat back and stared at the agent. Narrowing in on the handsome young man. "What makes you say that?"

Michael rubbed his hands together. "Um, my gut."

"You sure it isn't just gas?" asked Felicia.

"Ha ha," Michael said.

"Explain," Kelly said, turning her chair to face him.

All eyes were on him. He exhaled slowly through his nose. "I looked back over his file. The campus police made some notes regarding several phone calls Joseph had received from an old friend. His roommate said Joseph became more and more upset over the course of a few weeks. That's when he mentioned a girl to a few friends. What if Joseph was referring to Casey?"

George leaned forward, resting his elbows on his knees. "If that's the case, our guy has been keeping tabs on everyone involved in the party. And that means the victim pool just got a hell of a lot larger."

Derek stared at the case board. "Not necessarily," he said to George. "If our killer is targeting those at the party, he would be targeting the kids from the school, not everyone. In the conversation with Baily Hodges and his lawyer, Baily mentioned a kid harassed Billy. Billy threatened to shut him up, but then weeks later, the kid had a new sports car. What if the car was a payoff for keeping quiet?"

"Based on what Klint and Baily have said, that makes perfect sense. Especially knowing Billy's dad stopped at nothing to keep him out of trouble," George said.

Felicia snapped her fingers. "Arthur Brandis' murder looked like it had been related to one of his cases. What if his murder had everything to do with his helping Billy's dad cover-up things?"

Derek scribbled on his case board. "Let's go with this. Whoever this kid is he has the means to hunt everyone down. He knows where they are, and he can get to them. I would think to pull something like this off, they would have to have a lot of money."

"Well, that's the entire graduating class. Every one of those kids came from really rich parents," Kelly said.

"Not all. Baily Hodges said Casey came from a well-off family, but they weren't filthy rich. So, if this kid ended up with a new sports car, maybe his family wasn't as rich as the rest of the students," Derek said, trailing off. "He may be wealthy now, but I'm betting back in school he wasn't." He turned back to the whiteboard.

Emma, who had sat quietly for a while listening to everyone, chimed in. "You know, Londonvale has a program to help pay either some or all of a kid's tuition, allowing kids who don't meet the minimum requirement for tuition to attend the school. All a parent has to do is apply for it. I remember hearing about it."

Everyone stared at her.

She giggled. "What?"

Felicia looked from Derek to Emma and back to Derek. "Why didn't we know this?"

Derek chuckled. "I never even considered it. Tell us more, Emma."

"A lot of things have to be in place for the kid to get the money. If I remember correctly, the parents couldn't make above a certain amount of income." She shook her head. "I remember the child had to have excellent grades and take some kind of IQ test. Those scores and scores from other tests qualified them for the program. The newspaper ran a big story about it years ago. They were trying to put forth the idea the school cherry-picked its kids. But they were still giving less fortunate kids a chance to attend. And it's a private school they can do what they want."

Derek sighed. "Do you know the name of the program? Did it have anything associated with it?"

Emma cocked her head to the side. "I'm not sure what you mean?"

"Like a club or organization?" Derek asked. He didn't even know what he was looking for. How would Emma know what he was looking for?

"Oh. I don't know." Her brow wrinkled. "I think the kids had to do so many volunteer hours—kind of like working for their scholarship. Let me see if I can find the story."

"That would be great." Derek walked towards the kitchen. "I'm going to get a drink." As he walked into the open space, his head throbbed with a sharp, stabbing pain right behind his eyes. He searched the cabinet for some pain relief medicine. "Damn. I need to remember to bring some from home." Grabbing a soda from the fridge, he leaned against the counter. He rubbed the sides of his head and breathed slowly hoping the pain would recede.

He heard a loud crash next to him and turned to find the woman from his car standing right beside him. Her bloody, broken hand reached out to grab him. When she touched him, a flash like from a grenade went off. In an instant, he was transported to the backseat of a car.

CHAPTER FORTY

Screams of a woman pierced his ears. A man shouted, frantically gripping the steering wheel. The car swerved from side to side. The man overcompensated, trying to regain control of the vehicle.

The man's voice boomed out. "I can't control the car."

"Hit the brakes!" The woman cried out as she braced herself against the dash.

"I am! They aren't working!"

Derek saw the canyon walls flash past the windows.

The screams blended with the whirling sound of air and screeching metal as the car collided with the railing. Everything moved in slow motion as the car nosedived off the edge of the cliff.

Moments before impact, Derek felt as if he floated. The sunlight reflected off a pink stone hanging from the rearview mirror. Mesmerized by the prisms cast by the angle of light, Derek was oblivious to the canyon floor rushing towards him. For a split second, all sounds in the car ceased. No screams, no metal crunching. Only silence.

Slamming into the boulders on the canyon floor below, the crushing force pushed the air out of Derek's lungs before the full impact of his body smashed into the dash of the car. Every bone in his body seemed to splinter into a thousand pieces. Within moments, the car burst into flames as the metal crunched like an accordion.

Derek's legs gave out just as the last bit of air left his lungs. When his knees hit the floor, the jolt brought him back to the kitchen. Sweat beaded down his back, making his shirt stick to his skin. The food he had eaten moments ago threatened escape. He gagged on the bile, quickly trying to regain his composure. He glanced around. No woman. No car. No canyon. Laughter echoed from the front of the old church.

Derek stood, picked up his unopened can of soda, and leaned against the counter. His body shook as he let his head fall forward, and his hand braced him over the sink. The woman from his car was Billy's mom. "I'm losing my fucking mind."

"No, you're not."

Derek waited a moment before he cocked his head to the right. Chrissy sat on the counter. She held a daffodil in her hand. The cut across her neck had fresh blood on it. "Why are you bleeding?"

She smiled at him. "It seems to bleed now and then. Not really sure why. Maybe it has to do with you."

Derek sighed. His head throbbed even more. "How does it have anything to do with me? You're not even real."

She looked at him. Her bright blue eyes still carried a sadness. A sadness he was responsible for. "I am so real. You know that. You need to just give in. You keep fighting it."

"I don't know what you are talking about." He rubbed his head, pinching the bridge of his nose. He winced. It still hadn't healed completely. He was sure this caused his headaches. Josiah had damn near smashed his face in. It's no wonder he had these horrible visions and talked to a dead girl. Maybe it was time to let Dr. Chelsea run a CT scan.

"Listen, I'm forever stuck to you. I don't mind, really. I need you, and you need me. Plus, it keeps me connected to this world." She looked down at her hands. "I guess I'm not ready to let go. I know that time will come. But it's not time yet."

Derek's mouth watered as the bile started its return up his throat. He opened his soda and guzzled. He was hoping to keep the vomit at bay. Sweat lined his hairline, the dampness inching its way across his scalp. "I don't feel so well."

"No wonder. Let them talk to you. Others need your help." She shook her finger at him. "It wouldn't be so bad if you just let them in. They are trying so hard to get your attention." She sighed. "You are the most stubborn man I've ever known. I thought my daddy was bad." Chrissy threw her head back and laughed. "He ain't got nothing on you."

"I buried my watch. It was supposed to end there."

"That part ended. The guilt for the girl long ago. The girl you hit with your truck. You had to let her go. Now you hold on to the guilt surrounding me. And others, like Michael's sister." She reached out and touched his cheek.

Derek reached up and tried to take her hand. It was a wisp of air through his fingertips.

"I was dead the minute that man took me from the carnival. There was nothing you could've done. Holding onto it is clouding your judgment."

Derek finished the soda. "I don't trust my judgment anymore."

"You should. Your instinct will never lead you astray. One day, you will trust it without a second thought. For now, you have me." She smirked at him. "Gawd, this is way too mushy." She hopped off the counter.

Lola and Marc Anthony stood behind Derek.

He turned to see them staring at Chrissy, but neither barked. He watched as Chrissy patted their heads. "Okay, Mr. Mule. I can't tell you everything. But think about what you know."

"I don't understand. I don't know anything." Derek heard footsteps coming up the stairs. He turned towards Chrissy. "Help me. I don't understand."

"Think about what you do and how you do it. The killer can do the same thing. Also, someone has been hiding information from you. But you already knew this. And Billy's parents need your help."

"The lady from my car, that was Billy's mom. Is that why I saw her?"

Derek glanced over Chrissy's shoulder as Kyle popped up from the basement.

Chrissy smiled. "You know why, and you have all the answers. Trust yourself."

His brow wrinkled as he looked at Kyle. "What you got?" he asked.

Kyle flinched back. "You okay?"

Derek pursed his lips together. "Why wouldn't I be okay?"

"You look flushed. You don't look so hot." Kyle stepped up next to him, placing the back of his hand against his cheek. "You feel hot. Maybe you're coming down with something."

Derek swatted his hand away as he headed towards the main room. "What are you, my wet nurse now?"

Kyle laughed. "Hell no. I don't even know what I'm feeling for. My mom used to do that when I was a kid." He followed Derek to his desk. "I found something."

"Please tell me you know who the killer is?" Derek sat at his desk.

Kelly turned and squinted at her boss. "What's wrong with you?"

Derek's brow furrowed. "What's wrong with you?"

George leaned forward in his chair. "You look like something's wrong. Do I need to call Dr. Chelsea?"

"Oh, for crying out loud. You guys are driving me crazy." Derek took a deep breath, dragging his hand down his face, careful to stay away from his nose. "What do you have, Kyle?"

"First, the cabin. The reporter had all this information. In 2003, a company called Cabin Delights owned several cabins located around Lake Pleasant. They rented them out to vacationers. This cabin was the only one not owned by Cabin Delights. After Casey's death, they bought it at auction. They tried to purchase it before 2003, but the management company, called Evergreen, repeatedly told Cabin Delights it wasn't for sale," Kyle said.

"I dug through some records. The management company doesn't exist any longer. I'm not sure it really ever did." Kyle cleared his throat.

"Explain," Derek said.

"There is no record for Evergreen. Anywhere. I found the auction house which handled the sale of the cabin. There happened to be only one in the area, owned by...," Kyle glanced around the room, "can I get a drum roll, please."

Derek squinted at him. "No. Tell me."

"The owner of the auction house was Randall Smart." Kyle smiled.

"Who the hell is Randall Smart?" Derek asked.

"Yeah. Who is he?" Felicia asked.

"I'm getting to that. Randall Smart had several business numbers. One of those numbers listed in the reporter's notes belonged to the company known as Evergreen. Which only existed because of the phone number."

Kyle laughed. "Randall Smart is the brother-in-law to James Rockport."

Derek leaned against his desk. "You're killing me. Who is James Rockport?"

Kyle wiggled his eyebrows. "James Rockport later became one of Mr. Edmond senior's law firm partners." Kyle smirked at his boss' reaction. "He later bought the firm from Billy."

"That's one helluva connection to Billy's dad. Do you have current information on Randall Smart or James Rockport?" Derek asked as he scribbled their names on a notepad.

Kyle pulled a folded piece of paper from his jeans pocket. "I got them right here. I figured you would want one of these guys to call." He handed the paper to Derek.

"How did you find it?" Derek asked.

"I got very lucky. It seems the law firm did a pretty good job of hiding who owned the property, but they forgot the pesky little title transfer record. Pink Diamond Industries held the listing for the cabin, but someone still had to sign for the sale."

Derek's chest tightened. "Who and what is Pink Diamond Industries, and who signed it?"

"James Rockport. When this happened, he was two years out of law school working for Mr. Edmond. Pink Diamond Industries is a shell company."

Derek nodded to George and Kelly. "Here, you two take one. Call them at the same time. That way, they don't have a chance to speak to each other. See what you can gather over the phone. I'm sure we will have to have an in-person meeting. Ask about the incident."

He glanced between his two agents. "Whoever calls the lawyer, ask about Edmond Senior and see if he can tell you anything about the kid Klint mentioned who we think was paid off. I have a feeling this guy will clam up, but maybe he wants to save himself the embarrassment of being associated with covering up the death of a young girl."

"I will mention that," George said as he took the paper. "I'll call the lawyer."

Kelly nodded, taking the other phone number from him.

"I hoped you would say that." Derek smiled, turning his attention back to Kyle. "Do you know what Pink Diamond Industries did?" He couldn't take in a deep breath.

Kyle shook his head. "I'm combing through some files. I may have something in a few minutes. I may not."

"What about Dwight?" Derek asked.

"I followed him from Washington to Dallas and used facial recognition to comb through airport check points. I found Dwight as he left the concourse and picked up his baggage. CCTV picked him up again out front getting into a chauffeured limo." Kyle flipped through his notepad. "I tracked the limo exiting through the gates of DFW airport and saw the chauffer license in the window. I tracked it back to Fire Limousine. They have a contract with several high-end hotels in the DFW metroplex."

"Please tell me you have the hotel." Derek sat in his chair. His legs too unsteady to remain standing.

"I do. I also have video from the hotel picking Dwight up as he leaves the Anatole Hotel in a cab. I phoned the cab company and spoke with

Gerald Hanger. He informed me he wouldn't talk to me about anything over the phone. He didn't trust I was actually who I said I was." Kyle handed him a sheet of paper. "Here's all the information."

"I'll call Agent Lassiter. He's out of the Dallas office. I'll get him to get us some answers. In the meantime, hunt down our two girls and make sure they're still alive. Ask them questions. See what you can get out of them. This guy has to have an end game, and I need to know what it is. And give me whatever you get on Pink Diamond." Derek picked up his phone. He set it back down. His hand shook.

He rubbed his sticky, sweaty palms on his jeans. His pulse quickened. The vision of the car wreck clear as day now. The pink stone hanging from the rearview mirror was a pink diamond.

"I can do that," Kyle said, walking to an open computer at an empty desk.

Derek barely acknowledged him. His brain was on overdrive. He needed to take a pill. His head throbbed. The pain was right behind his eyes.

Emma stood.

Marc Anthony immediately ran to her, thinking he was going somewhere.

"How's my baby boy?" She patted his head. "I'll take you out in a minute." She walked to Derek's desk. "I found the article."

Derek beamed a big smile at her. "Really? That's great," he said.

She cocked her head at him. "You okay?"

"Yes. I'm fine. What did you find?" Derek kept his hands under his desk.

"It took me some time, but I found it. The scholarship program was started by Mary 'June Bugs' Falwell. She endowed a sizeable sum of money to the school to be used in her name as scholarships to local residents. You'll never believe what the club was called. I'm surprised I didn't remember it. The June Bugs Club." Emma giggled. "I remember now how odd I thought the name was until I learned about Mary Falwell. She came to Phoenix by way of the south. Texas, to be exact."

"I don't understand," Derek said.

"Mary's family was extremely wealthy. They were some of the original oil barons of Texas. Her father always called her June Bug. It's an old southern term used to describe a young person with no real-life experience, just kind of bumbling around. The name stuck, and she didn't want other less fortunate kids to bumble around in life, so she created this endowment at Londonvale." Emma handed the printouts she had. Including pictures of kids throughout the years who took part in the program.

Derek took the papers from her. "This is fabulous. Thanks, Emma."

She walked back to her desk. "My pleasure. I hope it helps." She gathered the leashes for the dogs. "How about we go for a quick walk?"

Lola and Marc Anthony wiggled with excitement, waiting for their afternoon stroll.

"Hold still, sillies," Emma said, laughing as she exited the building.

Derek chuckled to himself as Emma maneuvered the two big oafs. His gaze fell on the pictures of students in the Londonvale program. Shifting his thoughts from the kitchen to the photos, his breathing eased. The band around his chest was gone.

It was the second to last photo which caught his attention. Casey stood in the center of a group of kids. Three girls and four boys. She wore a t-shirt with a picture of a beetle-like creature. "Holy shit," he whispered. Casey's t-shirt clear as day now. The one she pointed to, had a beetle on it. Her arm draped over a young man. Everyone else in the picture stared forward for the camera, except for one boy in the back row. He stared at Casey.

CHAPTER FORTY-ONE

Kyle sat at his desk in the basement. This part of the job made it all worth it. He chuckled. "I should've been a criminal. I probably would make more money." He loved searching the web and uncovering nuggets of information. Information most people thought they hid from prying eyes.

"When will people learn?" He took a sip of the soda he brought down from the kitchen. Files and files scrolled across his computer. Several windows showed emails, interoffice documents, and page after page of correspondence between tons of people. Anything associated with Pink Diamond Industries popped up in windows. He quickly scanned files, closing ones which didn't pertain to what he needed. A picture popped up. One, two, then several. The same woman in all the pictures.

Kyle's throat seized from the instant dryness. He knew this woman. Her beautiful silver-blue eyes could pierce the soul of any man. She stood in a photo with Billy Edmond senior and Congressman Jackson. The caption said a night of celebration. As Kyle read the article, it became clear Billy's dad had some serious pull in the political world. William Edmond Sr., Billy's dad, had negotiated for a piece of land just outside of Phoenix. "This explains how Congressman Jackson knew Billy Jr."

The land deal would provide an opportunity for several groups to develop a property that had been deemed uninhabitable. It promised to open up previously untapped natural resources, jobs, and an economy that would increase the size of Phoenix.

Kyle sat back in his chair. His skin itched. "This makes no sense." He researched the area of this land deal, and there would've been no way they could develop this land. Just getting water to the area would've cost hundreds of millions of dollars.

As he read several other newspaper stories, another file popped up. He pulled it to the side and tried to open it. "Hmm." He looked at the file. For a moment, he thought it might be the file Kelly found earlier, but it didn't have the same extension or file lock.

Kyle opened a program on his desktop. "You can't hide from me," he laughed as he dragged the file to a program. While he waited for the program to crack the security code, he searched for more records.

At some point, a congressman, Rudolph Hagleman, had been indicted in a scandal alleging he had tried to scam money from several investors. When Hagleman took his life three years ago, the US government set up a hearing to close the case and lay the blame squarely on the shoulders of the dead congressman.

"No doubt burying everything under the rug. No one will ever know the truth. Whatever the truth is," Kyle said, typing on his keyboard. The US government could hide anything they wanted to, and he had firsthand knowledge of that power.

He stretched, arching his back and twisting his neck. Bones popped echoing throughout the basement. "That felt good." Kyle heard the ding of the program. He closed some windows he no longer needed. Shifting other open folders to the left, he opened the file.

"Oh shit." He trembled as he read a classified document. "Mother fucker. I'm in so much trouble."

CHAPTER FORTY-TWO

Wednesday evening 5:00 p.m.

George and Kelly stood in front of Derek's desk.

"This can't be good," Derek said. He spoke again when Lola started whimpering.

Everyone looked in her direction. She stood next to Marc Anthony, sad and droopy as she watched Emma put the leash on her best friend.

"We have to go home, Lola. But Marc Anthony will see you tomorrow." Emma glanced up to see the room staring at her. "I have to go. I'm having dinner with some of my girlfriends." She paused and frowned. "That is, okay? Isn't it?" She directed the question to Derek.

"Of course. Go. Have fun. We will see you tomorrow." Derek waved her off. "Lola, come here, girl."

Lola obeyed. Reluctant in her movements, she laid down next to Derek's desk. A sigh escaped as she settled down.

"It's not that bad, Lola." Kelly giggled.

"What's the bad news?" Derek asked Kelly and George.

"We didn't say we had bad news," George responded.

"Why do you jump to conclusions?" Kelly asked.

"I have a sneaking feeling. Tell me." Derek leaned back in his chair, interlocking his fingers on the top of his head.

George glanced at Kelly, who nodded. "Both Kelly and I can't speak to our guys. They are out of the country."

"Both families?" Derek asked.

"Yes," Kelly said. "The good news...."

Derek cut her off. "I thought there was no bad news? How can there be good news without bad news?"

"There isn't any bad news. Just good news." She smiled. "The good news is, they will be back this Sunday."

"And according to the housekeeper, for the Rockport family, the entire brood will arrive on Sunday at 4 p.m., and they are having a large family dinner. In which both parties will be present." George nodded. "See, good news."

"Okay. You two plan on making a visit there on Sunday. Get to the residence at 5 p.m. and interview them both. Two birds with one stone," Derek said.

"No problem," Kelly said. "Is there anything else you need?"

Derek sighed when he glanced at his new watch. A watch he hated. "No. Why don't all of you go? I'll wait for Kyle."

George snapped his fingers. "Sounds great. I'm talking to my dad tonight." He turned towards Kelly. "On Sunday, you want to get a bite to eat before we head to the Rockport home?"

"That would be great." She grabbed her keys and her gun from her drawer.

Felicia finished up a phone call, grabbing her keys. "Anyone want to go for dinner tonight?" She waited for an answer. Everyone shook their heads.

Kelly shrugged. "I'm beat. Going home and going to bed early."

"I'm having dinner at the main house, steaks," Michael said, walking towards the door. "Maybe tomorrow."

"Fine. I'll go home and go swimming." Felicia followed the others out the door.

"Make sure you guys come in by eight tomorrow morning. I want to track down as many people as we can," Derek yelled after them. Several raised their hands, letting him know they heard him. He glanced down at Lola. "We'll go home soon, sweetie."

Lola sighed without even looking up.

Derek opened the file with the picture of Casey. All those times, his subconscious told him about her. He must have seen a picture of her during the last few days of the investigation and cued in on it.

Still rattled by the car wreck scene, he rationalized what he saw. He'd remembered he saw a picture of parents at Billy's home. Maybe that and Dr. Callahan telling him about their car wreck made his brain fill in the rest. And the pink diamond hanging from the mirror, pure coincidence or conjecture.

"Derek. How's the day going?"

"Pretty good, Dr. Chelsea."

"Wait, you only call me Dr. Chelsea when you're talking to me professionally. What's going on, Derek?"

"I want to have that CT scan you've been hounding me about. But I want it off the record." Derek craned his head, listening for Kyle coming up the basement stairs.

"Derek."

"I'm not messing up my career for nothing. The minute I have a CT scan, I'm on desk duty."

Dr. Chelsea sighed into the phone. "Are the hallucinations getting worse?"

"Yeah. If that's what you want to call them. I'm sure it's my mind needing to heal. This bump on my head hurts. Listen, I just want to know. I promise, if something comes back, we can go through the proper channels and get it in my record. Just do this for me. Please." Derek slumped in his chair.

"I don't think this is a good idea."

"Fine. I won't do it at all."

"I didn't say I wouldn't do it. I simply said it was a bad idea. Give me a few hours. I have a friend I can ask. Can you be ready anytime?"

"Yes. Just say when and I will be there." Derek paused. Silence filled the line. "Thank you, Ronald." He hung up. He didn't want to answer more questions. He knew Ronald would help him. He pushed his chair back to check on Kyle when he heard the footsteps coming towards him.

Kyle rounded the corner.

Derek looked up, smiling. Kyle's face drooped, and his shoulders hunched over. "Oh no, Kyle. What did you do?"

CHAPTER FORTY-THREE

Congressman Jackson walked into the bar on the Phoenix city limits. His party was seated at the back, tucked away in the corner. He took a seat across from the man. It was rare he would call for a meeting in such a public place. Why he was even in Phoenix, Jackson had no clue. But they could write the meeting off as two friends having a meal together, should anyone recognize them.

"What can I get for you?" the server asked, looking at the congressman.

"Double whiskey on the rocks." Jackson peered at his colleague, who waved him off. "Thank you." He waited for her to be out of earshot. "What are you doing here? And why did you want to meet?"

"I had to come out here for something with Director Jessup. And I needed clarification."

"What about Assistant Director Fretz?" Congressman Jackson asked.

"What about him?"

"Won't he be suspicious you're out here?" Jackson studied the man before him.

"No. I don't have to check in with him. He works for me."

"What clarification did you need?"

"Are there any files out there?"

"No. Not that I'm aware of. Billy had those scrubbed. Which should be clear since he received clearance for the hearing." Jackson glanced over his shoulder. The dinner crowd filled the restaurant. Turning back to his friend. "Why?"

"I'm worried about Reed." The man took a sip of his water.

"Don't worry about him. He's only after Billy's killer. He has no interest in the Balderro case."

"How can you be so sure? That man is like a bulldog with a fucking bone. He doesn't let anything go. I still don't know why you requested him."

"Because I owe it to Billy's dad. He helped me get to where I am. I wasn't going to let his son's killer go free." Jackson smiled up at the server. "Thank you." His gaze shifted. Tilting his head slightly, he watched her walk away. He turned his attention to his companion. "Not after what happened to Senior."

"I couldn't stop that. He got way too greedy. If he had just done what was expected, none of this would've happened. There wouldn't be a fucking case in front of Congress." The man pulled an envelope from his pocket. "This should remind you of what's important."

Congressman Jackson opened the envelope. Several pictures of Elizabeth and her family fell out. He lifted his stare and focused on the man sitting across from him. "You touch her or her family, and you will disappear."

"Don't threaten me. I will not go to jail for this. I have my career to think about."

Jackson reached over the table and grabbed both of the man's wrists. His vice-like grip made the man squirm. "You got into bed with someone you shouldn't have. That's on you. But if anything happens to her, jail is the last thing you need to be worried about." He stared at the man. "I know all about your role in the Balderro case. And if you think I don't have a piece of insurance out there to protect me and those I hold dear, then you are more stupid than a box of rocks."

The man yanked his hands away. Rubbing each wrist. "You said there were no files."

"There aren't any files that anyone can find. I didn't say I didn't have any files." Congressman Jackson swallowed his whiskey and stood. He leaned over and flicked the man's ear. "I'll say it one more time. Let sleeping dogs lie, and you won't have anything to worry about. Touch her, and you and your family will disappear. Am I clear?"

"I just want to protect what I have. That's all."

"Well, then I suggest you play nice." Jackson walked out of the bar. The sunlight, bright and hot, was beating down on him. He couldn't wait to get out of Phoenix. He brought in Reed for more than just Billy. But no one will ever know that. He inhaled the sticky air. Just one more day and back to Washington. And hopefully back to Elizabeth.

CHAPTER FORTY-FOUR

Kyle pulled a chair over and sat in front of Derek's desk. "I didn't know."

"Didn't know what, Kyle?"

"I searched for anything regarding Pink Diamond Industries. It pulled in stuff from all over. Some had nothing to with what we wanted."

Derek watched as his agent struggled. "Kyle. It can't be that bad. Tell me."

"It's bad. Lizzy may be in trouble."

Derek sat up straight. "What do you mean?"

"She knew Edmond Sr. And...."

"And what?"

"The congressman knew Senior as well." Kyle looked up. He blinked. "There's more."

"Start from the beginning." Derek reached into his satchel and removed a bottle of pills. He popped two into his mouth and washed it down with the last sip of his warm soda.

"There were several pictures of Lizzy with both Congressman Jackson and Billy's father, before he died. They were at several functions for Pink Diamond Industries. There were a ton of events celebrating a land deal."

Derek's pulse sped up. "Land deal?"

"Yeah. The Balderro land deal."

"Fuck."

"It seems Edmond Sr. spearheaded the deal. He had a shit ton of investors who put millions—I mean, mega millions into this deal. They were promised untapped resources and building Phoenix's boundaries out further. Allowing for all kinds of growth and production of minerals and other resources. But it was all a lie."

"All a lie?" Derek took several deep breaths.

"Yeah. There was no way they could develop this parcel. Just getting water out there would require a shit ton of money, it was a scam. I don't know if Congressman Jackson was involved in the actual deal, or if even knew it was a scam. However, he attended several events, and he's mentioned as part of the original team of investors."

Kyle leaned back in his chair. "Derek, the search revealed a file. I thought nothing of it. It wasn't marked with any official markings. At first, I thought it might have been the locked file from earlier. The one Kelly found, but it wasn't. Hell, it shouldn't have even come up. I guess my search tapped into a file on an old server."

"I'm not following. And old server, where?"

"In the FBI." Kyle couldn't catch his breath. "I ran the file through a filter which unlocks secure files. It opened this one."

"Okay. Can they trace it to you? I mean can they find out you were on the system?"

Kyle shook his head. "No. They can't. When I search," Kyle winced, he knew he would be in trouble for this, "Whenever I search for files, I'm a ghost. I can get in and get out, and no one will know."

Derek's eyes squinted. "You're a hacker."

"Yeah. In another life. I got into some trouble in college. The FBI wanted my help with something. I traded jail for this."

Derek laughed. "Holy shit. Does anyone know this? I know it wasn't in your file."

Kyle shook his head again. "No. Only Director Carlson. My files were wiped clean. I attended the Academy as a special enlistee. I coasted through it—all under the guise of a techy position. Carlson retired shortly after. My life went on as a tech agent."

Derek stared at him. His blond hair, a little long for the average FBI agent, made perfect sense now. "I don't want you to breathe a word of this to anyone. Not your skill set or what you found. Not a peep. Am I clear?"

Kyle pretended to twist a key in front of his lips. "You won't hear me mention it."

"What's in the rest of the file?"

"Someone in the FBI knows the truth. I could tell from the files a lot of money went into bank accounts. There aren't any numbers, account numbers, but you can tell. There are ID tags identifying banking codes. Listen, someone in this organization was in on the deal. They knew it was a scheme. I can't tell where the file originated. Whoever hid it thought they were hiding it on a secure server." Kyle ran his fingers through his hair, pulling on the ends. "I only use my skills to find the bad guys. I promise."

Derek's face softened. "Listen, I don't question your character one bit. Don't worry about that. And this goes nowhere. But I need your help."

"I'm willing to do whatever you need," Kyle said.

"Hide the file. Somewhere only you can find it."

"I don't have to. My searches clone files. I never remove the original file. I duplicate it. The original is still where they hid it. Unless they have a hack do what I did, they will open it and see the file and not even have a clue." Kyle breathed out.

"Can you put a tracer on the file?" Derek asked.

"I can. But that may increase the chance of being caught. I can embed a tag on the file to send me an alert when the file is opened. It can tell me the IP address the person used while accessing the file. It can't tell me who, just where. If a computer geek stumbles on it, he might think it's there because someone opened it at one point."

"Do you think the person who hid the file has skills?"

"No. They would've hidden it better," Kyle said.

"Okay. Put a tracer on it. Whatever you think will work. Maybe someone will open it." Derek thought about what he asked Kyle to do. It could blow up in their faces. "I need something else from you."

"Whatever you need."

"I need you to find out all you can on Jackson. I also need you to see if you can get any records or activity on Edmond Sr.'s vehicle before it crashed. Any maintenance reports. Anything at all. There's no hurry, wait until after this case is finished. I just need you to get me the information." Derek eyed the agent.

"Why? What do you think happened?"

"You know, from this case file, Billy's parents died in a car crash outside of Phoenix. But what you don't know and what no one knows is I think someone tampered with the car. I can't tell you how I know. But I just know. And now, with what you have told me about his involvement in the Balderro case, I'm sure they were murdered. I think we have two separate cases about to converge. The Edmonds are smack in the middle of both." Derek sighed.

"This is going to get nasty. Who in the FBI has the power to make this go away? You realize, someone we work for has not only helped set this up, someone took out Billy's parents and Congressman Hagleman. He was the only one indicted for the Balderro scandal." Kyle's brow wrinkled at Derek's expression. "What did I say?"

"Wait, Congressman Hagleman committed suicide three years ago."

"I don't think so. The reports said he hung himself over the banister of his mansion. I looked at the photos." He pulled a jump drive out of his pocket. "Everything is on this. I didn't go through every file. I stopped after I realized what I had." He slid it over to Derek. "Someone covered up his murder. There is no way he committed suicide. Any first-year medical student could look at the markings on his neck and see from the angle. Someone lifted the man over the railing then dropped him. Look at the file, Derek."

In for a penny, in for a pound, Derek thought. "Listen, I need to find out something else. But I want it kept between you and me. At least until I have more information." Derek took the picture of Casey and the other kids from the June Bugs club. He pointed to the kid in the back row. The one who stared at Casey. "I need to know who this kid is. Actually, all these kids, but him in particular." "I have nothing to go on. I can't ask anyone from the school about him."

"I don't understand? Why not?"

"I don't know if our killer is in this group, but I think our killer has skills. He either knows how to chase people or find out information on people. I'm not sure but I can't take the chance of him finding out what we are doing."

Kyle inhaled, blowing out the air through his pursed lips. "Get the fuck out. How? No one put anything in the file."

"And it won't go in the file. Just trust me. I think our killer has some kind of security clearance. Or, he has the same abilities you do. Don't ask me how I know." Chrissy flashed in his mind. "Right now, it's just a hunch. He may not work for us or have anything to do with us. But if I go looking for him, he will know. I can't risk him getting away by going underground or killing more people. He's after something. He has to finish this. I can't have any more dead people on my conscious, I have enough already."

Kyle frowned at his boss's statement but knew better than to push it. "I'll see what I can do. I can run backgrounds on everyone. Most of this information is in the school files. What isn't, I can find fairly easily." Kyle stood.

"Don't let anyone know you're looking at him. I'm not sure about this guy, but something about him has me thinking he isn't your average private dick." Derek stood and walked around his desk. "Don't mention anything about Pink Diamond at all. Anywhere. Put nothing you found regarding the land deal in this case file or anywhere on our system. Wipe it from yours."

Kyle nodded.

"Don't worry, Kyle. Knowing what I know of you, you covered your ass. I'll keep you safe."

"I believe you, Derek. I'm not worried about me. I'm more worried about you."

Derek crossed his arms. "Why me?"

"Congressman Jackson specifically requested you to handle this case. Now either he did it to monitor you or to place himself in a position of power. I don't know if he thought you would uncover the Balderro connection, or you would just solve the murder of his friend. Either way, I don't think it was coincidence he asked for you not to mention the connection to Lizzy. Something isn't right."

"Kyle?"

"Yeah?" he said as he turned towards Derek.

"I sure am glad you're one of the good guys."

Kyle laughed. "Yeah, me too."

Derek looked at his watch. "Will you take Lola home for me?"

Kyle smiled. "Sure. C'mon Lola. Let's go."

Lola jumped up and ran to the door, following Kyle out.

Derek sat back at his desk and pulled out the SAT phone. He dialed a number and waited for the beeps. He put in his code and laid the phone on the desk.

It rang once.

"We need to talk," Derek said.

"Is it bad?" the man on the other end asked.

"Yeah. It's very bad."

CHAPTER FORTY-FIVE

Wednesday evening 5:30 p.m.

Dr. Chelsea tapped his finger on his desk as the phone rang on the other end of the line.

"Well, now. What can I do for you, Ronald? How long has it been?"

"Too long. You still owe me for that round of golf I won."

Laughter roared through the phone. "You cheated. You always do."

"Listen, I need a personal favor." Dr. Chelsea sighed.

"What's wrong, Ronald."

"Nothing's wrong. At least not with me. Jeffrey, do you still run the CT clinic on the south-side of town?"

"I do. I have another one closer to your office now. Just opened it. Not actually taking clients at the moment."

"Perfect. Would you be able to run a scan on a friend of mine?"

Dr. Jeffrey Coats huffed out a breath. "Are you still working with the FBI?"

"Yes."

"I'm guessing this can't go in a record?"

"No. I'll pay for the scan."

"No need. Give me a week. The new CT machine will be online then. We won't open the clinic for several weeks."

"I can wait. I can't thank you enough. I owe you for this."

"You could just play golf with me this weekend. I need a partner for a tournament. My guy backed out at the last moment."

"I could do that. Thanks, Jeffrey. I really appreciate it."

"I'll text the date and time. Oh, and Ronald," he paused.

"Yeah?"

"No cheating. Okay?"

"I never cheat."

"Famous last words."

Dr. Chelsea laughed when the line went dead. "Everyone just hates to lose to me." He texted Derek. Letting him know it would be a few days until he could get the scan. Ronald wondered what made Derek change his mind about getting it after weeks of arguing with him. A small pang of worry settled in his gut. It had to be bad, if Derek was willing to risk his career to find out. A career Ronald knew Derek couldn't survive without.

CHAPTER FORTY-SIX

Wednesday 6 pm

Derek parked his car on the backside of the National Memorial Cemetery. The sun had begun its descent in the westward sky. Looking back towards the south and Phoenix, the Piestewa Peak area made the perfect backdrop for the dark burnt orange colors bursting across the sky.

Mesmerized by the hues of color, Derek lifted his head towards the evening sky, inhaling the crisp fresh air. The cemetery and the distance from the city limits filled him with a calmness he hadn't felt since this case started.

As he turned to head to his meeting, the calmness and peaceful moment dissipated. The man across the lawn waited for him. His silhouette was shadowed by the darkening sky. His pulse increased, racing and thudding against his temples as he walked. He nodded as he stepped off the pathway leading to his friend. "Thanks for coming out here."

Assistant Director Fretz stretched as he moved away from the Eternal Flame memorial. "I figured if you wanted to meet here, it had to be important."

Derek positioned himself where he could see the drive leading to the center of the cemetery. "I need you to be straight with me. Did you know Edmond senior scammed millions from investors regarding the Balderro deal?"

Assistant Director Fretz bristled. His lips pursed together in a tight, thin line. "I don't know what you're talking about."

"Bullshit. That's complete bullshit, and you know it."

The AD looked towards the sky. "I think this area has some of the most beautiful sunsets I've ever seen."

Derek stuck his hands in the front pockets of his jeans. "Don't fuck with me on this. We go back a long way. A very long way. I expect you to be honest. If nothing else."

"Derek, you need to stay away from this."

"I can't. Not when Lizzy may be in danger."

Assistant Director Fretz's brow wrinkled. "I don't know what you mean. She has nothing to do with this. Never did."

"She went to several functions with both Billy Sr. and Congressman Jackson. Even though she may have had nothing to do with the scam directly, someone who knows her connection to the congressman could mistake her involvement in the handling of the money."

He shifted his weight. "Someone took out Edmond Sr. and his wife in a car crash and made Congressman Hagleman's murder look like a suicide. I don't for one minute think they won't take out anyone else they think knows something." Derek watched the AD's facial movements.

"Where did you hear they were murdered?"

"C'mon. You have to know. You're a fucking director in the FBI. If you looked at any file on this case, you had to know."

AD Fretz shook his head, waving his hands through the air. "No. I don't have a fucking clue what you're talking about. I know only about the scam. And from what Associate Deputy Director told me, Hagleman scammed everyone. Now, maybe William Sr. played a part in getting the money, but I never saw the file on Hagleman's death. That was classified above my paygrade." The AD paced. "I knew something was off. I just wasn't in the loop." He squared up with his friend and colleague. "You have to believe me."

"Tell me what you do know."

Fretz sighed. "I had heard about the land deal. I paid little attention to it. I didn't care. I knew Edmond Sr. had a lot of connections. When he and his wife died in the car crash, things changed regarding the land deal.

"Information was slow in coming, but right away, things shifted. What once was the deal of the century for several well-connected politicians became a big mess. Congressman Hagleman, who had been directly associated with the investors, started speaking publicly about the land deal. He started mentioning he thought there was no validity to the plan."

Derek squinted at him. "And what happened when he started saying all this—regarding the others involved?"

"Things started moving, and fast. News releases started coming out about Hagleman and his involvement in trying to scam money from investors. The more he yelled he had nothing to do with it, the more shit came out against him."

"How can you sit there and say you didn't know what was going on?

It doesn't take a rocket scientist to recognize the beginnings of a cover-up."

AD Fretz paced again. "I wasn't involved in any of the dealings. The Associate Deputy and his fucking cronies handled all that. I'm an assistant director. I only know what they want me to know. Information flowed out to the department heads on a need-to-know basis. And I wasn't in the loop."

"Have you seen any files on the land deal?"

"Only scrubbed files. Again, the need-to-know basis. I was told enough to help with getting Billy Jr. ready for the hearings."

Derek zeroed in on his boss. "What exactly was Billy Jr. going to testify about?"

Fretz hung his head. The silence hung heavy.

"Just tell me."

"Billy Jr. had information about the dealings from his father's files. He produced information for a meeting when he was notified the Justice Department wanted an accounting of money during that time frame. Billy said he had proof his father never received money."

"What did you see?"

"Derek, let this go."

"I can't."

"Damn it. I should've trusted my gut." The AD pulled a pack of cigarettes from his pocket.

"I thought you quit?"

"I did."

"Why should you have trusted your gut? Something had to make you question what the hell was going on."

"Billy Jr. had been vetted, meaning the committee cleared him to testify. They took all the evidence he provided and decided he had viable information to help get the heat off several high-ranking officials involved in the land deal."

"Except for Hagleman," Derek said.

"I knew when Billy Jr. had all suspicion against his father dropped, and the committee cleared him, essentially giving him immunity from anything that may come out while testifying, I knew Hagleman was the sacrificial lamb."

"And you did nothing?"

"Are you fucking kidding me? Do what? Take my hunches to my boss who was the one spearheading all of this shit? I'm not like you, Derek. I don't just do what I want. I have a family to think about. It had nothing to do with me."

"That's a fucking copout. What about doing the right thing?"

"Tell me, Derek. What would that do? If I took my theories to my boss, whom I'm pretty sure is up to his fucking neck in this shit, and I told him what I thought. What the hell do you think would happen to me? To my family? Especially if what you said about Hagleman's suicide is true."

Derek took a pack of gum from his pants pocket. He placed two pieces in his mouth while he inhaled the last bit of cigarette smoke lingering in the air. "This is all kinds of fucked up."

"How do you know any of this?" AD Fretz asked.

"Information I've found while searching for Billy Edmond's killer, who by the way, is killing several people because of a fucking prank gone wrong in high school. This information led me to a file regarding Pink Diamond Industries."

AD Fretz's posture straightened. "How did you find the company?"

Derek cocked his head to the side. "Why does that matter?"

"Derek, that company was tied to Hagleman. It should have nothing to do with your murder case."

Derek laughed. "Well, now. I guess whoever was involved in this didn't do his fucking research when they were setting up the coverup. Pink Diamond Industries was a shell company Billy's dad used to help hide the accidental killing of a young girl in high school. That's what led me to find the information about the Balderro case."

"Bury what you know. Don't mention Pink Diamond Industries in any report. If you do, you will have a target on your back and Lizzy's as well."

Derek's stomach rolled. Bile crept up his throat. He glanced around the cemetery. The hair on his neck stood on end.

"Can you keep it out of your files? And it's not to protect me. I know I did nothing except not speaking up, but no one knows you know this information right now. Keep it that way."

Derek put another piece of gum in his mouth. Shaking off the feeling of being watched. "I can do that."

AD Roger Fretz winced. "You have to believe me. I didn't know what was going on behind the scenes of the Balderro case until it was too late." AD Fretz lit another cigarette. "My wife doesn't know I'm smoking again. I'm more afraid of her finding out than this fucking land deal shit."

Derek chuckled. "I'm only going to put what I need to in the files for this case. I'm not giving any information to Congressman Jackson, either." He pointed at his boss. "And I don't want you giving him any updates at all. I don't know what his involvement in the Balderro case is, and I don't trust him."

"This is your case. You run with it. Just don't mention Pink Diamond or the Balderro connection to anyone involved in your investigation. I'll do whatever I need to," the AD said.

Derek glanced at his watch. "I need to head back to the city. You need to protect yourself, Roger. If you have anything, any file, any information you need to make sure no one knows. I have a feeling this is going to get ugly. I don't know where this will lead."

"I want you to know. I should've said something. But I had no proof. I had feelings, but feelings won't get you shit in this business." AD Fretz walked down the path with Derek. "I want you to trust me."

Derek stopped and turned towards his friend. "Do you have any information on Congressman Jackson?"

"I know Billy's dad helped him a lot when he first came on the political scene. He helped fund several of his campaigns over the years. From what I have heard, the Edmonds had connections most of us only dream of."

"Do you know if Edmond Sr. had ties to the Assistant Deputy?"

AD Fretz sighed. "I don't know. I think they had dealings before the ADD got to be the ADD. But I have never wanted to ask. I didn't know how or who to ask." Fretz reached out and grabbed Derek's arm. "If you think the ADD is involved in this, don't go asking questions. The ADD has some powerful friends. And he has ways of finding out everything. Just let this go, Derek. You have to let this one go." AD Fretz stopped at his vehicle. "Can you promise me that?"

Derek stood several feet from the AD. "I don't know if I can do that." He sighed, letting his shoulders droop. "I need to concentrate on this case. This killer isn't done yet. And I have to stop him. The Balderro case and all that goes with it, I'm going to set it aside, for now." He walked away and turned back to his boss. "I will promise you one thing. If Lizzy is in any kind of danger, I will protect her at all costs. And if that means I have to kill someone to do it. I will." He turned and walked back to his car.

The sun now gone, and darkness engulfed the cemetery. He watched his director drive away as he entered his vehicle. He spit out his gum before he closed the door. His thoughts turned to Lizzy as he sat in the silence. The only woman he has ever loved. The only woman he would love. He meant what he said. He would kill to protect her. Even if it meant he went to jail. Or worse.

CHAPTER FORTY-SEVEN

Derek walked into his house.

Lola stood waiting for him in front of the cabinet that held her dog food bin.

"Oh, girl. Did I forget to tell Kyle to feed you?" He placed his pizza and his satchel on the counter and filled her bowl. "I'm sorry, sweetie." He grabbed two beers and a bottle of water from the fridge, the pizza, his bag and headed to the living room.

Turning on the DVD player, he started another episode of Star Trek. Taking several bites of pizza, he opened the case folder. The entire file was on his laptop, but he always preferred the feel of paper when researching a case. Something about holding it in his hand made him feel more connected.

He thumbed through the notes, settling on the picture of the June Bugs group. He focused on one kid. "Are you my killer?" He had no clue if his assumption even had merit. However, this kid captured Derek's attention, and he couldn't shake the feeling he'd seen him before.

Tossing the photo on the table, he guzzled a beer. His head throbbed. He rubbed his temples before picking up another slice. Glancing down at his bag, he shook his head. "No. No pills." He threw a sizeable piece of crust to Lola. "Don't tell your mama how much pizza you eat."

Thinking of Lizzy, he mulled over what Kyle had told him. He didn't for one minute think she had anything to do with the land deal or anything illegal. In his heart, he knew she wouldn't stand for Congressman Jackson's behavior if she thought he did anything illegal.

Yet he knew men like Jackson. And he knew they could hide things. His mind drifted back to the cemetery and his conversation with his boss. He had known Roger a long time, and he believed him. Derek leaned back against the couch. The throbbing in his head, now an intense stabbing pain. He reached up and touched the bruise on the back of his head. He winced as the pain radiated outward. He breathed in through his nose and out through his mouth.

He continued breathing, finally giving in. "Screw it." He reached into his satchel and pulled out his prescription of pills. Staring at the bottle, he sighed, rounding his shoulders forward. Holding the bottle in his hand, he grabbed his beer off the table.

Lola stared up from her resting spot on the floor at his feet.

"Don't judge me."

The brown boxer twisted her head to the side, listening to him not with an air of judgment, but pure love.

"Stop it. You're making me feel guilty." He threw her a sizable piece of pizza. The heaviness of her stare gone; his body relaxed. His grip tightened around the pill bottle. He couldn't shut his mind off. The pills helped, and they helped with the pain. His phone rang as he was finishing off his beer.

"Reed."

"Agent Lassiter here, from Dallas."

"Agent Lassiter, what do you have?" Derek set the pills on the table.

"I got your email and called around. Your hunch was right. The ME's office had a John Doe. I took the information you had on your guy, Dwight Black. It's a match. Our dead guy is the guy you're looking for."

"What's the cause of death?"

"The ME said he believes he died from blunt force trauma."

"I don't follow. Doesn't he know for sure?"

"Well, this guy had some damage done. It looks like your killer had some fun before he bashed in his skull. The ME said he had been tortured before the final blows occurred. Several broken bones in his legs and arms. The guy's back had been broken in two places. Listen, you have a sick fuck on your hands."

"Tell me about it. I need all the reports. We will handle notifying the parents. Send me the name of who they need to contact to arrange for their son to be brought home."

"No problem. I have the file ready to go."

Derek heard typing on a keyboard.

"Just sent it," Agent Lassiter said.

"I appreciate your help. Tell me where he was found."

"There's a park outside Dallas proper. It's an old ballpark on the outskirts of town. He'd been left behind the dugout. It looked like a drug deal gone bad to the local cops. Anyway, you should have the file."

Derek pulled his laptop from his bag. "Thanks very much for running this down for me. I owe you one."

"I'm just glad it's not my case."

"I wish it wasn't mine either." Derek snapped his fingers. "One more thing. Did you find out anything about the limousine?"

"No. Dead end there. Whoever hired the company to pick up your dead guy paid in cash. By courier. They gave the owner a hefty tip, so he just took the job. Kept it off the books."

"Okay. That helps a lot. Thanks. I'll talk to you later." Derek hung up the phone. His leg bounced up and down while he checked his email. His headache gone, he grabbed another slice of pizza. Opening the file, he searched the notes from the ME. The injuries were similar to Billy and Greg Burks. All the victim's murders were up close and personal. Except Billy's parents.

"Why wouldn't you kill them like the others?" Derek asked. He scrolled through the file. "Did you even kill his parents, or did someone involved in the land deal do it?" He rubbed the back of his neck. His jaw clenched. "I'm missing something." He grabbed a second beer taking a long sip.

He scanned all the pieces of paper from the file. The picture of Casey watched his every move. He took a deep breath, calming his racing pulse. He leaned back against the sofa and closed his eyes, letting his mind drift.

This time, he didn't fight it. He let all the mental notes flash across his mind like a movie on a screen. His muscles tensed as he saw bits and pieces of the case. He pushed back, forcing himself to relax, to be vulnerable. His pulse quickened as he let himself go. Flashes of interviews, notes, pictures of crime scenes bombarded him. He shook his head, breathing deep.

Images of the dead, the blood, the destruction hit him hard. The tension in his face locked his jaw in place. He tasted the blood at the back of his throat. The smell of burning rubber and metal filled his nostrils as the images from Billy's parent's car wreck flashed before him. He heard the mother's screams. His body jumped as the car smashed into the canyon floor.

The image changed to Casey, crying in the closet. His chest tightened. His breathing labored. Just as fast, another sensory explosion hit him. Chrissy's throat bled. He heard her gurgling for air. The next vision had him in his truck on the old country road in Tennessee. The girl looked up just as he hit her.

His eyes popped open. He couldn't catch his breath. "Fuck." Sweat covered his skin. At some point, Lola had moved near him and her head rested on his leg. He rubbed her fur, trying to slow his pulse and regain himself. None of it made sense. He concentrated on what he saw, pushing the emotions to the bottom, along with Chrissy and Tennessee. He focused on the crash. It stuck out the most. *Why?*

He opened the file, searching for all the notes on Pink Diamond Industries. "Where are they?" He snapped his fingers. "They aren't in this file." He reached into the front pocket of his jeans and removed the jump drive Kyle had given him.

He didn't know what he hoped to find, but the need to search the drive was overwhelming. He felt the flush of heat on his cheeks. "It's got to be here. Something has to be here." He combed for anything linking to Pink Diamond, Casey, or Evergreen. He tapped the down arrow, highlighting file after file.

"Wait." He scrolled back up a few files. Derek stared at the computer. His pulse thumped against the sides of his head. His chest tightened as his fingers hovered above the file name. Everything around him slowed as if time crept to a halt.

CHAPTER FORTY-EIGHT

Late Wednesday night

Derek clicked on the file labeled Casey Evergreen. The file opened with line after line of payments made to an account. There was a partial account number but nothing identifying. At least that he could tell.

There were various deposits, but the first several seemed to be for random amounts—a few hundred here, maybe a thousand there. About two months after the payments started, the amounts became regular and for tens of thousands of dollars made monthly and sometimes twice a month.

"That's a hell of a lot of money," Derek said as he searched the rest of the file for anything, telling him where the payments came from and where they went. He could follow the money. One problem, if he asked for a warrant to search for this account, he would have to prove where the information came from. And this file didn't exist.

Derek thought of asking Kyle for help, but he had already asked so much of the young tech. He skimmed everything. He noticed the payments stopped abruptly. "Wait, why?" They started thirteen months before Billy's parent's car wreck and stopped when they died.

The dates for these deposits and withdrawals time perfectly with the Balderro case. Billy's parents have nothing to do with Billy's death. They were killed because William Sr. stole money. And someone didn't like that. Derek wondered what and how much Congressman Jackson really knew about the Balderro case.

Taking Billy's parents out of the mix, Derek concentrated on Billy. He grabbed the file from his table and searched for the financials for Billy. George had gathered everything from Aleshire earlier in the week. His knee bounced as he read through the record. "Nothing. How is that possible?"

He scrolled through the file on the jump drive. He found no other payments. He grabbed the file from the table, searching for what he wanted. "Fuck." He shuffled papers around. He opened the file on the computer. "I'll be damned."

A spreadsheet listing several of Billy's business accounts had withdrawals and deposits. Derek stared at the records. Billy started depositing odd amounts into a business account three months after his parents died.

Within a few months, he started paying someone five thousand dollars a month from this same account. "I bet you knew all along what your father did with the money from the land deal. You hid the money from Congress, to cover your ass. Didn't you, Billy?"

Derek guzzled the rest of his beer. The records indicated Billy made the payments for the same amount to various businesses. Although he believed these were to the same person, just different names to keep the questions at bay. Some were even listed as charity. He scribbled on his pad of paper. He would have to call Aleshire and ask some questions without raising red flags.

If Congress didn't see this account or thought nothing of it, he shouldn't have any trouble following the money from this account backwards. He paused. Did he really want to do that now? If he set off any alarms indicating he and his team were getting close to the Balderro case, he could put Kyle or Lizzy in harm's way.

"No. We can just take this at face value. We can see Billy shuffled money around to pay someone. If someone really wants to know who, they can hunt down Billy's financials." He opened his bottle of water and finished the last slice of cold pizza. He could at least find the account the payments were made to. That shouldn't be connected to the land deal and, if he was correct, it should be connected to the killer. He hoped Aleshire would have some information as to who received these payments. He didn't even know if they could find the account in question. Billy definitely hid his money well.

Searching the records, he found payments from Billy stopped a few months before his death. He opened another file on his computer, looking for the financials of the other victims. "I can't fucking believe this." His chest hardened as the breath of air stuck in his lungs. He and his entire team had missed this. He scribbled more notes.

Each victim had payments made to some sort of security business. They ranged in amounts. Some had regular payments of five hundred dollars, some a few thousand. None were the five thousand dollars Billy paid. All looked like random monthly payments. "This is how the killer funded everything."

Derek made notations next to each victim and when or if they paid, when they stopped payments, and when they died. The first three victims, Terry Curren, Xavier Blackman, and Albie Hawkes had small payments. Timmy Cowan and Arthur Brandis made small payments before stopping after about seven months each. Coombes paid nothing.

"That may have been what got you killed. That also may account for why the reports said you started freaking out at the start of some phone calls." Derek believed Michael was on the right track with Coombe's death not being a suicide.

Billy stopped making deposits into his business account shortly after the publicity started regarding the land deal, leading Derek to suspect Billy hid the rest of the Balderro money somewhere. He wondered if Billy hid the money to protect his father's legacy, or so he wouldn't go to jail himself. Either way, it seemed clear Billy knew his father stole money from the land deal. And Billy used the funds his father took to pay someone regarding what happened to Casey.

Greg Burks threw this whole theory out of whack, though. Derek saw from his financial records Greg had made regular payments of three thousand dollars to Camden LLC. Derek searched the internet for a Camden LLC and found nothing. Not that he had expected to. However, Greg stopped payments almost two years before his death. "Why didn't you kill him when he stopped the payments?"

Derek looked through the record but couldn't find anything to explain the gap in time. Again, he searched the internet. Skimming over the stories about Greg's murder, Derek found an obscure story about Greg Burks and his travels across Europe and East Asia. He had spent the better part of two years traveling abroad. Several interviews he did indicated he wanted to find himself. "Okay. Now I know why you had to wait."

Knowing this gave his theory credibility. Yet Derek didn't think their unsub killed because he didn't get his money. No, the money just gave him a reason to kill. "It gave you the permission you needed. Maybe even relieved you of the guilt."

Derek checked the other players from the team. Julian Mosley, Gordan Padden, Martin Lucey, and Klint Kenyon had nothing in their financials indicating they ever made payments. "Okay, that tells me our killer knew who was at the cabin and who wasn't. Or maybe he just held the inner circle responsible. And if that is the case, our killer must be very intimate with the team."

Something George had said about the coach thumped at the back of Derek's skull. He opened the computer file containing everything on Coach McMillan. There were no payments made to anyone via the Coach's financials. "This can't be right. And if it is, it throws my whole theory out," he said, tossing his pen on the table.

He scratched Lola's head as she laid next to him on the sofa. "If you killed them because they didn't pay you the money you wanted, why haven't you killed the coach? Or better yet, why hasn't the coach made any payments?"

Lola raised her eyebrows as he kept talking.

"If it isn't all about the money, then what is it about?"

Lola lifted her head and nudged him when he quit scratching her ears.

"What? Don't you have any answers for me?" He sat back, glancing at his watch, 2 a.m. "Shit." He closed his eyes, rubbing them as he rested his head against the sofa. Some pieces of the puzzle were falling into place. However, now he had more questions than ever before.

He kept coming back to what Bailey Hodgens said about Coach. He wasn't a good guy at all. Baily said he would do anything to save his ass and earn a buck. This entire case kept coming back to the coach, but he didn't know why or how.

He struggled to shut his mind off. He thought about moving to his bed, but he couldn't muster the energy to be bothered. Star Trek played in the background, and his relaxed body wrestled with his overstressed mind. His biggest concern came back to how he would move forward, keeping what he knew about the Balderro case hidden and keep Kyle out of harm's way.

Lying to his team weighed heavily on him. He didn't like it; he didn't like when people lied to him. But he was also aware the more people who knew, the more would be in danger. He drifted into darkness as his body sank into the sofa, and his mind rested.

Jolted awake by his phone ringing, Derek blinked, trying to wake up. Fumbling for his phone from his satchel, he grunted as he answered. "Reed."

"Agent Reed, this is Sargent Mullens with the Arizona State Police. We had an alarm go off at your FBI office. It looks like they have arrested an armed intruder."

"I'll be right down. Keep the officers there until I get there. Please."

"Will do. They have him in custody. They'll wait for you."

CHAPTER FORTY-NINE

Thursday early morning 4:30 a.m.

Kyle rubbed the sleep from his eyes. Unable to rest, he had come in early. He saw Derek asleep on his sofa and almost woke him to talk but decided against it and came to the office instead. The events of the day before had him rattled.

Sitting at his desk, he pulled up each of the students in the photo. He figured this would keep his mind occupied and his worry at bay. Plus, knowing who this kid in the photo was might go a long way in helping to close this case.

Starting with the one kid, Derek suspected, Kyle started the search. As data scrolled across one screen, he set up searches for the other kids in the photo. He had their names from the school records from the year in question. Quickly looking over each kid's grades, these were no dummies, Kyle thought. Each kid carried a GPA of 4.0 or better.

"Wow," Kyle said. "You guys were super smart brainiacs." Report after report scrolled across the screen. Kyle grabbed a soda from the little fridge under his desk. He grew tired of running up the stairs for a drink and purchased it two days ago. Only big enough to hold about a twelve pack. It held enough to satisfy his soda pop addiction.

Pulling the tab on the can, he took a big gulp. A picture caught his eye, and he coughed, choking on the drink. Fizz burned his nose. Once he regained his composure, he stared in disbelief. "Get out."

The kid in the photo, a young man, was now a woman. Mesmerized by the beautiful lady in front of him, he shook his head. The boy, handsome in his own right, was now an incredibly gorgeous woman. He couldn't believe the difference. When he rechecked the name, just to be sure, his brain had a hard time wrapping around what he had in front of him. "This case just a got a lot more interesting."

Kyle printed out the information and set it aside. He continued searching for the other June Bug members. Most had nothing in their pasts to make them stand out as a serial killer, but he knew better. Printing each person's bio with updated and current information, he waited for the last guy's information and thumbed through the notes on each member.

One had a car dealership. One girl had become an orthopedic surgeon, and another had become a plastic surgeon. As the last member's information printed out, he grabbed it without looking at it. Putting it at the bottom of the stack, he set it aside. He started another search for something else when he heard the alarm go off, indicating someone was at the front door.

He glanced at his watch. Just barely 6:00 a.m. Not sure who would be here this early, he headed upstairs. His stomach rolled as a queasiness filled his gut. Kyle stopped at the bottom of the stairs. His heart thumped against his chest. "There shouldn't be anyone here this early." It came out in a whisper. He crept back to his office and grabbed his weapon from the holster hanging next to the door.

He checked the magazine. Full. He pushed it against his stomach as he cocked the weapon. Hoping to muffle the sound, he cringed as it echoed throughout the basement. He blew out a breath through his nose, forcing himself to slow his breathing. Cocking his head to the side, he closed his eyes as he concentrated on the silence, searching for any odd noise.

Dead silence filled the building. Another alarm sounded. This time, several beeps filled the church. Kyle knew someone had tried to access the keypad and unlock the door but didn't have the code. He maneuvered up the stairs, hanging back at the top of the landing. He eased his head through the doorway, peeking around the edge. A quick look to the right confirmed an empty kitchen. Glancing to his left, the front of the building and what he could see appeared to be empty. The security screen above the doorway showed all the cameras and their views of the property.

Kyle squinted, trying to focus on the little squares at the other end of the room. The one showing the front entrance had a person in a hooded sweatshirt trying to break into the keypad. Kyle wondered why the system hadn't sounded the main alarm. If the keypad had too many unsuccessful entries, it would lock down and sound a horrendous alarm, along with notifying local authorities and Derek.

His pulse quickened. He knew the person at the door had no way to see him, so he moved towards the front, focusing on the camera view. He knew the security system recorded every movement, but he wanted to make note of the guy's attributes. The would-be intruder didn't seem very tall, however, he hunched over the keypad, trying to gain entry.

Kyle went to the intercom system on Emma's desk. As he reached out to push the button, the alarms went off, and a siren sounded.

He watched as the man ran away. Kyle reacted and unlocked the door, running out into the parking lot. The siren blared as a dark SUV peeled out of the lot. He watched as the guy drove off. Not three minutes later, two police cars roared into the parking lot. Before Kyle could react, they had their weapons pointed at him.

"I'm Agent Kyle Marcum." He held his weapon at his side, next to his thigh.

"Drop the weapon!"

"I'm FBI Agent Kyle Marcum."

"Drop the weapon! Now!"

Kyle laid his weapon on the ground and placed his hands on his head. "I can't believe this. I'm an FBI agent. I work here."

"Get on the ground!" The cop yelled at him as he approached him.

"I'm an FBI agent. I have my badge in my pocket."

The cop kept his weapon trained on him. The other officer flanked his right side.

"Guys," Kyle said as he laid on the ground. "I'm an agent. My badge is in the front pocket of my jeans."

The closest officer ignored him. "Cross your feet, and place your hands behind your back."

Kyle sighed as he followed the directions.

The second officer came up to Kyle, kicking his weapon away from his reach. Holstering his own weapon, the officer kneeled down, grabbing Kyle's left thumb, bending it awkwardly.

"Ouch, man. Can you not. I'm a fucking FBI agent."

The officer placed the cuffs around Kyle's wrists, then yanked him into a kneeling position.

Kyle lifted his head, about to say something when a car pulled into the lot and parked. He moaned as his boss exited with a big smile on his face. "This isn't funny, Derek."

Walking towards the officers flanking his agent, Derek muffled a laugh. "Officers, what's going on? I got a call and an alert about a break-in?"

Before the officers could answer, another car pulled into the parking lot.

Felicia stepped out. She bit her bottom lip to keep from laughing. Kyle's head hung low. "This is so bad."

CHAPTER FIFTY

Derek eyed his agent. "Officers," he said, nodding towards them. "What has my agent done? Is it really necessary to place him in handcuffs?"

The officers glanced at each other.

"I'm Officer Porter. We received a call regarding an attempted break-in at your facility. When we arrived, we found," he cocked his head to the side towards Kyle, "we found him outside armed with a gun."

"That's because I'm an agent, man." Kyle's nostrils flared as he glared at his boss. "I told them this about a hundred times."

"Take off the handcuffs, Officer. He is an FBI agent," Derek said. "I know he looks suspicious, but I promise, he is one of the good guys."

Officer Porter released the cuffs. Stepping back, he ogled the agent. "Don't take it personally. You don't look like an agent."

Kyle rubbed his wrists. Harkening back to his younger days, he didn't remember those bracelets hurting so much. "Well, I am. And I told you that. Several times."

Officer Porter shrugged. "Criminals tell us they aren't criminals all the time. We would've figured it out soon enough."

"Yeah, hopefully before trigger-happy McFly over there shot me." Kyle nodded towards the other officer.

"Kyle, tell us what you know." Derek folded his arms across his chest.

"I came in around 4:30 a.m. I parked in the back parking lot. Which probably helped make it look like no one was here." Kyle took his weapon from Officer Porter, who picked it up off the ground. "Thanks."

"What else?" Derek asked.

"I'm in the basement, and I heard a beeping noise. I figured someone came in early like me. But that didn't make sense, so I grabbed my weapon and came up the stairs. I could see someone on the screens trying to access the keypad."

"Could you make him out?" Officer Porter asked.

Kyle's brow wrinkled. He glanced at his boss. "No. He wore a black hoodie, hunched over the pad. Something wasn't right, though."

Felicia stood next to Derek. "What do you mean?"

"Why are you here?" Kyle asked

"Couldn't sleep," she said.

"What wasn't right?" Derek asked.

"The alarm. I watched the guy messing with the keypad for a few minutes, and I kept hearing beeping, but no alarm. This guy knew his way around this system."

"What makes you say that?" Derek asked.

"I can't really say except, he had to have been able to delay the alarm from sounding. Giving him a few minutes extra to hack the code. He had a small box in his hand."

Kyle walked over to the door. He pointed to the pad. "He connected it to the pad, trying to crack the number code. The only thing he didn't realize is you need the code and a thumbprint to unlock this. If he had a few more minutes, he may have been able to bypass the thumbprint."

Derek saw the worry flutter across his agent's face. He started to tell him he didn't think it had anything to do with what he'd found earlier but stopped himself, remembering the mixed company.

Officer Porter jotted in his notebook. "What do you need from us?" he asked Derek.

Derek held out his hand. "Nothing. I appreciate you and your men coming out here."

"That's our job." He turned towards Kyle. "I am sorry about the misunderstanding."

Kyle shook his outstretched hand. "I would have thought the same thing. No worries."

"If you need anything, let us know. I will send over a copy of our report for your records."

"Thank you, officer." Derek watched as the patrol cars left the parking lot. He turned back to Kyle. "You okay?"

"Yeah," he said. "Man, do they have to put those damn cuffs on so tight?" He rubbed his wrists again.

Felicia chuckled as she stepped over the threshold of the door. "Don't like handcuffs, huh?"

"In the right situation, not so bad. With Officer Porter, no, I don't like them."

CHAPTER FIFTY-ONE

Kyle studied Derek as he inspected the keypad. "Did he do any damage?"

"None other than popping off the cover. The cool thing about this pad, these wires are a diversion. Everything needed to operate the electronics is on the backside. Either he got lucky, or he knew that. I'll have our security guys come out here and check it out. Put on a new interface just to be sure." Derek armed the system then used his thumb and code to disarm. "It seems to work okay."

The three of them walked into the church. Felicia headed towards the back to make coffee.

Derek pulled up the security recordings. He could see when Kyle entered the lot and the building. About twenty minutes later, a dark SUV pulled in and parked where the camera couldn't pick up the license plate.

Kyle leaned against Emma's desk. "Looks like a late model Chevy."

"I think you're right." Derek watched as the guy walked with his head down, obstructing the view of his face as he came up to the door. "He knew where the cameras were. Or at least had a good idea of their position." He watched as the hooded man tried to get in.

Kyle watched as the guy ran off when the alarm sounded. "I was about to speak through the intercom when he ran off."

Derek looked at Kyle. "You went out after him. Why?"

"I guess I hoped I could catch him."

Derek glanced into the kitchen. "After what we learned yesterday, don't do it again. You did not know if he came alone or if he carried a weapon."

"Yeah, you're right. It was a dumb move." Kyle's head fell forward. "I couldn't sleep because of what I found out."

Derek reached out and squeezed his shoulder. "You're going to be okay. No one knows about anything regarding the Balderro case. Just think a little more."

Felicia walked back into the main room carrying three mugs of coffee. She handed one to each of the men. "I know you drink soda," she said to the resident geek, "but I think you need something a little stronger."

He smiled at her. "Thanks. I appreciate this."

"Before all the excitement, had you found anything to make your early morning worth it?" Derek walked towards his desk.

"Oh heck. I sure did." He set his coffee on Felicia's desk and trotted off towards the basement.

Felicia hummed as she booted up her computer.

Derek watched as she sipped her coffee, then hummed some more. "You're in a good mood."

She shrugged. "I try to wake up in a good mood. Makes my day better."

"Why couldn't you sleep?"

She frowned shrugging. "I don't know. This case. New town. New boss." Felicia's eyes smiled over the top of her coffee as she took a sip.

Kyle rounded the corner.

Derek took the stack of paper from his agent. "What did you find?" he asked as he thumbed through it.

Kyle hesitated. Not sure how much the others may or may not know regarding Derek's assumptions, he chose his words with care. "Well, the kid from the photo, um well, is not the same person."

Derek's eyebrows wrinkled. "What?"

Kyle chuckled. "Look at the first photo. That's the kid in the picture with Casey. You know."

"Okay," Derek said.

"Now look at the second photo." Kyle waited.

"Holy cow!" Derek had to sit down.

"What? What is it?" Felicia asked.

Derek handed her the second photo. Now he knew where he'd seen the kid in the photo with Casey. And why he stuck out so much to him. "Does this person look familiar?"

Felicia's jaw hung open. "Oh my gosh." She glanced from Derek to Kyle and back to Derek. "Are you sure?"

Derek nodded. "This is the security guard at Londonvale."

"She was a he," she said.

Derek checked his watch. "I want to be there first thing and talk to her." He scanned the paper. "She goes by Rebecca C. Francis." He looked up at Kyle. "Do you know what the C stands for?"

Kyle shook his head. "No. I didn't get that far into her file before they handcuffed me. He pointed to the file Derek held. "Her bio should be the next paper. I put them all in order."

Derek opened the file to the paper in question. "Oh."

"What?" Kyle asked.

Felicia heard the tone. "Oh, what?"

"Her middle name is Casey." Derek thumbed through the rest of the file, but he wasn't able to concentrate.

"Now that's odd. And a little creepy." Felicia sipped on her coffee.

"It is. His birth name was Fredrick Marvin Goddard. No Casey anywhere." Derek leaned against his desk. The black coffee helped soothe his uneasiness.

"You think this guy is our killer?" Kyle asked, glancing between Felicia and his boss.

"I guess we will find out." Derek sat at his desk. The door alarm pinged.

Kyle jumped.

"Wow. PTSD much?" Felicia half chuckled.

"Not funny." Kyle stuck out his tongue.

Derek glanced at his watch. The rest of the crew filed in. All but Emma. "You guys are here early."

George smiled. "Wanted to get an early start."

"Same," Michael and Kelly said in unison.

"I like it. Get your coffees, snacks, whatever. Then I want to go over some things." Derek watched as everyone made their way to the kitchen. The sound of several soda cans opening had his mouth-watering. He liked coffee, but soda held his heart.

His crew filed back in. Laughter settled into soft, whispered conversations as he pulled the whiteboard over. Victim's pictures were still attached with notes from the last time he used the board.

Derek stood next to his desk. "Last night, I asked Kyle to find out any information he could on the June Bugs group." He held up the photo of all the kids. He pointed to the kid staring at Casey. "We may have a break in the case."

A buzz of excitement swept through the team.

"Nothing for sure, so let's keep it in check. A kid in the photo with Casey raised a few flags. And from the photo, he seems to have an infatuation with her. And we know Casey is the key to these killings." Derek set the photo on his desk. "I looked over the case file last night. We missed something."

Everyone shifted in their seats. Twisting from side to side as they glanced at each other.

"I missed it too. It seems all of our victims made payments to various companies or charities at regular intervals. On its surface, it isn't much. But the victims died within a few months of stopping those payments. I want each of you to look into the victims you covered and track their financials," Derek said. "Call parents or spouses and see if they can tell you anything about where the money went and if they know why."

Kelly raised her hand.

Derek nodded.

"Why don't we just get search warrants and pull everything?"

Derek made eye contact with Kyle. Quick and unnoticed by the others.

Kyle looked at his feet.

Derek exhaled. He couldn't tell them much, but he had to give them an explanation. "I don't want to raise any suspicions by getting financials via a warrant. I don't want to play our hand, instead, I want to keep this in this office."

"And away from Congressman Jackson?" George asked.

"Exactly," Derek said. "I don't trust him."

The team looked at each other.

"Neither do I," said George.

The others nodded in agreement.

"Just see what you can get. If it doesn't lead us anywhere, we can pull the information via warrants." Derek sat at his desk. He twisted the watch on his wrist. He wanted his other watch back. Regret filled him. He didn't have time to dwell on something he could never retrieve. He had forty-five minutes before the students would start their day at the Academy.

CHAPTER FIFTY-TWO

"Oh, Dwight was murdered in Dallas," Derek said.

His team stopped working and looked at him.

"When did you find this out?" Kelly asked.

"Last night. I had a field agent out of Dallas see if there were any John Does. He got lucky." Derek sat back and finished his coffee.

Michael sighed. "You want me to contact the family?"

Derek watched the agent. Family notifications were some of the hardest to do. He didn't feel comfortable making his youngest agent do it. "George, you've done notifications before, right?"

"Yeah. I can do it," he said.

"Take Michael with you." Derek nodded in his direction. "It's the worst part of the job. You need to know how and get as comfortable as you can doing it. Go with George." He leaned forward on his elbows. "If you think you can ask the parents anything, do it. If you think they aren't ready, let them know we will need to ask them some questions by this weekend if possible. And set up a time on Saturday. I'll do it then."

George stood and stretched, grabbing a piece of paper from his desk. "I'm going to go call them and make sure they're at home."

"Kyle," Derek said.

"Yeah, boss?"

"I need to search Coach McMillan's financials. Get everything you can without crossing the line. He is the only one I couldn't find any payments coming out of his accounts."

"I'm on it." Kyle rose to leave.

"Oh, check the records for the academy. He may have used academy money as well." Derek stood.

"Okay." Kyle headed to the basement.

Felicia picked up the coffee mug from Derek's desk. "You want me to go with you to the academy?"

Derek needed to clear his head. "No." He handed her the file with the June Bugs member's information in it. "I want you and Kelly to go through each of these people and see what you can find. Kyle has pulled all their info. Run through it and see if there is anything pointing to a suspect. Be thorough. I don't want to miss anything again."

She set the file on her desk. "We got it covered. We'll finish up the financials first. For all the victims. Then we will start on this."

"Sounds great." Derek reached into his pocket and remembered he'd left the jump drive in his computer, at his house. "I'm going to stop off at home after the academy. I need to get Lola and my computer. I left so quickly this morning I didn't have time to pack my satchel."

"No worries. We have things covered here," Kelly said.

The door chimed as Emma walked in with Marc Anthony.

The big dog ran around greeting everyone but seeking the only one who mattered. Lola.

"Good morning." Emma placed her bag on her desk. She glanced around the room. "Where's Lola?"

"I had to leave her at home. We had an incident here at the office." Derek patted Marc Anthony's head when he stopped at his desk. "Lola will be here later. I promise."

The dog sulked away, taking refuge in his giant bed next to Emma's desk.

"What kind of incident?" Emma asked.

"Someone tried to break into the office," Derek replied.

"Oh, my." Emma glanced at the door, then back down at her desk.

"There's nothing to worry about, Emma. I promise," Derek reassured her.

She shrugged halfway, shaking her shoulders. "Oh, I'm not worried. Just can't imagine what they were hoping to get."

"Probably case files. If they even knew this is an FBI office." Kelly faced Emma. "We don't have a signup, but I think everyone in town knows we're here."

"So basically, you just contradicted yourself?" asked Felicia.

Kelly spun around and glared at her. "Oh, shut up."

Felicia laughed at the snarl on Kelly's face.

"You're buying lunch for that," Kelly said.

"Fine. You big baby." Felicia made a pouty face.

Derek shook his head. "Can you guys finish the work together?"

"Of course. If I'm buying lunch, she's doing all the work," Felicia said.

"Pfft." Kelly waved her off.

Derek walked towards the door. "Call me if you need me. Otherwise, I will be back later." Even early in the day, the sun beat down on the pavement. Ripples of heat made the concrete look uneven. In his car, he set the envelope with the photo of the June Bugs club on the seat. He sighed as the AC kicked in. After pushing a button, the driver's seat cooled. He leaned back against the head rest enjoying the silence.

Once the car cooled off, he headed to the academy. Pulling into traffic, his phone rang, a smile pushed his mouth upward. "Hey, you."

"Hey."

"You sound tired."

"I'm so tired. We got into California last night. Very late."

"Are you still in Cali?"

"Yeah. Our pilot can't leave until tomorrow. He needs a day of rest. We should be in Philly by late afternoon."

"Babe, I'm so sorry. I know how hard this is."

Lizzy sighed into the phone.

He could hear her sniffling. "Lizzy, talk to me."

"This is so hard, Derek. Watching your mom slowly die in front of you, and there is nothing you can do but make her comfortable."

"I'm not even going to pretend I know how difficult this is, but I know you, and I know how strong you are. And I know how much being around your mom is helping her."

"I'm scared."

"It's okay to be scared. How's your sister holding up?"

"She's doing okay. We are relying on each other. My dad is glad we are coming home. He just wants to be with Mom as long as he can."

"Listen. You stay in Philly as long as you need to. Lola is fine."

Lizzy giggled. "I bet you're spoiling her rotten."

"I am. I sure have enjoyed having her with me. She misses you. I miss you. But you need to stay there." He heard her blow her nose. His heart ached for her.

"I do. I think I will stay until the end. If you're sure."

"Lizzy, you be with your mom and dad. They need you. And so does your sister. I'm here anytime. I don't care what time of night. You call me. If I have to come out there, I can arrange the trip."

"No. I know you have work. I'll be okay. Just hearing you has made me feel better."

"I love you, Lizzy."

She didn't respond for a moment. He could hear the sniffles starting again.

"I love you. You always seem to save me. From the first time we met until now. You're always there to save me."

"It's the best job in the world." He heard a muffled conversation in the background.

"I need to hang up. Mom wants to go to the pool. She amazes me."

"Go enjoy. Love on her. I will kiss Lola for you."

"Okay. Bye."

The phone went dead just as Derek drove down the lane leading to Londonvale Academy. As much as he wanted Lizzy home, he wanted her safe. And being in Philly was about the safest place for her.

CHAPTER FIFTY-THREE

Thursday 8:30 a.m.

Derek pulled into a parking spot outside the gate of Londonvale Academy. He stepped out of his vehicle, holding the envelope, he waited for several students to drive through the gate before he walked to the security shack.

As he approached, Rebecca stepped out and met him. "Rebecca Francis?"

Her brow wrinkled, and her gait slowed to a stop. "Yes? I guess you know."

"Yes. And I need to speak with you."

Rebecca glanced around. She pointed to a pathway just behind the parking area. "Do you mind if we walk for a bit? There's a sitting area on the other side of the tree line." She glanced over her shoulder back towards the guard shack. "I really don't want to talk about things within earshot of my coworkers."

"No problem at all. Lead the way." Derek followed her as she walked between two cars and a row of trees. A pathway opened up, and a large pond with a jogging trail came into view. Benches had been placed around the body of water with strategically placed trees to provide shade.

Rebecca took a seat on the first bench along the pathway. She grimaced, glancing at the agent, then turned her attention to the ducks on the pond. "What do you need to know?"

"What was your connection to Casey Redding?" Derek couldn't see her face from the front, but he saw the ripple of tension as her jaw locked into place.

"I haven't heard her name in so long." Rebecca wiped a tear from her face. "I haven't met anyone like her."

"Tell me about her." Derek's gazed drifted to the pond. Several ducks swam around while a few looked for snacks on the grassy area.

"Casey was kind and generous. She helped anyone who needed it." She chuckled, but it wasn't filled with joy. "She knew who I was before I knew who I was. And she accepted me. No questions asked."

"What do you mean, she knew you? You mean regarding your transition?"

She nodded. "I didn't think of myself as gay. I wasn't sure what I was, but I knew there was more to it than that. She helped me, be me. I wanted to be all girl. And she taught me all about being a girl."

Rebecca wiped her chin, rubbing her moist hand on her tan uniform pants. "We spent a lot of time together. Laughing, talking about boys. She was like the sister I never had."

"What about the cabin and the accident?"

Her head swiveled as if an invisible line had yanked it. "There was no accident. Those kids murdered her. They knew she had asthma. They didn't care. Especially, Billy Edmond."

Derek sat in silence, waiting for her to continue.

"His dad covered everything up."

"Tell me about what you know."

She shrugged. "He and Coach. They made sure nothing hurt Billy, and the chosen few."

"What do you mean, the coach helped?" Derek removed the pack of gum from his front pants pocket. He held it out, offering Rebecca a piece. She waved him off.

"Coach cared about Coach. And he did whatever he needed to keep his position."

"You mean his position as coach? His position here at Londonvale?"

"All the above. And the money. The Edmond's money."

Derek turned to face her. "Can you explain?"

"Coach and Billy's dad go way back." She looked at Derek. "You're the FBI. Surely you already know this?"

Derek shook his head. "Enlighten me."

"Edmond Sr. helped get Coach his job here as the coach and head of the athletic department. Coach worked for Billy's grandpa at his law firm for a long time during and after college."

"We found nothing linking Coach to Edmond's law firm. Are you sure about that?"

"I bet you were looking for Russell McMillan."

Derek raised his eyebrow, giving Rebecca a glassy stare. "Who should we have been looking for?"

She smirked. "Don't feel bad. I only know all this because of my former job. I used to work at a tech company and learned a lot about research. And I'll leave it at that. As for old Coach, he knew Billy's dad when they were in college together. He got in some trouble and was looking at serious jail time. Billy's grandfather, who was also a criminal attorney, got Russell cleared of all charges and helped him expunge his record.

"Not long after the incident, Grandpa helped Russell officially change his name. He used to be known as Harry Fredricksburg. I suppose you want to know what Harry did to get into so much trouble?"

Derek looked up from writing in his little notebook. "I would."

"Seems like Harry had a penchant for fraud, embezzlement, theft by intimidation, and later in life, you can add internet theft to that." She winked at Derek. "He's very resourceful. Anyway, in college, he found some dirt on a few people and tried to blackmail them. Unfortunately for him, he picked the wrong kid. His dad made Harry's life hell. That's when Grandpa Edmond got involved."

"I can't imagine it was out of the goodness of his heart." B

Rebecca laughed.

Derek instantly liked her because of it. Her soft, warm tone reminded him of Lizzy.

"Hell no. The Edmonds have no goodness in their hearts. Both Coach and William Sr. worked for Grandpa Edmond at his firm. Coach's job entailed hunting down information on people."

Derek raised his hand. "How do you know all this?"

She didn't respond, just stared at the pond.

"Rebecca, I'm not after you. I don't care what you have done."

"I did a little investigating several years back. I had a job that allowed me some research perks." She sighed. "Understand, after Casey died, my world crumbled. She was my best friend. I decided right then I would make all of them pay for it."

Derek sat up straight. "How did you do that?"

She smiled, then her brow wrinkled. "I didn't kill them if that's what you think."

Derek stared, stoned-faced.

"That's why you're here. You think I killed them." She fidgeted with the buttons on her shirt. "I wanted to, all these years. But I couldn't. I thought about ruining their lives with little tidbits of information I knew, like regarding Coach. But I didn't. No one knows who I was. They only know who I am now. And I want to keep it that way. I wish I had the courage to do something, though."

"Tell me about this club." He removed the photo of the June Bugs. "He pointed to Rebecca as a young man. "You were a handsome young man, and you are an exquisite young woman. Tell me about these kids."

Rebecca took the photo. Her hands trembled as she wiped her cheeks. Inhaling through her nose and exhaling through her mouth, she took a moment to gather her emotions.

"I can't imagine the anger and hurt you felt after Casey died."

"I almost left school. It was the worst time of my life. But I knew Casey wouldn't want me to quit." She stared at the photo. "I can't remember most of these kids. I didn't spend much time with any of them. But this kid," she pointed to one in the front row. "He's Coach's nephew."

Derek's jaw slacked. His breath hitched. "How do you know this?"

"I didn't realize it until I broke into Coach's personal life via the internet a few years ago. It's amazing what you can find when you know where to look." She handed the photo back to him. "His name is Ford Johnson. Remember, Coach changed his name. Grandpa Edmond helped craft a whole new identity for him, but he still had a family. The new identity was so he could move through life with no legal issues."

"That's how he could get this job." Derek placed the photo in the envelope.

"Yup. Anyway. Coach had a hand in recommending kids for scholarships, and he recommended this kid." She stared at the pond. "Coach never showed this kid any special attention. It was probably part of the deal. He was kind of quiet. He was really smart. Tech-savvy even for a kid in high school."

Derek jotted notes down. "Do you know what happened to him?"

"Last I knew, he had a security company. I think it was like home security. Surveillance for homes and businesses. That kind of thing. Ford had a huge crush on Casey. That kid wanted to marry her right then and there. But Casey had eyes for Greg."

"Greg Burks?"

Rebecca nodded.

"Rebecca, why did you come to work here?"

She leaned back against the bench, turning towards the agent. Not very handsome, yet something about him made him attractive. She found herself immersed in his green eyes. "I don't work for the school. I own the company that provides the security."

Derek watched the gleam in her eye brighten. "I didn't know. That's a pretty nice gig."

She laughed. "I bet I've gone to the top of your suspect list, haven't I?" She waived him off before he could answer. "I can provide you a detailed alibi of where I was when Greg Burks and Billy were murdered." Her eyes narrowed in on him. "I didn't kill them. I think the world is better off without them. But I didn't kill them."

"Does Coach know who you are?"

She shook her head. "No one knows. I'm not from around here. When I came to the school, I was living with my mother. My dad lived in Texas. I got the scholarship, kept my head down, and barely talked to anyone. I just wanted what this school could do for me.

"I left and went to college. Studied engineering. During college, my mom died, leaving me a nice little nest egg, allowing me to start and complete my transition. By the time I left, I was Rebecca. I changed my identity and wiped the old me off the face of the map." She tilted her head. "Or at least I thought I had."

Derek chuckled. "I got a guy."

"I bet. Anyway, I'm not sure why I came back here. I always liked this area. And I had a friend in college. I met her after my transition. She told me about a company for sale out here and thought I might be interested. I ended up buying it, and I've grown it into what it is now."

"What kind of security?"

"Onsite stuff. Security guards, mostly. I send people to training, then hire them. It's a win for both. They have to work for me for three years unless they pay for the training themselves."

"You're telling me, no one at this school knows who you were in your previous life?"

"Nope."

"What can you tell me about Coach now?"

"He's an ass. He uses his position here to insert himself into society. His nephew lives in this area."

Derek sat up. "Really?"

She nodded as she pulled the scrunchy from her hair. She shook her locks, rubbing her scalp. "He pops in once in a while. Never calls him uncle. Just Mr. McMillan."

"Have you seen him recently?"

"Yeah. Now that you mention it. He's been out here a few times over the last few months. We have summer school. This campus is always in session." She snapped her fingers. "I didn't think much about this. Remember, no one knows they are related. One evening, I was going over the grounds before I locked the front gates. I check all the doors and make sure no stragglers are left behind.

"I saw Coach and Ford at the front steps of the main building. They looked very animated. I couldn't hear them, but I had the impression Coach seemed angry at his nephew."

"Do you remember what day that was?" Derek scribbled in his notebook.

She sighed, pulling her hair into a loose bun. "The day you came to see him."

"This week?"

"Yes." She watched his reaction. "I guess it means something to you."

Derek didn't reply. He had a slight chill. For a minute, he thought a cool breeze blew. But the trees were dead still. His stomach sank. He didn't want to look up. He smiled at Rebecca as his gaze landed on the far side of the pond. "It does," he said.

He saw Casey waving. He couldn't help the feeling she looked happy. He turned towards Rebecca. "I know Casey would love the woman you've become. You chose her name as your middle name."

Rebecca blinked, trying to hold back the tears. "I miss her. I wanted to keep her close." She stared at the ducks. "Do you believe in the afterlife? Spirits? That sort of thing?"

Derek shifted his body. Placing the book in the back pocket of his jeans. "I don't think so."

Rebecca reached over and held his hand. "You should. I think you have a gift you aren't quite ready for."

He pulled his hand away when her grip tightened. He swallowed the pooling saliva forming at the back of his mouth.

"Trust your gut. And let them talk to you."

Derek pulled his hand back. His fingers were icy to the touch. Rebecca seemed unfazed. As if she hadn't been holding his hand in the first place.

"Is there anything else, Agent Reed?" she asked, standing.

He stood, stretching. "No. If I need anything, I'll call."

She handed him a business card. "Call me at this number anytime. If you want to grab a drink, off duty, of course, I would love it."

He grinned. "I'm flattered. I will keep this."

She laughed again, lifting her chin. "I guess that seemed awkward."

"Not in the least. You're a beautiful woman. I'm flattered you would even ask."

"You're a classy guy, Agent Reed. Kind, too." A full-face smile stared back at him. "If I can help you nail Coach. Call me. I'm sure your guy can take what I've given you and work his magic. I have one request."

"What?"

"Please bury my past life. When you can. Please."

They started walking back to the car. Derek stopped at his vehicle. "I promise, I will."

She winked. "Call me for that drink."

Derek sat in his car. His head hurt. His fingers grazed the raised lump as he touched the back of his head. He winced as the pain radiated outward. "Ouch." Rolling down his window, he spit out the stale gum. Backing up, he saw Rebecca standing at the doorway. She waved as she stepped back into the little shack.

Embarrassed that his team had found nothing out on Coach, Derek contemplated if his actions were the cause. Maybe he has been hyper-focused on the wrong parts of this case. Then again, maybe someone knew what they were doing when they buried Russell McMillan's former life.

Derek's stomach knotted, feeling as if a rock formed in his gut. Something still didn't sit right. He should be excited they may have an actual suspect. Instead, he mistrusted his own judgment. He wanted to flee. Pack up and run to Lizzy. But he knew as well as anyone he couldn't outrun it. Whatever it was.

CHAPTER FIFTY-FOUR

Thursday mid-day

Derek walked in with Lola. He'd picked her and his laptop up from his home. He expected the office to be a hustle and bustle of work. "Empty," he said as he entered the building. He'd parked in front, so he had no idea if anyone's car was parked in the back.

Lola ran around looking for everyone. She stopped and turned, looking at her master.

"I don't know, girl." He glanced at the screens. Two cars were parked in the back. "Okay. Maybe they went for lunch." He laid his stuff on his desk and walked into the kitchen. Staring at the fridge, he wondered what he could eat. His stomach growled, emphasizing his hunger. He grabbed a soda, some lunch meat and cheese and started making a sandwich.

Lola came up next to him, startling him. "Calm down, Derek. You have got to relax." He thought of his pills but decided he wasn't going to take them. At least he hoped he wouldn't need them. Placing the meat and cheese back in the fridge, he turned towards the counter. "Holy shit." He grabbed his chest. "How the hell did you get in here?"

Kyle stood there staring at him. "Um, I came up the stairs."

"Well, quit sneaking around." Derek blew out a long breath.

"What the hell is wrong with you?" Kyle laughed. "You're jumpy."

Derek twisted his neck from side to side. "Just this case, I guess." He grabbed his plate with a bag of chips from the cupboard. "Follow me. Speaking of this case, I got something."

"Awesome. Like a suspect?" Kyle sat in Felicia's seat.

Derek made a circle with his hand. "Where is everyone?"

Kyle glanced over his shoulder. "Well, Emma was just here. She must have taken Marc Anthony out for a walk. The girls went to get a bite to eat. They said they were tired of sandwiches."

Derek took a bite of his. "Me too." He took a sip of his soda. "I need you to do something for me after this case."

Kyle's nose wrinkled. "Okay."

"I want you to bury Rebecca's past."

Kyle leaned forward, resting his elbows on his knees. "Why? I mean, I will, but why?"

"Just make it hard for someone to connect the old with the new." Derek took another bite of his food. "She gave me a lot of information. I made a promise, so just make sure for me after the case is over."

"You got it. I know you don't make those often. Must have been important."

"It was. Is. I need you to run a deep search on Ford Johnson...."

Kyle cut him off. "I know that name." He snapped his fingers. Digging through the mess on Felicia's desk, he found the folder. "Yeah. He was in the June Bugs group." He handed the paper to Derek.

"Did you find anything suspicious in his background?"

"No. Should I have?"

Derek read the information. He set the paper on his desk. "In your research, have you come across the name Harry Fredricksburg?"

Kyle frowned, shaking his head. "No. Who is he?"

"Harry Fredricksburg is Russell McMillan."

Kyle's mouth hung open. Then he smiled. "No way. You're lying."

"No. And, he and Billy's dad go way back. Like when they were in college," Derek said. "Back in the day, Harry got in some trouble, and Grandpa Edmond helped him out. He kept him out of jail and later expunged his records. Then, he helped him change his name."

Kyle slapped his leg. "No way. I found none of that." He turned towards Felicia's computer. Pulling up a secure database he started typing. "It looks like someone, and it very well could be the coach himself, tried to erase all evidence of his former life from the internet. According to this, Harry Fredricksburg stopped existing around 1974. No death certificate just disappeared." Kyle continued typing.

"You need to pull everything on Harry and his nephew Ford." Derek leaned into his desk, lowering his voice. "I want you to check and see if Harry's name comes up anywhere in the Balderro case. Don't leave a trace."

Kyle turned around and scooted closer to his boss. "You think he helped with the money?"

"I don't know. But on the jump drive, I found payments into an account, out of the same account, and later a lot of money went into one of Billy's business accounts. That's an account he used to make monthly payments to various businesses. I believe those payments went to our killer. I think the money put into this account came from the Balderro case.

"As it pertains to this case, I only want to see if Harry moved sizeable sums of money since the death of Casey. And I want to see if they match up to Billy's business account. Anything you find, make sure it can be attributed to her or this case. Leave out anything remotely associated with the Balderro case."

Kyle nodded.

"Listen, don't worry. Okay?"

"Yeah. I'm trying not to," Kyle said.

The security system beeped as Emma opened the front door.

Lola bounded down the length of the room, sliding to a stop at Emma's feet. She howled and barked, dancing around her.

"Oh, my. You are so excited." Emma petted her at the same time she unhooked the lead from Marc Anthony's collar. She stood laughing at the two dogs. "They are silly." She smiled at Derek. "How did your morning go?"

"Great. Learned a lot."

"That's fantastic. Give me a list of things you want from the store. I'm going shopping in the morning after I drop Marc Anthony off here."

"You know you don't have to do that. We can all buy what we want." Derek slipped the jump drive from his computer into his pants pocket.

"I need a few things, so I thought I would go for everyone." Emma sat at her desk, reading her emails.

"Okay. Thank you."

"Hey," Kyle said. "I got something."

"On who?"

"Ford Johnson. He owns a security company that specializes in door alarms, high-end surveillance, and cyber security." Kyle continued typing.

"Rebecca mentioned he had a company. He would be familiar with the security lock on our front door. And, he would be well versed in internet stuff."

Kyle nodded. "Yes. Internet stuff." He muffled a giggle.

"Funny, you know what I meant. Now, give me the name."

"C. R. Securities." Kyle's eyes widened.

"I'll be damned. Rebecca said Ford had a huge crush on Casey. I don't think it's coincidence C.R. is in the name." Derek leaned back in his chair.

Kyle continued typing on the computer.

"Ford had to know who the inner circle of the baseball team was. Rebecca said no one knew he was Russell's nephew. But that didn't mean he didn't talk to his uncle outside of the Academy. What if Ford was the kid who got the car?"

Kyle spun around in his chair. "It has to be him."

"No, it doesn't have to be, but it makes sense if it is." He pulled his phone from his pocket. "Rebecca? This is Derek." He smiled into the phone. "Not quite. Can you tell me if Ford came to school driving a new car after Casey's death?"

Kyle watched as Derek's eyes widened. The security system beeped. He turned around to see George and Michael enter. Neither looked happy.

"It was him." Derek laid his phone on the desk.

"Woohoo!" Kyle said, spinning around in his chair.

"What? It was him, who?" George asked as he sat in his chair. An exasperated sigh escaped.

"How did it go?" Derek asked.

"It was horrible." Michael sat at his desk. "I don't want to do that again."

"They are brutal. Did you get to ask them anything?" Derek took a piece of gum from his pack.

"They were devastated. But the father answered what he could. He said he had no idea why Dwight went to Texas. He wasn't privy to his business dealings."

Michael took a sip of water from the bottle he carried in with him. "They said during high school, a group of boys from the team always hung out at the cabin. Then, one day, they all stopped. Dwight never explained why."

"Did they say anything else?" Derek asked.

George rubbed his bald head with a handkerchief. "No. We didn't push it."

"He found out who Billy paid off with the car." Kyle spun around in the chair again.

"Yeah? How?" George asked.

"Rebecca, the security guard at the academy. She also explained the kid in question, Ford Johnson, is the nephew of Russell McMillan, Coach McMillan."

George and Michael glanced at each other, then back at Derek.

"You're kidding? How come we didn't know that?" Michael guzzled the last of his water.

"Coach changed his name." Derek started to explain as Kelly and Felicia walked in. He waved them over and reviewed the new information regarding Ford Johnson. "Felicia, what did you and Kelly find?"

"The kids from the June Bugs had nothing in their financials at all. Not even our new suspect, Ford. His security company didn't have any large sums of money. He had a few major contracts with area business, but nothing that warranted a second look."

"What about the victims?"

Kelly pulled a piece of paper from her folder on her desk. "All the victims had payments. Random amounts. They matched up to what you found. Klint Kenyon, Christian Dawson, Humphrey Archer, Julian Mosely, Martin Lucey, and Gordon Padden didn't have any unusual activity on their accounts. Neither did the girls."

"That bolsters our theory this killer is targeting the inner circle of players. He glanced at his team, he pointed at Kyle. "You're going to have to look deeper. I know what they did was a surface scan on Ford and the Coach. I need you to nudge the line. I'll clear it if we need to. I want you to do the same with Coach and his former identity."

"Speaking of Coach. Under Harry Fredricksburg, he has a few accounts." Kyle scooted a little closer to Felicia, who sat on the edge of her desk.

"How many?" Derek asked.

"I found three. One from the late-70s. It doesn't look like it's been touched since the 70s. Two others were opened five years ago. To see every transaction, I will have to straddle that line."

"Do it." Derek felt sick to his stomach. He took a few deep breaths and sat on the edge of his desk. "George, Kelly, I still want you to go to James Rockport's house on Sunday. I want you to ask him about William Sr.'s relationship to Coach. See if you can get anything from them regarding what he did for him."

"Yes, sir," Kelly said.

Derek squinted at her, shaking his head.

"I'm going downstairs to hunt down these accounts." Kyle headed to the basement.

"Thank you," Derek called out to him as he rounded the corner. His phone vibrated in his pocket. "Derek."

"It's Callahan."

"Doc. What's up?"

"I looked over those autopsy reports from those cases. They definitely have some things in common. Why the ME didn't see that when he looked at them, I can't say."

"Time between cases. If he filled in, he may not have even remembered the cases. It's okay. We have a few leads." Derek moved to his seat. "Can you tell me anything about Billy's dad's time in college?"

"Not really. I didn't really know him that well. Why?"

"We found a connection between Billy's dad and the headmaster of the Londonvale Academy. Do you know any close friends of William Sr.?"

"Well, you're not going to like this answer, but Congressman Jackson would be your best bet."

"Shit."

Doc's laughter filled the phone. "I told you, you wouldn't like the answer."

Derek dreaded calling the congressman. "You sure you don't know of anyone else?"

"Listen, he wants the killer caught as much as you. He'd be willing to help. Call him. How's your head?"

Derek reached up, grazing the sore spot. "It's fine."

"You are a sucky liar. If it still hurts next week. We need to have it looked at."

"Okay. I need to go," Derek said.

"Fine. Next week, come by here so I can check it."

Derek laid his phone on the desk. Surely there was someone else he could talk to besides the congressman. How would he ever approach it? He turned on the desktop, pulled up the current case file on the computer, and input the new information he had gathered from Rebecca.

The queasiness from earlier settled deeper in his stomach. He never felt sick. *What the hell is going on?* He wanted to get a drink but didn't think he would make it into the kitchen without passing out.

Breathing slowly, he pulled a piece of gum from his pack. He spit out the one he'd been chewing. Glancing at his watch, he wondered if he should just bite the bullet and call the congressman. He reached for his phone as Kyle came around the corner.

"Derek," he said as he came up next to Derek's desk.

"What do you have?"

"I ran the bank statements from Billy's business account, and I matched a lot of payments to the same account under Coach's former identity. Harry. I couldn't find anything under the nephew. Nothing that stuck out anyway. Every penny he has accrued can be attributed to a business contract for his security company."

Derek blew out a long breath of air. "That makes no sense. I know the Coach didn't kill anyone."

"Are we sure about that?" Kyle asked.

"I received a call from Dr. Callahan. He followed up on the cases from five years ago. They all had similarities to our current cases. Leading him and me to believe the same person killed all of our victims. If we go with that, Coach has an alibi for Billy's murder. Making him less likely to be the killer of the others."

"I don't know. I couldn't find anything in the nephew's financials at all, so I double checked the girls' financials. Neither Katy nor Alesha made any payments." Kyle stuck his hands in his front pockets.

"What the hell am I missing?" Derek asked.

George heard the conversation between Kyle and his boss. "Maybe we have it wrong."

Derek lifted his head. "What do you mean?"

The other agents waited for him to explain.

"Just because the Coach didn't kill them doesn't mean he wasn't involved in their murders." George scooted his chair a little closer. "He could've paid for someone to kill them."

"I don't see it." Kelly stood stretching.

"I don't either," Felicia said.

Derek ran his fingers through his hair, tugging on the ends. He moved to the whiteboard, clearing it off. He scribbled the names of the victims. Then the other team players. He scribbled notes next to each group, listing the coach and his nephew. He included dollar signs next to Coach's name. In one corner, he listed Rebecca's name. He put Casey's name in the center, circling it. He drew arrows between Rebecca and the nephew.

As he worked, the others continued with their tasks, each glancing at their boss watching him.

Derek stepped back, picking up his phone. "Rebecca? I have another question for you. Did Billy and the others bully Ford?" He nodded into the phone as he faced the board. "Who was the worst offender?" he scribbled on the board, circling Billy's name and connecting it to the nephew.

"One last question, did he ever confront Greg after Casey's death?" he scribbled again on the board. He circled Greg's name and made an arrow pointing to the nephew. "I lied. One more question. Did Coach ever step in and stop his nephew from being bullied?" nodding into the phone, he smiled. "Thank you."

He spun around to the team. He focused on Kyle. "Are you sure you couldn't find any payments from the nephew? To any account?"

Kyle pinched the bridge of his nose. "I didn't find anything."

"Okay, can you backtrace Coach's accounts?" Derek asked.

"I could try. But to do that, I need to get into the bank's software." Kyle leaned forward. "I need a warrant. To do it legally."

Derek hit a button on his phone. "I need a warrant."

"Well, hi Agent Reed." The AD laughed on the other end of the phone. "For what?"

"Bank records."

"Well, you don't ask for much. On who?"

"Russell McMillan. He's the headmaster of Londonvale. I need it ASAP."

The AD moaned. "Let me see what I can do. It will be a limiting scope. Only his accounts. You can't go poking around the rest of the bank files. Limited scope."

"Thanks. Email it when you get it."

"Wait for the warrant, Derek."

"Yes, sir," Derek said as he hung up. "Go." He pointed to Kyle. Follow the money from McMillan's accounts and see if you can track where they originated. Go back through the nephew's accounts. Look for anything. Check the businesses and make sure they are real. If you find any links to Ford's account from the coach's, follow it. I'll make sure you're covered."

Kyle jogged downstairs.

Derek stood in front of the board. He circled Casey's name several times. "She's the key."

"How?" Michael asked. "I mean, I know it's her death that set things in motion. But I'm not seeing the big picture."

Smiling at his young agent, he sat on the edge of his desk. "Rebecca told me Billy was one of the worst when it came to bullying Ford. Although she said, all of them had a hand in it. After Casey's death, Ford confronted Greg. Said he killed her.

"Rebecca also said Ford punched Greg. About a week later, Billy and Greg cornered Ford and beat the snot out of him. She said the headmaster did nothing. He let Coach handle it. And Coach did nothing. Not a damn thing. He took the boys' side, not his nephew's."

Felicia twisted from side to side. "His own nephew. He didn't even stick up for his own nephew?"

"No. And we know the coach and Billy's dad were very close. We also know Coach spent time with them outside of school. Can you imagine how the nephew felt? What a slap in the face." Derek crossed his arms.

"Let's go question him," Kelly said.

"In due time. Right now, we have nothing but conjecture, and it won't get us very far." Derek set the marker on the ledge of the whiteboard. "We have to wait for the right moment. We need more information. If we go in now, we may tip our hand. Right now, the nephew doesn't even know he's on our radar."

"Do you think he was the one who tried to break in?" Michael asked.

"I do. But again, I have nothing to prove it. But his work makes it more probable than not he knew our system. And if it was him, then he may slip up because he's trying to cover his tracks." Derek took a deep breath.

He felt the electricity in the air. The puzzle pieces were sliding into place. Fear nagged at him, though. What if he had this all wrong? Waiting years to punish people for their sins had to mean something. And if Derek got this wrong, he feared his mistake would cost more lives. Just like his mistake cost Chrissy hers.

CHAPTER FIFTY-FIVE

Thursday late afternoon

Derek sat at his desk, bouncing his knee. He chewed through five pieces of gum and would need to go to his car to get another pack at this pace. He wished he had a cigarette and bent over, reaching for his bag. Not wanting to rely on them to fix him, he decided against the pills. He hadn't even gotten the prescription from Doctor Chelsea filled yet.

He considered what Chrissy, or his subconscious, tried to tell him. He needed to trust himself. The last time he trusted his judgment, he failed miserably.

He stared at the board. Baily Hodgens said the coach didn't care about anyone but himself. Derek believed it, too. After learning he didn't stick up for his nephew, he had to think the nephew stewed all this time.

If that were the case, then Ford Johnson waited for the right moment. He waited until he could make his uncle and the boys pay for their mistake. If Derek had it right, the nephew had something planned for his uncle. Something to make his uncle suffer.

CHAPTER FIFTY-SIX

Thursday 5:30 p.m.

Derek looked up to find his agents working in silence. The dogs napped, and everyone looked tired. "Finish up what you have going and get out of here. We all came in early, and it's been a long day." He typed a text to Kyle, telling him the same thing.

Kelly yawned, stretching as she stood. "I am so ready to go to sleep. I may not even eat. I'm so tired."

"You need to eat." Felicia pushed her papers into a pile at the corner of her desk.

"How do you even know what you're working on? Your desk is a sty." Kelly smirked at her colleague.

"I know where everything is. It's my system." Felicia stood, grabbing her keys and gun from her desk drawer.

"You have no system." Michael laughed when she threw a wadded-up piece of paper at him. "I'm eating a big steak and going right to bed."

George holstered his weapon. "You sure you don't need anything?"

Derek leaned back in his chair, resting his interlocked hands on his chest. "No. Go home. Be here in the morning."

"Everyone, have your grocery list for me when you come in. I'm leaving after I drop Marc Anthony off here. I want to get it done first thing in the morning."

"Thanks for going for us," Felicia said as she walked past Emma's desk."

"Yeah, thanks." Michael laid his list on her desk with two twenty-dollar bills. "I think this should cover mine. If not, I will reimburse you when you get back."

Emma smiled. "No worries. It's not like I don't know how to find you."

As the three agents walked out the door, Emma leashed up Marc Anthony. She waved at them, then grabbed her things. "Derek, I will see you and Lola in the morning."

"See you in the morning. Be safe, Emma." He watched her on the security screen as she entered her vehicle and drove out. He waited for

Kyle. He wasn't about to leave him alone. Not that the man couldn't take care of himself. He just didn't want to risk it.

His phone beeped twice, then rang. "What's up?"

"Did you know the Assistant Deputy Director came into town yesterday?" Fretz asked.

"What? No. Do you know why?"

"He said he had a meeting with Director Jessup. I called Jessup's secretary, asked her if they met. She said no. Said Jessup was out of the office yesterday and today. Wouldn't be back in and available until Friday afternoon."

Derek's stomach churned. The queasy feeling surged again. "I know Congressman Jackson was in town yesterday. You think it's a coincidence or a planned rendezvous?"

"Derek, I honestly don't know. But he came here to see someone or to do something. I wanted you to be aware he may pop in if he is still here."

"Well, he will have to wait until tomorrow to do any popping in. We are heading out in the next five minutes." Derek checked the time on his watch. He looked over his shoulder. Kyle should be coming up, he thought.

"Keep your wits about you. I'll keep you posted if I find out anything."

"You too." The line went dead, and Derek walked to the front. He secured it, setting the locking system. It would require him to shut the system down to leave, but he didn't like knowing the ADD was in town.

Derek walked to the back of the kitchen. He listened at the top of the stairs. "Kyle?" No answer. He went down the steps and stopped. "Kyle?" He reached for his weapon. Empty. He'd left his gun in his desk. "Shit," he whispered.

His anxiety heightened with each step towards the open office at the end of the short hallway. He craned his neck to hear better. The hum of the computers filled his ear. "Kyle?"

As he neared the door, he contemplated his next move. Surprise. The element of surprise was all he had. One step from the threshold, he took a deep breath and jumped into the room. "Kyle!"

Kyle jumped up, ripping his headphones off. "What the hell?" his chair slammed against the wall and hit the desk. His empty soda can fell crashing onto the floor. The sound made him jump again. "What the fuck is wrong with you?" he yelled at Derek.

Derek held his chest. His heart about to explode. "Shit, you didn't answer me."

"So you thought it was okay to jump in here and scare the shit out of me?" He picked up the can from the floor.

Derek started to chuckle, then broke out in laughter.

Kyle stared at the man. Stunned. Then he realized how stupid he must have looked, screaming like a little girl. He laughed as he took his seat. "Oh, man. We both need to get a grip."

Derek sat in the empty chair next to Kyle's desk. "I'm sorry. I freaked out because you didn't answer. And then, after my call with AD Fretz. I let my imagination get away from me."

Kyle cocked his head to the side. "Why did AD Fretz call you? Did we not get the warrant?"

He didn't want to worry Kyle. "Yes. He called to make sure we got it." Derek smiled. "We got it. Do I need to get another one for the nephew?"

Kyle motioned for him to scoot closer. "Maybe. This is Coach's financials from an account under his old name." He pointed to all the deposits. "These were made from Billy's account. These payments start a few months after the first three victims were killed."

"Okay. That's when Billy started being blackmailed."

"I think so. I found payments to this same account from the other victims. Each deposit matches a withdrawal from their accounts. According to what we have already uncovered. I didn't have to do anything nefarious to get these."

Derek laughed. "I'm not worried. At this point, I'm really not."

"This account, listed under Coach's old name, seems to be the account associated with all the blackmail withdrawals. Thus, indicating Coach as the blackmailer. Now, this is where I may have stretched this warrant a tad. I found a payment from an account I couldn't match up. When I backtraced it, it came from the athletic department at the academy."

"Wait... there's a payment into Coach's account from the school?"

"Yeah. Here's where the stretching came in. I scanned the account from the school. It was created five years ago and isn't listed with the other school bank accounts. It's like someone opened an account then hid it from the school."

Derek leaned forward. "Can you tell me anything about the account?"

"Just the creation date and that it was done all electronically."

"Okay. How about the payments into this new athletic account? Where did they come from?"

"Here's where it might get sticky." Kyle pointed to several deposits. "These originated from a local bank here in Phoenix. I went as far as I could go without needing a new warrant. What I can tell you is this account," he pointed to the local bank account on his screen, "this account is tied to one of the companies that made a payment to the nephew's business account."

Derek's head spun. He closed his eyes, letting the information settle a bit. "Is the company a real company?"

"No. It links to an offshore account. And that's as far as I could go. Our warrant won't cover hacking a foreign country's bank." Kyle grabbed a soda from his little fridge. "You want one?"

Derek held out his hand. "Yes. Thank you." He opened the can and took a long sip. "We know the nephew is doing this. It's convoluted, but you can follow the crumbs and know he is moving the money. That tells me he's the blackmailer, but he's setting up his uncle."

"And he's doing a damn good job of it." Kyle clicked on a few other tabs. "This is from the Balderro case. I have only skimmed the surface. I will spend more time later. But your hunch is right. This account is from the jump drive. Billy's dad siphoned money from the land deal into this account. By the looks of what I have found so far, its millions."

Derek's jaw tensed. "Stop here. Make some notes, and we will come back to it."

Kyle nodded. "I did one thing. I hope you don't punch me."

"What did you do?"

"I didn't want to go into the congressman's account yet. I thought I would wait until you were ready to move on the information I gathered. But I checked Elizabeth's accounts. I wanted to make sure she was safe. If Billy was able to move money around to protect himself and his father, I wanted to make sure he didn't use her to do it."

Derek's face felt hot. He curled his toes in his shoes so he didn't punch Kyle. "What did you find?"

"Nothing. She's safe. I erased my tracks. I found nothing linking her to the money." Kyle looked at his boss over the top of his soda can. "You want to fire me?"

Derek sighed. "At first, I wanted to punch you. But I am grateful you care. I appreciate you giving me peace of mind. If anything happened to her or hurt her, I would kill someone."

"I would too. I've never loved someone like that, but that's what I would do." Kyle started to close down his system. "What do you want to do with this information about Coach?"

"I need a few printouts with the blackmail money. Tomorrow I'm going to rattle a few cages. If we can provoke the nephew or Russell McMillan, then we may get one of them to do something drastic. I think the fact that Ford Johnson tried to hack into our security system and gain access to our records makes me think he thinks we are getting close."

"I can print some of this out. Do you really think it was him at the front door?"

"I do. On paper, it fits. I don't have any proof, and I won't ever get it. But I can use it to make assumptions. After all, that's what profiling is. Making assumptions based on a set of behaviors and incidents to predict an outcome."

"What do you think he will do?" Kyle grabbed his gun and holster from his coat rack. He followed Derek down the hallway.

"I think he's desperate. I don't know what his end game is. Is it to kill his uncle or just see him go to jail for blackmail? Is it to ruin him first, then kill him?"

They walked towards the main room.

Lola slept in her bed.

"If he waited this long, I think he wants to inflict as much pain as possible. And I think he has nothing to lose. He has no way out. And when you corner an animal, the fallout is always much greater than anticipated." Derek grabbed his weapon and his satchel. Checking to make sure his laptop was inside, he shut down his desktop.

As they neared the front of the door, a limousine pulled up. Both men stopped and watched the security screens as a man in a rich-looking suit stepped out.

"Shit."

Kyle looked at his boss. "Who's that?"

"That would be Assistant Deputy Director of the FBI." Derek watched as he pushed the button. The chime sounded.

Derek looked at Lola. She raised her head but didn't seem interested.

"What are we going to do?"

"We are going to sit here until he leaves." Derek looked at his tech. Relief washed over his face. "You okay?"

"Yeah. I was hoping you would say that."

They watched as he pushed the button several times before the ADD pulled a phone from his pocket. Derek placed a finger over his mouth and turned on the intercom.

"Why am I not able to get into Reed's place? No, the office? Well, I want in. I don't care this is still FBI property. I need to be able to get in." He paced. "Well, next time, I want access."

Derek shut off the speaker when the man got back into his car. He looked at Kyle. "I need you to make sure all these systems are locked down. I don't care what you have to do. Secure these computers so our tech guys can't break in. I want your system downstairs as tight as you can get it. Make sure you delete any trace of you anywhere, except for cases we work on. That would look very suspicious if we don't have any trace of our work."

"I already have this place locked down. Did it the other day." Kyle watched as his boss shut down the system so they could leave. "What do you think he wants?"

"I'm not sure. But you can damn well believe I'm going to find out."

CHAPTER FIFTY-SEVEN

Friday morning 6 a.m.

Derek and Lola walked into the legacy unit. He hadn't been able to sleep, got up about 4 a.m., and came into work. His head hurt, and he needed a distraction.

Lola laid in Marc Anthony's bed.

"He'll be here soon. I promise."

She didn't move.

Setting his satchel under his desk, he booted up the desktop. His phone vibrated in his pocket. There was a text message from Lizzy.

Things here are good. Mom received some medicine, and she's perked up. The entire family is coming in next week. An impromptu family reunion.

That sounds wonderful. I'm glad she's doing better.

If you can come. Please do. Next weekend we will have a big party and lots of food. I miss you.

If I can, I will be there. Me and Lola.

I gotta go. ILU.

I love you more.

He checked flights to Philly for next Friday. Not bad on pricing. If he could get even one day to see her, he would take it. The stillness in the church this early in the morning eased his anxiety. The hum of the electronics and the AC lulled him into calmness. He placed his feet on the corner of his desk and placed his hands on his chest as he leaned back and closed his eyes. The day would start soon enough.

The smell of incense, used days gone by, permeated the room. Inhaling through his nose, he let the scent engulf him. His breathing slowed, and his body sank into his chair. He let rest come and overtake him.

The chime of the door woke him. He shot up, looking at the screens. Rebecca stood outside. "What the hell is she doing here?" the wall clock said 6:30. He rubbed his eyes, walked to the door, and used the code and thumbprint to open it.

"Rebecca. Come in."

"Something bad is going to happen. You have to help me."

Derek stepped back. "What's going to happen?"

"I can't explain it. I know something is going to happen." She stepped closer and wrapped her arms around his waist. "Hold me, Derek."

He lifted his arms and tried to push her back. Her grip tightened. "Uh, this isn't a good idea."

"Sure it is. Just let go, boy."

Derek's throat seized. He tried to scream, but he couldn't open his mouth. He reached up and felt strands of cord stitched through his lips. He wrestled free of Rebecca. Only it wasn't Rebecca. It was Josiah. Maggots and beetles crawled on his flesh. Derek looked down at his shirt. He brushed the bugs off him as he fell backward. His screams were muffled by his sealed lips.

Josiah threw his head back and laughed. "I'm coming for you, boy. I've been lonely too long here in the dark. I need you. I need you, Derek." He pointed a gun at him. "You remember this?"

How could Derek forget? It was his gun pointed at him. The one Josiah took from him when he ambushed him in the carnival tent. The one Josiah used to kill himself with. Derek reached out to grab it.

"No, no, no. You screwed up. It's mine now. Chrissy is mine, too. Ooh boy, she's a sweet girl. So innocent. You remember how you screwed up and killed her? You can't save anyone, Derek. You can't save Lizzy, either. I'll get her too." Josiah stepped closer and put the gun right in front of Derek's head. "Bye-bye."

Derek lifted his left hand to protect himself. The muzzle flash was the last thing Derek saw before he felt his head explode.

Jumping up from his seat, Derek pulled his weapon. His breathing was shallow, and his chest hurt. The pain in his head caused starbursts behind his eyes. He placed his gun on his desk and grabbed both sides of his head. It felt as if shards of glass pierced his skull.

"Aaaah!" he screamed as he fell to his knees. Panting, vomit hovered at the back of his throat. Gagging, he leaned over his garbage can, his morning coffee spewed out.

Lola sat at his side. From the first cries of pain, she had run to him. She nudged him, whimpering. She kept head butting his chest, trying to get him to acknowledge her.

He couldn't lift his hands. He sat on his knees. His arms hung limp at his sides with his knuckles resting on the cool concrete floor.

Lola scooted next to him, leaning into him. She maneuvered her head under his arm, snuggling close to him when it draped over her body.

"I'm okay, girl." He panted. Using what strength he had, he squeezed her body next to his. Tears ran down his face. He shook his head as he huffed out several quick breaths.

"I'm okay. I'm okay."

"No, you're not."

He knew Chrissy's voice. He also knew it was his subconscious trying to reel him back. "Yes, I am. I'm okay." He used the corner of the desk and Lola to help him get on his feet. Struggling, he fell into his chair. He laid his head on his desk. Sweat soaked his shirt.

"Something bad is going to happen. That was a warning."

"I can't stop something I can't see."

"You have to be prepared."

"How can I prepare for something I can't see? I can't."

"Don't push things."

"I don't know what you're talking about. Stop. Just stop."

Lola whimpered. She sat right next to him, glued to his leg.

He let his hand fall on her head. Her soft fur brought him comfort. The cool air washed over him as the AC kicked on. He took several deep, penetrating breaths to slow his breathing. He looked at his watch. The face had a crack in it and the time stopped at 6:09. He lifted his head and squinted. The clock on the wall said 6:25.

He tapped the face, and lifted it to his ear. No noise. "Hell. I must have hit it on the desk when I fell." He started to remove the watch, decided against it. "Fuck it."

He stood and got his legs under him. He leaned on the desk until he felt he could make it to the kitchen. He grabbed his trash can so he could clean it out.

Lola was right on his heels.

Setting it in the sink, he ran water, rinsing it. Using a handful of paper towels, he dried it and set it on the floor. Derek opened the refrigerator and grabbed a soda. He placed the cold can against his face. Looking through the cabinet, he thought about eating a granola bar. But the sour taste in his mouth gave him pause.

Grabbing his trash can, he walked back to his desk.

Lola sat next to him, waiting to protect him.

He glanced down and rubbed her ears. "What would I do without you, huh?"

She rested her head on his knee.

He closed his eyes. However, this time, he didn't fall asleep. At 7 a.m., the front door beeped. "Why are you here so early?"

"I saw you leave this morning and couldn't go back to sleep. I want to print out those papers." Kyle sat at Felicia's desk, booting up her computer. He turned and studied Derek. "You okay?"

"Yeah. I have a headache. Just took some aspirin for it. I'll be fine."

Kyle's lips pooched out. "If you say so." He focused on the computer. Logging into the network, he opened the file with the financials. After clicking a few screens, the printer roared to life. "That's all the financials putting McMillan in the middle of the blackmail. What do you think you're going to do?"

"I'm going to go see him at the academy. Show him what we found. Then I'm going to wait. And see how long it takes for him to call his nephew." Derek took the papers from Kyle. He read them. "This should work."

"You going to take someone with you?"

"Why? You want to go?"

"Yeah. Are you kidding me? I would love to see his face."

"Then be ready by eight."

Kyle's nostrils flared as a big smile filled his face. "This is going to be so epic." He went into the kitchen. "I'll be up in an hour, ready to go."

"Okay." Derek pulled his phone out and punched in the security code. He heard the beeps on the other end and waited.

"Did something happen?" The AD's voice sounded strained.

"Is everything okay? You don't sound so good."

"Tired. I know you didn't use the secure number for chit chat."

"Last night before I left, the ADD showed up."

"Are you fucking serious?"

"Yes. He rang to get in, but I didn't open the door. I turned on the intercom and heard him say he wants to be able to get into our facility when he wants to. Do you know why he has an interest in me?"

"No. I know what we talked about hasn't gone any further than the cemetery. I can assume it's because Congressman Jackson called you in."

"Well, I want it stalled as long as possible. I know he isn't out here much. Did you find out why he was in town?"

"No. I didn't."

"That's worrisome."

"It is. Keep your head down. Hide whatever you found. And get that tech of yours to lock your computers down."

"Already in motion. If you hear anything, let me know. Stay safe."

"You do the same."

He stared at the silent phone. Maybe that's the warning. Let the Balderro case lie. He could do that for a while. He had no problem setting it aside. Unless he had to protect Lizzy. Then, all bets were off.

CHAPTER FIFTY-EIGHT

By 7:45 a.m., everyone arrived at the Legacy Unit. Emma took the lists from everyone and headed to the store. Lola and Marc Anthony ran around playing and chasing each other. Derek gathered the papers he'd planned to take to the school. He'd given everyone their assignments and waited for Kyle to come up.

He pulled up the recent parking ticket the secretary from London-vale had received. He made a mental note this was her fifth ticket, and he saw none of them ever amounted to anything, not even a fine. "Know someone, do we?" He had no business investigating her, but Derek didn't like her and hoped he could ruin her day.

"I bet Kyle is excited to get out in the field," Kelly said, sipping her coffee.

"Like a kid in a candy store." Derek made sure his phone was in his pocket, and he had the folder. He looked at his watch. "Crap." He glanced at the wall clock. "Kyle! Let's go."

Kyle ran up the stairs and into the main room. "Let's get the show on the road."

Derek stared at his tech. "What is around your neck?"

Kyle looked down. He smiled when he looked up. "My shield."

Derek tilted his head to the side. He opened his mouth, deciding to let it go. "Okay then. Let's go, Agent."

Felicia giggled. "You are such a dork. Just wear it on your pants, or better yet, in your pocket."

"Nope. I've been waiting to use this forever." Kyle smiled. "I look hot. Go ahead, say it."

Everyone chuckled.

"You look like a dork. Cause you are a dork." Felicia winked at him.

"I know you love me." He blew her a kiss as he followed Derek outside. In the car, Kyle whistled. "I knew this was a nice car, but man, this thing is sweet."

"No, I didn't steal it."

"I didn't think that. I know how suave you are at getting shit." Kyle messed with every button he could find. He smiled at his boss. "The backseat is dope. How much did it cost?"

"Several thousand. They had to reinforce the base to hold the bucket seats. I had them shorten the trunk area, allowing the backseats to lie down flat like the front. If you lay both down, they allow a six-foot man space to sleep. Great stakeout car."

"This is so dope. Why did you get into this? I mean, being a profiler?"

Derek pulled onto the main thoroughfare. Traffic still heavy from the morning rush into downtown. He took the turn, leading him to the academy. "Fell into it, I guess. I joined the FBI right out of college. I have a forensic psychology degree. A position opened up at the BAU. It fit, and I fit."

Kyle messed with the radio.

Derek swatted his hand. "Don't you know, the passenger can never mess with the radio. It's an unwritten rule."

Kyle ignored him and put on a classic rock station, turning it up as loud as he could. He glanced at Derek. He couldn't help but laugh at the look of sheer anger spreading across his boss' face before he turned down the volume. He laughed. "The look on your face was so worth it."

"You're like a kid. Can you behave?"

Kyle straightened up. "Hell yeah. Just messing with you." When the car turned onto the long drive into the academy, Kyle's mouth hung open. "Holy cow. I only dreamed of going to a place like this."

"You and most of society." Pulling up to the gate, Derek rolled down his window.

"Who are you here to see?" a young man asked.

"I'm FBI Agent Derek Reed. I need to speak with the headmaster."

The young guard searched the list. "I don't have you on the list."

"I'm a Federal Agent. I don't need to be on the list. Open the gate before I arrest you."

The young man stuttered. "Uh, uh, yes. Yes, sir." He stepped inside the shack and opened the gate.

Kyle howled with laughter as they drove through. "I so want to be you when I grow up."

"Seriously?" Derek laughed.

"I know I'm not a badass like you guys." Kyle sank into the seat.

Derek pulled into a parking spot. "I need you more than I need a badass, Kyle. You have skills that are unmatched. Often the fight against crime is done behind the computer screen. I wouldn't be as far along in this case without you on my team."

"Thanks. Now, I want to be the bad cop."

Derek roared back in laughter. "Okay. If you see an opportunity to make McMillan squirm, have at it. Just don't tip your hand."

Kyle gave him a thumbs up as they walked up the steps.

Several high school girls walked by and smiled at Kyle.

Looking more like a surfer, Derek thought about using him under-cover sometime. He definitely didn't look like an agent.

Outside the door to the headmaster's gatekeeper, Derek leaned into Kyle. "I get to make her cry."

Kyle didn't understand, and he didn't have time to ask before Derek pushed open the door.

The headmaster's watchdog glanced up over the rim of her glasses. She huffed out a curt breath. "Agent, you don't have an appointment to see the headmaster."

"Ah, Harriet. I can tell you're glad to see me. I guess I have to remind a few of you here at Londonvale I'm an FBI agent. I don't need an ap-pointment. Now, could you please let the headmaster know we are here?"

"No. He is on an important call, and I will not interrupt him. Not even for you."

Derek stepped closer and stooped down. "Harriet. I understand you have a proclivity for speeding. And from what I can see, you have never paid a fine. I wonder what that would look like in the society paper. Long-time secretary for prominent private school uses her position to thwart the law." Derek looked over his shoulder at Kyle. "Isn't there a federal statute we could slap on her?"

Kyle nodded. "There is a federal statute for just about anything. If you really want to, I bet you could even get some jail time out of it."

Derek smiled at her. "You know, you might look good in orange, Har-riet." He stood up straight. "Now tell him I'm here, or I will arrest you for obstruction and anything else I can find to put your cranky ass in jail."

Harriet's eyes glassed over. "Yes. I can do that." She picked up the phone. "Agent Derek Reed is here to see you."

Derek didn't wait for the invite. "Very smart, Harriet," he said as he opened the door to Russel McMillan's office.

Russel came around his desk. "I'm not sure why you need to see me again." He acknowledged Kyle, then focused on Agent Reed. "How can I help you?"

"Well, let's talk blackmail. Shall we, Harry Fredricksburg?"

CHAPTER FIFTY-NINE

Derek stood staring at the man. For a moment, he thought Russell would drop to the floor. He didn't want the man dead. However, the first strike did what he'd hoped it would do.

"I think you've made a mistake." Russell's voice broke.

Derek looked at Kyle. "Agent Marcum, I don't think we made a mistake, do you?"

Kyle sat on the edge of Russell's desk. "Not at all." He nodded towards the headmaster. "We think we can erase stuff from the internet with a push of a button or the deletion of a file. But unless you look under every nook and cranny. You will miss things. And you missed a few things."

Russell McMillan swallowed. He sat in a chair. "I need a minute."

Derek sat across from him. "Take all the time you need. As a matter of fact, you can listen." Derek removed the folded papers from his back pocket. "During our investigation, we came across some interesting material. But before I get to that, can you tell me about your nephew?"

His eyes bulged, and he swallowed several more times. "My nephew?" His shaky voice cracked. Russell cleared his throat.

"Yes. Your nephew. Ford Johnson. You know, the one you helped get a scholarship? Can you tell me about the bullying he suffered at the hands of some of the baseball team players?"

Russell recovered quickly. "Okay. Yes, I helped my nephew get a scholarship to this academy. However, he didn't receive any special considerations. He had to go through the process like everyone else."

"I don't really care about scholarships. I'll leave that to the governing body of the school to take action against you. I'm more concerned with this." He shook the papers.

"Kyle, can you explain to Mr. McMillan what exactly we discovered in the course of our investigation?"

"Yes, I can." Kyle took the second seat across from the headmaster. "We know William Edmond Sr.'s dad helped you in college. Helped expunge your record and give you a new start. We also know he helped you get this job and your head of the athletic department job. Imagine our surprise when we found an account with several thousands of dollars hidden away. Under your previous name."

Russell's head swiveled between the two men. "I don't know what you're talking about. I think I need my lawyer." He stood.

"Sit, Russell. We aren't here to arrest you. But if you call your lawyer, we will do just that. Right now, this is an inquiry." Derek handed him the papers. "These accounts match up to money withdrawn from Billy and several other murder victims. It seems several boys from the baseball team paid you prior to their deaths. Can you explain how this is possible?"

"There's been a mistake. I have one account from my past life. I never closed it, and I didn't want to do it now and raise red flags. I left it alone. These accounts, I have never seen them before." Russell looked over the numbers. "This is crazy."

Derek noticed Russell's hands shaking. "Mr. McMillan, if you didn't create these accounts, who do you know who could've done this? Who would want to implicate you for crimes you didn't commit?"

Russell stammered. "I—I don't know. I don't have any enemies. I don't know who would want to hurt me." Water floated in his eyes. "I didn't blackmail anyone. And I sure as hell didn't kill anyone."

"Then you need to tell us who has the ability to create accounts and move money around so easily?" Derek waited. "I think you know. You need to tell us."

Russell stood and paced his office. "I never hurt the boy. I tried to give him chances in life I never had." He stared at the agents. "Why would he do this to me?"

"Your nephew?" Kyle asked.

"Yes. He has the ability to do these kinds of things." Russell handed the papers back to Derek.

"Maybe he blames you for the bullying." Derek watched his reaction.

"I never saw any bullying. Those boys were just being boys."

"Boys will be boys, huh?" Kyle asked. "Does that include Casey?"

Derek smiled inwardly. He shot a sideways glance to his agent. "Can you tell us about that night?"

"I'm confused. What does Casey Redding have to do with anything now?" Russell stood with his shoulders slumped forward.

"What happened to Casey wasn't an accident, and you know that.

Billy's father went to a lot of trouble to cover it up. He even bought your nephew a car a few months later, and the boys left your nephew alone. Why was that?" Derek asked.

"I don't know what you're talking about?" Russell looked down at his feet.

"Don't lie to us," Kyle said. "We have eyewitness reports who said your nephew received a car shortly afterward. That your nephew threatened to tell everyone it wasn't an accident. He even got beat up by Greg Burks and Billy Edmond. Something you never did anything about. Can you explain why you didn't help your nephew?"

Russell sat on the edge of the chair. "I did. He was a loose cannon. I had to protect my interests. If I had stepped in to help, it would have been seen as showing favor."

"And your secret would be out," Derek said.

"Yes. I regret that I didn't do something about the bullying. But I did get the boys to stop. And Billy's dad was gracious enough to give him a car as a peace offering." He wrung his hands.

"How's your relationship with your nephew now?" Derek asked.

"Strained. Ever since Billy died, he's been acting weird."

"Acting weird, how?" Derek sat on the edge of his seat.

"He's been pressuring me to give him some of the money I received from Billy's estate. He feels I owe him." Russell's head sunk into his shoulders, all but making his neck disappear.

"Do you know where we can find your nephew?" Derek asked.

"He's due back in town this afternoon. I can have him call you."

"Please do." Derek handed him his card. "I would like to ask him some questions. Right now, it's just your word against his. We don't have anything tying him to this. It's all in your name." He watched as the anger flared in Russell's eyes, then quickly burned out.

"I didn't do this. I will have him tell you. If he didn't do this, then someone is setting me up." Russell stood straight. "I think it's time for you to go."

Derek stood, along with Kyle.

"I do appreciate your time. I hope your nephew can help you clear your name. The next time we come to visit, it will be with a warrant." Derek smiled as he headed towards the door. "One more question. Have you ever invested in a business deal with Billy's dad?"

A spark of recognition fluttered across his face, dissipating just as quickly. "Not really. He asked me if I wanted to invest in a few companies, but nothing concrete."

"How about Billy? After the death of his parents. Did he ask you to get involved in any business deals?" Derek studied the man's face, looking for a hint of culpability.

"No. I would never go into business with Billy. He has a reckless streak." Russell's face relaxed.

"Thank you, Mr. McMillan. Get ahold of your nephew. The sooner we talk to him, the sooner we might clear you." Derek didn't smile as he walked past Harriet. He held her stare until he left the office.

When they stepped outside, Kyle laughed. "Oh, my gosh. This is so worth being an FBI agent. This. Right here."

"Get in the car." Derek unlocked the doors. Once in the comfort and security of his car, he let out a long breath. "You did good in there, for your first time at an interrogation in the field."

Kyle slapped his leg. "That was so much fun." He looked at his boss. "Most everything was a lie."

"Yes. We can lie in an investigation. Now let's hope he takes the bait."

"What exactly are you wanting?"

Derek drove out of the gate. He nodded at Rebecca but didn't stop. "I want him to confront his nephew. I think that will force the nephew's hand and get him to make a mistake."

"What if it backfires? What if it pushes him too far?"

Derek knew that was a possibility. He also knew he had nothing tying either of these men to several brutal murders. At this point, he didn't care how he stopped the killer. He just didn't want more deaths on his hands. "Let's hope that doesn't happen."

CHAPTER SIXTY

Friday 4:30 p.m.

Derek sat at his desk. He and his agents had been working all day. Their theory the nephew killed everyone and was setting up the uncle fit. But he had not one shred of evidence.

"George, did you get anything from the crime scene techs?"

He rubbed his face. "No. It seems there isn't one piece of physical evidence tying anyone to the bat or the crime scenes. They found the weapon used on Greg, but it had been thrown in the pool."

"How about the sous chef at Greg Burks' place? Did he have anything on who visited Greg the night of his death?" Derek asked.

George shook his head. "Nope. He delivered the food. He said Greg met him at the elevator and took the cart from him. The sous chef said he didn't see anyone around."

"Crap." Derek tapped his foot. "Kelly, anything?"

Kelly used the palms of her hands to rub her eyes. "No. And my head is going to explode from looking at my computer." She faced him. "Most just don't remember. And others weren't a part of their family member's life."

"Something has to break. Or he's going to get away with it." Derek searched for a piece of gum. "Felicia? Anything?"

"Not yet. I don't know if Michael found anything. All I can tell you is, you would think if people were going to put in a surveillance system, why can't they put in one that takes decent pictures."

"Exactly. I got nothing. I don't know how Kyle does this stuff all day," Michael said. "I haven't found anything with Johnson or his uncle or anyone remotely suspicious anywhere in the vicinity of the victims."

"Let's hope Kyle found another account. If he does, we can get a warrant." His tech had come back from the meeting with Russell, determined to find something in Ford Johnson's financials for his business. Derek knew a warrant couldn't happen without substantial evidence pointing to a cause for the warrant. He didn't have that. Ford Johnson knew enough to cover his tracks and lay part of the blame at his uncle's feet. Ford Johnson was the killer. Of this, Derek was sure. "I need a drink. Anyone need anything from the kitchen?"

Kelly yawned. "Something with caffeine."

"You got it." Derek grabbed two sodas and a granola bar. Along with two bones for the dogs.

Kyle came up the stairs. "Boss."

"Please tell me you got something?"

"Nothing concrete, but I think I found another company."

"This is good."

Kyle followed him into the main room.

Derek's phone rang. Balancing the sodas in one arm, he pulled his phone from his pocket. "Derek."

"Agent Reed? This is Rebecca."

"Rebecca, what can I do for you?" He handed a soda to Kelly.

"Coach's nephew showed up an hour ago. They've been arguing in the office. I went in there a few times and checked on them. Coach assured me things were okay. But I don't think they are."

"Okay. Where are they now?"

"That's just it, I don't know. I only know they haven't left the school grounds."

"Are there students on the premises?" Derek snapped his fingers, getting his team's attention.

"A few from the band in the band room."

"Okay, Rebecca, I want you to get those kids off the property and keep the gates closed. Try not to let Coach or his nephew leave. Me and my team will be there in a few minutes."

"Okay. I can do that."

"Don't approach them. If you see them, just go to your shack and stay there. We are on our way."

"Thank you, Derek."

He pocketed his phone. "It looks like Ford Johnson showed up to talk to his uncle. They're at the academy now. Rebecca wants us to come out there and help diffuse the situation." He removed his weapon from his desk drawer and stuck it in his holster.

Kelly and Felicia did the same.

George stood and added an extra clip to his belt. He glanced at Michael. "You can ride with me."

"Great." Michael removed his weapon from his desk and clipped it to his belt. "You planning on a shootout?" he pointed to the two full clips.

"Always be prepared," George said.

"Felicia and Kelly ride with me." Derek turned and looked at Kyle. "I would appreciate it if you would stay and be my contact here if I need something." He took two radios off the charger and gave one to George.

"I have no problem staying here." Kyle sipped on his soda.

"Emma, you can go. Take Marc Anthony and go home." Derek scratched Lola's head. "Kyle, keep an eye on Lola."

"I got everything covered here." Kyle stood as they headed towards the door.

Derek turned back. "As soon as Emma leaves, lock this place down and do not open the door to anyone. Understand?"

"Yes. I do." Kyle watched on the cameras as they headed to their cars. He turned to Emma. "Go home."

"Not on your life, son. I'm staying right here with you. Now lock us in."

CHAPTER SIXTY-ONE

Kelly and Felicia climbed into Derek's car.

"I'm only letting you have the front seat this one time," Felicia said as she buckled her seat belt.

"Whatever." Kelly buckled in, glancing around the cabin. "This is a sweet car. You steal it or take it from a drug king?"

"Yes. Yes, I did." Derek flipped a switch under his dash, turning on a siren, and red and blue blinking lights built into his front and rear light casings. He checked his rearview to see George had placed a blue light on the roof of his car.

He dialed George using the Bluetooth.

"Yo."

"When we get there. I want Michael with me. You, Felicia, and Kelly. I'm hoping he's in a room and not a big open space."

"Sounds good. I'm right behind you."

Derek weaved in and out of the evening traffic. Thank goodness most were going the other way. Entering the academy grounds, he stopped at the guard shack where Rebecca met him. He rolled down his window. "Do you know where they are?"

"No. I've checked the main buildings. I have the auditorium and gym left. He's got to be in one of those buildings."

"Are they near each other?" Derek asked.

"Sort of." She opened the rear door to his car. She looked at the kid in the shack. "Lock the gate." Rebecca caught Derek's eye in the rearview. "Turn to the right and follow the lane. There is a parking lot between the two buildings."

Derek followed her directions and parked closest to the side entrance of the auditorium.

George pulled up next to him. "Where are we going?" he asked as he left his truck and stood next to Derek.

Derek looked at Rebecca. "Are all the doors open on the buildings?"

"Yes." She pointed to the sides of each building. "We can enter through these doors."

"Make sure the volume is down." He pointed to the radio. "You take Kelly and Felicia and go through the gym. If you find him, double click, we'll be there. Same for me. I have no idea what we're walking into." Derek turned towards Rebecca. "What's the layout of the gym?"

"Once you walk in, you will be right in the main weight room. You can go down either side, and you can find offices and yoga rooms. The pool is at the far end." She faced Derek. "When you walk in this door, you will be on the right side of the stage. If you turn right, you go towards the front of the building. If you go left, you can go backstage."

Derek pointed at George. "Remember, double click if you find him."

"Understood," he said.

Derek took stock of his group. "Rebecca, I want you to call the police. Ask for Sergeant McNeil. Tell him I'm on site, and we need them to keep their sirens off. We don't need an army, but some backup would be nice."

She pulled her phone out. "I have him on speed dial."

"Great." Derek smiled at her.

Both teams hit the doors at the same time.

Rebecca stayed back as she called the Sergeant.

Before he opened the door, Derek faced Michael. "I know how well you shoot. If you see an opening to take a shot, do it."

Michael twisted his neck. "No problem."

Derek pulled the door and motioned for Michael to head towards the back and make his way around. He went to the right. Moving slowly down the hallway, he could hear muffled voices. He hugged the wall that wrapped around the stage area.

He pulled his radio from his pocket. The voices were getting louder. Derek clicked the radio and slipped it into his pocket. He reached the end of the wall, placed his back against it, and peered around the edge.

He could see Ford and Coach in the center of the auditorium, near the stage. Derek had no idea where Michael was, but he trusted the boy's instincts. He took a deep breath before he called out. "Ford." He peered around the edge of the wall.

"Who the fuck is that?" Ford glanced around, trying to find the source of his name. "Who are you?" he kept his gun pointed at his uncle as he searched the auditorium.

"I'm FBI Special Agent Derek Reed. I need you to put down the weapon. It doesn't have to go down this way."

Ford shook his head. "No, no, no. You called the police? The fucking FBI?"

"No, Ford, I didn't. Security must have heard us yelling and called. They're just making sure no kids are harmed." Coach McMillan took a small step back.

"Stop. Stop." Ford pointed the gun at his uncle.

"Okay. Please. You don't want to shoot me." Coach stood still. "I'm not going anywhere."

Derek came out from behind the wall. "Ford. It doesn't have to end this way. We know your uncle blackmailed the players. You can rest assured he will have to answer for that." He moved slowly to close the distance between him and Ford. "Listen, the police are on their way. We don't want anyone hurt."

Coach started to back away again.

Ford grabbed him by his collar and pulled him next to him, pressing the weapon into his side area.

"What are you hoping to get by doing this? You've got your uncle where you want him. You've made your point."

"Do you know what this man did?"

"He let the boys bully you, and he picked them over you." Derek took a step forward.

"He was mean. Mean to me and my mother. Even when she was sick. When I came here, I thought he'd changed. But no. He cared only about the boys at this academy because they had money."

"That isn't true, Ford. You have things confused." Coach pleaded. "You can walk away if you just put the gun down."

"Ford. I'm on your side. But I need you to put down the weapon."

He waved the gun in his uncle's face. "You treated us like we were less than those boys you protected. You let them get away with everything, even when Casey died."

"I didn't let them get away with anything. It was an accident. A horrible mistake," Coach said.

"I loved her. She was so special. She was the only one who was nice to me. She included me in things. Those boys treated her like crap. They made fun of her and then locked her in a closet. You did nothing afterward."

"Ford, what could I do? I needed this job. Billy's father had the power to hide everything...."

"You could've done the right thing."

"Ford. Did you kill the boys?" Derek asked as he took another step closer.

"Stop. Stay where you are."

"Okay. I'm stopping. Did you kill the boys on the team?"

"Yes. They all deserved it. Every last one of them." Ford wiped the moisture from his face.

Derek heard the remaining members of his team. George and Kelly headed up an outside isle towards the back. Felicia ducked back behind the wall. Derek assumed she was making her way to the other side. He scanned the area but didn't see Michael.

"Ford. You need to put the gun down. Let us handle it from this point forward."

"I have nothing to lose. I'm not going to jail. Not over those assholes. Not over my loving, caring uncle."

Felicia rounded the far side of the stage, boxing the two men between herself and Derek. She didn't have a clean shot. She would hit Coach first.

Derek held up his clenched fist when Felicia stepped into his line of sight. "Ford. My agents and I have you surrounded. Just put down the weapon."

Ford focused on his uncle. "I want you to say it out loud. Tell them what a shit brother you were to your sister. Tell them how you treated her like crap while she slowly died."

"I didn't do that. I loved your mother."

"You can't even admit it now, with a gun in your face. What a bastard you are." Ford raised the gun and grabbed his uncle, pulling him in close, using him as a shield. "I'm not letting him walk out of here alive. I'm already going down for a shit ton of murders. One more won't make a difference. Maybe I should take one of you with me. I can get one shot off before one of your men shoot me. Maybe it should be you?" he pointed his weapon at Derek.

"You don't want to do that. You want your day in court. You want everyone to know what an asshole your uncle is and you can't do that if you're dead." Derek searched for Michael. He couldn't see him and he hoped he had a clear shot. He wanted the coach alive. If nothing else, he needed answers regarding Billy's father and the Balderro case.

"We can guarantee you get to have your say." Felicia said as she moved towards Ford and his uncle.

He pointed the weapon at her. "Stop."

She did. "There's no way out."

"There is always a way out."

Michael could see everyone from where he stood. Just off to the right and at the back of the stage. He wanted to get close enough to tackle them from behind. But to do so, he would have to cross an open stage.

Ford wasn't going to last much longer. Michael didn't think he would hesitate to shoot Derek. He couldn't let that happen. As he inched forward, he saw Ford was using Coach as a shield. If he shot him through the back, he ran the risk of the bullet going through Ford and hitting Coach in the back. He did have one perfect shot. Michael moved forward. Positioning himself towards the left, he could shoot and not risk hitting anyone else.

Ford tightened his grip on his uncle. "You deserve everything that happens." He lifted the gun, holding it to his uncle's head. "I'm not going to jail, and my uncle isn't leaving here alive."

Michael didn't wait. He raised his weapon took a deep breath, and on the exhale, pulled the trigger.

The gunshot echoed throughout the auditorium. Within seconds cops ran in.

Coach couldn't move. His hands shook. He felt the brain matter and blood on the side of his face. He gagged and fell to his knees.

Derek ran up to them, kicking away the weapon. "Are you hurt?"

Russel McMillan lifted his head. "I don't think so. Please get this stuff off me."

"We will. Just wait." Derek searched the stage area.

Michael stepped out from behind a heavy upholstered curtain. "I had to take the shot."

Derek jumped up on the stage. "You did good." He looked over his shoulder. "Felicia, come here, please."

Felicia came up next to him. She smiled at the young agent. "Great shot. You had to do it. What do you need, Derek?"

"Take his weapon for me." He placed his hand on Michael's shoulder. "This was a clean shoot, and nothing is going to happen. You'll be on desk duty for a while."

"I know. I'm not worried." Michael sighed. "I didn't want to do it. And I don't even know if Russell McMillan deserves to be saved. But he didn't deserve to die. At least not today."

CHAPTER SIXTY-TWO

5 days later

Derek walked into the Liberty Scan clinic. The last-minute touches were still being put in place before it opened to the public. Some friend of Doctor Chelsea owned it and said he would do the CT scan off the record. He almost thought of not going through with it, but his head hurt too much.

"It's about time you showed up." Dr. Chelsea squeezed Derek's shoulder. "How's Michael?"

"He's doing well. He passed his psych eval, so he's back on active duty." Derek whistled as he scoped out the clinic. "This is mighty fancy."

Dr. Chelsea laughed. "There is a lot of money in medicine."

Dr. Jeffrey Coats came out of one of the rooms. "Hi, you must be Agent Reed." He held out his hand. "Nice to meet you."

"Same. And thanks for doing this." Derek said, shaking the man's hand.

"Anything for my friend, Dr. Chelsea. Let's walk and talk. The CT I'm going to use is down the hallway. Tell me what you are experiencing."

"I've been having some nasty headaches. Visions or hallucinations. Odd auditory sounds." Derek followed the doctors through a set of double doors.

"Dr. Chelsea told me about the injuries you suffered during your previous case. Are you still healing?" Dr. Coats handed Derek a hospital gown. "Put this on."

Derek stood by a chair and disrobed, keeping his underwear and socks on. "My nose still hurts. And my cheek sometimes aches."

"Broken facial bones can often take a long time to heal. Even the smallest fracture can take months. He also mentioned you fell and hit your head this last week?"

"I did."

Dr. Coats glanced at the back of Derek's head. "That's a nasty bump. And for it to be this swollen this long, you probably gave yourself a concussion." He waved him over to the table. "Lie down, placing your head in this cradle."

Derek did as instructed. "How long will this take?"

"As long as it takes." Dr. Chelsea stood with his arms crossed.

"What are you? The enforcer?" Derek asked.

Dr. Chelsea stepped next to Derek. He noticed his watch. "Why are you wearing a broken watch?"

"Long story." Derek tapped the glass. "I need to get my old one back. I'm just now sure how to do it."

Dr. Chelsea cocked his head to the side. "You need to tell me about this, sometime."

Dr. Coats strapped his head in the cradle, then placed straps across his body. "This helps hold your head steady and keeps you centered should you fall asleep. We are going to take a series of pictures. I need you to stay as still as possible."

"No problem. Do people really fall asleep?" Derek wiggled a bit, getting comfortable. A tech came out and placed a warm blanket over him.

"Yes. Are you comfortable?" Dr. Chelsea asked.

"Do you really care?"

"No."

"Figures."

Dr. Chelsea placed a hand on his shoulder. "It's going to be okay."

As the bed slid into the tube, Derek closed his eyes. Soft music played. When a voice came over a speaker, he jerked.

"You will hear a few clicks. Then a loud motor. When I say hold your breath, try to stay as still as possible. I will tell you when to exhale."

"Got it."

"Okay, Derek. We're going to do one full pass. Inhale... hold."

Derek held his breath.

"Breathe."

He blew out the air, easing the pressure on his chest. Derek closed his eyes. He was oddly comfortable. His body relaxed, and his limbs felt noodle-like. It had been a long week, and this was the first time he felt at ease.

"Okay Derek. We are going to perform several more passes. This time you can breathe slowly, but remain still."

"I understand." Derek listened to the clicks of the machine. The whirling noises sounded like a dishwasher. A loud old dishwasher. He breathed slowly, paying attention to his movement.

"Derek, how are you doing?"

"Fine. No worries here."

"Great, I need to do a few more passes. Remain still."

"I will." Derek concentrated on the music. He could barely hear the words over the noise, but he could hear the rhythm. Having second thoughts about the test, he wanted it to be over. His head started to ache.

The hard cradle pushed against the sore spot on the back of his head. Derek twitched as his muscles relaxed, and he thought of Lizzy. He'd wanted to go see her this upcoming weekend, but with the shooting, he couldn't leave the unit.

Lizzy understood, but that didn't alleviate the guilt he carried. She still wasn't sure when she would be home. Her mother was doing better, and Lizzy wanted every moment with her.

Derek opened his eyes, straining to hear the music. It wasn't music, though. Not radio music. He heard a music box. The soft sounds of the metal prongs hitting the revolving cylinder echoed around him. "This is so weird," he whispered.

He listened, trying to place the song. Some lullaby, but he couldn't be for sure. He closed his eyes. The prongs hitting the metal sounded crisper. As if the music box sat next to him. He couldn't turn his head, yet he was sure the box set off to his right. He moved his eyes to the corners. Nothing.

He trembled when a blast of cold air swirled around him. Goosebumps spread across his arms, and his heart raced. He took a deep breath and looked towards his feet. Again, nothing. *I've got to stop doing this.* He wondered what was taking so long. Surely the CT scan would be over by now. "Are we almost done?"

No one answered. "Dr. Chelsea? Dr. Coats?" Derek waited. "Hello?" he reached up to take his straps off, but they were already unhooked. He braced himself as the table slid out of the tube. "What the hell is going on," he said as he swung his legs over the side. "Dr. Chelsea, this isn't funny."

He moved to the chair to get his clothes and started dressing but stopped when he heard something. "Hello?" The little room where the doctor sat during the scan was dark, except for an eerie red blinking light. Derek peered through the window, but there were too many shadows. He heard a muffled cry from within but still saw nothing.

Derek followed the sound. He reached out to open the door. The stench of blood hit him first. He tasted the iron at the back of his throat and covered his mouth. Pushing open the door, he stepped inside. A young girl lay on the floor. Her stomach had been ripped open, and a ribbon wrapped around her neck. Her hands were outstretched, and she looked posed. And she held a music box in her hand.

He turned around to grab his phone from the chair when he heard someone say his name. "Hello?" he glanced around the room. He turned back to the girl; she was gone. Derek stepped into the little closet-like room. "What the hell? Where did she go?" he stood there wondering if he needed medication. "If this is Dr. Chelsea's form of a joke. It isn't funny."

Derek spun around when he heard the music box again. The girl stood before him, her entrails hanging like rope from her midsection. A ribbon around her neck covered a gaping wound from which blood seeped onto her chest.

"Please help me," she reached out for him.

"Derek, wake up." Dr. Chelsea gently patted his cheek.

Derek jerked but didn't wake. His breathing increased, and he had rapid eye movement.

"Is he having a seizure?" The tech asked.

"Music box. Pretty music box," Derek mumbled.

Dr. Chelsea became frantic. "No. I think he's dreaming. Derek? Derek?" Dr. Chelsea called out to him. "Derek, wake up."

Dr. Coats came jogging in. "Sorry, it took me a minute to find some." He snapped the small vial and placed it under Derek's nose.

Derek's hands waved in front of his face as if he were swatting away a gnat. "Go away. Go away. I can't save you. You're dead. You're already dead."

"Derek!" Dr. Chelsea shouted at his friend.

Dr. Coats waved the vile under his nose one more time.

Derek's eyes bulged open. He tried to sit up, but the straps kept him secure. His eyes darted around the room, trying to orient himself. The scanner bed had been rolled back to its starting position. "What the hell is going on?"

"You tell us?" Dr. Coats said, unhooking the straps. "Swing your legs over the side."

With help, Derek rose to a sitting position and dangled his legs off the bed. His head throbbed. "Did you see anything on the scan?"

Dr. Chelsea gave a sideways glance to his colleague. "We'll get to that in a moment. What happened after you got into the tube? I need you to tell me."

"I guess I must have dozed off. I had a dream or something." He rubbed his neck as he twisted his head from side to side. "This block is very uncomfortable." He pointed to the bed.

"Tell me about the dream," Dr. Chelsea said.

"No. You tell me about the scan first." Derek crossed his arms. Still sitting on the scanner bed, he waited.

Dr. Chelsea looked at Dr. Coats. "Go ahead. Tell him."

Dr. Coats smiled. "Aside from a few healing fractures, all you have is a severe bruise on the back of the head from when you fell over. I think you have one of the most severe concussions I've seen in a long time."

Derek's jaw tensed. "There isn't anything weird going on in my head to make me see or hear things?"

"The concussion and the bruising are severe. That could be the culprit for some. The medication you've been taking doesn't do you any favors. From now on, take Ibuprofen. If you are still having problems in a few weeks, I want to do a second scan with contrast this time. It may show something I'm not seeing now. Plus, some time will give the concussion a chance to heal." Dr. Coats stepped out of the room.

Standing, Derek wobbled slightly. "I'm okay," he said when Dr. Chelsea reached out to help him. He pulled on his jeans, then sat in the chair to put on his shoes.

"Tell me about the dream." Dr. Chelsea crossed his arms again. "Now, please."

Derek cringed at the tone. "Fine. What is wrong with you?" He tied his shoe. "Can we at least step out of here? I don't like this room."

Dr. Chelsea outstretched his hand. "Lead the way."

The bright lights pushed the dread feeling down a little further as they walked into the hallway. Derek inhaled, exhaling slowly. He heard Dr. Chelsea thank his friend before he came out.

"He will get me the report later next week. At least we know it's nothing serious that will keep you from working. Although, you do need some time off."

"Not going to happen." Derek walked towards the front entrance.

The hallway seemed to stretch out.

Dr. Chelsea grabbed his wrist, stopping him. "Tell me what you saw."

"A dead girl. Her stomach ripped open, a ribbon around her neck, and a music box in her hand." Derek rubbed his wrist. He watched as Dr. Chelsea's color drained from his face. "Ronald, what's the matter?"

"Tell me about the girl. What did she wear? Was it a nightgown?"

"What, I don't know." Derek shrugged.

"Think!" Dr. Chelsea grabbed both his arms. "Think. Close your eyes and remember the damn dream."

Derek closed his eyes. "She wore a flowing nightgown. Almost see-through, but not in a raunchy way." When he opened them, Dr. Chelsea stared through him. "What's going on?"

"It can't be him. It's been almost ten years."

"Almost ten years. Ten years since what?"

Dr. Chelsea paced the little hallway. "We never found him. But the killing stopped. Four victims later, the killing stopped." He quit pacing. "How could you know? You never worked on the case. The bureau didn't publicize it either. How did you know?"

"Ronald. I don't know what you are referring to. It's been almost ten years since what? What happened ten years ago that you think my dream was about?"

Dr. Chelsea's hand shook as he touched Derek's arm. "It's been ten years since we found the last victim of the Music Box Killer."

THE MUSIC BOX KILLER

Lullabies and Murder.

When two women are found with their throats slit and a music box left at each crime scene, the FBI worries a killer from the past is back.

Agent Derek Reed has an uncanny ability to solve cases that no one else can. When his friend Dr. Chelsea begs him to take over the high-profile case, Derek knows this case may ruin his career.

As the investigation unfolds, some have questioned how Derek knows things that only the killer or the victims would know. He tells everyone it's just his way of looking at things. But his team suspects there is more to it than that.

Faced with coming to terms with a gift he never wanted, he has to learn how to control it. If he doesn't, not only could it cost him his job, a job he can't live without, it could cost him so much more.

It could cost him his sanity.

Order The Music Box Killer

Links to books:
The Damien Kaine Series
The Derek Reed Series
Other Books

ABOUT THE AUTHOR

Victoria M. Patton lives with her husband of twenty-five years, two dogs—Bogart and Georgie, and two cats—Squeakers and Pumpkin.

Her years in the Coast Guard doing Search and Rescue/Law Enforcement and her BS in Forensic Chemistry helps her figure out the best way to hide all the bodies, and then write thrilling stories to keep you up at night. If she has any free time, she drinks copious amounts of whiskey and binge watches Hulu and Acorn TV.

Check out her blog Whiskey and Writing where she tries to help new authors navigate the indie publishing world. If all else fails, she provides great whiskey recipes.

Email her at: victoria@victoriampatton.com.
Check out her author website at www.victoriampatton.com. Be sure to join her Email List for updates on her latest book.
Follow her at Facebook @WhsikeyandWriting
Twitter @victoriampatton and on Pinterest.